I0525709

LESSON OF THE FIRE

By Eric Zawadzki and Matthew Schick

Other titles by
Eric Zawadzki and Matthew Schick:

Kingmaker

Available at
fourmoonspress.com

Lesson of the Fire © 2012 Eric Zawadzki and Matthew Schick.
All rights reserved.
Cover art © 2011 by Alan Gutierrez.

This is a work of fiction. Names, places, characters and events are used fictitiously,
and any resemblance to actual persons, living or dead, places or events
is entirely coincidental.

 Dedication

For my sister, without whose influence the fire never may have been lit in me.

Matthew Schick

For Brian, Heidi, and Adam, who know why I named the town Rustiford. Without your willingness to play those elaborate games of pretend with me there could have been no Marrishland.

Eric Zawadzki

 **Foreword**

The following is an account of the Takraf War, written as what Mar scholars describe as a narrative history in the tradition of the Gesyk Philosophy. This means it is both a history and a story about the people who played a role in that history. Like a "pure" history, it is based on eyewitness accounts of events. Numerous scholars labored over it to ensure every detail is as accurate as possible. The account describes all the major events of the Takraf War, as well as the causes and consequences of each.

Its focus, however, is on the people who played important roles in that conflict — their motives and their relationships to each other. While it is easy to see nothing but a civil war between factions vying for control, those at the center of it were passionate people fighting ideological battles. In particular, the account explores why the war's outcome mattered so much to each of them that they put their own lives at risk.

Most of all, it is the story of Mardux Sven Takraf himself — a genius or madman, a hero or tyrant, depending on whom you ask — and of the humble storyteller whose tales of Takraf's life shaped its outcome by teaching him the lesson of the fire.

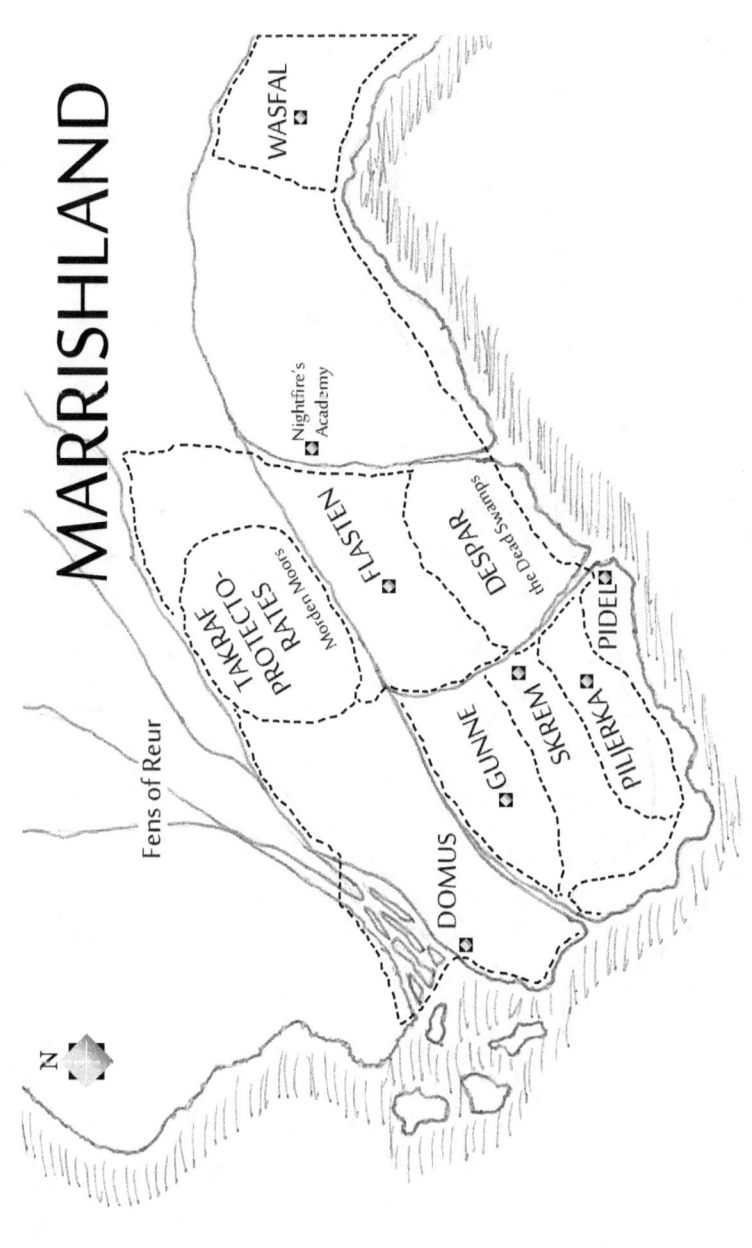

MARRISHLAND

WASFAL

Nightfire's Academy

Fens of Reur

TAKRAF PROTECTO-RATES

Worden Woods

FLASTEN

DESPAR

the Dead Swamps

PIDEL

GUNNE

SKREM

PILJERKA

DOMUS

N

 **1**

"First-degree wizards wear bright green cloaks. As a wizard rises from first-degree to seventh, the color of his cloak changes to reflect his rank — green, auburn, blue, amber, cyan, lavender and yellow. A wizard who reaches the highest rank, eighth-degree, wears red."

— Nightfire Tradition,
The Magical Tradition of Marrishland

Eda Stormgul walked the broken stone streets of Domus Palus, the capital and largest city in Marrishland. Swamp grass grew from cracks in the street, and to one side, a tree grew in the crumbled remains of a centuries old building's foundation.

Even in the midst of high civilization, the swamp encroaches, she mused.

The wizard wore thigh-high leather boots over her thick brown pants. Her tan shirt clung to her body in the early summer heat, and the clean leather utility vest and thick cyan-colored wool cloak she wore only made her sweat more. Heavy leather gloves hung from her belt, and the hilt and gouger of a marsord peeked through a slot in her cloak just above the knee.

The suffocating night air only added to the sense of being smothered as the crumbling stone buildings leaned in around her. Eight lesser wizards followed her in loose formation, the colors of their cloaks — six wore bright green and two auburn — barely visible in the light from a dozen constellations. None of the lesser wizards carried a marsord, the rare, two-bladed weapon that only the rich and powerful could afford to have crafted from what little metal was found in Marrishland. Eda knew she wore hers at the pleasure of her eighth-degree patron. She had no delusions about her status.

The patrol walked the night-shrouded streets with no torches. Eda glanced up, feeling watched. Overhead, the constellation of Marrish stared down at her from the moonless sky.

The stars, souls of our greatest heroes, Eda thought, remembering her father's stories. He had believed they continued to guide the Mar in death as they had in life. Most of the wizards living in Domus Palus regarded it as superstitious nonsense only taken seriously by rural mundanes, and Eda had lived in the city long enough to question her beliefs.

At home, we shunned slaves and wizards. Here, I am a wizard, with two slaves, and though my father might be watching me from above, he might also be feeding the swamp.

The gaze of the stars felt accusing now. Her boot caught on a crooked cobblestone, and she stumbled. One of the green-cloaked wizards caught her before she fell. She thanked him and turned her attention from the stars to the path ahead.

A flash of white light, like a lantern suddenly lit, filled the square. Shielding their eyes, the wizards hesitated.

This is what we have waited for, Eda thought, grasping the hilt of her marsord and drawing the finely sharpened hacker from its sheath. A form materialized in the light. A man crouched on the ground in the center of the light, his red cloak tight around him. He kept his head down as he recovered from teleportation sickness.

Eda reached for a bottle on her belt, nodding to her wizards. She poured a few drops of the bitter brown liquid onto her tongue and blinked her eyes a few times as the torutsen took effect. The wizards followed suit.

All around, a sea of colored motes appeared — green, blue, auburn, amber, cyan, lavender, yellow and red — drifting lazily across the square like dust caught in the sun. Near the wizards, it whirled as they gathered it with silent will. This was the myst, the source of magic, and though Eda knew it was always there, only torutsen allowed her to see it like this. She had heard some people say that, with enough training, one did not need torutsen anymore.

The man rose to his feet before she was ready.

Some of the greens shot small bursts of fire that quickly turned parts of his cloak black. The auburns hollered for a direct attack, but Eda shook her head.

He recovered too quickly, she thought, raising her marsord.

The first real flame erupted from the stone near the man and immediately went out. Other bursts exploded against an invisible shield thrown up absently even as the red wizard expanded the circle of white light surrounding him.

Eda joined the attack, tearing at his defenses with counterspells.

The explosions and steam drew six more auburns and two more greens to the square. They were seventeen against one as the new wizards created a cocoon to entrap the man. He disappeared from view in their cloud of smoke and flame.

Eda stepped away from the cocoon, nodding to the auburn in charge of the reinforcements. *They will take care of the rest.* She ordered her patrol to fall back, but kept her eyes on the white cocoon surrounding the intruder.

"He must have suffocated by now," someone said.

Eda nodded grimly. *At least his blood is not on my head.*

"Where is that light coming from?" a green whispered.

The white light had not faltered.

"Get back!" she shouted to the auburns, raising her marsord.

Too late. A circle of green flame exploded from the cocoon, engulfing the reinforcements in a wall of fire that stopped just short of Eda and her patrol.

When her vision cleared, the man was already moving toward her with incredible speed.

She cut at him with the hacker and he swept the blade aside with his arm. Leaning in, she reversed the marsord and lunged for his ribs with the gouger, but he caught the short blade with his left hand, lifting his right hand at the same time as he met her eyes.

Eda's eyes widened as she saw his clean-shaven face.

The greens in the square picked at his back with sparks and skin rashes — weak attacks were all they could manage, right now.

"Is it you?" she started, and he closed his fist.

An unseen hand slammed her down to the uneven stones. The marsord was wrenched from her hand, clattering to the stony pavement.

Stunned, she watched him calmly pick up the weapon and turn his back on her — one red-garbed wizard against sixteen greens and auburns, who howled as they charged with knives. He lowered the loosely held marsord and raised his left hand as if such a gesture would halt them.

She shouted at them to stop, but they didn't hear her.

The wall of flame they ran through was white-hot. Their screams turned from rage to agony as they writhed on the ground.

She reached for the myst through the wall of cyan motes that their adversary had built around her. The motes of green and blue passed through the barrier in an insignificant trickle. The red wizard took two quick steps toward her and pressed her marsord against her throat.

"Surrender!" he demanded, his face clearly familiar to Eda now that the fight had subsided. His head whipped up as someone groaned in the square.

She swallowed. "Yes."

He glanced at her two auburns, who were healing the wounded. In a few more minutes, someone might be able to fight.

"Tell the others to do the same."

"Obey him," Eda called to them.

The auburns nodded and continued their healing.

He helped her to her feet and handed her back her marsord as though giving a bowl of soup to a guest. Then he helped the auburns heal the injured. She followed him. Two of the greens had died, their faces seared to the bone. Eda turned away.

How hot is his fire, she thought, *if it cut that deep?* Mar magic was best at healing surface wounds, and fire seldom burned to a deadly depth.

"What is your name?" he asked her after all the wizards had been healed. "And why did you attack me?"

She cleared her throat and met his green eyes. *Maybe it is not him. No, it is him. How could he forget me?*

"Eda Stormgul," she said. "Our master has ordered us to kill all eighth-degree wizards entering Domus Palus until the Chair is secured by his allies."

Rage flashed across his face, but it wasn't directed at her. He glanced at the dead greens. "Who sends greens and auburns to fight reds?"

Eda had been asking herself that question all day. "We have received many strange orders lately. Rumor has it one of Nightfire's apprentices intends to try for the Chair — the one man the Dux of Flasten fears."

The red smiled at the flattery. "He does not fear me, yet, but he will."

She had to ask. "You are Weard Sven Takraf, yes?"

He nodded. "Inform your peers and master that the one they hoped would not come to Domus Palus has arrived. There is no further need to attack arriving wizards."

She raised her right hand to the level of her cheek. "By the Oathbinder and with the heroes as my witnesses, we will do just that."

Sven weighed her with a glance.

She met those hard green eyes. "I, too, studied at Nightfire's Academy."

He lowered his gaze. "I remember you from Rustiford," he said softly.

"Horsa and Katla are also in Domus Palus."

He glanced up, eyes wide, although Eda couldn't tell which name had surprised him. He recovered quickly, seeming to digest this news. "You always liked to be on the winning side, Eda. If you would stand with the victor, stand with me after I take the Chair."

"If you seize the Chair, I will follow you into the Fens of Reur. Remember me when you are finished."

"I will."

 **2**

"The first day of summer in Marrishland marks the start of Duxfest, and it is the only time when the Mardux's power can be challenged. Any eighth-degree wizard not on the Council may win the Chair by defeating the current Mardux in a magical duel. If a wizard wins the Chair and holds it against all challengers for one full day, he becomes the new Mardux."

— Nightfire Tradition,
The Magical Traditions of Marrishland

Weard Sven Takraf, eighth-degree wizard and graduate of Nightfire's Academy, had a marsord because of his power, but he had not brought it to Domus Palus. He knew he could defeat anyone who would be Mardux without it, and the challenge of retaining that position would not trouble him. He had no intention of allowing it to.

Three days of challenges and still no Mardux, Sven thought. *Nightfire would have returned to the Academy if someone had been able to hold the Chair, which means the magocrats are divided. The gods could not have crafted a clearer omen.*

He smiled grimly. *And how long has anyone thought of Nightfire as anything but his name, when it is truly just the title of Marrishland's arbiter of the Law.*

Sven wore knee-high boots turned down at the tops all the way to his calves. His loose pants were dark green, tucked in and bunched up above the boots. A leather strap served as a belt, and thick, studded leather gloves hung from it. His brown shirt had a collar — also turned down — and long sleeves with drawstrings at the end to tighten them. His leather utility vest showed years of wear. All his clothes had travel stains, but old ones.

Close-cropped brown hair and dark, almost mud-colored, skin surrounded his green eyes, hawkish nose and sharp mouth. Green eyes — Marrish's eyes, as the mundanes called them — were rare among Mar, but Sven knew of three others besides his parents who had them.

So much coincidence cannot be coincidence.

Domus Palus was the seat of the Mardux, the not-quite king of Marrishland and ruling magocrat. The city on the coast was the center of Mar civilization, and home to thousands of wizards, six times their number in mundanes and the largest slave population in the country.

And like our civilization, it stagnates around us, Sven thought as he passed a square reclaimed by the swamp. There was even a suckmud willow in it.

The slaves — mostly convicts whose crime had been reneging on an oral agreement — lived outside the ancient city. The mundanes, Mar who had not studied magic, lived throughout the city. Sven only cared about one group right now, the wizards, and they were at the citadel.

The "palace" of Domus Palus.

In the center of the city, eight tall steps led up to a wide walkway crossing between the citadel and the temple of Marrish. On that walkway, many of the most powerful magocrats in Mar history had fought for the position of ruler of Marrishland. Most contenders died simply because killing a powerful wizard was far easier than subduing one.

Sven heard the sounds of battle before he saw anything.

The massive citadel came into view, its stone and iron bulk in marginally better condition than the buildings around it. Crowds of wizards appeared, a milling mass of city officials on a holiday. Most wore green and auburn, but he could make out patches of blue, amber and cyan. This late in the night, slaves kept torches lit, filling the air with oily smoke.

What a waste of energy, Sven thought, shaking his head sadly.

He picked out and counted the lavender and yellow wizards, those one or two ranks below eighth-degree. As he reached a hundred, he stopped. Then he sought the bright cloaks of eighth-degree wizards and found them on the walkway. Two fought in the center, marsords flailing as fire burst between them. Sven judged the battle nearly over.

There were fifteen besides the two fighting — a group of five on the citadel side, two standing near them but separate, and eight standing in front of the temple, perched like a bunch of greedy, terri-fied scavengers waiting for the damnen to finish its meal.

Sven pressed forward, the color of his cloak making the crowd bend around him like water around a bubble of marsh gas. As he reached the foot of the steps, one of the red-cloaked men on the walkway drove his marsord through the other.

The victor — hands bloody, face blackened by burns — cut off his opponent's head and kicked it to the feet of the eight scavengers, a dark scowl on his face. Sven searched the victor's eyes and found the tiredness there. The foremost of the eight, the Dux of Flasten, Volund Feiglin, glared murderously at the victor and nudged the young man by his side.

Ketil Wenigar, Volund's son. Sven wondered who the challenger had been.

"Would anyone else like to die before sunrise?" the victorious wizard called hoarsely.

Volund scowled at Ketil before speaking. "There will be a chal-lenge tomorrow, you can be sure."

Nightfire stepped forward, part of the pair behind the victor. "Does any other wish to challenge Einar Schwert tonight?"

Einar wiped his marsord on the corpse of his opponent and sheathed it. None of the reds at the edge of the square stirred.

"Weard Schwert will return at noon. If no challenger defeats him by this time tomorrow, he will be Mardux."

The bloodied wizard turned on his heel and marched to the cita-del. The stiffness of his dirty red cloak betrayed a limp he had not yet healed. The group of five parted to let him pass, following only after Nightfire and his companion caught up to Einar. Sven crept up the stairs as Volund, cursing loudly at his son, stormed after them into the citadel. Ketil followed meekly.

Ignoring the six bickering reds and their seventh-degree companion, Sven joined the yellow-garbed priests of Marrish as they began disposing of the body.

Ketil hesitated because Einar just killed his brother, Sven noted as they moved the head. *Volund cannot take the Chair while he is on the Council, but he would have a son there. And what brings a borderland weard like Einar Schwert into this?* Sven glanced at the six reds.

A tall one with burning grey eyes was watching him as though all the Mar's troubles could be laid at Sven's feet. He turned to shout something hotly into the discussion.

They seem to want the Chair as well, but they let Volund's son fight first. Why?

As Sven eyed them, he gauged their strength. Surely any eighth-degree could defeat a tired eighth-degree. He shook his head. *Gobbels will eat their own if it is the least dangerous source of food.*

The crowd began to disperse. The eighth-degrees who still disputed Einar's claim to the Chair and their attendants did not stir from their place by the temple.

Sven thanked the priests as they blessed him in Marrish's name and gently moved him away from the corpse. He walked over to the vultures as the crowd and priests began to disperse. They did not notice him immediately.

" ... Must have gotten a message out of Domus before Duxfest," the angry, gaunt man was saying.

"A pest to the last, our Rorik Beurtlin," a man adorned in gold rings and necklaces said. "Like a konig worm infestation."

"Dux Feiglin's gambit has failed like his son," the obese man said. "Weard Schwert will hold the Chair tomorrow."

The only woman in the bunch frowned and opened her mouth to speak, but the gaunt man cut her off.

"We will be in the Fens of Reur before snow flies, am I right, Weard Faul?"

A slight young Mar balled his hands into fists and opened his mouth to speak. He closed it when the yellow — a pale-skinned man with straight, black hair — touched his arm.

The one with the jewelry sneered. "I did not see you step forward, Vigfus Vielfrae. Why did you bother traveling to Domus from Flasten if you had no intention of making yourself useful to your dux? Surely it caused you some ... strain."

The rotund man's face purpled in rage. "And what of you, Solvi Zorn? If you had challenged Einar in his weakened condition ..."

The gaunt Mar cut him off. "And make an enemy of Flasten? I may take the Chair tomorrow, but not without consulting my allies first."

He noticed Sven then, and all eyes turned to the newcomer. Sven kept his face expressionless.

"Solvi Zorn of Domus?" he asked quietly. "Perhaps you can tell me how many challengers Einar Schwert has defeated."

The gaunt Mar's grey eyes narrowed, and Sven did not need Fraemauna's eyes to guess the man's next move. "Do you think you can topple the old man?"

"It was a simple question," Sven said.

"We do not even know who you are," said the yellow smoothly, head and body swiveling to catch all the glaring eyes. "Young wizard, tell us your name."

Sven felt the slightest brush of a spell against his cheek and instantly snapped at the myst. *The yellow is trying to calm me with his magic.* Sven took an involuntary step back.

"I am Sven Takraf."

Vigfus gave a dismissive snort, but Solvi leaned forward a little, intrigued. The woman leaned over to whisper something to the gold-encrusted man, and the yellow stepped behind the frail, young wizard as though attempting to vanish.

I remember you, too, Robert Wost.

"Sven Takraf?" Solvi asked. "Of Tortz?"

"Ask your friend Dux Feiglin about me, Weard Zorn."

"Your ears are sharp, Weard Takraf," Solvi said. "I suppose you heard my name and Vigfus Vielfrae's. The thin one is Weard Ari Faul, and his man there is Weard Robert Wost. The woman is Weard Arnora Stolz, and her friend with the rings is Weard Valgird Geir. The silent one with the vacant expression is Weard Horik Neid."

"He is drunk on narcotics," Vigfus said. "He is a worthless piece of Domin's own dung, is that not so, Horik?"

Horik opened his mouth, but only drool came out.

"Weard Takraf, we hear the renegade Brand Halfin imprisoned you four years ago at Tortz."

"Volund Feiglin was there," Sven said. "I am sure that you can learn the story from him. If you cannot answer my question, I can go ask Nightfire or some other member of the Council."

"Einar Schwert defeated Ozur Betrun this afternoon, and two opponents tonight."

Sven nodded. *A fourth opponent surely would have finished him, yet none of them stepped forward. These are the ones who will challenge me, and they do not trust each other. It is a wonder anyone ever wins the Chair.*

"Do you intend to challenge Weard Schwert, Weard Takraf?" Solvi asked, voice too smooth for Sven's liking.

They want more power, and they do not even know how to use what they already have. Yet, they live for power. They would do anything to acquire more for themselves.

Memories of Tortz pressed in on him. He forced them away, gritting his teeth.

Or to keep others from having any.

Sven clenched his hands into fists at his side. "I will be Mardux because you cannot defeat me." They all started talking at once, but Sven spoke over them. "Weard Vielfrae would have to break a sweat, so he will not fight. Weard Geir is too weighted down with gold to step forward tomorrow. Weard Stolz would require many nine-day spans to plan a way to eliminate the danger of her defeat. Weard Faul cannot think for himself. Weard Neid does not even know what the Chair is. Weard Zorn, you fear my reputation too much to step forward. A mundane has more courage than any of you, and a mapmaker possesses more wisdom."

He started walking away.

Solvi hollered after him, "We had an agreement with the dux! His sons would go first!"

This is why I have come here, Sven thought. *This is why the gods chose me for this path. This is why the Mar need me.*

He walked into the citadel.

Nightfire must have noticed me while I watched the end of the battle.

Sven sent a slave to find him. The boy couldn't have been older than twelve, with dark eyes and calloused hands.

What crime could he have committed? What oath could someone so young break?

Sven waited in a room that might once have been a meeting hall. Several centuries of ivy had eaten through the ceiling. The flagstone floor was a mass of cracks, and bare earth peeked through in places. A second-story hallway opened to the room across the back, resulting in a crumbling balcony large enough for the entire population of Rustiford to stand on.

He imagined it whole once again.

I will commission a tapestry of the gods giving the Guardian his tasks, and the Guardian will have my face. No one will forget Mardux Sven Takraf.

"You will challenge Einar Schwert."

Sven did not turn to welcome Nightfire. "Of course, master. Marrish said I would be Mardux. Fraemauna convinced me. Seruvus stood there, and even the gods must fulfill promises brought before the Oathbinder."

Nightfire stood next to Sven, followed his eyes to the gaps in the ceiling through which the stars shone. He was a much older man. His hair was streaked gray and black, his skin much paler than Sven's for lack of sun. Under his cloak, he wore an outfit similar to Sven's, and he had not brought his marsord with him, either.

There are no Drakes in Domus Palus, Sven thought, *and Nightfire is a scholar, not a magocrat.*

He noticed that his master's companion had joined them. Katla Duxpite was Sven's green-eyed sister and four years his senior. She had worn the red a year longer than Sven. Education had transformed her as it had him, but in different ways, and they had barely spoken since Tortz.

"Weard Schwert is not your enemy. What will you do when you are Mardux that he would not do?" Nightfire asked softly.

"Unite Marrishland. Defeat the Mass. As the gods said I should." Sven couldn't keep the hesitation from his voice.

"And?"

Sven met his master's piercing green eyes. "And they said I will succeed you."

"You cannot be the arbiter if you are the Mardux."

"I will change the Law. I will remove the distinction between magocrat and mundane."

"Did the gods truly ask for that?"

"It is necessary." *They implied it. They want it.*

Nightfire frowned deeply. He took several steps away from Sven and turned around.

"You asked to see me. What is it you want?"

"I need your support when I take the Chair tomorrow. No one must doubt I am the Guardian."

"You speak as though you have already crushed your enemies!" Katla snapped.

Sven ignored her. *Her master is no threat without Volund.* "I have told you this day would come, master."

Nightfire shook his head. "As many times as I have supported you, Sven, you know I cannot take a side in this."

"Then tell me about Einar Schwert. You say he is not my enemy. Why does he seek the Chair?"

Nightfire glanced at Katla, and they sighed almost in unison.

"Please join us, Sven," Katla said finally with a weak smile. "We have some soup."

 **3**

*"Auburn is for Wisdom. Few Mar can use Wisdom well,
but its power is that of illusion and deception. Though it
may not seem as practical as Energy, Power or Vitality,
do not underestimate Wisdom's power. Farl enchanters ruled kingdoms in Flecterra on the strength of their
command of Wisdom."*

— Nightfire Tradition,
Nightfire's Magical Primer

Einar, wearing a new red cloak, regarded Sven coolly from the other end of the walkway. His marsord hung at his right knee, the gouger and hilt peeking out through the gap in the front of his cloak.

An overcast sky hid the noon sun. The six reds and Robert stood between Sven and the temple. The Duxess of Pidel and the Duxes of Skrem, Gunne, Piljerka and Wasfal, as well as Dux Feiglin and his son — the entire Council — blocked the way to the Citadel. Nightfire and Katla stood to the right of the Council.

"Weard Takraf," Einar said, drawing his weapon slowly and examining the saw-toothed hacker. "I warn you to step down. You are a legend whose blood I do not want on my hands."

Sven's gaze never left Einar, though he adjusted the leather gloves on his hands. "Weard Schwert, I admire your devotion to principles so much like mine, but I must be Mardux."

Einar nodded and extended the marsord toward Sven in challenge. "Then let the duel begin."

Einar's approach to duels, Sven had found out at dinner the previous night, was an enhanced warrior gambit. Power to strengthen the sword and his body, and increased speed to get to his opponent before a spell was cast. Sven had devised a defense. Before Einar even moved, he set a spell his opponent would trigger. Einar rushed him, raw force surrounding the blade, feet leaving a trail of lightning on the ground. Sven built a shield of force and braced himself. The two crashed into each other in a blaze of blue motes, but the force of Einar's rush threw Sven backward.

He rolled to his feet even as Einar brought the gouger down on his back, below his ribs.

Sven gasped, fell down and rolled over. A healing spell began as flames crackled in the air, aimed at his opponent's midsection, but Einar had moved in a flicker.

Sven's triggered spell struck Einar blind. Momentarily confused, he froze, and Sven used that moment to heal himself fully.

Einar began the counterspell, but Sven, anticipating it, twisted and corrupted it delicately. Einar regained his sight, but now he saw six Svens standing before him, none of them real.

Abandoning his enhanced warrior gambit, Einar launched spheres of fire at the illusions Sven had placed in his mind, forcing Nightfire and the other reds to counter the attacks before they hit the audience of greens and blues below. Using this moment of uncertainty, Sven added more subtle components, though he felt the strain of working with illusions in spite of his preparations. The Mar were weakest with those parts of the myst, and using them quickly tired a wizard.

To all appearances, Einar stood in one place, completely immobilized by the phantasms of his corrupted spell. Sven locked a shell of countermagic around his uninjured opponent. A murmur drifted through the crowd as Sven casually took off his gloves and plucked Einar's marsord from clutching fingers. Even the other eighth-degrees seemed ill at ease.

They are uncertain of what I have done.

Sven ceased gathering the myst, turning the marsord over in his hands absently. The sword had a blade on either side of the hilt. The longer blade, known as the hacker, was serrated on one side and finely honed on the other. The shorter blade, or gouger, was thicker with grooves on it to let blood drain. It was a weapon for use against Mar, Drake or swamp. Sven wiped his blood off the gouger.

He knew he possessed the power to kill this man. It was the way of duels. No one was foolish enough to leave a rival alive.

Out of the corner of his eye, he saw Ari lean forward in anticipation of the inevitable.

What interest do you have in this man?

Sven looked at Einar carefully — the aged face, the brown eyes, the grey hair. The red cloak was still clean and free of wrinkles. He checked his magic. The illusion would fade soon — half a minute, at most. He would have to choose quickly. Last night, in talking with Nightfire and Katla, he had learned much more about Einar than his fighting style, and even then, knew what he would do if his gambit worked today.

You guarded our frontier once before. I will give you a chance to do so again.

Sven placed the tip of the marsord against Einar's chest, prepared to summon magic if the man resisted, and waited. The crowd held its breath, watching him and looking for the killing blow. Einar came to his senses with a jolt, eyes wide in shock.

"How did you ...?"

"Einar Schwert, you are defeated. Yield."

Einar attempted to cast a spell, but the shell held his magic at bay. He stared hard at Sven.

What are you thinking, old man? Sven kept his face passive. *Are you thinking, why would Sven Takraf want the Chair? Or why tell me to yield if you are going to kill me anyway?*

Finally Einar nodded. "You have indeed bested me, Weard Takraf. The Chair is yours if you can hold it against them."

Sven did not stir. "Swear your loyalty to me."

The crowd murmured. Robert whispered something furiously to the other eighth-degree wizards.

"I understand." Einar raised his right hand solemnly. "By the Oathbinder, and Marrish, my patron, I swear my fealty to you, Sven Takraf, Guardian of Marrishland."

The signs are everywhere! How many others have noted them as he has?

Sven removed the blade and returned it. "You serve your patron loyally, Weard Schwert."

Einar stepped back and out of Sven's way. Sven stuffed the gloves behind his utility vest and drew out another pair from the pouch at his side.

As he put them on, he met Nightfire's eyes, skimmed past the Duxess of Pidel and the duxes of the southern duxies and rested on Dux Volund Feiglin. Volund glared back in undisguised fury and prodded his son, Ketil, forward.

Sven deliberately turned his back on Ketil and spoke to the remaining six reds.

"Who disputes my ascent? Step forward and speak."

Solvi looked past his shoulder at the spurned dux's son and stepped forward with a confident smile. Vigfus' smile had finally reached his eyes. Sven sized up his opponent, considering this man's value to his plan. Alive, Solvi would turn against him someday. Dead, then. But … Sven steeled himself.

You will make a valuable lesson for my enemies.

"I warn you, Weard Zorn," Sven said coldly, stretching his fingers out in front of him. "Yours will not be the fate of Weard Schwert if you oppose me. Step down and swear fealty to me, and I will spare you."

Solvi sneered. "You may have survived Tortz, but you will not survive me, now that you have exhausted yourself with farl tricks."

Sven kept his left hand up, stretching the fingers wider. "Then let the duel begin."

Solvi was still readying his first attack as Sven closed his hand into a fist and a green beam of fire burned into his challenger's throat, melting it closed. Solvi clutched at his neck, all thought of attack forgotten. He mended his windpipe and prepared to throw up a hasty defense. Sven didn't wait for him.

Slices of fire slapped off Solvi's hands and cauterized his wrists. Tiny beams of light burned out his eyes. Invisible hammers snapped his shinbones and kneecaps. Knives of force filleted his skin. Bolt after bolt of intensely focused energy struck the wizard, hacking him limb from limb. The smell of burnt flesh made Sven gag. Ari whimpered. Someone at the edge of the square vomited.

They have seen my mercy. Now I will live up to my reputation for ruthlessness.

Numbly, Sven continued. After the eighth or ninth bolt of fire, the man was surely dead. But he continued until there was little more than a steaming pile of burnt flesh bubbling on the walkway.

Sven stripped off his gloves to dead silence and stuffed them behind his vest, retrieving a fresh pair from a pouch at his side. He turned to the other five reds. He could see the uncertainty on their faces and knew the reason why. Wizards never put on such displays when fighting for the Chair, because it was imperative they save their strength for the large number of challengers they might face. The use of illusions to subdue an opponent would have worn out all but the most powerful wizards. To win the second duel so flamboyantly might be possible for the strongest magic-wielders, but afterward, a green could defeat them.

And they are right. The duel with Einar should have left me too weak to set dry tinder alight.

"Are there any others who would challenge my authority?" he demanded. His voice could have frozen the swamp.

Prodded by his comrades, Horik stepped forward hesitantly.

They test me, Sven thought.

He allowed Horik two nervous steps, and the challenger was looking back at his companions when Sven struck. The melon-sized fireball made barely a noise as it struck, leaving sparks licking the other wizards' robes. A headless Horik Neid slumped at their feet. Ari turned and vomited.

"A challenge must be issued!" Volund exclaimed. "That was cold-blooded murder, and the weard should be tried for it."

From his place at the back of the pack of reds, Robert granted Sven a small smile.

I learned your lessons, but I was never your pupil.

Sven turned away from Robert to face Volund.

Nightfire spoke. "Weard Takraf issued the challenge. Weard Neid took the step forward. The Law says nothing about waiting for your opponent to be ready. That is a courtesy developed from centuries of challenges." He glared at Sven.

Courtesies are well and good, but the Law is the part you must follow, Sven thought. He considered if they would change the Law for this.

It will do them no good, for I will change the Law more dramatically.

"We will be back tomorrow," Volund said.

"Then you will lose another of your sons to me, Dux Feiglin," Sven replied disinterestedly.

Ketil shivered, turned to his father and whispered hurriedly in his ear. Volund slapped his son away. He made no effort to mask his hatred. "We will be back tomorrow."

Volund grabbed Ketil by the arm and stalked away. Sven waited as the carrion eaters passed him to follow the dux. Vigfus offered him a shaky grin while sweat poured off his brow. Arnora nodded respectfully, and Valgird ignored him. Ari's head was bent in almost supplication, but Robert met Sven's eyes with a knowing smile that sent a chill down his spine.

Yellow-garbed priests took the bodies of Solvi and Horik. Sven started toward the citadel, but Katla approached him in the middle of the walkway. The audience remained hushed, and even Nightfire seemed on his heels, ready to stop what appeared to be a challenge.

"You are trying to boil soup in a wooden bowl," she said quietly, stepping in very close as though congratulating him. "When it burns through, you will have neither bowl nor soup."

Sven leaned back and met her stony green eyes. He looked away, annoyed. "I refuse to show mercy to Marrishland's enemies."

"Volund and his reds are not Marrishland's enemies — only yours."

"Nor are they Marrishland's allies — only your master's."

She frowned. "The path you are taking prevents you from taking any other roads."

"Are you now my enemy, too?"

"A fire does not refuse to bend in the wind. It bows that it might spread more quickly."

"A friend of mine tried that, once. The wind snuffed him out."

"Mother would have said ..."

Sven's patience slipped. This was an old argument. "Mother was enslaved by your precious dux before I was eight," he said coldly. "Tyra Gematsud raised you, not me."

She closed her mouth. Her eyes glistening with tears, she teleported away.

Sven marched toward the citadel, Einar at his heels.

"Old lover?"

Sven opened his mouth to answer but changed his mind. *If he knows who she is and who she serves, he may yet turn against me.*

"I am in no mood, Weard Schwert."

Sven knew he should be horrified by the day's activities, sick to his stomach for his behavior on the square. Two men dead by his hands, but he felt nothing.

It was the only way to win three consecutive duels. My display of superhuman power today will keep other wizards from challenging me each year. My enemies will have to find other ways of fighting me, ways that don't force me to give away my weaknesses.

Sven removed the gloves from his utility vest and returned them to the pouch at his side. He had killed men who had done nothing wrong before, as he protected innocent people from the wrath of a magocrat. Horik and Solvi had deserved their fates.

For Marrishland, I must beat those who would be her enemies. I must learn their strengths and weaknesses and use that knowledge against them. Now I am the most powerful wizard in Marrishland. I must use this position to my advantage.

Slaves and mundanes of the Citadel stepped forward until they surrounded him, asking his command. Sven flinched slightly at this servility in fellow Mar.

This, too, will I change.

He gave them instructions patiently, asking for food and a room. Sitting at a table before a narrow opening, he ate the soup they brought. It was delicious and thick with meat. He ate it in silence, noting with some sadness that it was the best he had ever tasted.

While many mundanes risk their lives daily in the swamps to feed themselves, the most powerful weards do not even have to boil their own soup.

He vowed he would not allow such meals to become a habit. Wild rice and laurita soup with a little meat had sustained him all his life. There was no reason he should eat better food than that.

If I did, I would be no better than Vigfus.

When he had finished his meal, he withdrew to his quarters to rest. He stayed awake just long enough to offer a prayer of thanksgiving to his patrons for his success in battle that day, and for the gifts they had given him.

 4

"The oldest Mar stories are more symbolic than literal. Oral tradition loses details of fact in just a few generations, replacing them with details that reinforce existing values. When these stories are written down, it preserves them, but traps the tales in time. As the centuries pass, the symbolic details lose their strength as metaphors and come to be regarded as literal facts."

— Weard Eira Helderza,
Unavoidable Problems in Literature

Sven Takraf's dramatic victories over three contenders for the Chair on his first day effectively ended all formal resistance to his ascent, and he faced no further challenges the next day. Existing political pressures, clever planning and turns of good fortune often attributed to divine intervention allowed him to lay the foundation for his rule after only one forty-five day month as Mardux.

Sven chose an ideal year to seek the Chair — the same Duxfest when more than a dozen reds conspired with Dux Feiglin to topple Mardux Rorik Beurtlin. Five reds died at Rorik's hands in two days before he fell to Ozur Betrun. Rorik's old friend and master duelist Weard Einar Schwert arrived from the frontier to issue a challenge of his own.

Volund's allies were still implementing a revised plan to take the Chair when Sven Takraf arrived in Domus Palus. By the end of Sven's first day of duels, nearly a third of all the reds in Marrishland lay dead in the year's battle for the Chair. If he had not spared Weard Schwert, though, he may still have faced more challengers. However, while the remaining reds could not know with certainty that Weard

Schwert would issue a fresh challenge against anyone who defeated Sven Takraf, no point of Law forbade him from doing so. Dux Feiglin and his surviving supporters decided not to take this risk.

Minutes after Nightfire announced Sven's ascent to the chair, the four hundred seventh-degree wizards belonging to the priesthoods of Domus Palus' temples arrived at the citadel without warning or explanation to swear loyalty to Sven. The priests had not given an oath of loyalty to a Mardux in a century, and few people knew that one of Sven's friends, Weard Horsa Verifien, was behind it. Some saw divine approval of Sven's rule in this gesture, but no one could ignore the magic resources hundreds of yellows represented.

Sven acted quickly to consolidate his power within Domus Palus. The Mardux was little more than a dux of duxes. He was the dux of Domus, equal rank in rank to all the other duxes, except that by law and tradition, the ruler of Domus led the Council. His authority ended at the edge of Domus. But as a stranger to Domus, he wanted to make certain of his people's loyalty.

He ordered all wizards to attend a banquet celebrating his ascendancy to the Chair. During the days-long celebration, he greeted all in the government, stripped them of their ranks and titles and demanded an oath of fealty like those the priests and Einar had given him. He banished anyone who refused from the Duxy of Domus and confiscated their property — the Law wouldn't let him execute them. While his education and experience had not equipped him to analyze and restructure the bureaucracy of the capital after banishing so many wizards, he gave Einar and Horsa full authority to act on his behalf. Sven personally and severely punished any magocrat in the capital caught committing an act of bad faith, and the others soon learned he had no patience for the tears and pleas of corrupt officials.

Eighteen days into his rule, Sven met with the Council to tell them of his plan to unite Marrishland. He met fierce resistance from Volund. Nightfire and the Duxess of Pidel reiterated their neutrality. The Dux of Wasfal offered suggestions but would not declare his loyalty outright. The Duxes of Skrem, Gunne and Piljerka swore fealty with little encouragement.

Little noted but of great importance to the course events would take was the arrival of the Traveller and storyteller known as Pondr. He played only a minor role in spreading the Mardux's legend, but his stories had a profound effect on Sven that may have altered the course of Mar history.

The celebratory banquet evolved into something else during the fifth nine-day span of Sven's reign. He stood on a balcony overlooking the revelry, viewing the celebrating crowd. Einar stood at his shoulder.

"I should stop this soon," Sven mused. "It is devouring resources we will need later."

"Food and drink can be replenished," Einar said. He swept an arm out over the crowd below. "These are the resources you must watch most closely."

"They have all sworn their loyalty to me before the Oathbinder. Even a mundane knows the consequences of breaking such an oath."

Einar chuckled.

"You do not trust their word."

Einar shrugged. "I trust it for what it is — a promise to obey you as your position demands."

"Many of the faces out there are my students and friends. They did not have to come all the way to Domus Palus to swear fealty to me."

"Wizards flock to powerful leaders for many different reasons," Einar said, leaning against the crumbling stone rail of the balcony. "Some are here for you. Some hope for money or advancement. Some may even join you because you share an enemy with them. Most just want to keep the positions they have here in the city, and they really did not have any choice but to swear fealty to you."

"Will they resist me?"

"Some may, but most will not risk your wrath. They did not keep their posts this long by refusing to bend in the wind."

Sven gazed down at the colorful crowd of magocrats.

Normally, the greens would have outstripped any other color, but at this function, the bright green had soon been weeded out and ambers and higher colored the room. Amber, cyan, lavender and yellow made lively patterns across the floor. Among them, Eda Stormgul — the woman who had led the patrol the night Sven had arrived — wandered, no doubt currying favor from her new superiors while commanding those now below her.

She joined me because mine was the winning side, Sven thought.

Rustiford had given eight others besides Sven to Nightfire's Academy, and none would have gone willingly. He frowned as the thought crossed his mind.

I went willingly, he thought, a part of him trying to recall why. *For knowledge,* he decided, *and to protect Erbark, who is not as intelligent as I am.*

Below, a man of middling years gained the stage and gathered his grey cloak about him in a flourish. Sven peered at him. The man was no Mar, but it was hard to place his origin.

He began speaking and then singing in adhi tetrads, and the crowd became fixated.

> "Oh come sit by my hearth tonight
> And warm your hands near golden flames.
> Here, have some meat and soup as well.
> Sit, eat, and hear what I will say:
> I am not ready yet for sleep.
> The night is just as long as day.
> What stories do your people tell?
> Who are your heroes? Give their names.
> For it is hours 'til morning's light."

We are known for our love of the legend, Sven thought, smiling. *Perhaps that is another reason so many have sworn to serve me — to be a part of my story.*

The crowd, too, from lowliest slave to highest yellow, was mesmerized already. The speaker raised his hand toward Sven and appeared to stand taller.

"I tell of our Mardux's humble beginnings," he cried, and the crowd roared approval. The storyteller appeared to be waiting for

Sven's permission.

Sven was surprised by the choice. *Is this a story to tell now? But the people below do not know me well yet. Let them hear what I have done. They will see soon enough what else I can do.*

He waved the storyteller on, and the man bowed extravagantly as the wizards cheered.

"Sven Takraf was born i'the wild'ress of Gunne, a secret child of Marrish an' Fraemauna. Seekin' to protect her lover from the wrath of his wife, Dinah, Fraemauna aban'oned her son. Seruvus, who sees all, took pity on the babe, blessed the boy with his own memory an' gave him to Pitt Gematsud to raise as his son."

All worries of the storyteller vanished from Sven's mind. The man certainly didn't know any truths, if that was how he began. And though he spoke in the rural, uneducated Mar dialect, he certainly could have picked that up. Trained storytellers could do many things.

"Pitt an' his wife had no child'en, an' they were happy to do as the god asked. But they didn't reckon on the jealous wrath of the Bald Goddess. Dinah called a ban' of damnens to raid the villages of Gunne, promisin' them all the slaves they could catch as lon' as they killed any child with Marrish's eyes of green fire."

Now Sven found Eda, her back to the storyteller, her brown eyes seeking him. Another face was turned toward him, a man not three years older than him, wearing yellow. *Horsa Verifien,* Sven thought. *There were six of us who finished: Brand and Tosti, who are dead, Eda, Horsa, Katla and myself. Is it coincidence these two are here now? The gods have played their games with me before.*

"The list of people taken an' green-eyed child'en killed grew daily, an' th'ones left lived in fear of Dinah's child'en. The people of Gunne cried out to the gods for deliverance, an' Seruvus heard them an' brought the message to Fraemauna.

"She sent her servant, the great wizard Nightfire, to spirit her son to safety in his Academy. The son of Fraemauna would receive the gifts of Marrish an' become a wizard who would be the Guardian of Marrish-land — the one who'd lead the Mar to vict'ry over Dinah an' Domin."

Sven started at the line. *Can he know that I believe this too? The storyteller paints myth as truth, and truth as myth. What does he really know?*

"Marrish objected. This wasn't how wizards chose their students. Fraemauna's son would have to prove himself worthy of his father's gifts, first. The goddess saw the wisdom i'this, but she didn't wish to leave Sven an' th'other towns to Dinah's damnens. Actin' as her han's, Nightfire led Pitt Gematsud an' all the other Mar through the Dead Swamps an' to a new place near his Academy. Many didn't survive the journey, but those who did foun'ed a town at the edge of ravit territory, which they called Rustiford.

"Grateful to Nightfire for deliverin' them from the damnens, the villagers asked how they could repay him. 'Every year on Weardfest, you must give me a slave,' he told them. 'The slave must be eighteen years old an' must volunteer to serve me for eight years.'"

Sven's hands gripped the stone in front of him, his knuckles shading to white. His chest rose as he took a deep, calming breath, and when he exhaled slowly, he thought his breath moved the storyteller's cloak, so far away. The memory rose in his mind like a bubble of marsh gas.

The green of Rustiford had seemed so large to Sven when he had set himself on the path to Mardux, years ago. The mood that night was a mix of somberness, relief and fright. The elder told the story during Weardfest, and this time, it was Finn's turn to play the role of Brand. Sven would get his chance, though.

I remember ...

 **5**

*"Each color of the cloaks worn by wizards corresponds
with those of the eight kinds of myst, which is the source
of Mar magic. Green is for Energy, which is used to create or negate heat, light and sound. It can also increase
the duration of other spells. Most Mar find Energy the
easiest magic to use, and producing a tongue of flame
at the tip of the finger is almost always the first application taught to an apprentice."*

— Nightfire Tradition,
Nightfire's Magical Primer

"The villagers heard Nightfire's terrifyin' words an' flinched," de-
claimed the elder on the green of Rustiford. "The price the wizard
asked was too much! Many townsfolk grumbled, an' it may've come
to blood an' fire, but Bran' Halfin shouted over them all."

"Hold, neighbors!" Finn Ochregut called tremulously, walking forward from his seat in the crowd and reciting his part of the story.
"We couldn't have made it here without Nightfire, an' we would've
died if we'd stayed. We know the Law an' what it demands for a life
preserved. We must do as he asks."

"But who'll go with him?" the villagers demanded as one.

"I'll go first," Finn announced in an uncertain voice.

A younger Sven watched Finn from a log near the fire. Cloaked
in black, he sat with three others, all one year younger than Finn.
Across from them, two villagers sat. They were Finn's age — safe
from slavery to Nightfire and torn by guilt at Finn going instead of
them.

"Nightfire heard the boy's words an' smiled," Sveld, the elder, continued. "He allowed Bran' a few hours to bid his family an' frien's farewell before takin' him from us.

"Ev'ry year, Nightfire has come to collect, and ev'ry year, a brave young man or woman has stepped forward to pay Rustiford's debt. Bran' Halfin was the first. He was my gran'son, the son of my daughter, Tora Halfin, who fell during the passage to Rustiford."

All the names were repeated, as they were every year. Rustiford had sacrificed seven young men and women to Nightfire, and now an eighth would go. None had ever returned.

The names were branded on Sven's soul, and his eyes were rooted to Finn.

Had I thought, eight years ago, that I could be the one chosen? Maybe I did know.

Eda's eyes were still liquid brown in his mind, and Katla's fiery green. Brand was a distant memory, a young man more like an older brother than a playmate, but strong and stern.

The first to choose.

And Horsa, who had taken Sven in like a younger brother when his sister had made her choice.

The elder paused for a long time, looking at the small crowd that was the whole population of Rustiford.

"This year, Finn Ochregut has offered himself as the tribute to Nightfire. This town is in his debt an' the debts of all who've gone before him."

To Sven, Finn looked more like a man who would sooner plunge his head in a marsh pond than do this. Whether he had made his choice to gain honor or because he owed a debt, Sven could tell that the ceremony was the only reason Finn wasn't fleeing. Though Mar distanced themselves from immediate family at a certain age — community was key to survival — Finn's mother was crying.

"The Weardfest has en'ed with the night. Today comes the wizard who will take our tribute an' leave us t'our grief."

The crowd did not stir as Sveld walked slowly away from the dying embers of the bonfire. When he reached Finn, the elder raised his right hand, palm open to near his own shoulder in a deferential blessing and salute. Finn returned it automatically, sweat rolling down his face despite the cool air. Others in the crowd did the same.

Some spoke to him in hushed tones, but most could not find words.

Finn's mother looked into her son's eyes, tears streaming down her face. She seemed on the point of clutching him in a crushing embrace, but thought better of the embarrassing display of physical affection in public and settled for placing a hand on his cheek before walking past.

Sven and his three companions, Erbark, Hauk and Lori, made no move to leave, waiting for the two across from them. Finn's peers left without speaking to Finn, without saluting him and without inviting anyone else to join them. Sven watched them, and at first he thought he alone saw them touch hands when they were nearly out of sight. He caught Erbark looking in the same direction, but his friend quickly pretended not to notice.

"Th' people of Rustiford came here to avoid this," Lori said quietly.

Sven huddled closer to them nervously, looking over his shoulder. He thought the great wizard could hear them.

Dad said the Duxy of Flasten used to raid our town, and all the towns around us, to take our people for slaves. That was years ago, when Sven was just a child, and halfway across the swamp. His father had said they had lived in a town with clean water and flat fields on the edge of two duxies.

"We came here because of this," Erbark said dully. He sat up straight, but his eyes were staring after the two who had just left.

They took us as slaves, Sven thought. Two kinds of slaves were allowed under the Law — tribute slaves and oathbreakers. Tribute slaves, like the ones Nightfire took, volunteered their service to repay a debt. Oathbreakers served as punishment for a crime, repaying their debt to the Oathbinder for breaking their promise to obey the laws of their community. A slave was supposed to serve a sentence of no more than eight years.

Flasten's slave-takers were magocrats who came to town and arrested whomever, claiming they were oathbreakers. The judge was a Flasten magocrat. The sentence was always the maximum. But it was worse than just lying about oathbreaking. Flasten then sold the slaves to foreigners, who did not understand the Law. No one ever returned.

"I feel so bad for them," Lori said, and everyone's eyes turned to the log Finn's peers had sat on.

"I feel relief," Sven said, letting his thoughts spill out. "They say we were starvin', that all the people Flasten took left us with not enough han's to feed an' clothe ourselves. That Dinah's Curse was runnin' through us like water through mud, an' we were on the edge of death, when Nightfire came an' saved us."

Across half of Marrishland, he added to himself. *Dad said thousands of us left with the great wizard, and there's less than a thousand in this town.* He looked at Finn, standing alone briefly. *And soon to be one less.*

He put his arms around his friends as they huddled together.

One of us four next year, Sven thought darkly, his breath puffing out in front of him. *We are the only four who will be of age.*

He remembered there once being seven kids his age. The trek from their old town took one kid, and two more had died from Dinah's Curse after Rustiford had been founded. He shook his head and stood up, his friends' eyes following him. *There had been six when Katla had chosen to go. There were three for this year. Next year, there would be four.*

And the year after that?

Sven realized he could not recall the number of sixteen-year-olds in Rustiford.

Brand will return to Rustiford next year. It's only eight years.

But eight years seemed like an eternity right now. Eda had told him of her plans to stay away from all the men in Rustiford until she could volunteer to join Horsa as Nightfire's slave in just a year. Two months later, though, deep in despair over her loss, she had come to Sven for comfort. Sven still wasn't sure which he regretted more — that he didn't refuse her or that she still volunteered to go with Nightfire the next year.

No. Eight years meant that by the time he returned, many people here wouldn't even remember him. It would break his father's heart, his father who had already lost his wife and daughter to the wizards.

Erbark helped Lori stand, and silent, giant Hauk, who had a tear on his cheek, grasped Sven's hand to pull himself up. Sven looked at his companions, his friends, and saw his fear mirrored in their faces as they left the green behind. They knew it, too.

Erbark broke the silence, "This is our last Weardfest together."

They walked, their boots breaking the frost on the ground, their breaths puffing out in clouds. The morning sun crawled out from behind the horizon as though it had overslept. The tall homes of the first adult citizens gave way to the shorter cabins of newly declared men and women.

"I'm scared," Lori voiced what they all felt.

"I'm not tired yet," Hauk made a universal suggestion.

"I've some soup," Sven invited.

"All right then," Erbark agreed for them.

They walked through the village. The sun struggled over the trees, slowly shedding light on the town. The smoke from scores of chimneys hung against the blueness of the clear sky. A brief gust of wind from the north moaned through the trees. Their heavy boots clunked up the stairs to the door of Sven's house.

Sven turned the latch and pushed the door open. The sun had not yet become bright enough to light the cabin, so he lit a lamp and stirred the hearth fire before hanging a small pot of soup over it. The four of them took a seat in a circle near the hearth.

They sat without speaking for a long time. Hauk lit a pipe, inhaled deeply, blew a stream of smoke through his lips and launched into a brief fit of coughing. Lori pulled the strip of cloth away from her hair, allowing the dark strands to cascade to her shoulders. She produced a brush and began brushing the black, curly hair rhythmically. Sven stirred the soup, watching as the flames engulfed the wood with greedy hunger. Erbark sharpened a dagger along a small whetstone.

Long moments passed in this way — the scrape of the metal, the crackle of the fire, the spoon against the bottom of the pot, the coughing fits between puffs of smoke and the whisper of hair against the brush. Then Sven spoke.

"The soup's ready."

The other three looked at him, a little surprised. With tired smiles, they accepted the meal offered them.

The soup was mediocre, being leftover from the previous day. It was a mixture of rabbit and root vegetables with just a hint of laurita, a wintertime soup that they would soon grow to detest. None of them complained, however. They merely ate quietly, even slurping up the last of the broth in their bowls.

The hum of voices and the scrape of walking feet on sandy paths alerted the four that Nightfire had arrived. Much of the town would turn out to watch Finn depart. Sven did not stir from his place in the circle, and neither did anyone else. They would not be going this year. It was important they stay together today.

"Which one of us?" Lori demanded. "It has to be one of us, so we might as well decide now."

None of them spoke for a minute, staring at Lori. She didn't blush.

How could you feel embarrassed about this? Sven thought. *It's like asking who'll go hunt for food or who'll boil the water so we can drink.*

"I can't go," Hauk said. "I've a duty to my neighbors."

They all knew what he meant. Hauk had trained with Thorhall, the blacksmith, for years. Thorhall was becoming too old to do smithwork, and Hauk was doing most of the work now. He was irreplaceable.

"I don't want to go, either," Lori said. "I want to raise a family."

Each one of them knew how important Lori's family was to her. She had been the oldest of nine children, making her practically a mother already. She had made it her duty to see that the children of the village did not wander into the swamp. The parents in Rustiford depended on her and trusted her.

But someone could replace her, Sven thought, but he forced his mouth to stay shut. *Is there an argument for everyone not going?*

He opened his mouth to speak.

"I'll go," Erbark broke in suddenly. "Perhaps he'll even let me visit Rustiford sometime."

He smiled and leaned back casually. Lori did not react so favorably.

"He's never let any of th'others visit, Erbark!" she snapped. "For all we know, he's sellin' all his slaves to the Dux of Flasten or findin' a reason to keep them longer than eight years."

"Not all wizards are slavers," Erbark said, testing his dagger's edge with one finger. "If he tries to cheat me, well … " The blade flashed in the air and sank into a knothole in the far wall.

"He's a wizard!" Lori cried. "He'll just hurt you if you fight him."

Erbark shrugged, and Hauk laughed so hard he pitched into a

coughing fit.

It's a fantasy, but what else do we have left? Sven thought, but he chuckled and pulled the hood over his head, his green eyes gleaming red in the firelight.

Lori stood up, pulled on her boots and stormed to the front door.

Erbark hurried to her side. "Where are you goin', Lori?"

"To watch Nightfire take Finn away from us with the rest of th'adults i'the town. When you're done talkin' like mapmakers, let me know."

Then the door opened, and Lori was gone. Erbark paused, deciding, and then returned to his chair.

Sven, Erbark and Hauk regarded each other in silence, suddenly uncomfortable. For a long while, none of them spoke. The sounds of Finn's departure filtered into the cabin, interrupted only by the occasional pop of the fire in the hearth.

Hauk stood up suddenly. "I'd better get some sleep. Thorhall might want me to make some nails this afternoon."

It was a weak excuse. Compassionate almost to a fault, Thorhall would spend the day consoling Finn's mother. It was unlikely he would work at all. But Erbark and Sven empathized with their friend. They all needed some time alone, now. Sven opened the door for Hauk and wished him peace and comfort in Marrish's name. Hauk murmured a blessing in return and plodded toward his house.

Sven returned to his seat and watched the flames of the hearth fire. His hooded head nodded once, and he woke instantly. He looked around his cabin, re-familiarizing himself with the room. Erbark's grey eyes were still open, but the eyelids were heavy, his expression blank. The fire had burned low, leaving only hot coals and ashes. There was little firewood left.

Not yet ready for sleep, Sven found that he was glad of the chore of chopping wood. Ignoring the crowd of people gathered at the distant village green, he began chopping vigorously, splitting the logs into flinders with heavy-handed blows. When the well of energy in his stomach had died down, he gathered the wood and returned to his fire. He fed the greedy flames until, it seemed, they would accept no more wood. He kicked off his boots and sat on his chair, satisfied, watching the fire dance madly around the logs, devouring them.

He sat there feeling the heat on his face — fascinated, horrified, afraid for his life, helpless.

"You or me?" Erbark asked suddenly.

Sven did not answer, could not.

"Your dad's already lost Katla to Nightfire."

Sven turned his head to face his friend. "An' your mom lost both your brothers to ochres on the way to Rustiford." His eyes shone in challenge. The very memory of the mossy, muck-covered Drakes would not be enough to shake his friend.

Erbark paused and looked at Sven intensely. The smile vanished, and a look of understanding replaced it. "You're a good man, Sven. None doubt your courage. You won't take Lori or Hauk away from their duties an' dreams any more than I will." Erbark leaned back in his chair and closed his eyes heavily. "But I'm goin' with Nightfire next year. Rustiford'll need someone as smart as you when you're old. You're a good man, Sven."

Sven did not respond. *But you're in love with Lori*, he wanted to remind his friend. But he knew it would be useless to argue.

A light snoring filled the room. Sven turned back to the fire. It crackled and smoked heavily in the still-wet wood, fingers of it seeking the cracks that would lead to the logs' dry hearts. It snapped wildly throughout its cage — yellow and red on the outside with sharp blue at the heart. Not for the first time he wondered whether the colors of the wizard's cloaks came from the colors of the fire. Sometimes he thought he saw deep reds and dark greens and black on the logs themselves. He knew the colors Mar wore were protective, helping them blend in and hide from Drakes. The wizards, though, wore bright colors that made them stand out. The brighter the cloak, the more powerful the wizard.

Nightfire wears red, so he must be very powerful. But why do they choose the colors they wear?

The room grew warm, and Sven became drowsy. His head dipped and did not rise for a long while.

The flames painted patterns on his closed eyelids, sending him strange, disturbing dreams of a burning town and swarms of attacking gobbels and ravits. He saw Lori at the center of a throng of children, trying to shield them all from the poisoned darts of the small, bristly ravits. Then he saw Erbark watching them all, too far away to help her.

He woke with a deep sense of guilt. He had missed Finn's departure. He had not objected to his friend's self-sacrifice. Sven turned to check Erbark, jaw open and head back. Then, as silently as he could manage, he pulled on his boots and slipped out into the cold morning air. He knew what he could do. He could save his friends from separation. He might even be able to put a stop to slave-taking in Rustiford.

A dark cloud loomed over the sky to the north. The leaves of the trees, painted with the colors of fall, danced along the ground as the north wind hurled itself against them. Sven closed the door softly behind him and began to walk, cloak flapping no matter how tightly he held it.

Fear strangled his stomach as he thought of Lori's words. What did Nightfire do with the slaves he had taken? Even if he obeyed the Law, what kind of master was he? Was he kind? Cruel?

A fog hung lazily in the air, drifting along in the wind without rising. He reached the homes of the town's founders.

I can stay here in Rustiford. It would be far easier than volunteering. Erbark has made his decision.

The sun battled to shine in spite of the thickening clouds, faltered and sank into the darkness. He approached his father's house.

He felt suddenly very stupid. How could he possibly hope to stop the wizard's slave-taking? A wizard could be killed, yes, but there was no doubting their power to defend themselves against Mar like himself. And if he stopped Nightfire, what would prevent some other wizard from demanding the same tribute? He suddenly felt very small and helpless.

The sun peeked through a small hole in the darkening clouds.

I can save just one person, Sven thought as he steeled himself to knock on the door. *If I go next year, Erbark can stay here and marry Lori.* He smiled at the thought of his friends being happy together. He could not help himself. They deserved to be happy. The sacrifice of one person would bring joy to two.

He knocked. A long pause before a very drowsy Pitt answered.

"Father, I've come to volunteer to go with Nightfire next year."

"An' Sven Takraf stepped forward an' volunteered to pay Rustiford's debt to Nightfire with his own life, never thinkin' of his own fate, but only that of his people."

The storyteller's voice trailed off into silence. Sven wasn't sure he heard it finish. A part of his mind — the part that remembered everything it heard — began recounting the various lies and stretching of truths the man had told, sorting it with the other knowledge he had acquired and might one day use.

He touched his forehead with his hand as the crowd applauded, leaving the past behind. A bead of sweat glistened there.

I know my own story. I know why I began. But to do what I am destined to do, I must sacrifice more than myself to save just one person. I must sacrifice others to save all of Marrishland. I continue as I began.

 **6**

*"Nightfire acts as arbiter whenever a wizard is accused
of breaking Bera's Unwritten Laws. He alone determines
guilt or innocence and passes sentence. In the case of
capital offenses, Brack also observes the proceedings
and carries out any death sentence."*

— Weard Sigrath Brennan,
Models of Power and Authority

Weard Katla Duxpite opened the door to Brack's main library,
where the wizard sat writing vigorously, his hands shaking.

She was a slim woman with curly brown hair and green eyes. She
was plain and bookwormish but had exited her thirties more grace-
fully than her brother Sven would, with nearly unwrinkled skin.

"You wanted to see me, master?"

Brack looked up from his work. He looked like he had aged ten
years in the last two-month season, and he had never looked a day
younger than seventy for as long as Katla had known him. His frame
looked brittle enough to shatter in a strong wind, and the lines of his
face made Nightfire look young by comparison.

"Have a seat, Katla." He set down the pen as she took the chair on
the other side of his desk. "I have been called to meet with the Delegates. They have heard much about Mardux Takraf from the Hue,
none of it good."

Katla frowned. The Hue was the gobbel tribe that had claimed
the Morden Moors as its territory until Sven had driven them out to
found his Protectorates, long before he decided to become Mardux.

Brack nodded, his expression severe. "You can see why it might
take me some time to placate them."

"What will you tell them?"

He shrugged. "Mardux Takraf will soon anger his fellow reds, and someone will defeat him next Duxfest."

"Sven won every duel with ease. I do not think his enemies will have the stomach to challenge him next year."

"I agree. However I cannot exactly tell the Delegates that." Brack smiled knowingly, but the tension never left his eyes.

"It is a delaying tactic."

"Yes. This gives us a year to find another way to topple Mardux Takraf from the Chair without breaking the Law."

"And if we cannot invent one, will the Delegates mobilize the Mass to defend their territory?"

"The Mass only attacks, and it only attacks with overwhelming numbers. The Drakes know the limits of Mar magic." Brack stood up and took a fine red cloak from a hook on the wall.

Katla allowed herself a small hope. Brack spoke about his meetings with the Delegates often, but he had never let her meet them. "Are you taking me with you?"

Brack slipped into the hisses of the Drake common tongue. *"Yee Ka Lah is not yet ready to meet the Delegates."*

"Stop that, Yee Roh Yeh. Yee Ka Lah no longer needs to practice."

"Yee Ka Lah is still a Mar. To speak to the Delegates, you must prove to them that you are a Yee."

Katla resisted the urge to roll her eyes. The Mass assigned Drake names to everyone and expected them to respond to these names, and this included any Mar the Delegates had reason to discuss. All names had three syllables — a tribal or racial designation followed by a two-part personal name. Brack was Yee Roh Yeh, and she was Yee Ka Lah. The Drakes called the Mar the Yee, so all Mar names began with that designator.

Brack liked to juxtapose the two names for the Mar. The Mar were proud, ruthless and savage, he claimed, but the Yee were humble, polite and eager to serve the Delegates.

"If Yee Roh Yeh does not think Yee Ka Lah is ready to face the Delegates, you should go to them, instead." Katla returned to the Mar language. "Now, if I have proven that I can speak Drake, could we please continue this conversation in a language that does not feel like I am

gargling snails?"

Brack didn't acknowledge her question, but he did switch languages. "Never fear. I will bring you to the Delegates as soon as we have neutralized the Mardux." The old wizard adjusted the cloak on his shoulders and returned to the desk.

If indeed they even exist, Katla thought. *Brand certainly never believed in them.*

She met his eyes with a hard stare of her own. "I am your only apprentice. You have named me the successor to your post. Why do you continue to shield me from the Delegates?"

"You will meet the Delegates soon enough, Katla, but this is not the time."

"I have heard that too often since I became your apprentice."

"Do you recall how unprepared you were to face the reality of a Drake civilization when I first brought you here to Tue Yee?"

Katla lowered her eyes. It had been astonishing, seeing the Drake city of Tue Yee for the first time, and learning just how civilized the Mar's eternal foe really was.

It was not that long ago …

She had been a junior administrator climbing the ranks to become Nightfire's right-hand weard and, eventually, his replacement. Whatever Sven's aspirations, she had intended to be Nightfire's successor.

Only one of many possible paths to the fulfillment of my oath.

But despite Sven's mistakes at Tortz, Nightfire began to lean more heavily on his star pupil. In her research, Katla had discovered the truth of a few rumors, and when she approached Nightfire with a plan, he had sent her off without even his trademark weighing glance.

Now, deep in the Fens of Reur, she began to second-guess her motives for choosing another path and agreeing to apprentice herself to the red-cloaked figure before her, blindly following wherever he led.

Nightfire had said Brack may be too empathetic to the force he was trying to control, that the power to control the Drakes might be going to his head. The stories she had read said Brack controlled the Mass, which Nightfire had not dismissed despite refusing to answer her.

At Nightfire's Academy, she had been a fourth-degree with a suite of rooms to herself and three classes to teach. Out here, no shelter existed. She was covered in bug bites and the humidity made her hair stick uncomfortably to the nape of her neck.

They had walked and canoed for five days across rivers and muck. She dulled her marsord daily clearing a path for them, and Brack spoke only in the evenings. She asked him when they would arrive at their destination. His lips only twitched, and he wouldn't answer. She was about to refuse to do any more work for him when he pressed past her purposefully. She saw the smoke, then, over a rise near the horizon. She heard the humming of raucous conversation long before they found the source of the smoke.

It sounds like a city. But there should be nothing here. And that hum sounds like conversation, but those are not words, I think.

They topped the rise, and Brack stopped so she could see the town. A hundred paces away, rotting boards and thatch created some kind of road on top of the muddy ground. It looked like some kind of market community, with hundreds of thatched-roof stalls selling all sorts of things, and a dozen great buildings near the center. Giant, stinking bonfires kept bugs away from the marketplace. But the most astonishing thing was what populated the place.

Stocky, tusked gobbels. Scrawny, long-limbed ravits. She saw an ochre, a sickening pile of muck that somehow had life. A giant winged insero, towering over the stalls, eyes the size of her entire body dominating its triangle face. And dozens of species of guer, the reptilian species that came in a scary variety of sizes and strengths. *Drakes! A whole army of Drakes!* She nearly dropped her marsord as she prepared to defend herself, but her companion gripped her arm tightly, his fingers like ropey tendons.

"Civilization comes from all directions," he said. "The Mar never understood that."

"These are the creatures of Domin," she hissed at him, afraid they would hear her. She quelled it, pulling her arm away from his.

This is why I followed Brack here — the path of my patroness, Dinah.

"Why is Domin any worse than Seruvus? Seruvus makes slaves. What does Domin do that is any worse than that? The gods do not show up unless you call on them, Weard Duxpite."

"Why did you bring me here?"

His hand encompassed the whole bazaar. "This is Tue Yee — the most important spiny-tailed guer city in the Tue territory. It is a major hub for trade between the other territories." He stroked the deep lines on his face. "What do you know of the Mass?"

"Nothing," she lied, knowing that Brack was said to believe in such nonsense. *He had to, though.* His brown eyes bored into her green ones, and she wavered.

"Nothing, she says." His cough sounded like a laugh. "Not even the lies taught you as a child?"

"They are lies," she said, steeling herself for what he would say. "They must be, if they never told of this True Tee." Her hand swept the bazaar.

"Tue Yee." He snorted and turned away, leading her into the market. "The Mar have the Mass to thank for their freedom. In the dark days when the Gien Empire ruled Marrishland, even the mightiest Mar wizards were ground beneath imperial heels."

A couple of short, scaly guer looked up at them as they passed and bared their teeth at the two wizards, hissing. Katla flinched, but Brack hissed back. An apparent stand-off continued for several seconds before Katla recognized it as a conversation in a language she had never heard.

"Through it all," Brack continued once the lizard-like guer had returned to their own business, "the Drakes retained their independence by fiercely defending their swamps. Rural Mar had their freedoms, too, but the Gien Empire never laid claim to these lands, nor to the dead swamps of the lost Duxy of Despar. It is a pity, really, that the damnens still refuse to send emissaries here even after all these centuries."

"The Giens regarded the Drakes as monsters," Katla said. "They were unworthy of conquest and only fit to die. Sending armies into uninhabitable swamps was a waste of their time. This history is written. The Drakes damn themselves whenever they attack a town."

Brack's eyes burned, but he kept quiet, feigning disinterest. Katla wanted to scream at his fake complacency, but she kept her patience.

They passed a spiny-tailed — a short guer with two well-muscled lower legs and two long arms, its most prominent feature was its long, thick tail covered in small, stinging spines — Katla cringed at the grotesque proportions of the creature. It seemed to be engaged in a fierce discussion with a pair of ravits in the same hissing, spitting manner that Brack had used earlier.

Brack strode by, acknowledging Katla's surprise. "The Drakes have a common language, as the Mar do. They are not monsters, and neither am I for dealing with them."

"You seem as much at ease killing Mar as they are," she observed.

He only acknowledged the barb with a small smile. "You may suffer more surprises while you are here. Many Drakes speak Mar more fluently than many of your rural mundane do." He spoke louder as she opened her mouth. "Not many Mar have ever considered the possibility of negotiating with Drakes. In the days before the Giens arrived, most of the Mar who knew anything of the Drake language were considered mapmakers. Some mapmakers had even mastered different dialects."

"I am no mapmaker, but I will learn their languages," Katla said firmly, making the quick decision. She was, after all, here to learn what she could from this wizard.

"You will first learn their history with the Mar. The fall of the Gien Empire marked a revolution in these relations."

"Tryggvi Fochs."

"Yes. Those who spoke Drake tongues were often those who lived on the fringe of Mar society, but not always. A few scholars collected knowledge of that sort, as you have learned. Nightfire has never had a reputation for discarding knowledge, however forbidden it might be. The Brack who preceded me was an avid scholar of the Drake languages when he was a young wizard."

"You are Brack the way Nightfire is Nightfire, then." *Over hundreds of years, a name becomes a title — are not all of us weards named for the first wizard, Weard Darflaem? Nightfire is the title of the person who is the arbiter of law among weards.*

"Yes." He touched the braided gold and silver ring on his finger. "Domin's Favor marks me as his successor. Brack learned to despise the Giens after he witnessed the Flasten Massacre."

"The what?"

He ignored the question. "It changed Brack, made him a hard, ruthless man who would stop at nothing to destroy those who opposed him. He organized a rebellion among his fellow wizards, which failed, before fleeing into the swamps. When he returned, it was with an army of Drakes at his back."

Brack's Rebellion.

They entered a low building separated from the others. A fire already crackled in the hearth, a tall stack of peat to one side. Two chairs and a table were the only furnishings.

"Brack wanted to liberate Marrishland at any price," she said.

"He learned the Drakes' common tongue. He befriended the leaders of many of their tribes. It would be presumptuous to say he is the reason the Drakes united peacefully, but he was there the first time the Delegates met to discuss how to deal with the Gien problem. The Mass was the result of that first debate."

"A treaty."

Brack nodded. "A delicate one forged in fear of the Gien invaders. Brack fanned that fear daily. He painted them as barbarians with powerful magic who would not rest until they had slain every Drake on the subcontinent. The Delegates' power grew as more tribes joined them out of fear of the Giens."

And then Domin came to him, Katla thought bitterly. *Brack, a brilliant strategist, led what to the Gien mentality would be a sizable force to attack a northern town far from the capital. When the Giens committed a majority of their forces, Brack led the rest of the Drakes along the coast from the east, leveling every city in his path.*

"His rebellion succeeded at an incredible cost to the Mass. The Drakes defeated the Giens and liberated the Mar. That is when matters got out of control. The Mar turned on their saviors, and Brack convinced his allies to leave Mar lands alone."

The Mar turned on the Drakes, monsters of the northern swamps. That was not surprising. But, then Brack would have had to convince them that the Mar were not Giens, despite what the Drakes must have seen as mass murder and betrayal.

"Many Mar and Drakes branded Brack a traitor, and someone

surely would have killed him if the Delegates had not sheltered him. Many Drake tribes withdrew their support for the Delegates and went to war with the Mar. They caused a lot of unnecessary bloodshed that drove a wedge between Mar and Drakes, and even mapmakers stopped talking to the Drakes."

Katla stared at Brack's aged, wrinkled face. *Everything he has just told me conforms with the histories as I know them.* Out loud, she said, "That was centuries ago. What have you and your predecessors been doing since then?"

"Keeping it from happening again. We spread and reinforce the legend of the Mass to discourage expansion beyond the Fens of Reur. We seek out magocrats who are sympathetic, or who can be bought, to tell us when a threat to the Drakes is beginning to grow. When possible, we eliminate the threat before the Delegates ever hear of it. Our magocrat allies serve that function, too."

"Dux Feiglin is one of them."

A short nod. "Nightfire, too. Many more magocrats than you'd likely believe."

"A conspiracy." The word was bitter in her mouth.

Brack sat in a rocking chair and gave her a wry smile. "More like a delicate treaty forged in fear to prevent the Mass from eradicating the Mar." He waved at a chair on the other side of the fireplace.

They could invade. History tells of such incursions. The Mar had never stood a chance during these battles, yet the Drakes only rarely take a city. But widespread belief is that they are too stupid, little more than livestock, to take a city. If the Mass is real …

Katla sat. "If the Mass could wipe out the Mar whenever they wished, why haven't they?"

"The tribes are no more united under the Delegates than the duxies are under the Mardux. The Delegates are a real political force, but they have limited control over the tribes who make up the Mass." Brack gave her a conspiratorial wink. "And that is my other duty — to keep them that way."

Katla lowered her voice. "You serve the Drakes among the Mar and the Mar among the Drakes."

"Both sides hate me for it, yes." Brack leaned forward and steepled his fingers. "As long as the Mar are weak, and the Drakes are not united, the uneasy peace persists. In the absence of a threat as powerful and aggressive as the Gien Empire, the Delegates cannot send the full power of the Mass against the Mar."

"And if one were to emerge?"

"Then we may have to choose between breaking the Unwritten Laws and the extinction of our entire civilization."

"If Tue Yee cannot prepare me for the Delegates, then take me to the Delegates. How else can I learn their ways?"

Brack shook his head. "This is not the time to introduce new faces to the Delegates. Besides, I could be gone for some time, and I need you to be my representative among the Mar in my absence. Dux Feiglin is our most cooperative ally. Convince him of the wisdom of overthrowing Mardux Takraf before the Delegates grow ... restless."

Katla chewed her lower lip thoughtfully for a moment. "It likely will not be as simple as duels for the Chair."

Brack smiled, but his eyes held deep sadness. "I am all too aware of that. The fire must find a way to keep burning."

"The fire will find a way," Katla promised.

Brack picked up his cane and took a few experimental steps, not even aiding himself with magic. "I will return here when I can."

Even though he could teleport with ease, he walked out of the library like a mundane Mar, leaning heavily on a cane.

 **7**

*"I maintain a series of journals because I am driven to
express my feelings and tell my stories, but often am in
want of an audience. I read my journals to remember
those lessons I once learned, but might have forgotten. I
share my journals in the hopes my mistakes and failures
will help others avoid repeating them."*

— Pondr,
Collected Journals, edited by Weard Asa Sehtah

Weard Einar Schwert fingered the hilt of his marsord as he
strolled through the citadel, the storyteller Pondr at his heels.

Once a place of functional beauty — the seat of power of an empire — the citadel now went mostly unused. Three whole wings had
been left to the ravages of nature. When a ceiling had caved in, one
wing had completely separated from the building. Many resident
wizards would fight for that space, as close to the citadel as they
could be without being Mardux.

Einar owned a marsord out of duty. It was expected of a frontier magocrat to carry one, and Einar had no illusions about that.
It was duty, too, that had led him to pursue the Chair. He had
known Ozur Betrun from schooling, and Marrishland would have
been less for him. The man had been Flasten's creature and would
have dismantled everything Einar and Rorik had fought for their
whole lives.

Mardux Sven Takraf's methods, questions and proclamations
spoke loudly of the weard's dedication to his ambitions. He certainly
had no intention of surrendering the northern frontier to the Drakes.
If the tale the mapmaker Finn Ochregut had brought to Domus Palus

of Weard Takraf's early days held any truth at all, Sven and Einar shared many political interests. Einar was certain the Mardux was readying Domus and its allies for war, and that could only mean an expansion into Drake territory.

Einar knocked on the Mardux's study door.

After a long pause, Sven spoke. "Enter."

Einar did so, noting the piles of records on the Mardux's desk. He knew they would be records of Domus Palus' holdings. Einar had frequently heard Sven reading accounts and notes aloud. According to the mapmaker's tales, the Mardux had Seruvus' memory only for what he heard, not for what he read.

Sven's red cloak was now emblazoned with his seal — a broken marsord consumed by flames. A former student of Sven's had come up with the idea to show the Mardux's ascent to the Chair, but Einar suspected Sven saw it as a reminder of a different sort.

"Weard Schwert," Sven addressed him with a nod. "You have brought the storyteller."

"The Traveller, Mardux," Einar corrected quietly. It had taken a forty-five day month to track down the right one. He was not the only member of the wandering race in Domus Palus.

"That explains some." Sven gazed at the fire. "Let him in."

Even as Einar approached the door, the Traveller stepped inside. He hastily sidestepped Einar and bowed at the same time. It was an overly complicated gesture, and Einar wondered how the man did not fall down.

"What is your name, Traveller?" Sven asked.

The Traveller sat in a chair across from the Mardux. He smiled and seemed to relax a little. "Do you play the Game, Mardux?"

"I have heard of it," Sven answered, coolness enveloping his voice. "We do not play it here in Marrishland."

"I see." The Traveller smiled slightly. "Call me Pondr."

"Very well, Pondr. You told a remarkable fabrication of untruths when last you were here. Enough of it was close enough, barely stretched, for me to wonder as to your whereabouts at the time. How much do you really know about me?"

The Traveller leaned back and clasped his hands across his chest and looked back at Sven. "You are a very different person now than who you were when Nightfire came for you. How much have you blocked out?"

The Mardux's face hardened. "I have Seruvus's memory. I could not forget even if I wanted to."

Pondr held up a finger. "I know of this quirk of memory. Some remember all that they see. Others, all that they hear. But none remember all they thought or felt." He steepled his fingers and leaned forward. "Can I tell you more about yourself? You might enjoy it."

Sven raised an eyebrow and hunched his shoulders. "More fabrications?"

"How much do you remember about your first days at Nightfire's Academy?"

Sven glared at the man. "How would you know any of that? How could you know anything about me?"

The Traveller spread his hands, sitting straighter. "Stories of you, Mardux, have spread, in one fashion or the other, throughout Marrishland. I consider it a trifle if I hear these stories and pass them along. There are huge chunks of your life unopened to me. Maybe I can hear these words from your own lips, or you will let me talk to those nearest you.

"This tale, however, I can trace to the slave who heard from the mundane who heard from the mapmaker who heard from the wizard who heard from the apprentice who heard from another slave who came to Nightfire's Academy soon before you did. Their names are unimportant. Surely you are versed in the strong Mar oral tradition? I find it fascinating, myself."

Einar did, too. He watched Sven to see if the Mardux would prefer this conversation to be private, and he rubbed his thumb over his belt absently. Sven appeared nervous about something, but the only threat was of a story. Einar waited.

Sven seemed to digest this. "Why would I want to hear any more about a life I have already lived? Despite your words, I do not forget as easily as others do."

Now the Traveller sat forward, his hands gripping the chair. "Even great men cannot see themselves through another's eyes."

Sven's green eyes searched the Traveller's blue ones. The Traveller began to speak, and Sven was drawn back into his memories.

Sven pulled the black cloak around his naked body to deter as many insects as he could as Nightfire led him barefoot to a narrow gate in the palisade. He could almost feel the konig worms burrowing into the soles of his feet as he walked lightly across the soft, goddess-cursed ground.

Nightfire's a wizard. If he can heal me after all that he just put me through, maybe he can protect me from Dinah's Curse, too.

He touched his bald scalp gingerly but felt no pain. The blisters on his hands and arms had vanished, too, leaving him hairless but uninjured. Nightfire followed Sven's eyes.

"You can bring nothing of your past life into the place you are about to enter," Nightfire said, voice heavy with the repetition of a ritual. "The Sven Gematsud who left Rustiford is dead. He is ashes as surely as your clothes and boots are."

Sven looked at him with uncomprehending eyes, trying to make sense of what Nightfire hoped to achieve. His temper flared. "If slavery's death, I'll only stay dead for eight years," he snapped.

The wizard smiled as if at a secret joke. "Come, Sven. I will show you where you will be staying."

Nightfire, red cloak swirling around his ankles, led Sven to a huge four-story building and opened one great double door. They stepped into a room that could easily have housed everyone Sven knew. A bonfire burned brightly in an immense hearth, casting light and shadows in equal measure. A handful of Mar without boots looked up at them in surprise from where they were scrubbing the clean floors. Nightfire acknowledged them with a nod, and they returned to their tasks.

Perhaps Rustiford isn't the only town in Nightfire's debt.

Nightfire took a lantern from a table and led Sven upstairs to a dark room. The room seemed a closet compared to downstairs, but it was still as large as his home in Rustiford. *Not mine anymore. But I will go back, someday.* The room had one small window covered with sheer cloth to keep out insects, a sturdy bed and a dresser. Sven stepped inside and looked around.

Such luxury for slaves' quarters.

"Dress, and then I will show you what to do," Nightfire said, leaving the lantern and closing the door behind him.

"But the konig worms!" Sven protested. The wizard did not respond.

Sven frowned deeply and wiped his feet off as thoroughly as he could with the cloak Nightfire had given him. He knew cloth couldn't wipe away Dinah's Curse, but it felt a little better not to have mud on his feet.

He tossed the cloak into a corner and wriggled his toes, feeling the firm wood beneath his feet. He rummaged through the dresser, which had clothes in many sizes. He dressed hastily in a rough shirt and baggy breeches, which he cinched tight with a length of rope. He searched the room for a pair of boots and found none at all. He glanced at his bare feet, bare feet that might already be filled with nests of konig worm eggs, and gritted his teeth.

"Is there a problem?" Nightfire called from the other side of the door.

Sven yanked the door open. "When're you replacin' the boots you burned?"

Nightfire regarded him mildly. "You will have boots when you need them."

"An' I'm to risk Dinah's Curse until then? Or am I cleanin' floors with th'others?"

"You will stay in this building until I have a use for you elsewhere. As long as you obey me, I will protect you from Dinah's Curse."

Sven's irritation rose. The wizard, for the moment, had him trapped. He pressed the emotion away with difficulty, reminding himself of Nightfire's last demonstration of power.

"Come."

Sven followed grudgingly. Nightfire led him up another flight of stairs and opened a door.

"I will give you instructions," the wizard said as Sven peered into the room, which was lit just enough for Sven to tell it was full of shelves covered in bottles. "You must perform all the tasks I give you. You will move the fifth green bottle in the fourth row on the third shelf on the west wall to the second row of the first shelf on the north wall."

Sven nodded.

"Do you want me to repeat it?"

The young Mar shook his head, irritated. He stepped into the room. Nightfire did not move, but something held Sven back.

Magic, he thought.

"You will begin these tasks tomorrow. Come."

Nightfire led Sven from one cluttered room after another, pausing at each one to point out a single object that needed to be repositioned — stools, tables, painted blocks of wood, cloaks hanging on pegs, clay pots, metal pans. Each object was different from every other, but Nightfire always pointed out a specific one.

"Move the copper cauldron to the fireplace." Sven repeated each of the more than one hundred instructions quietly to himself, simplifying Nightfire's instructions, still amazed at the size of this building. "The green cloak over there goes on the blue peg here."

The wizard didn't comment on this. "Now," Nightfire said in a hard voice when they returned to the entrance of Sven's room. "I want you to do everything I told you to do before I return. Is that clear?"

Sven nodded, and Nightfire departed. When he was gone, Sven set his mind to work.

He's testing my memory. For what purpose, Sven was not yet sure. Better treatment, perhaps, or maybe greater responsibility. *If I'm to get my boots, I need to prove myself.*

Sven gave silent thanks to Seruvus for the memory he had been born with: a mind that remembered everything it heard. The next morning, he set to work, quickly completing each tedious task. The other slaves made no mention of his confident appearance late in the day.

How could they know what I've been doing?

Nightfire didn't return that night, so Sven set out to meet the other slaves. He recognized only one slave from Rustiford. Finn Ochregut, who had volunteered a year earlier, scrubbed floors with the rest of them, his grumbles long and loud. He gave a grudging tour to Sven, introducing people and explaining the uselessness of their duties at great length. He hadn't seen anyone from Rustiford, but they might be in one of the other buildings.

The building housed twenty young tribute slaves from towns like

Rustiford who had taken Nightfire's deal. None of them had been there for less than a season, and none wore boots, not even the woman who had been there for nearly eight years.

"Does he ever let us leave?" Sven asked her.

"Oh yes," she said with a toothy grin. "Some get boots in just a few days. Some in a month or two. An' he keeps the Law, too. The ones who came before me went free, an' soon I'll be free, too."

Sven grew more thoughtful as the days passed. Through the windows, he could watch the regular hustle and bustle of the compound. It was like the cities in some of Sveld's stories — hundreds of buildings, most of them larger than any in Rustiford. As Sven began to place voices with names, people would leave. New ones would replace them. Many of them wore bright green, though an equal number wore black. There were dozens wearing auburn, and several in blue. Occasionally, a cyan- or lavender-garbed Mar passed by, carrying heavy books and talking ferociously to the air. Sven puzzled over the strange flow of people for days before he came to a clear conclusion about his enslavement. It took another day for him to make his decision.

On the eighth day, Nightfire returned, entering Sven's room without so much as a knock.

"Have you completed your tasks? I understand you spent quite a bit of time helping the others."

Sven nodded confidently.

"Show me," Nightfire said, motioning for Sven to lead the way.

Sven retraced his steps precisely, pausing outside each room to recite its assigned task. The wizard offered no comment, but he looked suitably impressed when Sven finished.

"How did you remember?"

"I can remember anything said to me."

If Sven had not been watching the man's green eyes, he would not have seen the surprise that vanished as quickly as it appeared. He nodded. "Seruvus' memory. That is quite a gift."

Sven took a deep breath and blurted, "I passed your test, didn't I?"

"What test?" Nightfire asked, feigning confusion badly.

"The test to see if I'm worthy to be taught your secrets."

Nightfire closed the door. "Explain your reasoning."

Sven took a deep breath, composed his thoughts.

"Well, the house of slaves doin' nothin' useful helped a lot. Why keep slaves if you don't use them for anythin'? Then there's the people outside wearin' colors too bright to be anythin' but wizards. Plus ev'ryone here is youn' except you an' a few others who're dressed in lavender or yellow. You make me remember a really long list of jobs just to see if I can. Put it all together, an' I know I'm in a magic school, an' you make the slaves who pass the test your apprentices. Am I right?"

Nightfire leaned against the door and took a deep breath before responding. "You have not mentioned that most of my apprentices come to my Academy willingly in search of an education. But you could not have drawn that conclusion based on the information you have been given. You have quite a talent for drawing reasonable conclusions from incongruous information."

"What?" Sven asked. It had sounded like a compliment, but most of the words were new to him.

Nightfire smiled patronizingly. "Sorry. I forgot myself."

"You haven't answered my question." *I think you haven't.* "At least not directly."

"You are right. This is the most prestigious academy teaching the art of magic in Marrishland. Every magocrat would gladly pay the considerable tuition to send his children to study here, but we only accept the most promising students."

"Tuition?" Sven asked, repeating the unfamiliar word precisely.

"Something of value they give us in exchange for receiving our knowledge."

"Like metal an' food? Or coins?"

"Something like that," Nightfire said with a slight shrug. "It is our tradition, though, to enroll a small number of gifted youth from rural villages."

"Your slaves," Sven said, surprised by the anger in his voice.

Nightfire's eyes glittered with fire for a moment and then cooled. "Magic is a secret knowledge. The rules for picking apprentices are very complicated. Those slaves who do not pass the tests never learn magic."

"Why didn't th'other slaves tell me about the test?"

"They do not know about it. One test is keeping the existence of the tests a secret from the others. If you can pass that test, you will receive a chance at education."

The wizard stood up, his red cloak making him appear taller and more imposing. His voice took on the qualities of a seasoned orator. "I warn you the path will not be an easy one. The rigors of obtaining an education are more than many can bear, and you must compete with those who have spent the early years of their lives in learning. No concessions will be made for your rural upbringing, making your task all the more challenging. Think long upon the implications of your choice, Sven." Nightfire moved to the door. "I will give you three days to decide if you wish to accept this apprenticeship."

"I accept it," Sven said levelly.

Nightfire turned to face him. He waved his hand in Sven's face. "This is not a decision to make lightly! There are responsibilities and implications you cannot even begin to comprehend unless you are a wizard. And by then, it is too late to hide in ignorance."

Sven did not flinch. "I've thought about this long enough, an' I tell you, I'll accept your offer. Then I can return to my home as a wizard who can protect his family from the trials of the swamp an' keep magocrats like the ones that took my mother from makin' them slaves."

Nightfire opened his mouth, and then closed it. At last, he spoke.

"One day, you will think differently, Sven. Your love for your friends and family and the grudge you bear magocrats might provide you with the sense of purpose you will need to succeed in your studies. I will not deprive you of your desire. But you must still wait a few days before a pair of boots can be provided for you. If you change your mind, do not hesitate to refuse my offer."

"An' so Sven Gematsud became Nightfire's apprentice. His intelligence an' enthusiasm served him well i'the classrooms of the Academy. His warmth an' energy earned him the respect an' love of his fellow students, earnin' him the nickname 'Takraf,' which means 'energy.' For eight years, Sven studied at Nightfire's side, learnin' the craft an' theory of magic. So absorbed by his studies was Sven, he didn't notice that no more slaves had come from Rustiford."

The Traveller's story ended, and Einar realized Sven was gripping the edge of the writing desk with white knuckles. The chancellor himself wanted to hear more, but was grateful Pondr had stopped, for Sven's sake.

"No one tells of your apprenticeship at Nightfire's Academy. Or they do, but it is entirely unbelievable." The Traveller's earnest blue eyes watched Sven closely. "I do seek that margin of truth you discerned in my other story."

"So I see." Sven's eyes hardened. "You should not try to leave, Traveller. Before you could get far in any direction, there will be blood spilt." Sven rose and opened the door for the man.

As Pondr turned to leave the room, Sven clapped him on the shoulder. "If only for the satisfaction of seeing the story unfold before your eyes," he said with a hard smile, "you should stay."

As the man left, Einar stepped forward. "What is wrong, Mardux?"

Sven's hands shook as he gripped the back of a chair. "The Traveller's story reminded me that I need to leave Domus Palus for a few days."

Einar weighed the Mardux with a glance. He recognized that worried expression, recalled how it had felt on his own face not so many years ago. "You have a family. You think Dux Feiglin will try to use them against you."

Sven nodded mutely and swallowed hard.

"It may be too late," Einar said, wincing at the Mardux's stricken look. "You need to be prepared for that."

"I will only be gone a few days. As the only other red in Domus Palus, you will be seneschal in my absence."

Einar spoke slowly, in awed tones. "I am honored by your faith in me, Mardux."

Sven frowned. "Do not mistake my trust as affection, Weard Schwert. You are a competent man." He smiled grimly. "The Oathbinder himself will assure me of your loyalty. Should you break my trust, I will lay my full wrath upon you, and this time, I will hand you over to Domin. What, then, have I to fear from you, Weard Schwert?"

Einar mastered his anger at the insult only with a force of will. "I will do as you command, Mardux," he said stiffly.

"Yes," was all Sven said, and then he vanished into the Tempest.

 **8**

*"The blue myst is Power. It creates raw telekinetic force
— lifting, carrying, crushing and producing barriers.
Wizards use Power to attack almost as much as they
employ Energy, especially if they intend to capture an
opponent. Power is a versatile tool and the most effective defense against physical attacks in any wizard's
repertoire."*

— Nightfire Tradition,
Nightfire's Magical Primer

Erbark Lasik was a formidable man. He projected "mapmaker"
the way a calloused handshake radiated bootmaker. His broad limbs
and careful walk spoke of years fighting enemies toe to toe. He had
the thick black hair and sun-darkened skin of a mundane from one
of the least civilized towns in Marrishland, but his clean-shaven
face proclaimed him a wizard even if his dark green cloak had not.
His brown eyes were fearless and confident. He had a penchant for
speaking only when necessary, and only his fellow Rustifordians recognized this as something he had learned since leaving home.

Erbark carried a marsord out of loyalty to Sven, who had given
it to him at the end of his warrior's apprenticeship. He only used it
where Sven and his conscience directed, such as when navigating the
Morden Moors, or in the current situation that he found himself in on
his way to visit Sven's family at Nightfire's Academy.

"Are you Weard Lasik?" demanded the auburn standing in Erbark's path. There was nothing friendly in the man's stance.

Erbark nodded once.

"I have a message for Weard Takraf. Could you take me to his house so I can deliver it?"

"I'll deliver it." Erbark caught a movement out of the corner of his eye but did not turn to look.

"I was instructed to place it in his hands myself."

"Then I can't help you," Erbark told him, moving to walk past the auburn.

"Oh, but you can." The auburn waved a hand, and four greens moved into the space between the trees. The auburn smiled. "And you will."

Erbark took in their cloaks with a glance and snorted a laugh. None of them carried a weapon. "A few miles outside of the Academy, and you expect me to be impressed by an auburn and a few greens?"

The auburn frowned, and the first fist of Power threw Erbark backward. The warrior tucked himself into a ball and let its momentum roll him back to his feet. A pillar of fire erupted in front of him as he reached his feet.

"Alive. Alive!" shouted the auburn.

Erbark took two quick steps and buried his fist into the stomach of the nearest green, who doubled over and fell to the ground wheezing as if he'd never encountered physical pain.

The warrior yanked a flask of torutsen out of his pocket and pulled the stopper. Another fist of force hit his hand. The flask somersaulted out of his fingers, its contents showering the ground. He cursed silently and charged the nearest green.

Erbark slammed into a wall of Power at full speed. Despite the spots in his vision, he rolled quickly to one side and around the barrier. The green on the other side opened her eyes wide in shock before Erbark smashed her nose. There was a crack and a splash of blood, and the green clutched her nose with a moan.

A fist of force struck Erbark in the back, and he felt a rib crack. He winced but moved around the green with the broken nose. She abruptly stood up and turned to him with a smile, the injury healed except for the blood on her cloak.

That's it, Erbark thought. *Wear yourself out healing yourself instead of attacking me.*

He drew a javelin from the sheaf on his back and slammed it into her thigh in a single smooth motion. She howled in pain and fell to the ground as her bone shattered.

The auburn and the other two greens surrounded him, and blows fell like rain. The javelins flew from their band on his back to well out of his reach. His belt of knives snapped and crawled away into the swamp. Erbark tried to move forward, but walls of Power blocked him at every turn.

Then the injured greens recovered enough to join in, lashing at him with whips of Power. One green's face scrunched up in concentration, and Erbark's left arm snapped just above the elbow. He fought the instinct to curl up on the ground, knowing it wouldn't ward off the attacks.

Niminth, you know I tried, Erbark prayed silently.

He called the myst — not to soothe his wounds or attack his enemies, he wasn't skilled enough to do that without torutsen, but he could insulate himself. With torutsen, he could see what he was doing and could have countered the incoming spells while still using other magic. Blind to the myst, he had to grope and hope he gathered enough of the right motes. The shell of countermagic would hold for a minute or two, and that would have to be enough.

As soon as the fists of Power stopped striking him, Erbark stood up straight and turned. The greens wore expressions ranging from surprise to confusion to unmistakable fear. His gaze fell to the auburn, and Erbark stepped forward, the wall of Power disintegrating at the touch of his defensive shell.

The auburn simply sneered. "Five on one, and you have no magic? You can't win this fight."

Erbark smiled grimly. "Try telling a damnen that."

The auburn's eyes widened slightly, and Erbark used the distraction to close the distance and slam a knee into the auburn's groin. His marsord's gouger bit tender flesh, and any thought in the auburn's mind turned to agony.

Erbark didn't give him a chance to recover. He grasped the blood-covered hilt and drew the hacker out, pulling the long blade against his fallen opponent's throat. Blood sprayed, then pumped, and finally stopped.

Marsord dripping wizard blood, Erbark rose and gave his attention to the greens behind him. His lips curled in a snarl.

"Who's next?"

The greens fled. With a heavy sigh, Erbark rummaged through the dead auburn's pockets. He regretted the necessity, but the greens might regain their courage. Eventually, he found the flask of torutsen and took a swallow.

Erbark scanned the myst around him, watching for any irregularities in the motes' movement that might indicate a nearby wizard readying a spell. He saw none, so he released the countermagic shell and called new magic to heal the worst of his injuries as he collected his scattered equipment. He got as far as the broken ribs before the myst stopped answering his call.

He looked at the corpse with a frown.

"I should have tended you first, I know," he said softly. "But there is no dry wood out here, so hopefully your friends will come back after I leave to do the honors."

He closed the dead man's eyes and pulled the edge of the auburn cloak over his face. Wincing at his remaining injuries, Erbark continued along the path to Nightfire's Academy.

The dux's magocrats are getting bolder, Sven. I hope you come home soon.

Erika Unschul watched the flames in the hearth consume the wood while she waited for the soup in the pot to boil. She could hear Asa and her friends playing "Academy" in the nursery. Their muffled voices drifted to Erika.

"Today," Asa began in her high-pitched, serious voice, "we are going to learn to use Energy."

Erika smiled in amusement. Her daughter reminded her so much of Sven — intelligent, outgoing and eager to teach whatever she learned. Asa could already read and write paragraphs in both Mar and Middling Gien, the language the magic textbooks were written in. Her vocabulary was still quite limited, but she was only three and a half years old, after all. Yet, the bright-eyed girl had a fascination with magic that rivaled her father's. Already, she made use of most of the words wizards used to describe their use of magic.

"Energy can be used to make heat or cold, light or darkness. It is all the green specks in the myst and is the easiest for a wizard to use."

"I don't see nothin'," complained a young boy's voice.

That would be Ottar Verunigsud, the class skeptic. Ottar was a constant thorn in Asa's imaginative little boot, refusing to pretend that her dreamed-up characters and things were really there. Now, Erika knew, Asa would either find a way to punish the boy's honesty or dismiss his opinion completely.

If nothing else, Asa will teach him to feign creativity.

Erika's brown eyes sparkled in the flickering light as she waited for the expected response. As she moved closer to the fire to stir the soup, her shadow on the wall swelled, almost filling the entire room.

"What's taking Sven so long?" she murmured.

Her husband had left the Academy with promises to return as soon as his business to the west was finished. That had been an entire season ago. She knew Sven often got so caught up in his latest project that he tended to forget his family.

It's a fault in him, Erika thought. *He should be here with us, raising his daughter.*

The fire's heat waned slightly. Erika picked up a log from the small pile of wood stacked nearby and fed it to the flames. The flames licked the new wood experimentally, still clinging to the familiar fuels at the bottom of the pile. After a few moments, the flames all but abandoned the old wood in favor of devouring the new. She basked in the warmth.

Where is he? Asfrid Staute and the other Protectorate wizards can renew the spells without him.

The fire soon grew so hot it began to hurt her face. She sighed as she picked up a broom and started sweeping the wooden floor. As she put the room into order, Erika noticed the silence emanating from the nursery. Aware that this was not a normal state for children, she decided to check on Asa and her "class."

"Sven Takraf, why can't you just stay home for a little while?" she asked the air.

As Erika moved away from the hearth, her shadow shrank. By the time she reached the door to the nursery, the fire illuminated the entire room. A knock on the front door interrupted her as she reached for the nursery latch. She glided to the entrance and opened it.

A mud-covered Erbark grinned at her from the darkness outside. His left arm hung in a makeshift sling, and his face was a mass of bruises. One eye was swollen shut.

"Erbark!" Erika cried. "What happened to you?"

"I thought I'd visit Lori."

"Olver attacked you again?"

He shrugged.

Erika knew the story of the warrior's love for this townswoman. Erbark visited Rustiford three or four times a year, if he was not busy in the Protectorates, all for the sake of Lori and her twelve children. The Rustifordian must be on her way to forty, yet he proclaimed her the most beautiful woman alive. Erika was somewhat jealous of this man's devotion to a woman not even his wife.

Sven could learn from Erbark.

"Come in. I've some soup."

Erbark obeyed, carefully setting his travel pack and javelins near the door.

"Sven hasn't returned yet?"

She shook her head as she ladled some of her rabbit and wild rice soup into a wooden bowl. Of course, the main ingredients weren't the most important. When it came to soups, seasoning was every-thing.

"Whatever he's doing, it's important. You know how he is."

"I know, but two months without even a message?"

Erbark ate his soup, watching her as she fussed with her apron.

"I see him little enough already. He's always off adding a new town to the Protectorates or researching some new spell. He's so wrapped up in thinking about ways to help everyone else, he forgets the simple stuff. I can't remember the last time he chopped wood or weeded our vegetable garden."

"I'd be happy to do those things while I'm here."

"That's not the point."

"If it bothers you, tell him."

"I'd have to find him."

"I guess that's true," Erbark conceded.

"I don't know what to do with the man, Erbark."

The fire cracked and popped in the silence.

"Do you remember your wedding?" Erbark asked suddenly. "Half-way through his hunting, he finally figured out how to improve the defenses of the Protectorates using Blosin wands. How long did you wait for him then?"

"Six spans." She blushed. *But he made it worth the wait.*

Erika had remained confident that despite the six-span delay, Sven would return to fulfill his proposal to her. Each day, more people told her she was wasting her time on him, that he had abandoned her for some woman on the other side of what was being called the Takraf Protectorates.

But each day brought word of him, in its own fashion. As Sven renewed the spells protecting the forty other towns in his tiny duxy, people heard of his wedding. The Morden Moors had become safe around Leiben, and many people were able to attend the event. Mar trickled into Leiben by the day, each bringing vegetables and a pot. It was the job of the groom to bring the meat. Erika's mother, Batha, collected every pot to cook the wedding soup in.

"Saw him headin' to Erscht," an old woman told her. "Blesse' is the day you're wed."

"Took his time makin' us extra safe, 'cause we're on the border," a man said, scratching his hair and checking his fingernails, as if lice could live where Sven walked. "We're on the ... perry-me'er, he called us."

Through it all — the hustle and bustle of preparation, the disparaging remarks and sideways glances — hope burned in Erika.

He will return for me, she told herself. *He is a good man, a man who doesn't go back on his word.*

When Sven finally returned to Leiben after six spans of absence, it was all she could do not to throw herself on him right there. She had to settle for a quiet handclasp, and then she gasped with the rest of the crowd in attendance.

Trailing along behind Sven, like slaves to a master, were four piles of deer, rabbit and duck. They were suspended on nothing.

"Unload it," Batha said quietly. Then, louder, "Come on. We've seen him do it before." To suit her words, she grabbed two ducks by their necks and took them to the space reserved for whatever the groom had managed to bring back.

He is splendid, Erika thought, keeping her eyes downcast and her hands busy on her shirt. But she sneaked glances at him. *Look at what he can do.*

Then his eyes caught hers, and the smile on his face was gorgeous.

"Are you nervous?" he asked her. "Tonight ..."

"Ah, Sven!" Erlend, Erika's father, cried, clapping him on the shoulder and neatly separating them. "Groom can't be stan'in' aroun', can he? C'mon, we're to get firewood." Erbark joined Sven at the opposite shoulder with a smile for Erika, and the three men left her there.

But Sven's words hung in her mind. *Tonight...* They would be wed. Erika set about her tasks, trying to make time move faster.

The meal could feed hundreds. The meat was more than enough for the soup. Wild rice and roots, onions and spices were added to make the blend plentiful. By rights, a gathering this size should never have had enough food for more than a bite for anyone, but whole cauldrons were still full when people finished their seconds.

Hundreds of people congratulated Sven and Erika as they sat side by side in the center of it all, eating their soup. She beamed back at them, her heart and mind focused on him like a bootmaker to her craft.

As the meal finished, the tale-telling and laughter began. Elders from two dozen towns and villages within the Protectorates began an impromptu contest, each striving to tell the better tale. Stories and songs of Marrish and Dinah, Niminth and Sendala, even the comedy of Mytaraza — the heroine who had orchestrated a rather unusual protest among the women of Marrishland and the Gien Empire in order to convince the two nations to make peace. And every tale was bawdier than the last — a squeamish foreigner might even say cruder. But by Seruvus they were funny!

Ordinary people made fools of a hundred pompous magocrats. Mapmakers set out on a thousand ludicrous misadventures and almost always ended up dead by the end of the story. Men masquerading as women. Women pretending to be men. Men disguising themselves as women disguised as men. Mistaken identities. People pretending to mistake someone's identity. The tales went on and on all afternoon and into the evening.

"Did you hear the tale of the mapmaker who survived twenty-four missions into the Fens of Reur?" asked one storyteller. "Neither has anyone else."

"What do you call six mapmakers at the bottom of a pool of quicksand?" countered another. "An expedition."

"How many mapmakers does it take to start a fire during a thunderstorm?" a younger woman asked the crowd. "One. Lightning always strikes a mapmaker first."

Sven sat next to Erika and laughed heartily, and she laughed with him. At one point, she brazenly snuck her hand into his, and he stopped laughing immediately, his eyes softening as they turned to look at her. Green eyes that held the world met her own. He took his hand away and theatrically raised his arms above his head, pretending to yawn. She shivered a little.

He's moving the wedding ceremony on, she thought. Next to her, Erlend and Batha were speaking quietly to themselves and laughing. They knew what he was doing.

"The fires're gettin' hot. I think I could use some cooler air," Sven said after a minute.

Erika pressed a hand to Sven's forehead. "It feels like you might have a fever. Perhaps you're comin' down with somethin'. Maybe you should lie down."

Erika helped him to his feet and led him to her house. They brushed the mud from their boots, and she lifted the hide door open for him. She let it fall behind them, leaving them both in the dark and quiet of her hut. The hearth fire had been extinguished. She directed him to the side of the bed and helped him undress. He lay down. She pulled off his boots, rubbed his feet gently.

Now it was his turn to tremble. She bent over his naked body in the darkness and kissed him softly on the lips, lingering just long enough to make him eager for more before she disappeared back into the dark.

"Just try to get some sleep," she said and then giggled. "Isn't this silly?"

"It's tradition," he said quietly, his hand holding hers.

"I know," she answered, removing his hand. "So you'll just have to wait a few hours." By the door, she saw his boots. She grabbed them and took them with her.

Outside, Erlend and Batha watched her return. Batha smiled at her, and Erlend nodded.

"The first sign of a successful marriage's the wife's willin'ness to take her husban's boots," Batha said.

"An' the second sign's the husban's denial that anythin' ever happened," Erlend laughed.

Erika laughed, too.

"A strong marriage begins through waitin'. If the wife trusts the husband to return from the hunt an' does not fool aroun' while waitin', the marriage'll be strong. If the husban' respects his wife's right to take his boots, the marriage'll last," Erlend said. "It's the same for all the Mar. We trust an' respect each other, an' it makes us strong. When that trust dies, so do the Mar. This's why the ceremony's the way it is."

"We know how impatient you are, Erika, but you've got some waitin' to do," Batha added.

Slightly embarrassed, Erika said with mock anger, "He made me wait six spans! Let's see if he can handle six hours."

Erlend gave a low chuckle. "Your mother could only wait two."

Batha smiled. "An' your father didn't return with enough meat to feed a mapmaker. Isn't that right, Littlehart?"

"The mapmaker was sick! You wouldn't let him eat any meat!"

All three of them laughed.

Erika allowed herself to be distracted by everyone she knew, seeking out friends and family, letting Erbark guide her around to meet people from other towns. As time passed, people left to sleep. Finally, she was left with some of her dearest friends, at a small fire in front of her house.

"Do the last bit there, dear," Batha had told her daughter. "It'll drive him crazy."

The soup was at near boiling, the herbs she had gathered on

her own added. It was certainly a bowl of flavorful soup, the "love draught" she was supposed to be making him. Would she be able to wait as patiently as him while he waited for the soup to cool?

Fidelity, respect, patience — these are the things one needed to survive. And to marry.

Taking a deep breath, she went inside. *Tonight...*

 **9**

"Cyan is for Elements. Often considered a 'farl magic,' it is among the most versatile of the myst colors despite its arcane name. Elements can block, modify or counter other spells, which is useful enough when facing an enemy wizard. It also synergizes very well with every other kind of magic, especially Knowledge."

— Nightfire Tradition,
Nightfire's Magical Primer

"You should take better care of yourself, Erbark," Erika said as they went to the front door. "You're a wizard, remember?"

He tied a knot in the broken knife belt and reached for his green cloak. "Seems unfair using magic on someone who can't."

"That's not what I mean. You let Olver beat you broken, and you don't even heal yourself on the way home?"

Erbark shrugged. "Pain punishes my mistakes. Scars prove how often I've been wrong."

"We all earn our legends in different ways," another voice said from the living area behind them.

Both of them whirled in surprise.

Sven sat by the fire, red cloak emblazoned with a broken marsord engulfed by flames. He sat sideways in the chair, watching them. The fire flickered to his left, illuminating half of his face while plunging the other in shadow. He smiled at her — the light side warm and affectionate, the dark side sinister and filled with rage.

"How have you been, my love?" he asked slowly, as though very weary or uninterested.

Does he think I've been unfaithful? Erika flushed. Not that she hadn't thought about it, but she knew Erbark would never betray Sven. *Would I?*

"Fine, Sven." Erika shifted nervously. "Where have you been?"

Sven fingered his red cloak. "Domus Palus." His right eye caught a glint of firelight, transformed it into an orb of red light to contrast the deep green of his left.

"Domus Palus?" She was confused.

"Yes." He paused. At last, he gave a soft laugh that sounded almost like a rasp. "You might find this hard to believe, Erika, but I am now Mardux."

Behind her, Erbark released a held breath. "That explains some things."

Sven's face turned a little to look at him directly, and the shadow clouded his entire face. "Thank you for taking care of my family in my absence, Erbark. I know what it has meant to you."

"Will you be here tomorrow?" Erbark asked.

"Yes. We will talk then."

Erbark nodded, turned on his heel and vanished into the night, closing the door behind him.

Erika swallowed. "If you've taken the Chair that means ... "

Sven nodded grimly. "I preserved one opponent but was forced to slay two others. I have come to take you and Asa to the citadel with me. It might no longer be safe for you here."

Her patience slipped. "But we're comfortable here, Sven. Asa's playmates are here. I've made new friends of all the women at the Academy. I've almost finished my studies. And Domus Palus is so far away from Leiben, I'd never get to see my relatives."

She knew there had to be a better argument for staying, but she was too angry to come up with any others.

He shook his head firmly. "That is not important now. My enemies know you are here. They will try to use you and Asa to get to me. I cannot bear to see my family suffer, but nor can I surrender to my opponents. If they captured you and demanded my abdication as ransom, I would be forced to make a choice."

Erika began to cry. "Oh Sven, why can't you ever be happy? Why do you always need something bigger to do? Aren't we good enough for you?"

Sven's green eyes flashed red in the firelight and then changed to an eager green as he wrapped his arms tenderly around her. "Shh. My dear, I am doing this for you, for Asa, for our children's families. You have to understand. I started the Protectorates to improve the lives of the Mar. Zerst, Leiben, Tortz — they were all kindling for the flame of change. Now, the fires have gotten strong enough that I can add larger logs. I have enkindled the flame of change in Domus Palus in the last several spans. The wet wood is just starting to burn a little. All it needs is someone to fan it, and then real change can happen in Marrishland. But if I leave it unattended, the whole fire will go out, and I'll have to start again with kindling. I have to bring warmth and illumination to the Mar. It is my destiny!"

Erika tried to formulate an argument that would sway her single-minded husband, convince him that maybe so much change was not good all at once. But she knew from previous discussions that nothing could convince Sven to abandon his ambitions. He needed evidence, not appeals to tradition or emotion. How, then, could anyone change his mind?

From the nursery came the frightened squeals of children.

"Oh by Fraemauna, Asa!" Erika cried.

Her husband momentarily forgotten, she raced to the door. She yanked it open to find the room filled with smoke. Tendrils of flame snaked up one wooden wall. The children huddled in the opposite corner, sobbing in terror. Asa looked up at her mother in surprise and relief.

Erika gathered Energy, hurled the magic at the flames to extinguish them. Then she grabbed her daughter in a crushing embrace. "What happened, Asa? How'd the fire start?"

Asa burst into tears. "It was an accident."

Erika ran her fingers through the girl's hair soothingly. "Tell mommy all about it."

The girl spoke between sobs. "We were playing Academy. And I was teaching them magic, but Ottar couldn't see the myst, so I gave them all torutsen. Then the green motes were all around me, and I got scared, and everything was on fire."

"There, there," Erika said softly, though inside she was as shaken as the children. "Everything is all right, now. We'll take care of this in the morning. Right now, it's time for your friends to go home. Their parents will worry about them."

Asa nodded weakly.

The woman addressed the entire nursery. "And I don't want to catch any of you drinking torutsen again."

A six-year-old squirmed. "It was Asa's idea."

"Unn!" Asa moaned, betrayed.

"Home, all of you," Sven rumbled from the door.

"Daddy?!" Asa cried in joy and terror.

The children scampered past him and out into the night.

"And Asa."

The girl looked up at her father nervously. "Yes, daddy?"

"You are to go to bed right now. We will discuss your behavior in the morning."

Asa hung her head. "Yes, daddy."

Erika kissed the girl on the forehead. "You go to sleep. Everything will be all right."

Asa nodded and hugged her mother's neck. Then, not meeting her father's burning gaze, she retreated to her bedroom, whispering, "I missed you, daddy."

Sven examined his wife's face carefully.

She did not flinch. "You could at least have spent a few minutes with her after being away from home for so long."

He ignored the comment. "How long has she been playing this game?"

"The last three months." Then, bitterly, "If you were at home more, you'd know that."

"Three months, and she's already stealing torutsen and playing with the myst?"

Erika nodded silently.

"Where did she learn to use magic?"

"She's grown up at a wizards' academy, surrounded by magic. She's very bright. It was only a matter of time before she learned to do it herself."

"I could get in a lot of trouble if someone found out about this."

"Your daughter almost burned to death in your house, and you're worried about what would happen to you?" she raged, turning her back on him.

He must have caught the bitterness in her voice, because he softened. "I'm just afraid my enemies will try to do something to her. This might give them an excuse."

Then his arms were around her, and his lips pressed against the back of her neck tenderly.

How can a man so gentle be so cruel?

"I understand," she said, even though she really didn't. She touched the back of his hand with hers, and he clasped it, their fingers weaving together.

"Then you see why we must go to Domus Palus. I can protect both of you there. I can finish your apprenticeship myself, and we will both work to raise our daughter where it's safe."

Safer than being here where everyone loves you and would never let anything bad happen to her? Erika thought, but his lips were seeking her cheek and then her mouth.

She turned in his arms and slipped her hands around the back of his neck. His chest pressed against hers as he breathed deeply, inhaling her scent. His boots fell to the floor, and she could hear her own heart pounding in her ears as they made their way to the bedroom.

"Well? Will you?" he whispered in her ear as the fingers of his left hand kneaded the small of her back.

She barely heard him as she undid the clasp of his cloak and let the red cloth fall in a bundle at their feet. Her mind was filled with the thought of having him close again.

He suddenly pulled his head away from hers and studied her face in the darkness. She couldn't see his eyes, but she knew how they were looking at her — how they were searching for her understanding, her approval.

She could offer him neither, but she laid one hand on his arm. "I love you, Sven Takraf. I would gladly follow you to the Dead Swamps if you asked."

He planted a long, grateful kiss on her mouth. They separated for just a moment to undress.

His hand touched her bare shoulder. She sighed heavily, which he seemed to mistake for eagerness, for he pulled her close.

"Please promise you will never leave without warning like that again," Erika murmured almost absently.

He froze like a rabbit in the path of a gobbel, and she immediately hated herself for it.

He recovered quickly. "I promise," he whispered in her ear.

But even in the darkness of their bedroom, in the heat of the moment, Erika knew this promise could not bind for long. Her husband was not a guardian of home, hearth and family. He was a visionary, a champion of the Mar and now the Mardux. She had married him thinking she had found a good man, but he had turned out to be a great man, and she couldn't say whether what she felt was more pride or disappointment at that knowledge.

 **10**

"Amber is for Knowledge. Knowledge serves two extremely useful functions. First, it can gather a wide variety of information about the physical world, allowing a wizard to view the myst without torutsen, track enemy movements from great distances, and much more. Second, it can be used to create triggers for other spells by reacting to measurable circumstances, granting magical effects rudimentary intelligence."

— Nightfire Tradition,
Nightfire's Magical Primer

Katla Duxpite strolled through the halls of Volund's keep at Flasten Palus as if she did not wish death on every red living there. That it had been built of wood, not stone, was not a reflection of its shortage of wealth or power, she knew, but a purely practical consideration. Flasten Palus was not built on a foundation of coastal-quarried stone as was Domus Palus or Pidel Palus. The Duxy of Flasten was almost entirely a flat marsh reminiscent of the Fens of Reur, but with shallower water. Stone would have sunk into the mud within a decade.

When I am finished, Volund will wish it had sunk, and him with it, Katla vowed fiercely.

Flasten's primary product was wild rice, which had little demand in the rest of Marrishland and virtually none outside of it. By rights, it should have been as much of a poor satellite of Domus as Piljerka, Skrem and Gunne. Volund's ancestors, in fact, had lived in a glorified grass and mud daub hut for four generations. The only reason it had risen above its obscurity was the "innovation" of Volund's grandfather, who first hit upon the idea of selling enslaved mundanes captured just beyond Flasten's boundaries to foreign traders from Manerem and Aflighan.

Katla could hear arguing voices even from outside the council chamber, and she paused to listen.

" … has given us nothing but empty promises for nearly a year, while Sven Takraf's power grows. When she comes in here, I will … "

Katla pushed the door wide open and swept into the room. She fixed her eyes on Vigfus Vielfrae.

"You will what? Send more greens to abduct a Mardux who surrounds himself with hundreds of yellows?" She snorted in laughter.

Vigfus said nothing, but Katla now had the attention of the entire room — from Volund and his sons to Arnora, Ari, Valgird and Robert.

I see you finally exchanged your yellow for red, Robert, she noted absently. *Do you think the Mar would salute you if you took the Chair?*

Power slammed the doors shut behind Katla with a boom. She strode toward the long table as she spoke with contempt and anger made all the more convincing because she utterly loathed them all. "While you have been wasting time with your pathetic schemes to corrupt minor bureaucrats in Domus Palus, my master has been holding back the full fury of the Mass with nothing but his honeyed tongue. Do you know what he has promised the Drakes?"

Volund's face looked placid, which could only mean he was masking real fury at her tone. Ragnar was less successful at it and seemed on the point of objecting. The other wizards looked serious but clearly took their cues from the dux.

"Results." Katla tapped her finger on the table for emphasis. "Duxfest is only two months away — ninety days. Will the Mass get the results it demands of my master, or will hundreds of thousands of Mar die because of your incompetence?" She directed these last words directly at Volund, and his control faltered for just a moment.

"Weard Duxpite, we appreciate your … perspective on this matter," the dux managed with a thin smile. "If you would please have a seat, we would be all too happy to discuss our options."

Katla wanted to refuse. Brack's prestige among these wizards granted her considerable influence over them, even if she was only his apprentice. She wanted to hurl more insults at the Dux of Flasten under his own roof.

She recalled Brack's words on diplomacy. *Pull when they expect you to push, and push when they think you will pull. People are most at your mercy when they think they are directing the negotiations.* She sat at the foot of the table.

Volund folded his hands on the table and tried to look like he was in easy command of the situation. "We do not have the numbers to take the Chair this year. Even if we succeeded, Weard Schwert will only topple whoever defeats Weard Takraf. Nor can we abduct the Mardux or his family unless we can lure them away from their bodyguards. We have no remedies that are within the Law."

As if you ever respected the Law! Katla thought fiercely, but she said nothing.

The dux continued. "We can suggest solutions, but they are all ... problematic, from a legal perspective. Whoever succeeds Sven Takraf on the Chair needs to be sympathetic to our current plight."

"You want a Mardux who will grant you amnesty in spite of your crimes," Katla supplied.

"Yes."

Katla nodded. "That is only fair, though I doubt it will trouble you. Weard Schwert is the only red who openly supports Weard Takraf. Defeat them both, and you will decide who next sits on the Chair."

Valgird smiled slightly, as though he thought Volund would pick someone other than one of his own sons for the task.

Of course, it could happen if some accident befell Ketil before then, Katla mused.

Volund took a moment before responding. Perhaps he had noticed her knowing smile, too. "We will invade the Takraf Protectorates. Weard Wost assures me he can dismantle the automated defenses, and the handful of lesser wizards the Mardux has charged with protecting it poses no threat to a force of a thousand weards."

"And then what?" Katla prompted.

Volund seemed surprised by this question. "He will not abandon his Protectorates. Even if he does not go there personally, he will send some of his bodyguards in his stead, and that will make him vulnerable."

Katla laughed. She couldn't help herself. *Just because Sven doesn't mind getting his hands dirty doesn't mean he does it very often. He surely has a contingency for this. But would Volund know this?*

The reds in the room stared at her with a mixture of anger and confusion, and she managed to contain her amusement. "Three seasons! Three seasons, and you still have not gotten past your original solution of abducting the Mardux or someone he cares about?"

Confusion turned to embarrassment.

Ragnar retorted hotly, "Would you rather we all teleport into Domus Palus and assassinate him?"

Don't even think about it, Katla thought, but instead she spoke with heavy sarcasm. "That is a brilliant idea, Weard Groth! Surely Weard Takraf would never expect you to murder him when he is literally sitting on the Chair."

Ragnar stood up, face flushed. "I grow weary of your presumption, Weard Duxpite."

"She is right," Robert said. "The Mardux will have anticipated such a move."

Katla stared at the farl, hoping she didn't look as surprised as she actually was.

"We could try invading the Duxy of Domus," Ketil said in a small voice. "He'll have to defend his territory."

Volund shot him an irritated look. "We have already been over this, and it is out of the question."

"Why?" Katla asked, feigning confusion. "Let the battles be fought on their lands, at the expense of their towns, farms and mundanes."

Ragnar smirked at her apparent ignorance. "The Duxy of Domus has a long-standing treaty with the duxies of Gunne, Skrem and Piljerka, two of which share borders with Flasten. If we commit most of our forces to the invasion, the Duxy of Flasten will be vulnerable. And those duxies will invade, I can assure you. They have no love for us."

As many times as you've invaded them on your little slaving expeditions, you've given them good reason for that, Katla thought, but she waited, maintaining the push.

"Then there are the Drakes of the Dead Swamps to the south," Ragnar continued. "The gobbels have overwhelmed our perimeter defenses before, and ochre raiders dig under them quite regularly."

"And those are the obvious dangers," Arnora added. "What if the damnens invade? What if Wasfal, Nightfire or Pidel side with the

Mardux against us?"

"That is unlikely," Ragnar said. "The damnens have not left the Dead Swamps in centuries, and the other three have been neutral in political conflicts for nearly as long."

"Perhaps," Arnora conceded, "but if you rule out as impossible anything that is merely unlikely, you increase your risk of catastrophe."

Katla's respect for the woman increased fractionally, but she shared Ragnar's skepticism over the damnens involving themselves. While she had a healthy fear for a member of the Drake race who did not join in the Mass and still survived, they preferred to keep to themselves. The giant, clawed monstrosities combined the worst of most Drake traits, from immunity to Dinah's Curse to near-perfect camouflage, and on top of those, they were immune to magic. Any wizard would run before them, and all mundanes would die.

"Brack and I had hoped it would not come to this. Watch the myst carefully with Knowledge. I have something to demonstrate." Katla allowed them only a moment before reaching into the folds of her cloak and withdrawing a short, straight twig. "This is a Blosin wand."

Robert's eyes widened, and he opened his mouth, but Katla gave him no opportunity. She touched a small knot near one end. A jet of flame shot from the other end, leaving a black scorch mark on one wooden wall.

The other wizards did not react well to this sudden display, gathering the myst to counter whatever spells Katla might produce. *If killing you was all I hoped to achieve today, I would have done it by now.*

Even after they calmed down, Katla could tell they didn't yet grasp the implications.

"A slow device," Vigfus commented. "A green could work such magic more quickly."

"The magic is inside the wand, so a ready supply might prevent fatigue," Ketil offered.

"I do not understand how this solves any of our problems, Weard Duxpite," Volund said, but he at least looked interested.

Robert looked neither perplexed nor thoughtful. He stared at Katla with undisguised fury.

Would you like to explain to Dux Feiglin that you are the reason

Sven took the Chair so easily, Weard Wost? Katla thought, avoiding his gaze.

"I do not believe she had magocrats in mind when she created this wand," Robert said, and if his face showed emotion, his voice certainly did not. It was a lecturer's tone. "The magic is in the wand itself. Mere contact between that mark on the wand and a living tor activates it. Anyone can use it."

Valgird reached the conclusion first. "Mundanes." He smiled, no doubt imagining ways he could exploit this spell, once he knew how it worked.

"But it is against the Law to teach mundanes to use magic," Ari said.

Robert pressed his lips together, and Katla knew Nightfire had already forbidden him from giving wands to mundanes. *Otherwise you would have had an army instead of a few slaves.*

But Valgird answered with a sleek smile. "Yes, but this is not teaching the mundanes anything about magic. Eventually, the magic will run out, and the wand will not function until it is enchanted again. How many uses would you say it has, Weard Duxpite?"

"A few dozen."

"Still, we would be giving the mundanes weapons by equipping them with such devices," Arnora objected. "What is to keep the mundanes from turning the wands against us?"

Valgird and Robert looked at each other, and mutual recognition crossed their faces.

Valgird spoke, "Unless wand-wielders had a strong numbers advantage, I doubt they would be a match for actual wizards."

"This would give us an advantage in an invasion of the Duxy of Domus, Weard Duxpite, but it still is not enough to negate all our disadvantages," Ragnar said.

"Ah, but you must not march on the Duxy of Domus with these wands," Katla said. "The Drakes do not know the difference between a wizard and a wand-wielder. If you march toward the Fens of Reur with an army large enough to capture Domus Palus, the Mass will certainly interpret it as an invasion."

"Then what purpose do you have in giving us these wands?" Ragnar demanded.

"We will use the gobbels of the Dead Swamps. They can use the wands as easily as a mundane could. I will negotiate the deal personally."

All around the table, eyes fell. Wizards shifted nervously in their chairs.

After a long pause, Ketil spoke. "The Drakes and Mar have been at war for as long as Fraemauna has ruled the sky. To make such an alliance ..."

Katla sniffed. "Perhaps you have forgotten that it was an army of Drakes who drove the Giens out of Marrishland."

"And also razed all of our cities," Ari muttered.

Volund waved him to silence. "Go on, Weard Duxpite."

"If the gobbels in the Dead Swamps were armed with wands and — for that price — were convinced to invade the Duxy of Piljerka, the Mardux would have to deal with it using his army of wizards. Before he could even get there, Piljerka and Skrem would have fallen."

"Then we invade Gunne and Domus," Ragnar said, leaning over the table.

"The Mardux would see us gathering wizards long before, if we hoped to invade at the same time," Arnora said.

"Weard Stoltz is right," Katla said. "But, Weard Feiglin, you offer to help the Mardux. Then your people are amassed in the open, until they rival the Mardux's own. And you have permission to cross the border. You will be stronger than his army and, if you plan it right, between him and Domus."

Murmurs of approval swept around the table.

"What do you need from us?" Volund asked.

"I will need two of your reds to accompany me to the Dead Swamps. I will teach them to enchant wands so they can equip the gobbels. I will then report our plans to my master."

"Ketil and Weard Stoltz will go with you. Ragnar and Weard Vielfrae, you will lead the invasion. I will go to Domus Palus when the Mardux calls the Council to address the gobbel attack." Volund turned to Robert, Ari and Valgird. "The three of you will stay here in Flasten Palus to deal with any problems."

Valgird rose slightly from his chair. "Dux Feiglin, while I agree this plan is better than the one I originally recommended, one does not exclude the other."

Volund waved for him to continue.

Valgird licked his lips. "All I ask is permission to lead an invasion of the Takraf Protectorates once Weard Groth begins the real attack. As Weard Stoltz said, even if there is only a small chance that it will force Weard Takraf to take steps to defend it, I think it is worth doing."

"It is not a bad idea, Weard Geir, but I cannot spare any of my magocrats."

"I am willing to hire mercenaries from the Duxy of Wasfal," Valgird persisted.

Volund compressed his lips into a narrow line but nodded. "Very well." He took in the room. "Unless there are further comments, let us adjourn. Tomorrow, we move."

Katla, Arnora and Ketil teleported to the edge of the Dead Swamps, and after a day of searching and waiting, they stood negotiating with a gobbel chief who claimed to speak for the other gobbel chiefs.

The Dead Swamps had once been a duxy in their own right, until the damnens had claimed them. They looked no different from any other stink-filled, oozing part of Marrishland. The trees were perhaps a little thicker, the canopy maybe a little denser, but the standing water and konig worms were the same. Katla resisted the urge to run her hand along the soft green moss covering a giant root of the tree next to her. Who knew what the moss might do to her?

Katla Duxpite wore a marsord as a disguise. Few people had ever seen Katla for who she really was. The people she loved feared and distrusted her, while the ones she hated never doubted she was their ally. Even now, as she actively pursued his downfall, Volund had allowed her to plan his war strategy for him. She had no doubt that when Brack finally introduced her to the Delegates, the Drakes would misjudge her, too.

Katla recognized that and embraced it, even though it was sometimes painful. Her patroness had fashioned her into the perfect instrument of revenge, as suited Katla's purpose beautifully.

I did not devote myself to the most loathed and feared of all Mar goddesses because I hoped to be a miner or mapmaker. The Bald Goddess is generous when moved by injustice.

In addition to her reign over earth, Drakes and disease, Dinah was the goddess of vengeance. Hers was not the polite, civil justice Seruvus oversaw, but the ruthless, overwhelming revenge of one who has been wronged so badly that no reparations would ever set things right. The Bald Goddess dealt most harshly with those who abused their power — the prouder and stronger the tyrant, the more humiliating and absolute his demolition.

Katla could appreciate a patroness like that in a way she could never devote herself to Marrish or Fraemauna. Nightfire had been uncomfortable with her choice, and she knew many Mar would consider her a traitor if they knew, which was why she so seldom swore oaths to her patroness.

If I succeed, wizards like the ones who took my mother away will pay in blood for their crimes. I will break their power. I will diminish their numbers. And I will place them at the mercy of the mundanes. Sven seeks that goal, and I will ensure he achieves it, even if I must make enemies of every Mar to do it.

She smiled grimly at the thought but shuddered slightly as well. She pushed the thought away and concentrated on the matter at hand.

The needle-toothed gobbels of the Dead Swamps were driving a hard bargain. Their leader, a tall, broad-shouldered beast clad in the decomposing hides of alligators, wore a sheathed marsord at his side. That message was clear: This gobbel had won a battle against a powerful weard. As she spoke forcefully to him in his native language, though, Katla knew she would convince him.

She held out the wand to him in offering, glancing sideways at her two companions, whose looks were dubious even if they knew whom she represented.

Perhaps even more so because of whom and what I represent.

She glanced at the swamp around her. Gobbels stood in every direction. They had wide, flat noses and lips that curled up in a permanent snarl that revealed their sharp teeth. It was no wonder the

Mar considered them both aggressive and stupid. Katla knew better. They had learned how to fight Mar over the last several centuries. She noted the characteristic tactics.

They stood in groups of no more than ten or twenty, none more than a hundred feet from each other nor nearer than fifty. It was a formation that allowed them to forage on the march, but more importantly, it made it difficult for a wizard to attack more than one group at a time. In battle against weards, the members of each group would scatter. Now, they were all watching. All muttering.

Listening. Waiting for one of us to make a mistake.

If the wizards attacked, gobbel spears would be in the air too quickly to gather myst for teleportation. The edge Katla walked with Arnora and Ketil was sharp.

After a long pause, the big gobbel nodded and motioned to his bodyguards — eight thick-armed warriors dressed in rust-colored fox pelts. One of them stepped forward to take the wand from her hand. He pointed it at a small kalysut and touched the mark on the twig.

A jet of flame engulfed one branch of the tree, reducing its leaves to ash.

The leader of the gobbels nodded and laughed, shouting to the gobbels all around. The cry was taken up, echoing through the trees. Several thousand gobbels surged forward. Katla saw Arnora's face whiten and her knees buckle as several passed close to her.

"Well?" Arnora hissed, coming closer to Katla.

Katla spoke in Middling Gien, *"Stay here with the gobbels. I will bolster the perimeter defenses in case the gobbels try to betray us."*

"What did you say?" Ketil asked.

Arnora sniffed in disgust. "Do not tell me you cannot speak Middling Gien!"

He shrugged. "Read? Yes. Speak? That is not so easy."

Katla frowned at him, trying to think of another way to get her point across without undoing her negotiations with the gobbels. "You'll find that many of our allies speak Mar quite well. Be polite to them."

"What are your instructions, Weard Duxpite?" Arnora asked in Middling Gien.

Katla smiled slightly and matched languages. *"Do not underestimate the gobbels, and do not do anything that will provoke them. They will eventually lose. Do not be here when the wizards defeat them."*

"Will the gobbels blame us for their defeat and kill us?"

"The gobbels will flee when the day is lost. The Mardux's magocrats will accuse you of treason against Marrishland, however, and you must admit they have a pretty convincing case."

"Thank you for the warning, Weard Duxpite," Arnora said, and she sounded like she meant it. *"I will keep Volund's son under control."*

Katla nodded and disappeared into the Tempest. Instead of returning directly to the Flasten border, however, she went to the ochres. Katla found them easier to persuade than the gobbels had been. Of course their wands would be more effective against wizards — counterspell wands to tear down the perimeter defenses. Ochres were intelligent enough to grasp the implications.

 **11**

"It is not the goal of this Academy to teach Mar to use magic. The truest measure of a weard is not what he knows, but what he is capable of teaching himself. At my Academy, you young men and women will learn how to learn. Those of you who master learning might decide to take the next step, which is to learn how to teach others to learn."

— Nightfire Tradition,
Apprentice Addresses

Sven sat on the Chair overlooking the seasonal meeting of the Council. "What is the next order of business? Yes, Dux Verlren?"

"We estimate forty thousand gobbels have breached our eastern perimeter," Yver Verlren, the Dux of Piljerka, explained as though the spring rains had come a little early.

"How did they get past your border defenses?" the Dux of Skrem asked as though this was of purely academic interest to him.

"That is unknown at this time, Dux Zaghaf," Yver said. "We are investigating, but many of my frontier magocrats have not responded to our inquiries."

"Is there any chance they abandoned their posts, Dux Verlren?" Volund asked with a concerned expression.

Yver shook his head. "More likely, their towns have already fallen, although I'm surprised more did not teleport away."

The dux of Flasten managed a sympathetic smile. "You know frontier wizards. They always insist on being the last to retreat."

Sven studied Volund. The timing of this attack was too perfect, and based on his response, Volund seemed clearly involved with it. *But how had Volund convinced thousands of gobbels to attack Piljerka?*

Brack, he realized, glancing sideways at Katla. *No one else has any sway over the Drakes.*

She gave no sign of recognition.

Perhaps the old bogeyman was trying to make the Mass seem real.

"Do you need our assistance?" Sven asked Yver.

"Only your forbearance, Mardux. I am sending a thousand of my magocrats to break the invasion, so Piljerka may be slower in paying next season's tribute than I would like."

"I believe that is acceptable," Sven told him. "Does anyone on this Council have any objections? Yes, Dux Ratsell?"

Sven had a raging headache long before the negotiations ended. Wasfal was not as wealthy as Domus or Pidel, but it had ready access to more trade goods than any of the other landlocked duxies — a fact it used to its advantage. Every duxy owed money to Gruber Ratsell, every dux's debt secured by the sworn pledge of hundreds or even thousands of its magocrats. If the duxy defaulted on the debt, those magocrats became Wasfal's slaves for eight years.

Several other items of business came to the Council, but Sven found nothing interesting about any of it. When Nightfire, Katla and the duxes ran out of topics, Sven stood up from the Chair.

"I have one more order of business before this meeting of the Council ends. I propose an amendment to Bera's Unwritten Laws to allow Mar to use magic even if they lack the prerequisite education."

"I cannot advise against this action strongly enough," Katla said. "Your amendment would be a declaration of war against the Drakes, and the Mass will move against us." She sounded confident, but Sven caught a flicker of doubt in her eyes.

Or was that a wink of acknowledgment?

Sven went on. "I use the Takraf Protectorates as an example of the changes education can have. Disease, famine and danger have been severely diminished by my work there. There is no reason we cannot adopt such policy throughout the country. The quickest way to deal with this will be to teach all Mar to use the myst."

"Do you have any idea how many Mar would die if the Mass came down from the Fens of Reur again?" Volund snapped. "If we are lucky, only a few hundred thousand Mar would die in that war.

If we are not, there will be another dark age like the one after the Empire fell."

"Peace, Dux Feiglin," Yver said. "We have heard your rants before."

"You must have a unanimous vote of the duxes to change Bera's Unwritten Laws, and you will never have mine." Volund jerked to his feet. "Mardux, you have proposed this amendment at every meeting of the Council since you took the Chair. No argument will get me to change my vote." He stormed out.

Hand pressed to his temple to ward off the headache, Sven adjourned the meeting. As he shuffled to his offices, he smiled grimly. Volund had chosen the path Sven had laid for him. Yver Verlren of Piljerka, Wolber Verden of Gunne and Borya Zaghaf of Skrem always voted with him. Gruber was neatly in his pocket if only because he needed Domus to pay its debts more than Sven needed to repay Wasfal. Duxess Glyda Zaun of Pidel was, as usual, an enigma. And Volund voted against Sven no matter what the subject was.

The easiest solution was to get rid of Flasten. Would Volund be surprised to hear, while his army was in Piljerka, that Domus had taken the Duxy of Flasten?

And while Nightfire and Brack sat as judge and executor of the Unwritten Laws, they had no vote on amendments to it. As long as Sven did not break the Law, neither of them could challenge his authority.

"I am reminded of your return to Rustiford, Mardux."

Sven jumped when he heard the Traveller's voice. He turned around and saw the man sitting on the couch in the corner, playing with one of Asa's toys.

"I have no time for stories," Sven said and coughed. He surprised himself by sitting heavily in his chair. *A cough? When was the last time I was sick?*

"You are pushing yourself too hard. Your wife and daughter miss you."

"Do not mention them. It is too much you know who and where they are."

Energy made the fire blaze high in the hearth and lit all the candles. Power shuffled books and papers, rolled maps and charts in a swirl of paper until the desk was clear. Sven fell into a fit of coughing.

"Perhaps it will cheer you up," Pondr said, and began.

Sven's glared at the fire, but his eyelids drooped, and his mind followed the story.

Sven stepped out of the underbrush and into the clear area that surrounded Rustiford's palisade. He took a deep breath, inhaling the faint whiff of hearth smoke. He had almost forgotten that smell he had left behind eight long years ago. Smelling it now made him nervous. Even more than the fear he would not recognize the people he grew up with, Sven feared they wouldn't recognize him or wouldn't trust him. That dread sat in his stomach like a lump of cold clay.

He had been a different person then. The wizards of Nightfire's Academy called him Sven Takraf, but here they would still remember him as Gematsud after his mother — the name his father had taken for love of her. He pulled the green cloak of a first-degree wizard tighter around his shoulders as Heliotosis, the north wind, tugged at it, and walked calmly toward the palisade gate.

"Halt, wizard," called a voice from behind the palisade. Sven recognized it as Glum's — a boy two years his junior. "Who're you, an' why're you here?"

No longer a boy, Sven corrected himself. *All my peers and playmates are adults, now.*

"I'm Sven Gematsud, son of Pitt Gematsud. I've returned after eight years of enslavement to the wizard known as Nightfire."

"You don't look like Sven." Glum sounded suspicious. "Don't soun' like him, either."

Sven set his jaw. He couldn't say he hadn't expected something like this. Eight years was a long time, especially when you spent it at a wizard's academy while your friends spent it fighting to survive in a small town in ravit territory.

He forced himself to revert to his old dialect, the one Weard Kruste had all but flayed out of him. "Brin' my father to the gate. He'll remem'er me."

"Can't do that."

"Why not?"

"He's dead."

Sven would have been less shocked to find his hometown under siege by gobbels or occupied by an army of Flasten magocrats. Grief and regret washed over him, as well as completely irrational anger.

"How?" he asked, surprised by how cool and steady his voice sounded.

"Ravit attack. He took a dart i'the back, an' poison killed him."

Just like that, Sven thought, numb. *That's how we live out here. How I used to live. No time to care if we're ignorant, uneducated and poor. It is enough that we are alive at all.*

"Who's at the gate?" asked a second voice from within the walls.

"Some wizard says he's Sven Gematsud."

"Finn!" Sven shouted. "Finn, tell him I'm tellin' the truth."

"Is he?" Glum asked.

A new eye peered through the lookout hole. "Yeah. Open the gate, Glum."

"But he's ... "

"He's comin' home like th'others did. We've been over this. Open it."

A bolt moved and the wooden gate swung open to reveal a much larger Rustiford than Sven remembered.

Finn's unshaven face regarded him. Sven saw tension there, but among all the other faces that peered at him from the doors and windows of nearby houses, Finn's was the friendliest.

"Are the others here?" Sven asked. The town was larger, but seemed less well-kept than he remembered. He could smell the foulness of refuse mingled with the hearth smoke, and his nose wrinkled. He had forgotten about that.

"No," Finn said as the gate swung shut behind them. "You aren't welcome here anymore."

"Why?"

Finn pointed at the green cloak. "We've paid our debt. We're done with wizards."

"Then why let me in at all?" Sven asked, suddenly conscious of the number of people who had come out of their houses. Many of them held spears and knives at the ready.

Merciful Niminth, I can't fight that many. Not that he wanted to fight any of them. Many of the faces were faded memories, but some of the voices were all too familiar. *Maybe if I run.* He searched for holes in the crowd and found none large enough.

A new figure practically ran into the space between Sven and the gathering mob. "Enough!" he shouted in a voice clearly used to command.

It was Erbark, and Sven practically wept. *He was my closest friend, and I didn't even recognize his face!*

The townsfolk hesitated. "Back to your homes, all of you," Erbark ordered.

"But the mayor," a young man murmured. It was a voice Sven couldn't place, probably because it had belonged to a child when he had left Rustiford.

"I'll talk to her. Sven's not makin' trouble if he's with me."

"Erbark," Sven breathed.

"I knew you'd be back," Erbark said back, drawing Sven away from the crowd. "I have some soup."

"Thank you."

The taste of Erbark's soup brought back more old memories — rabbit and wild rice with too much laurita, though Lori had always preferred it to Sven's. Sven stared into the fire as he ate.

"I'm sorry for how they treated you," Erbark said as the spoon scraped the bowl. "Sorry about your dad, too. We lost a lot of good folk i'that war, but he was the best."

Sven swallowed hard. He still couldn't quite believe it. He hadn't seen his father in eight years. Numbly, he spoke. "Thanks, Erbark." With more energy he asked, "Who's mayor now?"

"Brita Ochregut took charge after Pitt died. She's Elder, too."

Sven sucked breath. "What happened to Sveld?"

Erbark shrugged and shook his head. "Sveld was old, Sven, as Elders tend to be. He caught Seruvus' Breath three winters ago. There was nothin' we could do."

Sven's eyes filled with tears as he listened to Rustiford being slowly annihilated by his absence. "Lori? Hauk?"

"Hauk's blacksmith now. Thorhall died i'the ravit war, too." Erbark paused, as though remembering some lost emotion. "Lori married Olver Winbrak."

Sven's jaw dropped. "Ugly Olver? You're kidding me!"

"They've three sons an' another kid on the way. Haki, Horik and Hrafn."

Sven still couldn't believe it. "She chose Ugly Olver over you? Perhaps we misjudged the strength of her sense."

Erbark's eyes became distant with regret.

Sven changed the subject. "And what've you been doing with yourself? I see folks finally listen to you."

"I was a scout i'the ravit war." Erbark's voice grew stronger as he spoke. "People thought I was crazy as a mapmaker volunteerin' for that, but then I kept comin' back alive. Killed a couple gobbels, too, three years back. No idea what they were doin' so far south."

"Sounds like you're halfway to your own star," Sven said, relieved that his friend did not dwell on Lori too much. He sobered. "It's probably good that you stayed here. I would've been useless in any kind of ravit war."

Erbark fixed Sven with a serious expression. "I never forgot that you went with Nightfire instead of me. You didn't even ask."

"You would have refused. I know you." Sven looked at the door. "What exactly happened here? Why does everyone act like they want to murder me?"

"Brand happened." Erbark sighed heavily. "I'm sure he meant well, but comin' back here an' tellin' Pitt what's what an' how to run the town was a mistake. Talkin' about turnin' Rustiford into some kin' of school, which seemed interestin'. I saw him usin' magic to haul stuff, which seemed awful useful. But not everyone wanted to go to his readin' lessons."

Sven remembered Nighfire's final words before he had left the Academy. *Do as I do. Help the ones who want your help. Enlighten those who seek enlightenment. Help those who can be helped, or you will merely end up wasting a lot of time fighting a losing battle against someone's comfortable ignorance. One at a time, Sven. Bring enlightenment to one person at a time.*

"But then he had to go pick a fight with the ravits after that one little skirmish. Dragged us into a war, which is how we lost Pitt an' a lot of others. Then Tosti came back wearin' green, and he was even worse. Burned another man with magic for lookin' at the girl he had an eye on. He an' Brand had a big magic fight that burned down five houses an' killed six people, includin' Tosti."

Nightfire's warning made more sense now. *He knew about this, but he didn't tell me. He knew I'd want to see for myself.*

"Brita said she'd had enough, an' she told Brand to leave," Erbark continued. "I think they would've killed Floki the next year if he'd come back a wizard. Thank Sendala he didn't. Greta, though. It's terrible what happened to her, an' she left right after. We banished th'one who did it, but that's not likely comfort to her wherever she en'ed up. Probably dead — she was headed right into ravit territory."

Sven's eyes went wide. "But she wasn't even a wizard."

Erbark spat into the fire. "No. Otherwise, he wouldn't have dared try it."

"What about the others?" Sven's voice shook. "Eda, Horsa?"

"Came an' went. Eda was mad, of course. Knocked out a few teeth before she left. Horsa, though, said somethin' about an omen an' walked back into the swamp like none of it mattered. Have you seen Katla? I wasn't here when she came back."

Sven nodded. "She's still at the Academy, teaching. I take it Brita welcomed Finn back?"

Erbark grimaced. "Yeah, but a lot of folks weren't so keen on th'idea. They wouldn't have let him stay if he'd been a wizard or if his mother wasn't mayor. That's for sure."

"And that goes for me, too, doesn't it?"

"It's stupid, but yes. People still remem'er Tosti an' the Flasten slavers were wizards. Why'd you come back?"

Sven managed a bitter laugh. "To teach people to read and maybe one day to use magic."

"What will you do now?"

"I don't know. Maybe find some other town out there where they're not afraid of wizards and teach them?"

"I'm goin' with you."

Sven looked at his friend but said nothing.

"Even if I don't owe you my life because you went with Nightfire, a lot of other folks here do because they'd be dead if I'd gone with him. So Rustiford owes you a slave. That's how it works, right?"

"I'm not going to make you my slave, Erbark," Sven said, appalled.

"Then teach me, an' I'll go wherever you go."

"Rustiford needs you more than I do. You said yourself."

"There's always new heroes. Marrish made the world that way. But you need someone to talk at, Sven, or you'll be talkin' at ravits before the month is out."

Sven looked at his friend's curious eyes and saw himself. His hometown had been poisoned against wizards, possibly forever. He'd have to start somewhere else.

"I'd be proud to have you as my apprentice, Erbark, and glad for your company."

One at a time.

 **12**

"Seruvus, the Mar god of water, is the only member of the pantheon who is considered omniscient, as water is everywhere in Marrishland. For each Mar Dinah's Curse kills in violation of the Bald Goddess's promise, she is condemned to serve Seruvus for another eight years. To this day, Dinah still bows to the whims of the Oathbinder, which is why any found to have broken their promises are taken as slaves for eight years by the magocrats."

— Weard Olga Fydelis,
Mar Legends

When Sven woke, the fire had almost gone out. He coughed behind his hand, and someone placed a cup of water on a small table next to him. He looked up, but Erbark was already headed to the fire, reaching for two logs.

"Pondr told me you wanted to see me," Erbark said as he used Power to split and crack the logs in the fire. Two more logs, and the fire regained its former heat.

Sven drank the water gladly, his throat dry from coughing.

A magocrat would never have fed the fire fuel slowly. A wizard would have placed all the logs on and then started the fire, which would have burned too hot to make the fuel last.

Erbark was watching Sven, who straightened.

"I fell asleep," he said, because there wasn't much else to say.

Erbark nodded.

"I did not summon you, but the Traveller must have known I would want to talk to you when I woke up."

"What did he tell you?"

"He told me about my return to Rustiford. He reminded me that I wanted to educate the Mar, that I had to start one by one."

"He opposes your amendment."

"It is necessary, Erbark, and you know it. You know the state of our wizards and how this war with Flasten will exhaust their patience." He coughed again. "And what I must do after that could take decades to bear any fruit. I am a powerful wizard, but even I can't hold the Chair forever."

Erbark poured himself a glass of water and drank it. Sven stared at the fire, his mind working.

The sleep was good for me.

"You're not a magocrat, Sven," Erbark said after a minute.

"What is that?"

"You're a teacher."

"Please do not test me, Erbark."

His friend dug in. "Remember when we left Rustiford? Remember Zerst, the first time? You just wanted to teach. To protect them long enough for them to learn to protect themselves. But even though they owed you their lives, you let them choose whether to accept you."

"What are you saying?"

"Nightfire didn't make Rustiford give him slaves. We did it because he helped us when we couldn't help ourselves. We thought we were paying him back, but he turned our tribute into a gift and gave it back to us. Even then, you didn't have to become his apprentice."

"What does this have to do with ... "

"I left Rustiford because you wanted to teach. And you didn't care who you taught, just as long as they wanted to learn. People owed you their lives, and you didn't demand anything from them in return."

Suddenly Sven knew. He spoke in a tight voice. "Those magocrats owe me their fealty. They could have left the Duxy of Domus if they had chosen. No oath binds you, Erbark. Do you want to end your service to me?"

Erbark shook his head. "Of course not. I'm just remembering how we started this."

Sven stared back at the fire. The Traveller's story was still fresh in his mind, burned in by voice and sleep. *And leaving Rustiford? Where did I go?*

Sven and Erbark headed northwest through the swamps sur-rounding Rustiford. Within a nine-day span, the heavy overgrowth of the swamps began to give way to the rolling wetlands of the Morden Moors.

While the swamp had presented its own dangers, the wide wet-lands ahead of them had completely different ones. Quicksand and sinkholes were more common on the moors, and grass and sedges often concealed such hazards. Not to mention trudging through knee-deep water filled with leeches and burrowing konig worms and tainted with Dinah's Curse.

They trekked a half-day back to find a tree to build a canoe from, but that would only solve some of their problems. They needed to find dry ground to sleep and repair their canoe on. There was no wood to burn, and peat would have taken too long to dry out. But they needed fire to boil water so they could drink and eat, even if fire would draw any Drake for miles like a mapmaker to uncharted territory.

It took them several days to adjust to this new environment. Fre-quently the water was too shallow to canoe in. Erbark's spear and javelins provided the majority of their food, though the warrior found it more difficult to stalk his prey in the absence of cover. Crouching made for slow movement, and Erbark dared not risk Dinah's Curse by crawling. Sven's limited study of botany helped him supplement their diet with a few berries he knew to be safe to eat, and fire fueled by Energy cooked everything.

Each night they ate their dinner, said their prayers and slept light-ly on the moors. On the ninth day, they spotted a tall hill amid the surrounding wetlands. Sven and Erbark paddled to the hill eagerly, reaching it before darkness fell.

"We'll be really dry tonight," Erbark said.

As if Seruvus had a sense of humor, the sky erupted in one of Marrish's famous summer storms, which drenched them and nearly washed them off the hilltop. Sven was thankful they had not been struck by a bolt of lightning during the tempest.

"We're lucky," Erbark said cheerily, when the thunder and wind had finally abated.

Sven joined him at the edge of the camp. The surrounding moorland had been submerged by the deluge, only the tops of the sedges betraying the presence of land below.

"Maybe it'll recede by morning," Sven suggested, not really believing it.

He was not in the least bit surprised when they discovered the water had not soaked into the saturated ground by sunrise. The pair gathered up their wet possessions and prepared to delve into the shallow pond at the foot of the hill when Erbark pointed excitedly.

"Look. Smoke."

Sven followed Erbark's eyes until he saw the pillar of smoke rising out of the moors to the west.

"A town?" Erbark guessed.

"Possibly. This is what we've been looking for." Sven squinted. Something was moving through the moors, heading for the pillar of smoke. Several somethings. "Looks like we didn't find them first."

Erbark gasped. "Gobbels. We've got to help them." He scrambled down the hill.

"We've got to be careful, Erbark. We're still on the moors. And now all the quicksand and sinkholes are hidden underwater. They must be a good league away."

Erbark gestured to the canoe. "Now it's easier, Sven. Let's get movin'. There're people who need our help quickly."

Sven struggled to keep up with Erbark's paddling. Waves of water splashed before them as their canoe crossed the submerged moorlands. As they approached the town, the ground grew firmer, and they leapt from the canoe. Sven could see the town walls clearly as they jogged forward.

Dozens of grey-skinned, mud-crusted gobbels with crude stone picks and shovels hacked at the earth wall surrounding the town. The townspeople within answered them with hurled stones and blowgun darts. But the Mar were too few and poorly armed. The rain had turned the wall to soft mud, and the gobbels were making short work of it. The militia began to abandon the wall, snatching up axes and javelins and racing to the widening breach.

Even with magic, what can two of us do against so many gobbels?

Sven thought, but he hurried after his friend, taking a sip of torutsen as he went.

Erbark drew one of the javelins off his back and took off as though there was no water ahead of him.

Sven called the myst. Green motes of Energy whirled around him like thick smoke. The town was a few hundred feet away now. A dozen gobbels turned as Erbark yelled, howling in surprise. He paused to hurl the javelin at one of them, which hit it in the thigh and dragged it to the ground. He shouted again and threw a second javelin. Sven winced as it sunk into a gobbel's white eye. Half the gobbels charged Sven and Erbark. The rest seemed to have not noticed them yet.

Sven focused the motes around a single hand and released his spell. A ball of flame leapt from his fingers and exploded amid the charging humanoids. Screams, like wailing winter winds, ripped across the moors. A cry of hope rose from the wall as the remaining gobbels realized they were being attacked from behind. The fighting grew more furious, but Sven had to return his attention to the three gobbels charging him.

Sven stood behind Erbark and gathered more Energy. His first attack had fatigued him, though, and the myst moved more slowly. He drew his hunting knife, but he knew it wouldn't be much good against axes. Erbark set his spear for the charge.

The oily grey bodies were twisted. They had wide, flat noses and lips that curled up in a permanent snarl. Sven shuddered, and then Mar survival instincts consumed all fear.

The lead gobbel fell upon Erbark's spear without hesitation. The Mar dropped the spear that held his impaled opponent and dove out of the way of a second gobbel.

Sven prepared to thrust his knife at the third but dove to the ground to avoid a thrown axe. He flinched as he hit the water, knowing the things that probably lived in there.

Deal with Dinah's Curse later, he thought absently.

The gobbel loomed over him, a second axe already in its hand. Sven lifted a hand, and flame leapt from it to consume the gobbel, which fell screaming to the wet ground. Sven bit down the urge to maintain the spell. He only had three or four of these left in him before fatigue rendered him powerless, and he needed to make them count. He crawled over to the still-writhing gobbel. It looked at him with terrified eyes a moment before he slit its throat with his knife. Blood pumped over Sven's hands.

Erbark had felled the last gobbel and was pressuring the gobbels attacking the wall already, spear jabbing and blocking. Sven could see the four warriors holding the breach, one with a broken spear.

It was a clear choice for the gobbels, and the leader shouted an order. The remaining gobbels retreated from the breach, one falling to Erbark's spear, and regrouped to one side. The town's warriors formed up behind Erbark, and Sven came closer to them.

He could count them now, lined up. *Twenty-six to six. But they listen to their leader. Which one is he?*

Sven was ready when the leader raised his weapon — a Mar knife. The wizard's hand rose just as fast and a javelin of pure, green fire silenced the gobbel.

Erbark gave a piercing battle cry and ran at the suddenly demoralized Drakes. The town's warriors followed almost on his heels. Sven collapsed to his hands and knees.

When it was over the gobbels were either dead or fleeing, Erbark took Sven's hand and helped him up. Sven glanced over his friend looking for wounds, then nodded. They burst out laughing, and cheers could be heard from the wall. The four warriors shared Erbark and Sven's exhausted grins, and a balding man dressed in a gray cloak stepped through the breach.

"Peace i'the swamp. May Fraemauna show you the path," the man said.

"Peace in the swamp. The blessings of the gods upon your village," Sven responded.

"I'm Valgard Ottarsud, Elder of Zerst."

"I am Weard Sven Takraf. My companion is Erbark Lasik."

"Peace i'the swamp, Sven, Erbark. I've some soup."

"Thank you, Elder," Sven responded with a salute. "But I wish to aid your wounded, first. I have some skill as a healer. Erbark, also, may be of some use. We are both at your disposal."

While Erbark joined a team of militiamen who were attempting to seal the breach made by the gobbel attack, Sven quickly set to work looking after the many injured of Zerst. He used what he knew of Vitality to close wounds and set bones, saving the lives of three men and erasing the wounds of a dozen others.

In all, only three warriors died. The villagers seemed to regard the town's survival as a miracle sent by one of the gods. Zerst's population numbered less than a hundred. Sven and Erbark had arrived just in time.

The town's squalor was evident. Children showed signs of malnutrition, and most of the adults were thin with hunger. The buildings were constructed of hardened mud. Fires burned piles of peat, the only readily available fuel on the moors. No system to dispose of waste seemed in operation. Erbark's breath caught in horror and pity. Sven could not help but feel relieved. Here, at last, his skills would be of use.

Valgard turned out to be a most gracious and grateful host, bringing the village's finest food before the two strangers. It seemed as though half the village watched the pair as they ate, stealing glimpses through the doorway of the adobe building.

"Life on the moors must be difficult," Sven said gently. "Your people are hungry."

The Elder, who could not have been older than fifty, sighed. "The gobbels often cut our huntin' expeditions short, an' Seruvus' Breath plagues us from time to time. We'd've died out a lon' time ago if we didn't know enough to purge Dinah's Curse from our food an' water. Even now, we lose some of the children to it — bare-footedness an' eatin' cursed thin's, mostly." Valgard held out his hands. "There's little more we can do. Our tools're limited to stone an' bone, an' food's often hard to fin' with all the gobbels about."

Sven sipped at the thin soup delicately, testing it to see if the boiling water was yet cool enough for drinking. It was not.

"I want to thank you both for your help. We might've been overwhelmed except for Erbark's spear an' your magic."

Sven looked up at the Elder, searching for some sign of hatred or terror, and seeing only curiosity. "Have you a magocrat?" Sven asked delicately.

The Elder shook his head. "I've been told of such thin's by my father, Weard Takraf, enough to know you as a wizard. Your cloak betrays you as surely as your displays on the moors."

Sven swallowed his fear. "I'm a wizard from Nightfire's Academy.

I've come to the Morden Moors to help other Mar with my magic." Sven paused to allow the Elder to voice objections. When he did not, Sven plowed on. "I don't want to rule Zerst. I just want to practice magic to help your people. I can make it safer and healthier."

"We're very poor, Weard Takraf," Valgard apologized. "We can't hope to provide for you when our own children often go hungry."

Sven held up his left hand and shook his head. "I demand no tribute, Elder. I ask only your permission to use magic and your patience in dealing with such an inexperienced wizard as myself. We will provide for ourselves. Do we have your permission?"

Here it comes. If he has heard stories of wizards who treat mundanes as animals, if he suspects us of any subterfuge, the citizens of Zerst will refuse me. To my advantage, Zerst has us to thank for its victory a few hours ago.

Valgard's face was thoughtful. At last, he spoke. "You may stay in Zerst for as lon' as it doesn't endanger my people. I'll fin' you a place to stay until you can build a home for yourselves."

"May Fraemauna reward you," Sven saluted him with an open palm. Erbark mimicked him silently.

This had been everything Sven had been hoping to find on the moors.

"Erbark, you know I have not forgotten the Protectorates."

Erbark nodded and tossed another log on the fire while Sven fought back a coughing fit.

"I wonder if a war with Flasten is really necessary," Erbark said.

"The only way to stop it would be to place myself at Volund's feet and beg for mercy. He'd chop my head off. And then where would my dream be?"

"A problem you created."

"No!" Sven almost shouted. "Volund's attitude is nothing of my doing! I was just ... learning ... at Tortz. I had people to protect. If they had been Volund's own wizards, I would have protected them. You know that."

"And Brand?"

"Erbark, enough. I have a favor to ask of you."

"I am your servant," he said, and there was no sarcasm in his voice.

Sven paused. *Erbark is utterly loyal. Had I questioned his loyalty? Erbark is my friend. He is trying to tell me my mistakes and at the same time obey me. I wish I did not have to send you away, my friend, but what I do next may offend you more than what I have already done.*

"I need Pidel's support. The duxess will not listen to me or any of the priests who swore loyalty to me. You are the only one who can convince her to side with me against Flasten — both in this war and on the amendment."

Erbark nodded and rose. "I will leave immediately."

"Go then, my friend."

It will work, and it will do so quickly. I must act now while the first fires burn.

Erbark saluted Sven. Sven returned the salute, marred only by a cough.

"By the Oathbinder and Niminth, my patron ..."

"No, Erbark. Swear no oaths to me. Oaths are for men who cannot be trusted, and I trust you completely. Your word alone is enough for me. Go in peace with my approval, friend, and may the gods guide you safely to your destination's end."

Erbark lowered his hand and departed, green cloak fluttering.

"He disagrees with you, so you send him away?" Erika asked softly from another doorway.

Sven turned to face her. She stood very still in the shadow of the arch, grey eyes sparkling in the firelight. She seemed taller than usual. With an effort, he straightened his back. It cracked twice, and he hunched over again to cough.

Worriedly, she took a step toward him, but he waved her off.

"You heard our conversation?"

She nodded. "You haven't answered my question, Sven."

He pursed his lips in thought. "Give me a moment."

She frowned. "You didn't plan to tell me about it, did you?"

He shrugged and shook his head.

The woman spoke slowly, reflectively. "I remember a Sven Takraf who told Erbark and me everything he had planned. Where has he gone?"

Sven winced and immediately wished he had the power to forget what his wife had just said. The words Marrish uttered in his vision so long ago echoed from the libraries of his mind.

We have determined what you will become, but only you can decide who you will become. What am I becoming? He shook his head to clear it. *The plans are already moving forward. If I stay my hand now, the tiny window of opportunity will be sealed forever. Wasfal, Flasten, Pidel, the Protectorates, Domus, Erbark, Einar, Drakes and gods — all will play a role in my plan. Some will be unwitting victims, others active participants, but all will help me create a new Marrishland.*

"Excuse me, my love. I have business that requires my immediate attention."

Sven departed. He went first to Weard Schwert, instructed him to check the Protectorates' defenses for weaknesses.

Even though it might not matter soon how well they are defended.

He pressed the thought aside. No, there was no other way.

He sent orders to his magocrats to abandon most of the lands north of Domus Palus and evacuate the mundanes who lived there. He couldn't afford to have any witnesses on that front.

For this, Domus Palus might come under siege by my enemies. The loss of civilian life would be catastrophic.

Again, he pressed the thought out of his head.

He sent a priest to Flasten Palus with a message that would probably enrage Volund.

Perhaps he will accept these terms.

He placed the thought low on his list of likely outcomes. Volund would sooner die.

There, it is finished.

Sven slumped into the Chair of the Mardux, exhausted. The foundation for change had been laid. There was no turning back now.

He stared at his hands, opened and closed them. They looked no bigger than they had years ago, but Sven knew they were now poised to tear down traditional Marrishland duxy by duxy, village by village, family by family, Mar by Mar.

He leaned forward to cough. Abruptly, the front two legs of the

Chair broke, pitching him forward. He fell to his knees and only bare-ly managed to keep from falling down the steps of the dais.

A priestess arrived.

"Mardux, a messenger has arrived from the Piljerka army. He begs to speak to you immediately."

Sven nodded silently and stood, jaw set firmly to receive the ex-pected news.

Too late to change my path, now. It no longer matters who I be-come, only that I accomplish the purpose for which I was chosen.

 **13**

"Yellow is for Mobility. Mobility is employed to increase or decrease speed and perceptions. It is essential to travel in Marrishland, and it is also a prime component of all forms of teleportation."

— Nightfire Tradition,
Nightfire's Magical Primer

Marrishland is a huge country, almost a continent in itself. At its widest, it is more than fifteen hundred miles across. It is attached to the main continent by a three-hundred-mile long, steeply sloping mile-high cliff. It is climbable, but like any travel in Marrishland, it takes a day to traverse, and a traveler has to carry plenty of fresh water with him.

Water itself is not the issue in Marrishland. There is water everywhere. Water rises from Seruvus-knows-where all along the northeast cliffs and generally flows southwest to the Huinsian Bay and the ocean to the west. Occasionally, it twists back on itself and empties off the northwest coast. But, as a rule, the rivers flow southwest.

Calling them "rivers" is a misnomer, too, and the word has bred a whole subculture among the Mar: mapmakers. The average lifespan of a mapmaker is a little more than two days after his first attempt to chart the rivers of Marrishland. There is a lot of danger associated with traveling the known swamps to begin with, let alone heading by oneself out into the unknown swamps.

The muddy water of Marrishland is filled with every imaginable aspect of Dinah's Curse, which in simple terms is a hundred horrible strains of sickness, easily preventable by boiling the water. As well, the water is rife with leeches, mosquitoes, stinging spiders, poisonous snakes, suckmud willow creepers and, of course, konig worms, which are tiny worms that burrow into flesh and reproduce. If they lay their eggs in a Mar's bloodstream, death is not far behind. Not even a wizard can save someone whose blood is infested with konig worm eggs. It is no safer on drier land, because Drakes roam everywhere. They come in all shapes and sizes, and are all intelligent enough to band together, to follow a leader or to attack at the best possible moment.

It has been said of Mar rivers that they merely travel overland, sometimes settling in a long puddle, other times seeping through the clay of a grassy hill. The Mar themselves note this only insofar as the stream's cross-country trek might evict them from their town because the community has been built upon a rise of land that the water is slowly sucking into the soft mud of the swamp.

Enter mapmakers — every year, the rivers change course, and every mapmaker goes out to remake the maps that exist. Every year, mapmakers die by the score because of some foolishness. A Mar joke goes: After the mapmaker got married, he couldn't stay inside any longer, so he ran into the swamp without his boots.

Outside of Marrishland, people laugh at the concept of a Mar joke.

With the lack of accurate maps, the sheer size of Marrishland and the dangers associated with travel, moving an army the almost one hundred miles from Piljerka Palus to the chosen site of battle took more than six spans.

Cyan-garbed Hallgerd Steln had been put in charge of the Piljerka army when it had left the city. Her orders had been direct: "Destroy the invading Drake force." Now she and her two ranking commanders — the other cyans in the army — stood in a tent and watched the reconnaissance stone with fixed smiles on their faces as rain poured outside on twelve hundred greens and auburns.

She pointed to a patch south and west on the stone, a magical map of the area devised by Mardux Takraf.

"What's this?"

Weard Flosi Recht squinted at it, brushing his gray hair over his bald spot. "A wild rice field, I think. See, these two towns would share it."

"We will make the battle there. Weard Nacht, gather a hundred wizards and direct the Drakes to meet us there."

"What was that?" Bert Nacht said, wiping his nose with his sleeve. "You said take one hundred and lead forty thousand Drakes to a rice field?"

"Yes, Weard Nacht. Did you not hear me?"

Bert shook his head. "But that's a whole lot of Drakes."

Flosi laughed. "You will only be able to see maybe a hundred at a time. Look at our army. I am not even sure where it ends."

Bert squinted at the reconnaissance stone. "Most of it is east of us."

Hallgerd took a deep breath. "They are just gobbels, Weard Nacht. What harm can they do you and a hundred wizards? All you need to do is distract them enough so they chase you."

"They move faster then we do."

"That is because we are twelve hundred city-dwelling, road-building Mar, and not forty thousand swamp-living, mud-eating gobbels," Flosi said.

"If you are not confident in this task," Hallgerd said, "I will send Weard Recht in your place."

Bert's face turned red. "I will do it." He still sounded uncertain, though.

"Then go! Go!" Hallgerd shoved the two men out of the tent. "We meet there in five days, yes? Go! If they do not attack us, we will assume the worst."

Bert slogged briskly through the mud on his way to the front line. He only fell twice before he was out of earshot.

"You scared him, Weard Steln," Flosi commented.

"He had better be scared," she hissed. "If those Drakes get by us, who knows what havoc they will wreak on the countryside?"

"They haven't touched anything so far."

"Shut up, old man. Get everyone moving to that rice field."

"Yes, Weard Steln." But Flosi's grin reached both his ears as he used his walking stick to push into the crowd.

The clearing was a portrait of Mar agriculture — a waterlogged field green with wild rice shoots. The plants stuck out several inches from the foot-deep water as though in contempt of Seruvus. The crops were not arranged in neat rows, but scattered helter-skelter over the whole area. In some parts of the field, where the water was too deep or too shallow, very little green grew. But in those areas where water depth and nutrients were particularly favorable to the plants' growth, the wild rice grew so thick it looked like an island of green in the grayish-brown water of the swamps.

Wild rice was as prolific as any of Cedar's creations, and harvest took place on a first-come-first-serve basis. An early arrival ate tough seeds, and a tardy farmer would find his portion harvested already. Sometimes the seeds dropped early, and the farmers were forced to rely upon their skills as hunters and foragers for a few months.

Twelve hundred wizards tramped across the field, their thick leather boots and magic working in concert to keep their legs dry and free from Dinah's Curse.

The first hundred wizards filled the clearing. As the rest began to flow around the first hundred, Hallgerd realized her misjudgment. The wizards had assumed a ragged circle with several dozen smug, well-protected first-degrees at its center, and that would not do.

It took two days to stretch the army out into a ragged curve several Mar deep.

During that time, the two towns that used the field sent parties to watch the bright ribbon of milling wizards and offer them gifts of food and thanks for their protection — beneath shaded eyes that spoke volumes about the death of the field and the insolence of the city wizards.

Flosi reported to Hallgerd.

"Weard Nacht has corresponded with me. He says the Drakes are headed this way. It appears the size of our force was enough to draw their attention."

"When?"

"Two more nights."

"Good."

"Why did the mapmaker run away from the wild rice field?"

"Why?"

"Because it looked so safe, he was certain it must be infested by powerful Drakes."

Hallgerd smiled.

"I've always heard it as 'because it had already been discovered.'"

The older wizard laughed. "There must be a hundred variations on that one. I've also heard it as 'because it looked like there was work to be done.'"

"Among the mundanes on our border with Flasten, it is 'because Drakes only eat their victims.'" The emphasis was on the action.

Flosi frowned. "They only eat them?"

Hallgerd smirked. "As opposed to kidnapping them and pressing them into slavery, I think. They don't have a very high opinion of magocrats out there."

Flosi grunted. "Let's see them fight the gobbel army then."

Two days. The wizards held their line for two hours, and then quietly broke rank.

It began as a soft murmur of small talk and rose to a series of introductions. This line of conversation quickly evolved into a discussion of favorite books and scholars. Soon, the wizards had broken off into small groups to heatedly debate topics of mutual interest with their peers.

Greybeards and tender youths fresh out of the academies alike made the best of a bad situation by trying to learn something interesting from their companions. They exchanged spells and told stories about their conquests and misadventures like mundanes at a rustic wedding. In speaking with some of them, Hallgerd learned that for many, this was their first time out of the city. Many were excited to see a live Drake for the first time.

Early on the second day, Bert returned, breathing hard.

"Well?"

He brushed leaves off his cloak and took a deep breath.

"They are maybe an hour behind us."

At last, Hallgerd decided it was time to choose a battle plan. Giving orders to Bert's hundred, she bade them spread the message.

"Good weards. Here is the plan: The gobbels will have to cross the field to reach us. Our goal is to kill as many of them as possible. They are not armed with bows, so we can afford to delay our attack until they come within javelin range. The wizards in the front rows will strike the enemy column's rear while those at our back will attack the Drakes' first ranks."

Hallgerd paused to consider whether further planning was necessary.

Drakes cannot use magic, so the wizards can easily annihilate them without meeting them hand to hand. Therefore, we do not need to designate healers.

"That will be all." She smiled knowingly. "You may go back to your conversations now."

The sun was in the gobbels' eyes, but it was an advantage lost to the army of wizards as dark shapes began to appear between the trees. They appeared one or two at a time, but soon there were thousands facing the wizards.

Hallgerd tried to admire the gobbels' discipline, but her breath caught.

"So that's what we look like," she breathed. Bert jittered at her side.

"If that's what we look like, then where are the rest of them?" Flosi asked, taking a few steps back.

Hallgerd calculated.

"They will only line up as wide as the field. In fact, they are probably not much wider than we can see and must stretch back deeper. Order the wings to move in range." The command went down the line, and greens edged forward into the unknown.

Something seemed wrong about the picture.

"Why are they holding twigs?" Bert said after a moment. "Where are their spears?"

At that moment, a messenger reached the commanders. "From the south, magic from the Drakes," the man said, a touch confused.

"I'm sure this got messed up in the relay. I'll ask for a resend."

Then the gobbels lifted their arms to a loud cry, and the world exploded in flames.

As the wall of fire was quenched by the pond in the middle of the field, Flosi raised his voice to speak over the murmurs from the wizards, who at this point grudgingly resumed their ranks.

"That was magic!"

"It came from the twigs," Bert said.

"How can you be sure?" Hallgerd asked.

"They all lifted their arms and waved the twigs at us. Drakes cannot use magic, so ..."

There were shouts from the south, and with a loud rustling noise, wizards appeared and started streaming past them. Hallgerd grabbed one by the arm.

"They are advancing!" Bert shouted.

"What is going on here?" Hallgerd asked the man she held.

"Fire at one hundred forty yards!" Flosi ordered. Wizards held their ground, but many squirmed uneasily at those running recklessly behind them, often tripping over their bright-colored cloaks.

The man's eyes were wide. "A thousand came from behind as we moved the wing forward and north. They struck us with twigs ... Energy. They have magic, weard. We cannot defeat them." He twisted free of her arm and ran.

Hallgerd looked at Flosi with fear in her eyes.

"Fire," she whispered.

"They are well out of range," the older wizard said.

"They have stopped!" Bert shouted.

"They are too far away," Flosi repeated.

"Fire anyway! Boost the damn spells!"

The gobbels raised the twigs again at a harsh order, and when the world became flame, people started screaming.

"Engage!" Hallgerd shouted until she was hoarse, but the ranks were fraught with confusion.

Mar fell and did not rise. Their companions were too distracted to bother healing them. Steam from burning bodies quenched in the water of the field filled the air.

"I can't see!" Hallgerd cried, rushing about until she slammed into a tree.

"We need to retreat!" Flosi shouted as he helped her to her feet.

"We can't retreat!" A boom as a fresh wave of fire engulfed the front line, less than ten yards in front of them. *If the Drakes take twenty paces forward ...* "If we retreat, the Drakes will be able to make it to the road!"

"We retreat and make another stand behind some walls!"

"Order it, damn it!"

The wizards obeyed all too gladly. Many enhanced movement with Mobility, leaving hundreds of their fellows to die at the hands of the gobbels. Hallgerd stepped forward as a knot of Mar slogged past her. She targeted the five gobbels chasing them, raising her arms and lifting the mud beneath them with Power until they drowned.

She turned, then, chasing after her own army. She nearly tripped over a corpse, the singed green of the cloak her only sign it was a Mar. Behind her, she heard a howl from the gobbels. A knot of them appeared to her right, their wands raised. Bursts of fire streaked toward her, and she could only fall to dodge them. She gathered the blue motes and flung it at them, missing, but hitting a tree that collapsed on them.

Hallgerd got to her feet, soaking wet, and automatically began to dry herself before another howl reminded her of the peril.

I am not made for this, she thought. *Mar do not fight against magic like this. Someone must survive to tell the Mardux.*

Sopping wet, afraid of the gobbels more than Dinah's Curse, she lurched forward. A group of gobbels was ahead of her, chasing a scorched auburn. Fists of Power snapped two of their backs and knocked a third down before the last ones turned to see the mud-covered, cyan-garbed wizard behind them.

Wands raised, and Hallgerd screamed, throwing up a wall of Power that flung the fire back at the gobbels.

Then she felt heat, itching and gnawing at her back, and looked over her shoulder. Blinding orange flames connected her back to three twigs in the hands of gobbels, and two more were running up.

Her hands were halfway up before the pain grew too much, and she lost consciousness, falling face-first into the mud.

🔥 14

*"The guer are any of several hundred species of lizard-
like Drakes dwelling in or beyond the Fens of Reur. They
are not unusually clever for Drakes, but the tendency of
many of their kind to bury themselves in the mud and
wait for prey to draw near has given them a reputation
only slightly less terrible than that of the insero and
damnens. Their camouflage is nearly perfect, and sight-
ing them as bubbles in the myst is nearly impossible
given the interference of several inches of mud."*

— Nightfire Tradition,
Catalogue of Drakes

"This is a Blosin wand," the Dux of Wasfal told the Council at the
emergency session in Gunne Palus the next afternoon. The dux held
a twig with a blackened knot on one side. Sven kept his silence, hoping no one would ask the obvious question. He was saved by Volund,
whose face was a masterwork of control.

"How could Drakes have been armed with these?"

But Yver and Borya, whose reconnaissance had picked up the
truth, looked thoughtful. Katla and Nightfire had not been available
on such short notice, but that probably worked to Sven's advantage,
and Pidel continued her conspicuous absence.

"It must be a renegade wizard who has chosen to give magic to
the Drakes," Gruber said. "A magocrat, probably, who has several others loyal to him."

"Obviously," Volund said with a snort. "But who made them?"

Gruber shrugged.

Sven spoke. "I doubt many wizards know how to make wands of

this sort. I have heard that they are common among farl enchanters."

The other duxes turned their attention to Volund, but Flasten's dux did not react to the implied accusation. He changed subjects deftly, "We can conduct an investigation at a later date. Right now, we must crush this Drake invasion. What kind of army can you create, Dux Verlren?"

"Ten thousand wizards from Piljerka, Skrem and Gunne have joined to fight this menace. There will be no difficulty in exterminating them," Yver said.

"It will not be enough," Volund said, echoing Sven's thoughts. "I have twenty thousand who can be at Piljerka Palus in one month. Is this adequate, or will the Drakes converge on the city sooner?"

Entirely expected, Sven thought. He knew the army was significantly more ready than that. Reports of wizards filtering into towns all along the Skrem and Piljerka borders with Flasten had been coming in for months now. The towns were overloaded with nearly ten thousand weards ready to move.

It shows how little they know about war that they do not question how close Flasten must be.

"Not soon enough, Dux Feiglin," Yver said. "A generous estimate of the Drakes' arrival would be one month, but we feel they will arrive in half that."

"You could send a thousand ahead, Dux Feiglin?" Sven suggested. "Teleport them? The priests in Domus Palus can provide the magical resources."

Not to mention the reds at his disposal.

"That will not be a problem, Mardux," Volund said with an icy smile. "A thousand weards will be at your disposal in two days, Dux Verlren."

Yver nodded his gratitude, and Borya and Wolber looked thoughtful. Sven stifled the urge to talk to them. *Piljerka, Skrem and Gunne must understand when Flasten betrays them.*

"The Mardux thanks Flasten, Skrem and Gunne for their help with the difficulties in Piljerka. May Fraemauna guide your footsteps and Marrish lead you to victory." Sven cleared his throat and straightened in his chair. The Council broke up after the closing formalities. Sven knew what the next move was. He had set the plan in motion long ago.

But I don't have to fight a united Flasten army.

One thousand more out of the way was a good start.

The long month was not lost to the Mardux. As soon as the Flasten army began to travel, the calendar was set for the projected arrival date. Sven ordered the Domus army to a position halfway to the Flasten border and on the edge of Gunne and Skrem duxies, ostensibly for backup as needed. Flasten's army entered the Duxy of Skrem after thirty-six days, and far north of where it should be.

The gobbels threw themselves at Piljerka Palus' stone walls on the thirty-seventh day. Piljerka, Skrem and Gunne coordinated the defense, waiting out the wands. But the gobbels were not as stupid as everyone thought, and teams, under cover of conserved wand fire, undermined one of the city's walls. Then the flood began — Energy from wands clashed with Elements from weards unused to working such magic, and the casualties soon numbered in the hundreds.

The last report sent to Sven was the most dire. Yver's messenger, a lavender-clad sculptor, was round, sweating and scared as she recited her dux's orders to retreat.

"Normal gobbels would turn and flee when faced with so many casualties," she said from memory. "But the flood of Drakes still comes. We must ... we will abandon Piljerka Palus and gather again at Skrem Palus. Mardux, we are lost." She implored him with frightened eyes.

Sven looked at Erika, who was watching him by the fire, and Asa with her dolls at her mother's feet. His wife understood. Rising, she took the lavender to one side, murmuring words of comfort. Sven went over and ruffled his daughter's hair.

If I can finish this for all Mar, I finish it for her, as well, he thought, taking another look at his wife before leaving.

In the hall, he teleported to Skrem Palus.

All of his vassal duxes were there, hovering over a reconnaissance stone and sending messengers out. Sven joined them.

"Mardux," Yver said, "I did … "

"The best you could, considering the situation," Sven said. "Now it is my turn. We will not wait here and let these monsters destroy everyone out there. I will take a thousand of your bravest weards and bring the Drakes here while you prepare your defenses."

"It is too dangerous," Wolber said, and Sven frowned.

Too dangerous for the Mardux, or too dangerous to fight a battle at Gunne? He suppressed the thought. These men had sworn fealty to him. *I can … I must trust them, now.*

Of the thousand wizards, five wore blue. The rest were auburn and green, in nearly equal numbers.

"Traps," Sven told the blues. "Explosions. Deadfalls. Space them far enough apart, because the first ones will make them wary. We can conserve our strength that way. And when they are nervous, we hit them from an unexpected place."

"Behind them?" someone ventured.

"Whichever side is closer to Skrem," Sven answered. "We are leading them here."

Satisfied they understood, his army marched. He felt the eyes of his greens and auburns, some hopeful, some hateful and many, many more frightened.

They are workers no less than the mundanes in Rustiford, he thought. *Accountants and bootmakers, smiths and cooks. They have families like any other Mar. Only their education makes them better.*

But he could not take mundanes to fight this battle. *We will need more weards before this is through.* He knew this.

The first encounter surprised the gobbels immensely. They walked, unsuspecting, among the dozens of traps. Power flung many aside and explosions of Energy sent more flying. The gobbels used their wands indiscriminately, but Sven had moved his army to the east, and there was no one for the gobbels to fight. The gobbel leaders gathered, and the Drakes' progress slowed to a crawl.

Sven grinned from his vantage point in a tree and teleported to his army.

"In the morning, we strike," he told his blues. "Like a spear. Jab, and pull back. We do not want to get caught among them. Make certain everyone understands."

The next day, the casualties for the Mar were higher than Sven would have liked. About one in five of his wizards did not pull back after their first attack, pushing their significant magical advantage into the fray. The gobbels reverted to their own tactics, though. Any group of them knew how to take down one green or auburn wizard. Almost fifty Mar ended up dead, although a vast amount of Drakes were also dead.

My people will learn, Sven thought that night. *This was a lesson they needed.*

They performed the same tricks, again and again, for spans, leading the gobbels away from population centers and deeper into the less civilized Skrem swamps. On rice fields and in murky marshes, among trees and open sky, Sven's wizards learned how to fight pitched magic battles. But most interesting was that the gobbels were using their wands less and less, and from this, Sven suspected their wizard allies had abandoned them, and he knew his forces would win the battle even as his cough worsened.

The morning of the battle of Skrem, more than half a year after the Blosin wands had first been used, Sven hacked up mucus into a pot in the corner of his rooms in Skrem Palus. He had been awake the past two nights with what remained of his thousand, setting traps in the path of the gobbels.

More than ten thousand gobbels dead. Almost four thousand wizards have died. Countless, countless mundanes and slaves have passed away. He fought back the tears, his hands scrubbing his dirty, haggard, unshaven face. He fought back self-pity, and drew his resolve. *Volund will move against me openly, and I will be able to remove Flasten's vote. All Mar will reach their potential.*

Is this the best way to achieve that goal?

It sounded too much like Katla's words to him. *What we lose in lives, we make up in time. Time is a finite resource. Lives are replaceable.* He hardened himself to the argument. *I am uniting Marrishland as only the Mardux, the Guardian, can.*

Scratching his chin, he left to join his vassal duxes where the army waited. Flasten's twenty thousand were still three days north. Domus' twenty thousand were more than a month away and still halted for the day. The Mardux scanned the ranks of the ten thousand in a wide semi-circle. Flasten's thousand had been incorporated a long time ago.

I saved a thousand of my enemy's men. We must watch them in case they turn.

Sometimes, since the gobbels had invaded, he wondered who the real enemy was. Was it Flasten, who opposed him in everything he did and stood in the way of the greater good of the Mar, or was it the Drakes, who slaughtered Mar mercilessly?

The gobbels straggled to a line just before noon, many with limbs missing. The traps had worked. They looked tired and defeated already, but the chiefs had pressed them. Sven's final victory would be tremendous.

The wands rose.

The wizards of the first rank erected a wall of Power and Elements to block the magic of the wands. Flames and bolts of power battered the barrier, but it held back the first wave. The second came and the third and the fourth. The wall began to collapse in places, forcing the second rank of wizards to send waves of flame to drive back the press of gobbel wand-wielders. The smell of burnt flesh filled the air as the fire consumed the enemies' first ranks. The wands could not keep pace with the wizards waiting for the Drakes.

The gobbel infantry surged into the breaches, spears penetrating the flimsy defenses still protecting the Mar there. The waves of fire broke off one by one as the wizards fell back. For a moment, it seemed the magocrats would fall as Piljerka Palus had.

Sven ran up and down the line, burning out the larger clumps of gobbels with streams of Energy. The officers followed his example, relieving their faltering greens and auburns long enough for the minor magocrats to regroup and heal themselves.

A voice somewhere among the invading army cried out over the din. Others answered it. The gobbel infantry took a few last thrusts at their enemies before falling back. The Mar made short work of those gobbels who had been cut off in the fray before sending bursts of fire to lick the heels of the retreating force.

"Hold your ground," Sven shouted, and the officers took up the call. "They are not yet finished fighting."

The Mar rotated their wounded to the back to heal themselves, while fresh troops moved forward into defensive positions, confident and dangerous even though only one wizard in a hundred wielded a weapon.

Across the field of burned wild rice and corpses, the Drakes lined up again, this time in groups of tens and twenties. The groups were mixed, with some wielding spears and others holding a wand in each hand. With a shout from their leader, the gobbels charged.

The Mar held steady until their enemies were nearly in range before erecting a new wall of Power and Elements. The gobbels raised their wands, but no flames licked the barrier between wizards and Drakes. Their spearmen pushed to the front, howling.

Elements wands, Sven thought.

"Brace for melee! Attack weards, gather fire."

Most of the Mar obeyed the order as it went down the line. Those who hesitated were soon skewered on gobbel spears. The others overcame the Elements wands and cauterized the gobbel infantry. Sven hurled flames against one clump of gobbels after another, shouting at the lines to hold.

The Drakes succumbed to the onslaught of fire and power. Those that survived beat a hasty retreat as the wand-wielders gathered in a line for another assault.

Sven smiled grimly, fully aware of what would come next. The Drakes shouted battle cries and surged forward.

"No walls!" Sven shouted. "Counter the wands themselves. Back ranks, ready fire."

The gobbels drew close, jumping over the dead and dying in their haste, sprays of water and burned wild rice racing ahead of them.

"Counters, now!"

The wizards looked solemn but did not stir. The wind tugged at their cloaks. The gobbels came to a halt several yards away from the line of Mar and raised the wands. Nothing happened. Sven thought he noticed more than a few wizards smile in amusement a moment before he spoke.

"And burn them."

The gobbels recognized their predicament too late to organize an effective retreat. Their wands now no more valuable than sticks, the wand-wielders vanished in an ocean of fiery waves. They tried to retreat, but walls of Power enclosed them, drowning them in flame.

When the Mar attack ended and the wind blew away some of the smoke, no sign of the gobbel army remained. Most were dead, and those who had held back on the far side of the field had no doubt fled back into the trap-infested swamps between here and the Dead Swamps. Not all would perish, but they would never assail Marrishland again.

This phase of the campaign was over.

Sven thanked his wizards and teleported to Domus Palus as the cheers rose across the fields. There wasn't much time.

The worst is yet to come.

"How did you know?" The Dux of Skrem shivered in rage as he and Sven stood next to the Mardux's master reconnaissance stone, a mammoth device supported by a half-dozen yellows that showed Marrishland almost to Flasten Palus.

Skrem Palus, in the same day as its victory over the Drakes, had fallen to Volund's army. Arriving half a day late, the Dux of Flasten's force, led by Ragnar and Vigfus, attacked the victorious city from three sides. Sven had ordered a full withdrawal from the city, mostly back to Domus Palus, and Flasten found only a token force of wizards waiting.

"Volund has abandoned the laws," Sven said, coughing. He spat something thick and bitter to one side. "He arranged for the wands for the Drakes. He took his time to come to the aid of Marrishland."

"He has been taking slaves for years." Borya's voice grated in rage.

Sven nodded. *Let the dux build his own rage. From him and his fellow duxes, I need a vote.* He turned to one of the yellows, a priest of Marrish.

"Go to the Domus army. Tell them to attack Flasten Palus. Any weard and any supporter of a weard is to be arrested if possible. Volund has forfeit his duxy."

My army should reach Flasten Palus two spans ahead of the Flasten army reaching Domus Palus, assuming Volund does not order Ragnar to turn the men back. Would he realize what was happening soon enough?

Sven dismissed Borya and shuffled up to the Chair, taking a seat heavily. His throat filled with mucus and his nose clogged. It was a simple cold, but it could turn to Seruvus' Breath if he wasn't careful. So Erika had said. He didn't have time for that.

She had offered to shave him. The look he had given her could have reduced a gobbel to ash.

Why should anyone else shave me except me? Can I get Seruvus' Breath from shaving? It was a mark of his anger that he had completely forgotten to shave. As his hand brushed his jaw, his darkened eyes widened a little in surprise. *This is three days worth of growth.*

A tiny force of a hundred wizards had entered the Protectorates from the Duxy of Flasten three days ago. *To make me split my army?* But he had known that would happen. He could trace in his mind the path the wizards would take through the Protectorates. Einar was there, and that gave Sven some time.

Pushing himself to his feet, he stooped over to cough up some mucus. As he straightened into a slouch, the door opened, and Eda Stormgul entered.

"Mardux," the brown-eyed woman said with a small salute. "A man has just arrived from the Protectorates. He seeks an audience with you."

The Protectorates? Sven sat back down. It was hard to sit up straight. "Show him in."

The man who entered was unfamiliar to Sven. That he was a mundane was obvious by his black cloak, his unshaven face and his smell. His hair was thick and curly and tied back with a leather thong. His irises looked like splotches of mud against the whites of his eyes.

"Who are you?" Sven asked.

The man bowed awkwardly and scratched his head vigorously, a smile playing on his lips. "I've no doubt you'll remem'er me after I've spoken but two words to you, Weard Takraf."

Voices meant more to Sven than faces, and his eyes widened. "Bui Beglin? Of Tortz?"

"I'm that, Mardux. One of the fifty mem'ers of the 'vacu'tion team. Twenty of us still live."

"You stayed in the Protectorates with the refugees?"

Bui shook his head. "We wen' north, crossed into the Fens of Reur an' waited for this."

"What have you waited for?"

"Re'emption, Mardux." His voice grew hot. "An' revenge on Volun' for what happened in Tortz."

"Brand Halfin taught you magic. He broke Bera's Laws."

"Volun' broke the Laws, first an' last. He took slaves before Bran' came, an' killed those who stayed with you."

"The wizards will still kill you if they know you use magic."

"We don't use magic anymore. I swear by th'Oathbinder that's true. The gods told us we could take revenge just as soon as we atoned, and we've done that."

"You have given up the use of magic."

"Yes."

"There are only twenty of you."

"Yes."

"What can you hope to do against the dux? He has an army of twenty thousand wizards approaching Domus now."

"Tactics, Mardux."

"What kind of tactics gives mundanes any edge over wizards?"

"Guer tactics, Mardux."

"You mean guerilla."

"That's what I said, guer. We bury ourselves i'the mud, an' when they get close, we strangle them. We draw some away from the rest, an' when they get close, we kill them."

"If even one wizard finds you first, you are dead."

"We know, Mardux. We just won't be foun'."

"What do you want me for?"

Here Bui seemed to get a little nervous. "We want a wizard to come with us to heal those who'ren't careful."

"You know we cannot bring people back from the dead."

He shook his head. "Fraemauna protects us from Dinah's

Curse, but sometimes 'saken worms get on us. An' we've heard of reco'orzance ..."

"Reconnaissance," Sven corrected.

"... An' a wizard can help," he finished with a hopeful smile.

Revenge. The Mar had fought battles against Drakes for as far back as history was spoken, but Mar fighting Mar was never spoken of. A good wizard duel was remembered for years, but Sven had read deeply into the histories in Domus Palus and only twice had come across pitched battles between Mar. The lessons learned from those fights had been severe as the Drakes took advantage of those towns' exhaustion.

Revenge was out of character for a Mar. Like the excesses of his enemies, revenge only led to destruction. It blinded you, turned your power with anger. It kept you from being focused.

And Volund is seeking revenge on me. Bui had reminded Sven of that. He watched the mundane from Tortz, considered the man's months-long trek to get here. His sacrifice, for leaving his others in the Protectorates. His bravery, for leading them to the Fens of Reur in the first place.

A wizard and twenty mundanes who know how to fight wizards. Can they be worked into the plan?

He knew they couldn't.

"Bui, I will give you your wizard," Sven said, turning his head and coughing.

The man beamed.

"In fact, I will send Weard Stormgul here and a priest of Marrish to teleport your men to us."

"Why'd we want to come here?"

"Because in payment for a wizard, I am going to ask you to deal with a different enemy. You see, Dux Volund Feiglin is leading an army to attack Domus Palus. I am going to ask your men, after a few days of rest and good food," he watched the man's smile, "to sneak behind their camp's lines and practice your tactics there."

"Mardux, how can we thank you?"

"You just do what you want to do. I will take care of the rest."

As Eda led Bui out, Sven rubbed his nose with his sleeve. *And while you are here in Domus, you will be kept safe and out of the way.*

For the duration of this war, this band will be locked up, because I can't afford to have anything happening outside of the plan.

He tried to stand up and fell back heavily into the chair. Confused, he tried to stand again, and this time made his feet. Light-headed, he took two steps and fell over. The last thing he saw before he passed out was Erika, running out of the shadows where she had been hiding, watching him, as she shouted for help.

 **15**

"Morutsen is the sap of the kalysut. It is a very sweet, golden liquid slightly thicker than water. It is moderately intoxicating — inhibiting reflexes and clouding thought much like alcohol. Sufficient consumption of morutsen leads to unconsciousness, but there is no known lethal dose. The tiniest sip of morutsen instantly arrests the ability to use magic for the next eight to twelve hours, although larger doses do not appear to extend this effect. For this reason, it is the shackle of choice when holding a wizard captive."

— Nightfire Tradition,
Nightfire's Herbology

"Give wands to the gobbels of the Dead Swamps and provoke them into invasion? That was your plan?" Brack ranted. He had just returned from a meeting with the Delegates that clearly had not gone well. He was impatient, and worse, he was powerless. The Delegates insisted he drink some morutsen before he would meet them, in order to keep him from using his magic.

Katla said nothing. She hadn't expected it to work, which was the point, but she couldn't exactly tell him that. She wasn't on Brack's side. She wasn't on the Delegates' side. She wasn't on Volund's side. She had thrown her lot in with Sven's vision for the Mar so completely that she was risking everything to achieve it. Hundreds of thousands might die. Thousands already had.

Brack paced irritably, leaning heavily on his cane. "This has complicated matters enormously. It is bad enough that Dux Feiglin is clearly taking advantage of the situation, but if the Mardux can prove

Flasten's involvement, he might convince Wasfal and Pidel to side with him in the conflict."

It had taken her a year to figure out how to do that. Convincing the Council to give her brother free rein to violate Bera's Unwritten Laws was an important part of her plan, but it would take a unanimous vote to do that. If Wasfal and Pidel sided with Sven, Flasten would be incredibly foolish to defy him.

"Neither Weard Wenigar nor Weard Stoltz were taken prisoner by the Mardux's allies. Dux Feiglin's son is safe in Flasten Palus," she said.

"And Weard Stoltz?"

"I am not certain, but she is resourceful."

"Resourceful enough to betray Weard Feiglin if he appears to be losing?"

Katla certainly hoped so, but she let Brack rant.

"She already switched sides once," he said. "She owed allegiance to Mardux Beurtlin and the Duxy of Domus before Weard Takraf took the Chair."

"Arnora knows what will happen if the Duxy of Flasten does not topple the Mardux. She knows the Mass will invade." *She probably doesn't think it's real any more than Brand did.* "Besides, implication in this invasion works both ways. The Blosin wand is the Mardux's invention, the application of an auburn magocrat trying to defend too much territory. He committed it to paper while he was at Nightfire's Academy."

Brack snorted a laugh. "Weard Takraf did not invent those wands. Farls have known the making of them for centuries. He could easily claim to have learned it from Weard Wost when he was at the Academy. I have heard Weard Takraf was one of his most beloved pupils, before he was forced to resign his post in disgrace."

She remembered that. Sven had caught Robert selling Nightfire's slaves in the Duxy of Wasfal instead of returning them to their homes. That Robert had survived Sven's wrath was a testament to Nightfire's ability to keep the peace at his Academy.

Katla shrugged. "It will take more than a civil war to draw Pidel or Wasfal into this. Even if they discover Flasten has broken the Law, they are not going to let the Mardux break it further by arming mundane with wands."

"What of this amendment?"

Brack feared her brother, Katla knew, which could only mean the Delegates did, too.

He is right to fear Sven. I see what my brother intends. By the time he finishes, it will be too late to raise an army. His changes will destroy Drake civilization. The Mass must invade or die.

"It is fen lights and nothing more," she assured him. "Even if Wasfal and Pidel radically altered their policy, they would never agree to such an amendment. Flasten is hardly going to vote in favor of it, and it would take a unanimous vote."

I just need to delay the Mass until Sven has broken Flasten. Pidel won't support the amendment, but they can't oppose him alone, and Wasfal has no stomach for an expensive civil war.

Brack stopped pacing. "The Delegates have given orders to mobilize the Mass."

"How soon before they invade?"

"The First Wave marches in a month."

Katla swallowed. *So much for delays.* "First Wave?"

She listened numbly as Brack explained.

There were millions of Drakes, like there were millions of Mar. Marrishland had shaped the majority of both into warriors. When the Mass invaded, the sea of bodies would be as spiky water drowning the land, Dinah's Curse come to life. Except the Mass was made of living, breathing beings that had to do a lot of the same things the Mar did: eat, drink, sleep, defecate, heal. The entire Mass in one place would starve to death inside of a span.

Therefore, as Brack explained in his aged voice, it was broken down into waves of more than twenty thousand apiece. Each had numerous scouts. The distance between the waves would vary based on the Delegates.

"The point, Yee Ka Lah," he finished, "is that there are more than three hundred waves, and the Drakes are not afraid to use all of them."

She gaped at him. The math was terrifying. The Mar could be extinguished.

But I knew that was a threat when I started this.

Brack's ancient face was grim. "I cannot hold back the river any longer, but I made a deal with them. The Mardux is still in Domus Pa lus. As soon as this morutsen wears off, I will teleport into the chamber with a squad of jabber guer and kill Weard Takraf and anyone else in the citadel. A headless damnen is a danger to no one."

"He has a hundred yellows guarding him at all times. Their counterstrike will be swift. How do you expect to escape once the deed is done?"

"I do not expect to escape." Brack removed the silver and gold ring from his finger and held it out to her. "If I succeed, you may be able to convince the Delegates to call off the invasion. So long as you wear Domin's Favor, they will recognize you as my successor."

Katla accepted the ring, the weight of the ancient metal heavy in her shaking hand. *How long have I waited for this moment? How long have I practiced and planned?* "And if you fail?"

"Then they will leave the Mar in a worse state than when the Gien Empire fell to the Mass."

Am I ready? Can I control the Delegates? Can I make the Mass attack when I need it to? He seemed to want her to say something.

"You seem to assume victory is inevitable, yet you said the Mardux might prove powerful enough to destroy the Mass," she said.

He turned away again, back straight and proud. "The Mass has never been defeated in the field. It will strike before your brother is ready."

Now, now! Katla raised her hands, fingers splayed, myst of every kind already gathered in great quantities along her fingers.

"By the Oathbinder and by Dinah, my patroness, this time, they will be, and my brother will lead them. The Mar will meet the Mass in the field, and they will drive it back across the Fens of Reur."

Determination filled her as her mentor turned, and fear washed away as his brown eyes hardened, so clearly pained at this seeming betrayal. Even if his magic had not been neutralized by morutsen, it would have made no difference. No one could evade morutmanon — a spell whose touch was death to the wielder's enemies and harmless to allies.

"With this act of war, you condemn Marrishland to a dark age. No duxy will be left standing," he said.

"Destroying duxies is easy. I do not need the Mass to do that."

The eight colors of myst merged together into a blur of blackness that fanned out into a thousand snaking tentacles of killing power, seeking her victim.

The black tentacles crawled up and draped over Brack's blood-drained face, unaccepting of his fate, then squeezed. They faded into his bubbling skin, and Katla held her poise as his eyes exploded and skin popped and boiled. The blackness seemed to grow within him, and ashes of his bones mixed with his smoking blood and flesh and the corpse finally collapsed, being consumed and crushed in its own heat.

Katla stared down at it. *He was always the enemy.*

Brack apparently had triggered spells of his own active in his home, for the library exploded into flames. Darkness clouded Katla's vision as the fire seared her. She recalled the day her mother had been taken as she blacked out.

I know you remember her, Sven. I know you remember her sacrifice.

Katla woke to the sound of her father putting on his boots, stomping them against the floor, but she pretended to be asleep. A chill hung in the air in their small home, and twelve-year-old Katla wasn't ready to come out from under the deerskin blanket she shared with her younger brother.

"Be careful, Pitt," Tyra, her mother, said too loudly, forgetting the children asleep by the hearth only a few paces away. "I want you home safe."

Sven stirred against Katla's back, and she thought for certain he would sit up, and then he would start asking questions.

Her brother had started speaking at so late an age that their neighbors had wondered if he might be deaf, but anyone who looked at his green eyes knew he heard perfectly. Other children began speaking in simple words — mama, dadda, no. Not Sven. His first word had been "why," and sometimes it seemed all his sentences ever since had been questions. From waking until sleep, always questions, and it seemed he thought Katla was there for no other reason but to answer them. If Sven woke, Katla would have to leave the warm blanket and begin her chores, and he would be at her heels the whole time, asking her to explain the world to him.

After a moment of rubbing his face against her back, though, his breathing settled back into the slow rhythm of sleep. At the door to their house, Katla's father spoke in a low, soothing voice too soft for her to understand.

It was his way. Katla had only heard him raise his voice once, and that had been to stop her from leaving the house barefoot. She knew he wasn't quiet because he was afraid of people. It was something else.

Her mother had tried to explain it to her, once. "Your dad talks quiet so people want to hear what he's sayin'. It makes them quiet. It makes them stan' close so they can hear — not just close to him, but close t'each other. Swind's whisper, they call it."

Katla hadn't understood it then and still wasn't sure she did. She knew her parents' chose the name Gematsud when they married, which meant "south-spirited" or "as warm and gentle of spirit as Swind, the south wind that brings summer," so maybe it had something to do with that. Her mother had that name, too, but Katla had heard her neighbors joking that it meant something else about Tyra.

Her mother tried to speak quietly, but Katla could still hear. "Domin take those wizards! Snatchin' people like we don't know who's doin' it." She sounded furious.

Katla's stomach growled, and she risked opening one eye to look at the fireplace. No soup pot hung over the flickering remnants of the fire. They had not eaten anything in two days except a bitter bark tea, and her parents had barely sipped that.

Pitt murmured something apologetic, but Tyra would have none of it.

"You couldn't have done anythin' if you'd been there. They've magic, an' you don't."

Katla knew the words had not been for her ears, even though she knew it was the worst winter anyone in their town could remember. Even during her short years, she had seen higher snows and felt colder nights, but she had learned many new words for winter hardships — war, magocrat, slaver, starve. People went out to hunt or collect firewood, and many of them never came back.

Her parents whispered back and forth, and Katla could tell they were arguing about something. Finally, her father let out a heavy, exasperated sigh. He was so agitated that Katla caught two words, "be back." And then he was gone.

Katla's stomach rumbled again, and a hollow pain seemed to sink teeth into her whole body. She began to cry softly into her blanket, hoping her mother wouldn't notice, fearing it would only make everything even harder for her parents.

Tyra came to the hearth. Her back was to her daughter, so Katla watched her stir the dying coals with a metal poker. It was the last of their firewood, and there were many days of winter left. Her parents might die. Her friends.

Sven shifted slightly against Katla. *He'd never get answers to all his questions,* she thought, and she couldn't suppress a sob.

Tyra turned slowly, her face a mask of concern. She held out her arms, and Katla flew into them, weeping as quietly as she could to keep from waking her brother.

"What's the matter, Katla?"

"Are we goin' to die?" she whispered like a secret.

Her mother cradled the back of her head and rocked her slightly. "What kind of question's that?"

Katla shook her head without releasing her hold. "I know what's happenin', Mom. We've no food. No firewood. There's bad wizards stealin' hunters, so we can't get more."

"Your father's gettin' us food and wood, baby. Not all the hunters got snatched. I brought you back a duck."

Katla relaxed a little. Maybe it was a lie, but her empty stomach forced her to believe it. "An' the fire?"

"If you'll let me go a minute, I'll show you."

Katla released her and looked around the room as if expecting a pile of sticks to appear out of nowhere. But there was no firewood or even blocks of peat to burn. Tyra walked over to a beautiful rocking chair Katla knew had been a wedding gift from her mother's father, who had been a carpenter.

Tyra ran a hand along one polished arm of the chair, traced the carvings at its back with her fingers. She had nursed her children in that chair, sung them to sleep. She looked at the chair thoughtfully for a long moment.

"I'll be right back," she said, and then she picked up the chair reverently and carried it outside.

Katla winced as she heard the hatchet fall, cringed at the splintering of wood meant for sitting. A short while later, her mother came in, her cheeks wet from crying, her arms cradling a pile of carved and turned wood like the broken body of a fond memory.

Tyra set the pile of wood down next to the fireplace and carefully chose a single, small shard. She caressed it, cupped it in her hand, and then placed it on the coals. A soft breath, and the faint orange lights glowed more brightly. Another, and the hot specks spread across the dark coals. A third, this one a little more forceful, and sparks flitted and spun in the hearth. Smoke curled up from the tiny sliver of the rocking chair. A few breaths more, and a tongue of fire burst out of the stick as if it had always been there, and Tyra had merely coaxed it out of hiding.

Tyra went to the door and collected her hunting bag. To Katla's delight, she withdrew not just the promised duck, but two fat rabbits, too. She felt her mouth watering in anticipation, and her mother smiled.

"Pluck it while the water boils."

"Yes, Mother," Katla said, taking the duck.

Tyra helped her cut up the meat and put it in the pot of melted snow with a little laurita from their winter supply of the herb. Soon, Sven was awake and asking his sister questions. Mostly, though, he spent the day asking when the food would be ready. Tyra urged him to be patient as she fed one precious piece of the rocking chair after another into the fire to keep it burning. By the time the soup was ready, they could no longer see their breath.

Their father didn't come home that night, though their mother was up most of the night waiting for him. He didn't come back the next night, either, and the pile of rocking chair shards shrank to a few chips of wood. Once, Sven asked about the rocking chair, which made his mother cry, but she comforted him with a story of how the Mar learned to make food sacrifices to the gods.

After Sven fell asleep, Katla crept out from under the blanket to sit with her mother. Eventually, Tyra fell asleep, but not Katla. She stayed awake, feeding the fire the chips of wood a few at a time.

The next morning, Tyra took the crib where her children had once slept out of the house. It took longer to dismantle than the rocking chair had, and soon they had another little pile of precious wood next to the fireplace. Tyra prepared a rabbit soup this time, and Katla fell asleep watching the memory-eating fire on which their lives depended devour the scraps greedily.

When she woke, the house was full of people — all of them murmuring, all of them afraid for the hunters and their families. The cyan-cloaked wizard who lived in the village had left days ago with promises to bring help, but she hadn't come back. Katla heard enough to know many people were dying of cold and hunger, and nobody knew what to do about the slaver wizards.

Tyra had no answer for that, but she told them about the chair and offered to share her soup. They accepted but only took a few polite sips before excusing themselves. The next day, some of the ones with no children brought food to Tyra's house — another duck, a bowl of wild rice, some roots and herbs. Nobody had much, but they shared it anyway.

"If everyone's hungry, why're they givin' us food?" Sven asked.

"They're not givin' the food to us," Tyra explained. "They're givin' it to the gods."

"So we can't eat it?" Sven asked, sounding a little petulant.

She smiled at him and brushed his cheek with one hand. "Don't worry, darlin'. You can eat it." She turned her face to Katla. "Do you un'erstan'?"

"It's a sac'fice. They go hun'ry to prove they believe the gods will help us. That's why you gave them soup, right?"

Her mother nodded. "An' I believe the gods will sen' the hunters back with enough food an' wood to last the winter."

"What if they don't?" Katla blurted out.

Tyra looked a little wounded.

"I b'lieve," Sven announced proudly, climbing into his mother's lap. No question in his tone, this time, and for once Katla missed it. Tyra wrapped Sven in her arms and held him tight while Katla contented herself feeding pieces of the broken crib into the fire.

Days passed with no word of the hunters. Furniture burned first.

Extra tools came next. In the end, even the dearest mementos that could burn fed the Gematsud hearthfire. Swind, the south wind, carried warmer weather, but they still needed to feed the fire. People who drank water without boiling it got sick from Dinah's Curse and died.

Katla and Sven weren't allowed out of the house anymore. Katla worried for her mother because she never seemed to eat anymore. Almost all Tyra's food went to her children, until she looked like sticks held together with mud — like something that would soon be chopped up outside and fed to the fire in the hearth.

Tyra stopped inviting neighbors inside for soup. They had no soup. They had started trying to boil just about everything in the house to make it into food — leather, reeds, even spiders and centipedes. They were hungry all the time. No one brought them any food, either.

Katla secretly stopped eating after two days like this, sneaking Sven her part of whatever barely edible food her mother gave her. If starving herself would bring her father back safely, that's what she'd do. She knew that soon she wouldn't have a choice. They would run out of food, and then they would all starve like so many of their neighbors were. The gods didn't reward Mar who starved because they ran out of food. That wasn't a sacrifice. For it to be a sacrifice, you had to have a choice. When she fainted from hunger, though, her mother forced her to eat — told her the gods didn't want children to make sacrifices like that. Katla was too weak to argue, and she ate the soup made with two boiled mice.

At last, they had nothing left to offer the fire. Instead of searching the house for a forgotten scrap of wood, Tyra put on her warmest cloak and kissed Sven and Katla on the cheek where they lay by the fire.

"Mom?" Katla murmured. "Where are you goin'?"

Tyra looked at Katla seriously. "I'm going out to look for firewood and maybe for some food, too."

"But the wizards," Katla whispered in a panic, hoping not to wake her brother.

Her mother cupped her cheek with one hand, her green eyes gentle but sad. "I have to. The fire won't feed itself."

"But Dad'll come back, won't he?"

Tyra crouched next to her daughter and spoke in a whisper. "I'll tell you a secret if you promise not to tell your brother."

"I promise."

"I don't know if your dad's comin' back. You an' Sven have t'eat, so I'm doin' ev'rythin' I can to get you food. If dad gets back first, good, but if the wizards took him, someone has to feed you, an' I'm the only one left. Do you un'erstan'?"

Katla shook her head and started to cry.

"You know how fire works, right? If fire doesn't have something' to burn, it goes out."

"Yes."

"People are a lot like fire. They have to eat or they die. Rem'emer how the fire burned Grandpa's chair, the spoons, your old doll?"

Katla nodded.

"Did it burn them any less because they were important t'us? No, because fire isn't picky. It isn't patient. It knows it'll die if it doesn't eat, so it burns ev'rythin' it can. That's what fire does — it burns for as long as it can."

Katla still didn't understand. She was crying too much.

Tyra sat on her heels and kissed Katla's forehead. "Take care of your brother, and keep the fire burning until I get back. You've watched me, right? Gentle breaths, first, an' then bigger ones. Little sticks and then bigger ones, but never too many at once."

"But there's nothin' left to burn," Katla objected softly, wiping her cheeks.

"You have to be like fire, Katla. You have to fin' somethin' to burn. But you have to be smarter than fire, too. Don't burn anythin' you don't have to. There's wood i'the walls, but if you burn it, you'll let i'the cold. Your blanket will burn, but if you burn it, it can't keep you warm at night. Fire will burn anything it can. That's what fire does. You have to tell it what it can burn an' how fast without lettin' it go out."

Katla nodded her understanding. Then Tyra kissed her again and left the house for the last time. The fire went out a few hours later, and only Pitt's arrival that night with food and firewood kept both children from dying of starvation or Dinah's Curse.

I have to control the fire. I have to tell it what it can burn without letting it go out. It can't stop itself from burning. That's what fire does — like the Mar, like the Mass, like Sven.

Katla woke to blistering pain, though the fires were no more. A ravit looked down at her. She opened her mouth to speak, but it hissed at her for silence.

"Yee Ka Lah, your wounds aren't healed. You need rest."

She squinted painfully against the sun and tried to summon Vitality. There were few burns magic could not heal. Her eyes widened in shock when nothing happened. The ravit shook his head.

"We have been feeding you morutsen to keep you from hurting yourself."

A hundred questions blurred through Katla's mind, some sincerely curious, others desperately worrying.

"One of the insero brought you out of the fire before it consumed you, but Yee Roh Yeh was gone. He did not complete his mission, so now the First Wave will march." The ravit seemed disappointed. "I will not be in it, but I will be in the Twentieth Wave. Will the Yee hold out for that long?"

And they would not find Brack. Morutmanon made certain of that, too.

One in a million wizards had the knowledge, discipline and magical strength to wield morutmanon. Sven made wand-like gloves that could mimic it, so in that respect, Katla was stronger than her brother.

Even the most militant reds largely scoffed at it as senseless overkill. It took too long to master, left the wizard exhausted and barely capable of any further magic and it was no deadlier than a hundred other attack spells that only used one or two magicks.

Katla knew the truth, though. Weards universally feared anyone who could wield morutmanon — not just because it required incredible skill and dedication, but because of the spell's legendary ability to recognize spies, traitors and even those who could easily be swayed. Legends claimed it sometimes spared an obvious enemy it knew could be turned or killed a close ally it knew would one day become an enemy.

And so, proof that I could never convince him to my cause. If it had spared him, instead, I would have gotten a different sort of message.

Coughing, she asked, "How soon ... ?"

"No questions now," another ravit said, gesturing to her guard to leave. This one was older. She crouched down near Katla.

"Once you have healed yourself, you will accompany the guer in the First Wave when they cross the Fens of Reur. If you kill Yee Seh Tah where Yee Roh Yeh failed, there will be no Twentieth Wave. Does Yee Ka Lah understand?"

So many questions! How soon will the Mass reach Domus Palus? How much time has passed? Will they ever let me meet with the Delegates?

The ravit watched her until she nodded, then left. The young guard remained, jabbering in his excitement. He seemed to think the Twentieth Wave would mobilize tomorrow, or in a span. Katla lay there, dredging up patience to cover her anger. Killing this guard would not help her, not now.

I cannot stop the invasion, but I can deny it surprise, at least.

When the morutsen finally wore off, she eliminated all signs that she had been burned badly enough to put her life in danger. Then she gathered the myst and fell into the Tempest, ignoring the young ravit's pleas to take him with her.

I must get the fire under control.

 **16**

"Lavender is for Presence. Presence deals with the manipulation of emotions. It is perhaps the most difficult magic for a Mar to use, but the farl enchantresses of Flecterra excel with it. In its simplest form, Presence can attract or repel the attention of those nearby. More advanced applications can generate intense emotions such as fear, love and rage."

— Nightfire Tradition,
Nightfire's Magical Primer

Einar checked the spells protecting Zerst, the last stop on his survey. Weard Takraf's defenses were intact. His twenty representatives in the Protectorates — an amber and some blues, auburns and greens recruited from Nightfire's Academy and the Academy of Domus Palus — had maintained them dutifully. Einar also noted those wizards were making progress toward educating the people of Zerst, Leiben and six of the other large villages. Hundreds could read and write Mar and Middling Gien relatively well, and soon a few of those would be able to teach others. In Zerst, a tiny handful of students were already beginning to learn the rules and Laws of magic.

This is Weard Takraf's real goal, Einar realized. *First the Protectorates, and then all of Marrishland.*

He smiled, the creases in his aged face deepening. In two years, maybe three, the Protectorates would graduate more wizards than the Domus Palus Academy, and those wizards had been groomed to teach others.

Working within the Law, the magocrats cannot touch him. Why has no other Mardux done this before?

The Mass.

But the Mass was just a legend — an excuse made by the magocrats like Dux Feiglin to protect their own precious knowledge. It was a religious myth invented by superstitious Mar after the fall of the Gien Empire. It explained why the Drakes had attacked the Giens and why they would never raze Marrishland again.

According to Asfrid Staute, the amber in charge of Sven's operations in the Protectorates, Drake attacks were increasing — mostly gobbel raiders with a few spiny-tailed guer. She mentioned it in passing, as if it were no more interesting than another raindrop in the river. The defenses held firm, after all. The Protectorates were the northernmost collective, even farther north than the Duxy of Domus, and yet Drakes had not come within eight miles of one of its villages in at least three years.

But it is only a matter of perception, Einar thought as he turned his attention to the town's reconnaissance stone. *The Fens of Reur have safe and dangerous times, too. My children learned that at a high price.*

The living things marked on the large, round slab moved in stop-time. Every four minutes, the spell connected to the device scanned the area in a nine-mile radius for all signs of life, especially noting those signatures belonging to Mar and Drakes. And every hour, the device exchanged its reconnaissance with all the other villages, making the Takraf Protectorates so well scouted that Asfrid's overconfidence seemed understandable.

From here, I could cast a spell on every Mar on the Morden Moors, if I wanted to.

Einar suddenly wanted to return to the Fens of Reur and implement these defenses there. His magocrats would have to become as comfortable working with Knowledge and Elements as they were with Energy, but with what he had learned from the Protectorates, the Mar could put an end to all the Drake attacks along Marrishland's northern border. The damnens could still leave the Dead Swamps whenever they wished, but the gobbels? The ravits? The guer? Those threats would end forever.

Why did the Mardux send me? These defenses could indefinitely hold anything less than a massed invasion of Drakes. Even if the Mass were real, the defenses would slow them down a month or more. Did he hope I would learn enough to retake the Fens of Reur?

He frowned at the stone in concentration, looking for the answer. The information updated, and Mar went about their daily business.

Does he not trust me to help him deal with Dux Feiglin and his duxy?

Suddenly, he had it, and the color drained from his face.

These defenses are designed to ward off Drakes, not wizards!

He viewed the myst, studied the patterns of all the spells on the stone. He was no farl enchanter, but he knew Knowledge-based reconnaissance spells could be altered by Elements. Many a magocrat had been defeated by simply mistaking information for truth, and the recon stones were just as vulnerable to misinformation as a wizard.

The spell radiated along a single plane, several feet above the ground, to a specified diameter. *To get around it, simply get above it.* Einar smiled grimly at that. *A little Power and Mobility to levitate me.*

I could kill one of their sentries and return with no fear, since the spell cannot detect the differences between Mar.

There is a four-minute lag between updates. With Mobility, I could run the distance in less than that.

For that matter, I could teleport in.

The actual defenses were another problem, but Einar saw holes in them as well. They were designed only to attack Drakes and wizards who did not fit certain descriptions. Any mundane army could walk right up to the walls and beat them down. Since wizards were often identified by their cloaks, any wizard who disguised himself with a different color cloak, hooded or grew a beard — Einar shuddered and fingered his bare chin — could easily get inside the defenses.

And, of course, once inside the walls, the defenses were useless.

These defenses have too many holes, Einar thought, running a hand through his hair. *Can I close some of the biggest ones?*

He knew he couldn't. Even the simplest of the automated spells demanded such a precise arrangement of Knowledge that only Elements could place the myst in the right shape. The triggered spells themselves weren't the problem. If he wished, he could incinerate all mundanes in the Protectorates instead of shielding them from Seruvus' Breath.

But the triggers are beyond me. I don't understand the theory behind them well enough to design new ones.

An apprentice or first-degree threw the myst around indelicately — calling the myst and activating it. Energy made fire. Power was a punch or a wall. Mobility increased speed. But there was so much more to magic than that. More powerful wizards learned to arrange the myst into patterns that changed its behavior — light without heat, lifting instead of pushing, true teleportation. They learned how to call different kinds of myst at the same time, which required an iron will and years of practice. The most powerful spells demanded both, and wizards had spent centuries designing magical applications based on the ways each color of myst behaved when arranged in a particular pattern.

Where did the Mardux learn to work with Knowledge and Elements like this?

He gave up the problem as unsolvable, for now. Weard Takraf knew Knowledge better than any wizard Einar had met, so perhaps he would have some ideas.

Ari watched as Robert carefully examined the information his spell had gathered. After a moment, Robert nodded and turned to Valgird.

"Well?" the gold-burdened wizard asked.

The enchanter smiled. "It is just as I had expected. Weard Takraf, like all Mar, is not as powerful a wielder of Knowledge as he is of Energy. The defenses of the Protectorates extend only nine miles from the outlying villages."

They stood on the northern border of Flasten, facing a broad swath of rolling brown that looked more like mud than water. Black things like sticks occasionally surfaced and made Ari wince, much to Robert's amusement.

A hundred low-ranking mercenary wizards stood behind them.

"Are you certain?" Valgird demanded, gold glinting off his fingers like the sweat shining off his forehead.

Robert flushed in annoyance, the blood showing clearly through his pale skin. "Yes, yes. I probed to the walls with Knowledge. It was not much more to find the exact spot of the nearest town."

"And what are we facing?"

"If we teleport, nothing. There are no spells functioning within the town walls."

"How can you be so sure?"

Robert regarded him coolly. "I know these patterns perfectly well. Where do you think your Mardux learned them?"

Valgird's brow furrowed, his face a mask of confusion. "Nightfire's Academy, I had assumed."

The farl snorted his contempt. "What they know about Knowledge patterns at Nightfire's Academy would not fill a thimble. I should know. I taught there for several years."

"He was Weard Wost's student," Ari supplied. Robert had told him the story when Ari had come to him to learn more about farl magicks — his second apprenticeship. "Back when Weard Takraf was just an apprentice."

"I taught him a few simple trigger patterns," Robert admitted with a nonchalant shrug. "He built the Protectorates on them."

"You farls have nothing like these spells protecting your towns," Valgird objected.

Robert smiled mysteriously. "We do not need them, but you are correct. Enchanters do not rely on violence to rule, as you do. Just as you Mar are useless with Presence, Knowledge and Wisdom because you have no finesse whatsoever, we have little reason to practice with Power and Energy. I have learned much in my time here, just as my students have learned much from me." His face clouded. "Unfortunately, not all my students respect the debt they owe me for their success."

"You had a falling out?" Valgird asked.

"You could say that," Robert said with cold fury. He visibly calmed. "On my mark, Ari will teleport the three of us into the town. You will deal with any physical threats, and I will handle the rest."

Ari called the myst for the teleportation. Elements shaped Mobility just so and held it ready. He reveled in how much less exhausting this had become since Robert taught him to hold spells together with Elements instead of relying on the attention-splitting exercises Ari's teachers had expected of him. Knowledge wrapped itself around the partial spell, calculating distance and finding a safe destination.

"Dux Feiglin put me in charge of this expedition, Weard Wost," Valgird grumbled.

"You are in charge, Weard Geir," Robert said with a smile. "Lead on. Ari, now."

Ari nodded, and Valgird vanished into the Tempest a few seconds before he and Robert followed. By the time they arrived, Valgird had already slaughtered the militia and set half the small village on fire. Ari blanched at the sight of dozens of burning corpses.

Robert merely clucked his tongue. "Is there any more resistance?"

"There might be a few waiting in ambush in some of the huts," Valgird warned. "I will drive them out, though."

It was too much on top of the stench of burned flesh. Ari's stomach heaved, and he fell to his knees vomiting.

Robert spoke quickly. "No need for that, Weard Geir. I will need a few alive to illustrate a plan of action I believe you might wish to take."

"They might have spears, farl," Valgird said with a laugh.

If the jibe offended Robert, his voice didn't betray him. "You killed almost thirty people in the town. There should be about fifty here. Head back to the army and bring enough people forward so the town's number match the original. The regional recon spell keeps track of the number of Mar in each town, and the sudden disappearance of several dozen citizens will raise an alarm."

Valgird shot the enchanter a cold stare but obeyed. Ari wiped vomit from the corner of his mouth with sleeve corner of his cloak and stood up. He followed on Robert's heels, hoping it would mean seeing fewer corpses.

Flames licked several grass huts. Ari could hear an old man's last agonized screams emanating from one of them. Bodies lay charred halfway out of doors, and near many of them was a dead-eyed, terrified child. Only three of the original twelve homes were undamaged.

With a regretful sigh at the waste of resources, Robert walked the dirt paths between the huts. Mar women and children came out of hiding and followed him, their eyes glazed over as though sleepwalking. With nearly two dozen children and elderly surrounding them, Robert returned to the green, where the last of thirty-six wizards had already begun tearing down the magical defenses with their crude knowledge of Elements.

"What is this suggested plan of action, Weard Wost?" Valgird asked, joining Ari and Robert. "Does this involve Blosin wands?"

Robert shrugged. "Somewhat."

"And you can maintain this," Valgird licked his lips, "enchantment until we have captured all the towns in the Protectorates?"

"This?" Robert gestured at the little gathering of children and greybeards. "This is hardly enchantment. For me, this is as easy as it is for you to lift a heavy rock with Power."

Ari knew that was an exaggeration, but not much of one.

The enchanter gave a little laugh. "I do not intend to maintain it that long, and I do not need to, Weard Geir. Let me show you a little real enchantment. I call it my Will-Breaker."

Ari had seen Robert use the spell a hundred times in the Duxy of Wasfal. Dux Ratsell prized the slaves the enchanter made with it. Even if Ari had been able to master Presence and Wisdom to such a degree and weave them together so delicately with Knowledge, Energy and Elements, he was pretty sure he wouldn't want to.

From listening to Robert describe it over and over again, though, he knew what happened. Each of those glazed eyes, now watering in terror and shock, faced Domin or Dinah, faced their failures and fears and their deepest secrets. It opened them to deeply rooted suggestions. Robert said Marrishland was a good place for this, because of its rich belief in the pantheon, but Ari always murmured a few words to Marrish and Seruvus to protect him in case Robert chose to use his Will-Breaker on him.

"Have you chosen to obey me?" Robert asked them with a patronizing smile.

They could not wait to answer him in the affirmative, their words tumbling over each other in a chaos of terrified sound. They begged him for instructions, assuring him that they would do whatever he wished.

The wizards at the edge of the green watched the exchange nervously. True, mundanes were not as strong-willed as a wizard. Ari knew their thoughts. *Could he break a wizard as easily as he dominated these mundanes?*

Valgird's mind traveled a similar path. After several moments of careful consideration, he opted for a change of tactics.

"Weard Wost, I see I have vastly underestimated your abilities. In all phases of this campaign, I will regard you as my equal in authority." He fiddled with a gold amulet. "How did you ...?"

Robert smiled, clearly flattered. "The human psyche is terribly frail if approached in the right manner. An advanced illusion complete with physical sensations of great pain has made them docile. They will do my bidding."

"What if they discover that it was merely an illusion?"

Robert touched a groveling girl's face, lifted her chin up to meet his gaze. She shivered, and then her eyes fell in fear and deference. "If you have ever stabbed yourself with a needle, you know that such an injury will soon heal. Tell me, does that knowledge give you the desire to stab yourself with a needle?

"And why? Because it is not the injury we fear, but the pain. These people have sustained no injuries, but they have all experienced more torment in an hour than you could inflict on a person in a decade. A torturer of the body must be careful not to kill those in his charge, neither by allowing them to bleed too much nor by causing irreparable damage to a vital organ. But the pain I inflict does not wound. It merely sets every nerve in the body on fire. It is a fine, and delicate art, good weards, but one at which I excel." Robert's smile was envenomed.

"Is there ... a way to break such an enchantment?" Valgird asked slowly.

"The beauty of the Will-Breaker is it cannot be unraveled without killing the victim — well, not unless you are a powerful enchanter, of course. To them, I am Domin — from his alligator head to his fatal touch to the tortures he inflicts on those who displease the gods. They will obey me without question or hesitation all the days of their lives."

Ari knew Robert could hand over that undying obedience to a buyer, too, but he knew why the enchanter skipped over that detail. He also suspected Robert was exaggerating the dangers of unraveling the Will-Breaker, although he had never had occasion to find out.

Valgird suppressed his curiosity about the Will-Breaker with visible difficulty. "What is your plan?"

"I will use my Will-Breaker to enslave the mundanes of the Protectorates one town at a time. You and the other wizards will make wands for them, and we'll use the mundanes as our army."

"That seems simple enough, if time-consuming," Valgird said, but his voice was deferential.

"Let me finish, Weard Geir," Robert snapped, all false humility cast aside. "The Protectorate defenses are a fully integrated network — like a spiderweb with every strand connected to the center. Do you know what I could do if we capture the central town?"

"Dismantle the defenses for all the towns in the Protectorates?" Valgird guessed, sounding like an apprentice instead of an eighth-degree wizard.

"Even better. I can use it to cast my Will-Breaker on every mundane in the Protectorates."

Valgird's eyes went wide. Ari resisted the urge to frown. He knew Robert well, but he had not quite expected this.

"But Sven's minor magocrats will be there, so it will be better to draw out some of them. The wand-wielders are no more than a distraction."

"And if the Mardux returns?"

"Then he'll taste Domin's burning duxy, too, and he will grovel before me."

"He will mistake you for Domin?" Valgird wondered. "What will you ...?"

Robert smiled poisonously. "It would be too difficult to believe unless you experienced the Will-Breaker first-hand. Are you truly curious, Weard Geir?"

He recoiled, shaking his head violently.

"I thought not."

17

"Red is for Vitality. Vitality involves the manipulation and mending of the body. It is very useful, but also limited. It is far easier to heal surface wounds than internal ailments. Most wizards can close surface wounds with ease, but have difficulty repairing shattered rib or cracked skull. Only the most skilled healers can cure disease or poison, and even for them, it is seldom a swift or easy process."

— Nightfire Tradition,
Nightfire's Magical Primer

Sven's condition worsened rapidly after his collapse on the Chair. Neither Horsa nor the other skilled healers in Domus Palus had ever seen a manifestation of Dinah's Curse quite like this, though they seemed intent upon hiding that from Erika, claiming it was only a case of Seruvus' Breath brought on by exhaustion. She knew better, though.

She knew her husband was slowly dying.

Now he lay in their bed with drapes around him, a priest in attendance keeping water steaming through the air. He rasped when he breathed and his chest looked expanded and red in the dim light. When his eyes opened, they were bloodshot and tight, and when closed, Erika could see his eyeballs jerking around. Sven had to be forced to drink water and broth every day, and if he didn't vomit it back up, someone had to help him relieve himself.

Erika brought their daughter, Asa, to see him every day when he was coherent, which was rarely, but she seemed uncomfortable with him and would squirm until she was allowed to leave.

Erika sat alone in the library where Sven spent much of his time, quietly weeping in the shadows of the bookshelves while she pretended to read the magical primer he had written shortly after Asa had been born. Tears magnified a few words of the Vitality entry as though everything Sven authored wished to be larger than it actually was.

"Tell me about how you and Sven met," Pondr said behind her, and she jumped.

"What?" Erika tried to surreptitiously wipe the tears out of her eyes as she closed the book.

"There are many holes in his story," he said seriously, his blue eyes catching a shaft of sunlight coming from one narrow window. "How you two met, the situation in the town of Tortz, and so on. You can fill one in for me. How did you meet?"

She wanted to tell him to leave her alone. She didn't feel like telling stories just now.

Can't he see that Sven is dying?

But she found herself blushing as she remembered it. "It was a silly thing, really," she said, and closed the book in her lap.

Leiben was a town that had survived for almost fifteen years in the forest shadowing the Morden Moors. In a straight line, it was four miles from Zerst, the first town of the Takraf Protectorates. But, so Sven had said later on, he had taken four days to find it.

Erika Unschul foraged for root vegetables. The town was bursting at the seams — a gobbel raid had destroyed Horm, several miles away, and the survivors had fled to larger, better-protected Leiben. There was a shortage of food. Even the wild rice was in short supply. So she had gone out on her own initiative, dressed in her black cloak and heavy leather boots.

Her thickly gloved hands rooted through the mud, pulling up a patch of onions. She could see white worms clustered around the root, all through the dirt, but she knew they weren't the ones she should fear. Konig worms were too small to see, and if any attached themselves to your skin, you lost that limb or died. It was safer to root through mud in water, because the water might wash the worms off, but then you risked leeches or Dinah's Curse.

A splash to one side made her look up. Ten yards away she saw a gobbel standing. She froze, but it had caught her movement, and now the greasy pig-eyes turned and saw her basket filled with the greens of plants.

If it's just the one, I might be able to fight it.

She tensed, steeling herself to grab the knife at her belt and fly at the gobbel. It turned its head and called out to some unseen companions, and Erika was off like a rabbit. It could be a bluff, but she knew she couldn't fight more than one gobbel at a time.

She clutched her basket against her as she ran, heading for a part of the woods choked with underbrush. Gobbels were strong, but they had poor eyesight, so maybe she could lose them.

A thousand tiny hazards covered the ground in the tangled mass — roots, rocks, slick patches of mud. The gobbels crashed through behind her, shouting as they tripped and fell, but she seemed to be falling down almost as much. Once, her foot got stuck and she fell forward on her out-stretched hands, the basket tumbling out of her hands.

Erika stood up again. She was breathing hard, tiring and sore from all the falls. But she grabbed the basket and collected its scattered contents. The first of the gobbels spotted her and called out to its companions.

Six of them, Erika thought with dread.

Tears streamed down her cheeks as she drew her knife and prepared to face them.

A wall of fire rose up in front of her, and Erika cried out in surprise. Gobbel voices shrieked in pain as the flames engulfed them. She ducked behind a tree and fell again on the slick mud, but crawled up to have a look at what was happening.

A Mar in a bright green cloak stood confidently to her left, arms held out before him. One gobbel rushed him, javelin rising into a throw, but the man didn't flinch. The gobbel's back arched as if it had run throat-first into a tree branch, even though there was nothing there. It fell backward and did not get up.

A motion of his hand, and a gobbel ten feet away from him crumpled as if a large rock had fallen on it. The last two gobbels died in balls of flame.

The wizard, for that was what he must be, had defeated six gobbels by himself. He had done it so quickly Erika's knife was still clean, and she felt ashamed for not helping.

I probably would have just gotten in the way.

He looked directly at her and smiled gently. He had the most beautiful green eyes. He approached her slowly, as if afraid she would run.

"Peace in the swamp," he said. "I'm Sven Takraf."

She nodded, wiped her face with her hand, felt the tears there. "I'm Erika Unschul." *Sendala, let me not look too bad.*

"Peace in the swamp, Erika. Do you live near here?"

She nodded. "I live in Leiben. It's not far. I was lookin' for food."

His green eyes widened a little. "Alone?"

Erika couldn't tell if he was horrified or impressed. She shrugged and deliberately set to collecting the fallen food into her basket. "Yes. It needs doin', an' I can take care of myself."

She half-expected him to argue that she clearly could not take care of herself, since the gobbels had almost caught her, but he didn't. He looked slightly wistful, as if the situation stirred some memory for him.

She caught herself picking nervously at the mud on her cloak. "I've some soup, Sven."

He focused on her, and a grin lit up his green eyes. "I'd like that."

"I flustered a little, then, because I thought he would want more than food because he saved my life, but the look in his eyes had nothing to do with that at all."

"What do you mean by the look in his eyes?" Pondr asked.

"You've got the same look right now. That earnest, 'all I want to do is learn' look. He just wanted to test out some new hunting spells. Between the two of us, we fed everyone in town, that night. Leiben was the second town to join the Protectorates." She looked aside and said more softly, "I never see that in him anymore."

In his sickness, Sven relived the past. Bouts of semiconsciousness followed torrential dreams and nightmares. What he thought about for the brief moments he was awake haunted him through hours of sleep.

Days passed, and he could do nothing.

Every day, he prayed to his patrons to give him back his health and strength. He just needed enough energy to get out of bed.

You said you would give me more Energy than any Mar who has ever lived. Why do you deny it me now?

There was no answer.

Are you punishing me, or is this the wrath of Dinah and Domin?

Sven swallowed painfully and waited for an answer in the darkness behind his heavy eyelids.

When was I last sick? When I helped Erika feed Leiben, and I caught Seruvus' Breath ...

Gudris, the mayor of Leiben, oversaw Sven's treatment personally, feeding him a gruel laced with bitter-tasting medicinal herbs for several days before, at last, the illness passed. Strength renewed, Sven went immediately to work on implementing changes in the town as he had in Zerst. There were three things the two towns needed first: defenses against Drakes, land to grow food on and protection from disease.

He constructed a spell to warn the town of impending attacks, allowing hunters a greater range. He used Power to help drain the lands near the town, making it capable of supporting vegetables. He carefully implemented a system of sanitation. Following a meticulous purgation of skin parasites from the townspeople, Sven established a magical screen to eliminate mosquitoes and flies that entered the village and spread diseases.

The people marveled at the magical wonders Sven had brought to them, especially the last. The children would spend hours watching the sparks flicker and crackle above the buildings as insects were reduced to smoking husks. True, the moors themselves were as wild and dangerous as ever, but at least the town was safer and healthier.

Sven smiled as he watched the children.

The future. And this is just the beginning.

He sat with Erika one evening by the fire. Since his arrival, she had not been very far from him. He would return from a hunting trip and see her waiting for him. He would turn a corner, and she would bump into him. He would stand up from sowing seeds and see just her head behind a house.

The looks she gave him, the way she watched him, her body movements were all obvious. But inside, he was conflicted. On the one hand, they were of an age when most people married. He himself was older than average. On the other hand, involving himself with her would only tie him down, and this was what he was trying to explain to her now.

"Leiben and Zerst are not the only villages that would benefit from my protection. There must be other towns on the moors, people who are suffering as Leiben once suffered. And winter will be here too soon. That will mean frequent gobbel raids, less food and more disease. The malaria will fade, but Seruvus' Breath kills so many Mar ..."

"But you don't know where any other towns are. How're you goin' to fin' them without leavin' Leiben at the mercy of the gobbels?"

Sven picked up a stick and made a mark on a patch of earth. From the mark, he drew a slowly widening spiral. "It will take time, but this will clear more of the moors of gobbels. And no town will escape notice." Sven's eyes flashed red in the light of the fire.

"Think of creating Leiben on a massive scale! Hundreds of towns free of disease. Starvation defeated. Gobbel raids just stories we tell children."

He felt the glow spread from him to engulf her. She could feel his energy and see his dreams before him.

She understands! he thought, and when it came time to leave, in private he pledged he would return to her.

From the fruitful womb of Sven's mind, the Takraf Protectorates was born.

He traveled from town to town, the spiral nearly flawless except for little jitters here and there. On the paths in between, gobbels and other Drakes who dared to stand before Sven were blasted into ash, until among their communities bright green became equal to red in terms of danger. After Zerst and Leiben, word had spread among the Mar of the wizard who walked the moors and demanded no tribute, who used his power to fend off disease and Drakes. And as winter progressed, representatives of distant villages met Sven in the wilderness.

By the beginning of spring, as Sven rejoined Erbark in Zerst, the Protectorates numbered fifteen. At that point, he had reached the limits of his ability to renew the spells, and he knew he would have to find other ways to expand his protection. After careful thought, Sven made efforts to introduce the mayors to each other. Mar and Mar communities were generally unsociable creatures, but, especially in the central communities, the lack of diseases to cure and monsters to defeat left much free time. Erbark had suggested using warriors from the inner towns to protect the outer ones, and the mayors, after a few months of debate and a handful of objections, eventually agreed.

And the travel between towns — safe, dry and occasionally enhanced by Mobility — gave the mayors and elders a taste of what magic could do for them. Sven added that as a bonus to all the dealings, because those he had started to teach how to read in Zerst were happily ready to teach others, in an effort to reach the ability required by Bera's Unwritten Laws — so they could use magic themselves.

When in Leiben, Sven and Erika spent as much time as he could allow together, which included many private lessons. She studied in earnest, soaking up everything like a starving Mar eating soup. She also had a knack for teaching and possessed a great deal of patience with students who learned so slowly that Sven wanted to give up on them.

In an effort to protect the towns more, Sven called upon his knowledge of reconnaissance, a word most Mar had never heard. They called it scouting, when they did it, though the word called mapmaker jokes to their minds because of the danger involved. But Sven wanted to take it a step further, and in Leiben, clearly as an excuse to stay by Erika longer, he built a hut and inside it made the first reconnaissance stone.

It was a simple flat, rough-edged disc, raised off the ground and made of clay. A spell that stretched the limits of Sven's skill sent rays of Knowledge in eight directions for a distance of three miles once per hour, identifying Mar and Drakes as specks of red and yellow light on the disc.

Sven knew its limits. Rays left too many gaps, especially at the edges of the reconnaissance. A field of Knowledge would be more effective. Also, an hour was too long an interval, especially with a range of only three miles. Many Drakes could march from beyond the spell's range to the walls of the town without being detected simply through lucky timing. It was the best he could manage with the knowledge at his disposal, but he never stopped looking for solutions to the problems.

Erbark studied with all the best warriors in the Protectorates, and he worked with them to develop a training program for all the members of the various militias. Officially, no town's militia answered to anyone outside the community, but in practice all of them acted on Erbark's suggestions and recommendations as though they were orders from a commanding general.

But warriors were easier to train than wizards and took far less time. Sven didn't even have time to instruct Erbark anymore, much less the masses of rural Mar in his protection. He was busy renewing magic, maintaining health and expanding the Protectorates. Occasionally, Sven would consider inviting a few younger wizards into the Protectorates to renew spells and cure disease so he could concentrate on these issues. But he was afraid they would try to take control. He remembered what Erbark had told him of how Tosti and Brand had fought over Rustiford. He couldn't afford that conflict. There had to be another way, another source of help.

A year later, less than a month before his wedding, Sven had a breakthrough. He turned a spell he had learned at the Academy as a sort of curiosity into the foundation for a system of defenses any duxy would envy. Not only did the fifteen towns already under his protection receive considerable infrastructure improvements, but the new spell allowed Sven to expand the reach of his Protectorates to thirty-nine towns.

Even so, he knew he couldn't expand indefinitely. Five more towns, maybe ten, and he would need another wizard — whether that was one of his apprentices or some outsider he could trust. But he kept adding new communities to the Protectorates in his ever-widening spiral.

Summer was in full flower when Sven at last stumbled upon Tortz, far south of Zerst. Even before he reached its walls, he knew it had a magocrat. The force of militiamen who met him before he was within sight of their village provided the first hint, but others followed closely thereafter.

 **18**

*"It is easy to tell whether a Mar is using magic by merely
viewing the myst by drinking torutsen or using Knowledge, since a wizard must move and use up the motes
to shape his effects. It is possible to conceal magic by
exercising the strictest control over the handling of the
myst, drawing motes only from the ground in such a
way that it is nearly undetectable. This was first perfected in Flecterra, but the number of Mar with the strength
and desire to regularly employ it can be counted on the
fingers of one hand."*

— Nightfire Tradition,
Nightfire's Magical Primer

Horsa Verifien, another man from Rustiford who had endured
Nightfire's tests, came into the room where Erika was reading. His
yellow cloak was emblazoned with a flame proclaiming him a priest
of Marrish.

"The Mardux wishes to speak to his wife," he said, smiling gently
at Erika. "If you'll excuse us, Pondr?"

But she was already through the door and into Sven's chambers.
When she reached him, she took his hand and looked deep into those
green eyes she had fallen in love with so long ago.

"Erika," he said slowly. "They said I have been sick for three spans
now, delirious."

She nodded. "You're still alive, right? That's important."

He coughed. "The army ... where is it?"

Nothing about me, she thought, but said, "It's just over the Flasten
border."

"Where is Flasten?"

Her eyes were wet. "Don't worry about it, Sven. Just get better. The Council knows how to handle war."

He shook his head, tried to sit up, but she was able to push him back down.

"Council doesn't know what war means," he said emphatically.

Suddenly his eyes blazed, at the ease she could push him down maybe, and all the candles in the room caught fire. The drapes blazed.

Erika screamed, threw herself away from the bed instinctively, and then rushed it as the sheets caught fire. The heat pushed her back. She scrabbled at the ground as heat began to pulse through the very stones.

"The Council thinks of battles!" Sven screamed, blood dribbling from the corner of his mouth. *"The Council doesn't know war!"*

Horsa fumbled with a spell, lost concentration as heat licked out at him, turning the bed into a pyre.

"Do something!" Erika screamed at him.

With a great inhalation, Horsa made a pulling motion with both hands, and Erika felt the heat draw past her, extinguishing the flames. A large section on the wall turned black and cracked loudly as Horsa pushed the heat into it. Erika fumbled through a medical kit, sought the morutsen. Finding the flask, she uncorked it, gestured to Horsa.

"Hold him down," she said, but Sven was unconscious.

His body was a mass of burns, except for his face. Only half of his face was blackened with soot, burned through to the bone. It frightened her, his eyelid a soft patch of red, seeming to glow from the white of the eyeball. The other side was a rictus of pain and dismay, but this side was just a blasted smirk. She dumped some morutsen down his throat anyway.

"Heal him."

Horsa laid his hand on the good side of Sven's face, and Erika watched as Vitality rebuilt the tissue on Sven's body. There were few burns Energy could inflict that Vitality could not heal, but she would never forget the blackened, bloody, bone-showing side of his face. The damaged eye did not heal, though, leaving a blank white orb that reflected the flickering light of the fading tapestry fires.

"Oh, Sven," she started to cry. "Oh, Sven, what have you done?"

Erika!

Sven felt the pain, felt it on his body and face as he felt it in his heart.

My love, did I hurt you?

And as he slipped out of consciousness, battling whatever diseases ate him on the inside, he wished he had told her about the army, and Bui, and the Protectorates, and inside, he cried out to his patrons.

Why have you struck me down when the Mar need me most?

"Stop where you are, wizard, or you face death!" called the eldest warrior of the group.

Surprised by this reaction, Sven obeyed, smiling and raising his hand in a gesture of peace that he had used to win over more than forty villages and family homesteads.

"Peace in the swamp. I am Sven Takraf. I come without malice."

In response, the warriors advanced upon him. Sven was certain he could protect himself from the four militiamen.

"Who sent you?" demanded a clean-shaven, middle-aged man whose hood hung low on his face.

Sven took a step backward, confused by this question, perturbed by the man's lack of facial hair. He scratched his own bare chin nervously. "No one sent me. I am the guardian of several villages north of here."

"A magocrat!" the clean-shaven man spat.

"No!" He did not want these people to hate him. "They make their own laws. I merely protect them from Drakes and disease as best I can." *Why did that voice seem familiar?*

Sven reached for Mobility in case he had to flee.

"Take him," the clean-shaven man shouted.

The warriors didn't move, and, for a moment, Sven thought they were afraid of him. Then an invisible force struck him in the gut, doubling him over. His spell tumbled away half-formed, and the world seemed to slow to a crawl. The militiamen stood stock still, and more attacks landed. Cheek, shin, knees, kidneys. Sven recognized Power attacks when he felt them.

He gathered Knowledge hastily. If he knew which of these men was the wizard, he could fight him. The colored fog of the myst materialized. Blue motes of Power shimmered around *all four of them! They're all wizards!*

Sven realized his mistake too late. His body was now a mass of welts and bruises. The barrage halted briefly before a wave of force knocked him to his knees. Then one of the militiamen was holding back his head while a second poured the contents of a leather flask down his throat. Sven spat out the sweet liquid violently. He tried to summon more myst, but none would answer his call.

He remembered a lecture from his days as a student.

Morutsen. I've already been pacified.

"I submit to your scrutiny," he shouted before the rough hands again pulled back his head, this time holding his nose.

The clean-shaven man bowed over him, pouring another vial into Sven's mouth. "And scrutinized shall you be, Sven Takraf."

Brand Halfin!

A sharp pain on his temple sent him into oblivion before he could greet the fellow student of Nightfire, the first slave taken from Rustiford and taught magic.

Tortz?

Sven woke again as someone moved him. A sickeningly sweet liquid was dripped in his mouth, and he tried to spit it out.

"Hold still, Mardux. This is for your own safety."

"Horsa?"

"The very same, Sven. Don't bother opening your eyes. There's no light in here anyway."

The words hung in the air.

What happened to the light?

And as he was laid back down, he fell asleep, the taste of morut-sen in his throat.

Why Tortz?

It is where I learned the lesson of the fuel.

 **19**

*"Bera's Unwritten Laws is that body of law dealing with
the teaching of magic to apprentices. The original laws
predate the invention of writing in Marrishland and
were passed by word of mouth from master to student
for generations before being committed to paper. For
this reason, they are still called the Unwritten Laws."*

— Weard Oda Kalidus,
Introduction to Bera's Unwritten Laws

When Sven woke, it was in near darkness. Only a small hole in the ceiling let in a dim light. Sitting up to look around, his head spun and pounded in fury. Sven squinted and rubbed his throbbing temples. He was in an adobe hut with no windows or doors. Even the floor had been covered in stone tiles sealed with clay.

This is a prison, built long before my arrival. What is Brand doing here?

They had left him only his clothes and cloak. He considered summoning the myst to see if the morutsen had worn off, yet, but decided against it. He didn't doubt Brand's people were watching him. It would only arouse suspicion if he used magic, and it would earn him another dose of morutsen, at best.

Torutsen helps us use magic and tastes bitter. Morutsen prevents us from using it and is sickly sweet. Both come from the kalysut tree. The gods love their mysteries.

The walls of the prison looked thick enough to withstand the hammering of Power, and Sven certainly lacked the skill to teleport to freedom. If Brand wished to keep him helpless, his wizards would give Sven more morutsen. If Brand thought he could trust Sven, his wizards might not. In any case, Sven would not have any opportunity to escape unless they let him out of this prison.

He found a chamber pot and made use of it.

There seemed little point in resisting his imprisonment. Brand had recognized him, at least. There was a good chance he would eventually talk to the prisoner. Sven stretched out on the grass-stuffed pallet and tried to get comfortable in spite of his bruises and other injuries.

My safety is in your hands now, he prayed silently.

At last, he slept.

"Welcome to Tortz, Weard Takraf," a gruff voice called down from the hole above, and a small flask tumbled to the floor. Sven recognized the voice as one of the militiamen from outside the town.

He sat up. It was morning outside his prison. "Peace in the swamp, sir."

"Peace i'the swamp an' good mornin'. The mayor'll talk to you. Drink that, an' I'll lower the ladder."

Sven obeyed, eager to get away from this prison cell. The flask contained morutsen, of course. Even if Brand was willing to talk, he wouldn't be careless with a wizard prisoner. Sven considered what he would do if their roles were reversed and discovered no clear answer.

And if this town was run by a magocrat I did not know? That was a dangerous path to consider. He climbed the damp rope ladder.

"Bran' Halfin was the first. We'll remember always his wisdom." The words were spoken every Weardfest in Rustiford, naming all nine residents whom Nightfire had taken. *And now Brand, a first-degree wizard, leads this town, Tortz.*

And he had taught at least four others here. He had been gone nine years from Nightfire's Academy, which meant he could have trained apprentices by now, following Bera's Unwritten Laws. *But they all speak with a mundane dialect.*

What about the disguises when I first came upon them? They wish to keep their knowledge a secret, which could also explain the rural accent.

What patterns do my observations suggest?

The warrior led him to another adobe building. Brand was waiting for them outside the door. He saluted Sven with his right hand.

"Thank you, Bui." Brand smiled warmly at Sven. "I have some soup, old friend."

Sven's eyes went wide as he realized what he had been missing. "The Unwritten Laws! Brand, what have you gotten yourself into?"

Brand sighed heavily. He held the door open and beckoned. "I'm sorry for your rough treatment yesterday. As you have already surmised, we have good cause not to welcome wizards with open arms. Come inside, and I will explain."

Sven obeyed grudgingly, not at all happy with the circumstances of this meal.

If Nightfire even knew I was here, he might not judge in my favor.

The soup was too hot to eat comfortably. He ate it anyway, eager to get the formality of the meal out of the way. "You offered an explanation," Sven prompted when his bowl was empty.

"You must have left the Academy quite recently." Brand's eyes watched the fire lick the blocks of peat in his hearth as he spoke. "Have you been to Rustiford?"

"Yes. They wouldn't let me stay because of what you and Tosti did when you came back."

"Tosti was abusing his power," Brand said without evident emotion. "I only did what I had to do to keep him from setting himself up as a petty magocrat. I only regret that others were hurt as a consequence."

"And the ravit war?"

Brand winced. "I can't make that right for you. I'm sorry. I had hoped to drive the ravits farther east, and we did that. Not everyone thought it was worth the price Rustiford paid."

"It wasn't," Sven snapped.

"What would you have done in my place, Weard ... Takraf you're calling yourself, now?"

"You kept your name at the end of your apprenticeship?"

"Shed your old name with your old cloak and choose a new one when you don the green?" He shrugged. "It seemed pretentious, so yes, I kept my name."

"In your place, I would have done as Nightfire advised and taught the ones who wanted to be taught, rather than making myself an educator magocrat."

Brand smirked. "I tried that, at first. My students got bored of learning math and reading when they had hoped I would teach them to use magic. They ran out of patience, and soon I had no pupils at all.

"I started going on hunting expeditions to prove my magic was useful enough to be worth years spent studying history and Middling Gien. I sold my magic to people in exchange for time spent in my classroom. Some people grumbled, but your father supported me. I think he knew it would be good for Rustiford to have its own wizards."

"He did," Sven said. "The town we came from had a magocrat. She treated us well, and it was only the war that forced her to leave us at the mercy of Flasten's slavers."

"Yes. Exactly. Anyway, everything was going pretty well until one of the hunting parties was ambushed by ravits. They killed Yrsa Lutig, Sven." Brand flushed in a mixture of anger and embarrassment that spoke of the strength of that relationship. "I didn't think of the consequences. I went out alone and used magic to kill the first group of ravits I found. Their tribe retaliated, and soon Rustiford had a war. A lot of people died, and most of Rustiford blamed me. They chose not to give Nightfire a slave the next year."

"That was when Tosti came back, and he made Rustiford dislike wizards even more. You fought. People died. Brita decided enough was enough." Sven spoke quickly, impatiently. "I asked for an explanation, not a saga."

Brand's eyes blazed a little at Sven's tone. "If you'd have a little patience, I'm getting to it."

Sven waved him on.

"After Rustiford, I gave up on doing it Nightfire's way. I picked a town beyond the duxies and offered to teach them magic. Instead of teaching them to read, I taught them to make torutsen. Instead of teaching them history, I showed them how to wield Energy and Power."

"You broke the Law," Sven said flatly.

"I broke the Law," Brand said, "because it makes no sense."

"It makes plenty of sense," Sven countered. "As with the ravits, you didn't think of the consequences of giving magic to the people of Tortz."

"The Mass?" Brand asked with an incredulous laugh. "That's a lie told by wizards to ensure they stay in power. Weard Darflaem taught magic to anyone who wanted to learn, and some of his own students killed him for it."

"The Mass wasn't the first thing that came to mind," Sven said airily. He spoke in earnest. "Even if the Mass isn't real, Nightfire certainly is. Whether you agree with the Law or not, the wizards will punish you if they catch you breaking it."

"I am well aware of that."

"Of course. That's why you have your prison. How many wizards have you killed so far to protect your secret?"

Brand hesitated.

Sven continued before the other wizard could reply. "Wizards usually serve another wizard, and those wizards ultimately serve a dux. One day someone will send a search party."

"There are many dangers on the Morden Moors," Brand said carefully. "It is not always possible to recover a body."

"But multiple disappearances in the same part of the moors? Eventually, someone will take notice. They'll send a dozen wizards to investigate. And if you kill them, it will bring even more."

"Enough!" Brand growled. "Few wizards come to Tortz. We've only had to kill three, and two of them were slavers, so pardon me if I don't weep over them."

What about the third? Sven thought, but he said nothing.

"The others leave none the wiser. We don't exactly show off our magic when we have guests."

"You certainly didn't hesitate when you spotted me."

"You scouted Tortz with Knowledge. We had no way of knowing what you were looking for, but we didn't want to take a chance that you were looking for illegal magic-wielders. Even then, we would have just driven you off if you hadn't called the myst."

"If I had been an agent of Flasten, you never would have gotten close enough to keep me from escaping. You met me too far from your town walls. I already suspected a wizard."

Brand nodded his acknowledgment of the point. "That's certainly a more rational reason than I expected. I was all set with a counter example to the 'dangerous tool' argument."

"Magic is a dangerous tool, and giving it to mundanes who don't have enough knowledge to wield it wisely only puts their lives in danger," Sven summarized. "And your response would involve the knife you've carried since you were a child — a tool whose utility outstrips the danger involved in carrying it."

"I've always been fond of the fire variant, actually, but yes." Brand grinned as though Sven was an honored guest and not a prisoner held captive with morutsen.

Sven hadn't forgotten that detail, but he had missed the company of other wizards since leaving Nightfire's Academy. He had enjoyed the heated debates over theory and practice where the best arguments won out, and no one had any hard feelings about being proven wrong.

He shook his head. "This is a real mess. You can't exactly un-teach them magic, and even if they swore off using it until they had the knowledge, the wizards wouldn't care. Under the Law, this is a capital offense for everyone in the town."

Brand looked at him hard. "What brought you here?"

Sven, certain that evasion of any sort would result in more suspicion, took a deep breath and began. "I have been systematically aiding towns, villages and homesteads on the Morden Moors. My assistance comes in the form of healing, sanitation, reconnaissance and parasite removal."

"And what do you demand in exchange?"

"Nothing."

"Nothing?"

Sven shrugged and spread his hands. "Education is simply one more service I offer. I started by proving how useful magic can be. I keep them safe, and they have more time for luxuries like learning."

"And how many villages are under your protection?"

"A few spans ago we added our fortieth."

"Forty towns!" Brand breathed. "And do you have other wizards helping you?"

"No. One green is unlikely to take orders from another. Erbark helps where he can."

"Apprentices?"

Sven wasn't sure where this line of discussion was going, but he liked it less and less. "A couple. None ready for torutsen, yet."

"How can you possibly protect so many without any help?"

Sven smiled mysteriously. "I've had to become very efficient."

"Dinah's shriveled teat! There has to be more to it than that." Brand waved a finger at him. "You're hiding something from me."

"Yes, I am," Sven admitted in a flat tone. "I think you can understand why."

Brand rubbed his chin thoughtfully. "I have been in Tortz for less than three years, and I no longer need to maintain the spells protecting this town, but you already know how I did it."

Sven shrugged. "Even if you knew my secret, you can't expand beyond the walls of Tortz for fear you will be discovered by the wizards."

"What if you die before any of your apprentices become wizards? Who will renew your spells? No one. And the lives of every person in those forty villages will be worse than they were before your arrival, because they will remember a better time. Everything you have done will come to nothing."

Sven considered arguing the point. The villages worked together now, but it would be harder without their only wizard. He waited for an opening.

"You go into the wizards' garden and pick its fruits for those villages, but you refuse to give them the key to the garden's gate. You will take the key with you to your grave, and then the fruits will cease to arrive."

"A colorful metaphor, Brand, but you've done even worse to Tortz. You may be elevating a few Mar from their mundanity, but the education you have given them is still far inferior to that of a wizard, and wizards are the opponents you will undoubtedly face once your crime is discovered, and you know it will eventually be discovered. Your handful of mundanes, while adept at a few applications, is not numerous or powerful enough to fight a force of true wizards."

"The wizards won't necessarily discover my adepts."

"Oh no, this is much worse than that," Sven assured him. "What is magic? It is an abstract energy form composed, to the appearance of one under the effects of torutsen, of eight concrete parts, none of whose function is discernable to the eye. A physical tool's purpose can generally be intuited quickly and with minimal experimentation. Unless the student knows the name and the color of each variety of myst, he must, in essence, reinvent the canoe. Moreover, unlike a physical tool, any application he discovers but does not pass on leaves no evidence of it ever having existed. Thus, magical knowledge gained without a reliable means of recording that knowledge is easily lost and, even in the best possible scenario, only very gradually increases. This is precisely why literacy and the development of a rational mind are so essential to the learning of magic."

Brand considered this for a long minute. "You're right," he said, at last. "I have been thinking in years when I should be thinking in decades, in generations."

Sven said nothing. He had the sense that he was no longer in danger of being murdered, but his chances of being executed for breaking the Unwritten Laws were rising by the minute.

I should turn him over to Nightfire for judgment. It is the only way to avoid being Brand's accomplice. If I so much as keep my silence about Tortz, I will be complicit.

"Secret or no secret, you must have difficulty finding time to teach your apprentices with forty towns to defend," Brand said conversationally, and Sven knew the renegade wizard had seen right through him.

He could already tell the course the conversation would take, the observations, the offers of compromise. And he knew he could refuse none of it. He had stretched himself too thin, and he needed Brand's help every bit as much as Brand needed his. *No, even more than he needs mine.*

"In that I fear you are correct," Sven said, jaw tight.

"I propose a compromise. Teach me your secret. I will renew the defenses of your Protectorates if you will stay in Tortz to teach my apprentices. Perhaps we can cover up my legal indiscretion before it is brought to light. Once they are wizards, they can teach the people of your benevolent little duxy."

Sven hesitated. *What if the magocrats find me in Tortz? They would hold me responsible for Brand's offense and might not believe me if I implicated him. In my absence, Brand could claim the Protectorates as his own. And will the wizards of Tortz be loyal to Brand or to the ideals he shares with me? Brand could seize control of the Protectorates that way, too.*

Was there some reason why he shouldn't let Brand put himself in charge of the Protectorates, or was it just his own pride in what he had already accomplished there? Of course he didn't want to surrender any control. He had friends there. A wife. Neighbors who treated him like family.

"One condition," Sven said finally. "You obey the Unwritten Law in the Protectorates."

"I've already told you. I'm not a very patient teacher. Besides, forty towns are more conspicuous than one, as you have already noted."

"I want your oath. No matter what happens," Sven persisted, voice hard. "No matter whether I am alive or dead, you will obey the Law."

Brand looked at him with a curious expression. A look of understanding crossed his face, then, and he raised his right hand in solemn salute. "By the Oathbinder, and by Cedar, my patron, I swear to abide by Bera's Unwritten Laws when visiting the lands under your protection."

"Then let's get started." Sven took a deep breath and explained the process for renewing the Protectorates' defenses.

Brand scowled the whole time. The defenses were complex to set up because they were so easy to maintain. An apprentice with his first taste of torutsen could do it. Sven didn't bother explaining how to set up any of the spells.

An hour ago, you would have killed me to keep the secret of Tortz safe. You didn't really think I'd give up the only leverage I still have, did you?

At the end of it, Brand simply nodded, and they both began their new duties.

 **20**

*"Any Mar, be he weard or mundane, who breaks my Law
shall be put to death by fire, as shall any student who
wields power beyond his understanding. Any Mar, be
she weard or mundane, who breaks my Law shall be put
to death by fire, as shall any student who wields power
beyond her understanding. Those who do not obey these
laws betray the shades of the dead, and the dead may
take vengeance upon them."*

— Nightfire Tradition,
Bera's Unwritten Laws

*I was right, and he knew it, but I didn't listen to my own arguments.
His methods changed mine. How long have I lived in the shadow of
Brand Halfin?*

Sven woke sweating, rolled on his side and hacked into a bucket
until the phlegm came out red. Someone was rubbing his back.

"Erika?"

"Yes, my love?"

He turned to look at her, dizzy. His left eye registered only a dark
patch. "What time is it?"

"Early afternoon. Welcome back to us. Horsa says your illness is
passing now."

He smiled at her beautiful face, her wonderful face ... *How could I
have forgotten that beauty?* "The war ... ?"

"Is happening." Her voice was too hard. "Get some rest."

She pushed him back down gently, and placed a cool cloth on his
forehead.

Then she was gone.

Erika ...

Sven took a piece of charcoal out of the hearth and began to write the alphabet on a piece of wood for the thirty Mar gathered in Brand's large house. "This is 'Wah.' It means 'nothing' in Middling Gien, which is what the Mar alphabet is based on. This is 'Zix.' It means 'darkness.' And this is 'Guel,' which means 'night.' This one here is 'Jah,' which means day. Now, the letters of the alphabet were arranged this way so that letters with related meanings were grouped together. 'Wah' is all by itself, but 'Zix,' 'Guel' and 'Jah' are grouped together because they all have to do with light or the absence of light."

"Um, Sven?" Askr Spertrag said hesitantly. "Did you say that 'Wah' means nothin'? But all th'other letters mean somethin' else, right?"

"That's why 'Wah's all by itself," Geir Tragget announced matter-of-factly.

Twenty-nine heads nodded at this, and it was all Sven could do to stop himself from shouting.

They hadn't all been this difficult. Three hundred magic-wielding mundanes lived in Tortz, and some of them had taken to education easily. Many were at least eager to learn, which certainly made them easier to teach. Not so much these thirty.

"No, 'Wah' is the word for 'nothing,' like the word 'nothing.'"

"I don't think I un'erstand," Askr said, not hiding his irritation very well.

The others murmured their agreement. Sven began to lose his patience.

"Never mind what it means, for now." He continued to write, the letters blurring as his left hand passed over them. "Wah, Zix, Guel, Jah. Myst, Tor, Ues. Lets, Frov, Her. Dih, Sen, Ud, Krah. Olf, Bik, Eep, Oud. Pleb, Nyp, Ahd, Rah. Oik, Ym, Ak, Ait. Ies, Xil, Veks, Es. And then Wah again."

They looked at him with a mixture of bored expressions and sheepish smiles.

Sven understood now why Nightfire was so careful about which mundanes he accepted as apprentices. In the Protectorates, only those who wanted to learn had come to him. Those who lacked self-discipline soon gave up and stopped coming, and it was no concern of Sven's.

"How do you know what order they go in?" Geir asked after a moment.

"They're grouped together by relatedness. Each letter means something in Middling Gien. Imperial Gien was pictographic, so the letters sort of look like what they mean. See this triangle pointing up? This is 'Sen'. It means 'water.' Can you figure out why?"

Some of them weren't even paying attention. The rest stared at the charcoal lines, faces set in concentration.

"A wave," Geir tried.

"Exactly," Sven said, pleased at this tiny bit of progress.

In Tortz, though, Sven couldn't allow any magic-wielder to quit his classes. If any of them failed the knowledge tests that came with an inquisition, he and Brand would both be executed.

Askr pointed at the first letter. "What's that one mean, again?"

Sven restrained himself with difficulty. "'Wah' can mean 'emptiness' or 'a lack of anything.'"

Geir suddenly laughed triumphantly. "Nothing! I see what you meant now."

Sven breathed a sigh of relief. "Yes, that's right, Geir."

Bui Beglin burst in through the front door, and thirty heads craned to look at him. "Weard Takraf! Brand's back. He says come right now."

Sven frowned at the interruption. He cleared his throat. "I want all of you to copy the alphabet until I get back. We'll learn to write your names tomorrow."

"I don't see much use in tellin' folks don't know you how to say your name," one of them muttered as Sven left, and laughter followed.

Why would anyone in his right mind attempt what Brand tried in Rustiford? Teaching apprentices who want to learn is hard enough, sometimes.

When Sven got home, he found Brand was not alone.

"Erika! What are you doing here?"

She flew into his arms and covered his face with kisses before answering. "Brand says you're goin' ... going to be in Tortz for a long time, so I'm staying here, too."

Sven shot Brand a look that could have set wet wood on fire, but Brand seemed not to notice.

"Your wife wants to help you teach the people of Tortz, and I agreed."

"You should have asked me before getting her involved in this," Sven said in a tight voice.

"You can't teach three hundred students by yourself," Brand said. "Nightfire has a staff of dozens, and there are only about a thousand apprentices at the Academy."

"What's wrong?" she asked, looking concerned.

"Nothing," Brand said at the same time as Sven said, "Everything!"

"I memorized the Unwritten Law as an apprentice," Brand said with the air of a lecturer, "and it was silent on pre-torutsen apprentices teaching post-torutsen apprentices."

"That's because it's never supposed to be possible!" Sven raged. "Do you have any idea whether this will get her executed for breaking the Law? Because I certainly don't!"

"Executed?" Erika asked quietly.

"You didn't tell her!"

"Neither did you," Brand countered.

"Tell me what?" Erika asked, more loudly, this time.

Sven and Brand looked at each other, and then Sven explained their dilemma. Erika listened in silence.

"You should have told me, Brand," she said when it was finished, but Sven saw no fear in her eyes. "I would've brought more teachers from the Protectorates."

"Do you have any idea what will happen to everyone here if the wizards find out?" Sven asked her. *I can't lose you! Not when I've only just found you.*

She shrugged. "I've some idea, but we have to do it." She gave Sven a serious look. "The longer it takes, the more likely you'll get caught, and I'm not going to let some wizard kill you for something that isn't your fault." She said the last fiercely, and he couldn't tell whether she meant the wizards in general or Brand in particular.

"She's right, you know," Brand said into the silence that followed. *Of course she is. Did I really think I could do this alone?*

Erika ...

"Erika?" Sven woke again, haunted by his dream of Tortz.

No one responded.

What time is it? What's going on? How long have I been sick?

He felt much better. Indeed, Horsa was not present, the water in the air was diminished, and the bucket by his bed was gone.

He felt weak, and just lifting his head to look around was an effort. Finally, he fell back again, and his dream continued where it had left off.

Tortz. I understand now. A single log cannot sustain a fire forever. I am hindering the spread of my light by not letting others add fuel to my fire. Now that I have solved your riddle, Fraemauna, will I be healed?

The goddess did not answer.

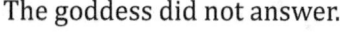

Six other Protectorate teachers volunteered for the task of educating the people of Tortz, which was most of the literate population of the Morden Moors. Sven impressed upon them the risks and warned them not to learn anything about magic from the magic-wielders who lived in Brand's renegade town. They assured him they understood, but Sven couldn't shake the fear that they would overhear something they shouldn't.

If you know too much about magic without knowing enough about everything you are supposed to learn first ...

It couldn't be helped.

Erbark stayed in the Protectorates as Sven's representative, and Brand spent nearly all his time wandering from village to village renewing the defenses. None of them slept much that fall. By the time winter crept in, Sven took over the defenses of Tortz. They simply couldn't afford to have so many of the magic-wielders maintaining the crude spells Brand had taught them, when a single recon stone could protect it much more effectively.

The warm breath of spring brought returning geese and ducks. By the midsummer holiday of Jaer's Hunt, Sven had mostly convinced the magic-wielders to stop brewing torutsen and limit their use of magic to life-or-death dangers. The defenses he had set up were more than adequate to keep Tortz safe and healthy.

Summer passed in storms and heat with little break in the routine of teaching, maintaining Tortz's defenses, and discussing the news from the Protectorates with Brand whenever the other wizard came back from a round of spell renewal.

Wainat, the first month of fall, brought visitors to Tortz less welcome than the icy breath of Heliotosis on the air would be — a wizard dressed in amber, traveling with a pair of greens. In Brand's absence, Sven threw the gates of Tortz open to them.

"Peace in the swamp, good weards. I am Sven Takraf. I have some soup."

The amber regarded him with suspicion. "Peace in the swamp, Weard Takraf. I am Arnlaug Saugen. What is the name of this village?"

"Tortz."

Arnlaug looked around casually, sizing up the people coming out of their homes to take his measure in return. After a moment, he turned his attention back to Sven. "Your village lies within the Duxy of Flasten. I have come to collect the dux's tribute."

Sven felt the tension rise all around him as eyes narrowed and muttered threats emanated from doorways. "I'm afraid you are mistaken," he said with more force than he should have used. "Tortz lies on the Morden Moors, which is not a part of any duxy."

"The dux's maps disagree, Weard Takraf." Arnlaug made an apologetic gesture. "I'm afraid I have no choice but to collect his levy — twelve pounds of common metals or a single slave."

Is this a slaver like the one Brand warned me about?

As if in answer, Tortz's militia arrived in a mob that formed around the wizards. Three wizards stood little chance against a few dozen mundanes.

Sven frowned at the amber. "Weard Saugen, we both know you owe no more loyalty to the Duxy of Flasten than I do," he said in a level tone. "I suggest you take your bowl of soup and then leave before there is blood spilt. Slavers and thieves are not welcome in Tortz."

Arnlaug took a step forward but stopped as the people of Tortz moved closer. He sneered at Sven in undisguised fury. "You are making a mistake. There will be consequences!"

Sven didn't raise his voice. "If you do not leave, those consequences will involve your corpse floating facedown in a river."

One of the greens gasped, but the amber actually smiled slightly. "You haven't been in Tortz very long, have you, Weard Takraf?"

Sven said nothing.

"Tortz's magocrat owed fealty to the Duxy of Flasten, but he stopped sending the tribute a few years ago. I think you murdered him."

"I really don't care what a slaver thinks," Sven said as nonchalantly as he could manage. *Is this wizard lying, or is Brand holding something back?*

"We will leave," Arnlaug announced to his two companions.

Sven watched the trio of wizards depart, monitoring their progress on the recon stone until they were out of range. He tried to push the incident out of his mind and focus on teaching.

He had turned his attention to history. Brand possessed only a handful of books, but Sven had memorized several texts while at Nightfire's Academy, and he recited them to his students. To his great relief, even the least attentive students absorbed these lessons with the ease of Mar children learning the legends of gods and heroes.

Thank Seruvus for our oral tradition.

Spring became summer again.

"Peace in the swamp. What news in my absence?"

"Brand, welcome back. How are the Protectorates?" Sven said in turn.

They shared information. The Protectorates had been forced to evacuate one of their towns — not because of gobbel attacks but simply because it had been built on land that had become unstable, and it was no longer safe to live there. Sven cursed the loss, but it was no catastrophe. None of the villagers had been injured, and they had already been safely assimilated into other communities.

"In all, it could be worse," Sven admitted. Then he reviewed the progress he and the teachers had made in the last season. It wasn't until the end that he remembered the incident with the slavers. He told the story to Brand almost in afterthought, but the other wizard's mouth was a tight line by the time he finished.

"What's wrong?" Sven asked.

"You just let them leave?" Brand sounded angry.

"I'm not in the habit of killing every magocrat who annoys me. I made a few threats, and they left without a fight. If they come back, maybe I'll be more forceful."

"If they come back?" Brand demanded. "They're Flasten slavers. When they come back, the dux will send a dozen magocrats with them."

"Why would he? Tortz is so small, and it isn't even ... " Sven stopped mid-sentence, realization dawning. He stared at Brand with fire in his green eyes. "We're on the other side of the border, aren't we? You killed the magocrat who was sworn to the Dux of Flasten."

Brand laughed mirthlessly. "Actually, no. I just never sent the tribute."

"You broke your oath of fealty," Sven said with barely controlled rage. *Oathbreaker. For all I know, he's been passing out torutsen all over the Protectorates.*

"Which I gave under duress," Brand amended, a little defensively.

Sven collapsed into a chair near the fireplace. "Which is why you broke the Unwritten Laws. You were already a dead man. Why not make it harder for Flasten to arrest you?"

"The Law is an unjust relic of the past." Brand sounded like he sincerely believed it.

Sven had no response to that. He watched the fire devour the blocks of peat.

Brand sighed heavily. "If you want to leave, Sven, I'll understand. This is not your war."

Sven rubbed his temples with one hand, contemplating his options. After a moment, he reached a decision. "I'm not abandoning Tortz."

"Thank ... "

Sven stood up and whirled on Brand in a flurry of green cloth. "I'm not doing this for you! You're an oathbreaker, a murderer, and you've broken Bera's Unwritten Laws. There is nothing anyone can do to keep you from the executioner's fire, least of all me." Sven pointed at the front door, toward the rest of the town. "But they've done nothing to deserve your fate. I'm staying in Tortz for the people of Tortz."

"The dux's magocrats won't spare them. Any they don't kill will go to Flasten Palus as slaves."

"I will hold Tortz against them until Nightfire comes to judge you and your apprentices," Sven said slowly, through clenched teeth.

Already, plans began to form in his mind. New spells emerged from pure necessity. Old spells found new meaning. Sven felt a smile creep across his face. This would certainly be the greatest danger he had faced since his graduation.

"How can you possibly ... "

"I can do it," Sven snapped, cutting him off. "I need you to do exactly as I say from now on."

"Of course," Brand said, but Sven could see doubt in his eyes.

"First, you need to identify every person in Tortz who can pass an inquisition."

"None of them can ... "

"You'd be surprised. Those who can pass stay. The rest evacuate. No one who stays can know where the evacuees are going." *Brand would not do it himself.* "Put Bui Beglin in charge of it. He has a veteran mapmaker's tenacity, but if his life ever depended on writing his name, well, he'd be a dead man."

"But you'll need him for ... "

"No, I won't." Sven paced briskly. "We'll keep teaching the ones who stay — get them ready for the inquisition. Based on the Law, I have some idea what questions Nightfire will ask."

"How do you intend to ... "

"Stop interrupting!" Sven shouted over him. "If you feel any loyalty at all to the people of Tortz, you will obey me without question." More pacing. "I'll handle the recon and defenses. We know how ravits fight, but maybe Flasten's magocrats don't."

Brand said nothing.

"Yes?"

Brand pursed his lips briefly. "What role will I play in this?"

The most unreliable and unpredictable of my allies? What indeed?

"Keep the fire burning," Sven said simply, and Brand winced as if struck. "Renew the defenses of the Protectorates and send Erbark here. I have an errand for him."

"Do you want me to take Erika to Leiben?"

Sven struggled fiercely with that for a long moment. She was one of the best teachers in Tortz, and he knew she could pass an inquisition.

I'm fighting wizards. If they're cleverer or luckier than me, I won't be able to protect her. This is the wrong choice.

"No," he said at last, suddenly more exhausted than he could ever remember being.

Brand left him, and Sven settled in for a long night spent redesigning the town's recon stone.

 **21**

"Any Mar who has observed the behavior of the Drakes can tell they are not the mindless monsters they seem in tales. Damnens are clever enough to capture Mar for use as herd animals. Gobbels with access to iron manufacture weapons. Ochres employ scouts and systematically test enemy defenses. There is not even enough space in this introduction to do ravits justice. Suffice to say ravits are the reason no duxy established between Flasten and Wasfal has ever lasted more than twenty years."

— Nightfire Tradition,
Catalogue of Drakes

Half a season later, in the autumn month of Heldnat, a force of twelve magocrats approached Tortz boldly, even recklessly. Sven monitored their advance from the recon stone in his home as he sipped his soup. The amber and green specks reached the outermost defenses, and two of the greens winked out immediately.

Walls of fire activated by the bright colors wizards wear, Sven thought, spitting out a sliver of bone.

Two other green specks vanished mere seconds later, and the remaining wizards withdrew several dozen yards. By the time Sven finished the last of his soup, the Flasten magocrats had retreated beyond the range of his reconnaissance.

They will drink some torutsen and return with counterspells, Sven thought, but they didn't. *They will circle around looking for a gap in the defenses and discover there are only traps on the southern perimeter,* he knew, but they never did.

Sven watched the recon stone until his eyes ached and the sun was low in the sky. He fingered a pair of gloves at his belt, felt the tiny lumps of iron inside. Before Tortz, he had only used them to set up the defenses that kept the Protectorates safe from Drakes — a way to compensate for his lack of experience wielding many magicks at once.

I just drove away eight wizards, including a fourth-degree! I did it without any help. From six miles away. While eating soup.

A chill crept up Sven's spine even as he fidgeted excitedly. He had won this first battle, not just decisively, but utterly. He had killed four wizards without getting up from his rocking chair, and that was horrifying. It was marvelous! It was ...

Too much. This is open rebellion. The dux can't ignore this. He'll send an army next time. How can I fight an army?

Autumn had turned to winter by the time Arnlaug Saugen, Flasten's amber, returned with an army of forty wizards and three hundred mundane warriors at his back. Geir Tragget reported their arrival to Sven as the wizard finished renewing the few defenses on the eastern perimeter of Tortz's reconnaissance.

Heliotosis moaned softly, whistling through the frozen branches of briars and dead sedge grasses. The cold was bitter enough without the wind. By night, the rivers froze solid. At the peak of the day's warmth, ice merely lulled a person into a false sense of security before giving way — plunging a Mar into the cold water. Winter was deepening. Snow clouds gathered in the sky to a size and color as threatening as a summer storm.

As soon as Sven saw the recon stone, he dismissed the three villagers watching it, urging them to silence. He saw the panic on their faces as they left, their unasked question the same as his.

How can we fight an army of wizards? We can't. I can't.

It was all Sven could do not to slump in defeat before he even closed the door.

What is taking Erbark so long? He should have reached Nightfire's Academy and come back by now.

He collapsed into the rocking chair and watched the recon stone.

The army had pulled back beyond the range of Tortz's reconnaissance, which meant the wizards were using torutsen to determine the limits of its range.

They'll skirt the perimeter in search of gaps. Most of the traps on the eastern and western sides are diversionary, and none of them will work on mundanes. If I could find some way to draw them into ...

Sven had an idea. He sorted through his supply of gloves and took a sip of torutsen before heading outside. Snow fell, and the wind quickly sucked at his body heat in spite of his thick winter cloak.

When he came within two miles of the edge of the enemy camp, he removed a stone as wide as his hand from a pocket and poured myst into it with one gloved hand. He dropped the stone into the snow and moved to another spot a hundred yards away, doing the same.

Each stone was a distillation of a principle of his reconnaissance stones. Instead of tracking enemy wizards, they actually ignited Energy in the air around them. Anyone who approached might get a light surface burn — no worse than touching a metal spoon left in boiling soup too long.

He was nearly frozen stiff by the time he finished the last of the stones.

Sven retreated to within a couple miles of Tortz and put on a final pair of gloves. They wouldn't do the job by themselves, so he had to call some of the myst himself this time. The snow was coming down more heavily now, and he had difficulty picking out the colors of myst between the flakes of white. He hurled four balls of fire to the heart of the Flasten camp, crackling infernos muffled and hidden quickly by the snow. He had no idea if they hit, but it would have to be enough.

Not many will die, but no one will get any sleep tonight, Sven thought as he made his way back to Tortz.

What he saw on the recon stone in his house shocked him. The bombardment of fire had done more than force the army to fall back or waste magic locating and shutting down the fire stones, which were no more than a lure anyway. The army was on the move in the dark and blinding snow, clearly convinced they were under attack.

You wake to fire coming down on you, then you see more explosions among the trees and think that people are out there fighting. But someone gathers you after the first few moments of confusion. And now they have bit on the lure.

The Flasten army tromped into the midst of Tortz's traps. Snares of Power and Energy grabbed those who blundered into them and burned them where they stood. Explosions of Energy with Vitality burned deep beneath the skin, making the wounds harder to heal.

Half a dozen wizards had winked off the reconnaissance stone in just a few short minutes, and the mundanes had suffered even more casualties. Sven stared at his pile of discarded gloves in shock, horror and renewed pride.

But surely they'll eventually notice each attack is on a regular time interval. Someone will figure out the attacks are coming from fixed points. At the least, they'll recon and realize there are no wizards out there in the snow — just another kind of trap.

After two hours of setting off traps on the southern perimeter, the attackers showed no sign of discovering the ruse. By the end of the night, a sizeable percentage of the army had fallen to the traps. The survivors were out of range of the recon stone and, no doubt, the fire stones, as well.

"What's happening, Sven?" Erika asked from the entrance to their bedroom. She sounded as exhausted as he felt.

Sven looked up at her and grinned in spite of himself. "It worked, Erika! A hundred mundanes and twenty wizards killed in one night by nothing but our perimeter traps. This should not be possible."

She recoiled slightly, but he couldn't understand the shock on her face.

"I think the heavy snow helped. They could not see the myst. Maybe now they will give up and go back to Flasten!"

At last, she found her voice, but it was faint, pained. "You killed ... non-wizards?"

Horror abruptly overtook Sven's glowing delight. He gave the gloves a look as if it had all been their fault, and then scrubbed a hand over his chin. He looked at his hands.

What am I doing? Protecting mundanes by killing mundanes? Buying the lives of Tortz's people with the lives of Flasten's mundanes? I should be ashamed.

He wasn't. He couldn't remove all the traps guarding Tortz's perimeter. There were too many wizards for him to fight alone, and if he didn't defeat this invasion, those magocrats wouldn't hesitate to enslave the people of Tortz. All but two hundred had evacuated, but Sven knew the Dux of Flasten would not stop here. If the dux's magocrats won too easily in Tortz, they would know the Protectorates were vulnerable — ripe for conquest.

"I cannot undo it," Sven said softly, head bowed.

"Come to bed," she said, and he heard a note of pity. "Leave the defense of Tortz in the hands of the gods for a little while."

The gods? There are still plenty of traps left, if they don't counter them all with Elements.

But he said nothing, merely obeying her. Outside, the snow whirled, and Heliotosis' icy breath bit even harder.

A whiter morning Sven could not have imagined. The snow had piled up fully sixteen inches and showed no sign of melting anytime soon, though the clouds had thinned out such that only a few flakes still descended from the realms above. The watch on the hills reported that the magocrats' army was now visible on the moors below, the drab clothing of the mundanes standing out no less than the green, auburn and amber of the wizards on the white blanket. Sven bundled up in two green cloaks and went to the top of one hill to wait.

It was obvious that the fifteen surviving wizards had completely run out of torutsen. A hundred mundanes marched toward the hills nervously, only slightly more afraid of the magocrats' wrath than they were of the renegade town's defenses. Many of the attackers looked on the point of dropping from exhaustion and the cold, as if the blizzard and the bitter wind had battered them even more than the traps had.

The amber stepped forward, and Sven immediately recognized Arnlaug Saugen. "Defenders of Tortz, we demand your surrender!"

Sven took a sip of torutsen, slipped on a fresh pair of gloves and stepped forward so they could see him on the wall. He tried to match the amber's haughtiness. "Weard Saugen, I warned you what would happen if I saw you in Tortz again. Do you remember?"

Arnlaug opened his mouth to answer, but Sven didn't wait. He wiggled a finger, and a ray of heat sliced off the amber's head. Arnlaug's corpse collapsed into the snow.

As easy as that. I expected him to be better-prepared.

The wizards took several steps back, their faces masks of shock.

You'd think I'd just used morutmanon, Sven thought. *Of course, no green could have done that, so I suppose they just don't know what to expect next.*

Something tickled his mind, telling him there must be more to it than that, but he pushed it aside, for now.

"These are Tortz's terms. Leave or die. Tell your dux this town owes him no tribute. If he sends another army, he will lose another army. Is that understood?"

One of the two remaining auburns nodded her assent, but none of them spoke. She jerked her head, and the withdrawal began. The greens collected the body of their fallen leader, and the remnant of the Duxy of Flasten's army returned from the direction they had come.

Not all of them reached the edge of Tortz's reconnaissance. Some fell prey to traps, others to Heliotosis' wind or Dinah's Curse. Dissent and desertion would plague them on the way back. But most of them would return to Flasten Palus to tell Volund of their defeat at the hands of a single green.

A green who had killed the dux's youngest son in cold blood without hesitation or remorse.

"Why did you not tell me he was Dux Feiglin's son before I killed him?" Sven demanded.

Brand drummed his fingers on the arm of his chair. "Would it have stayed your hand?"

Sven considered this, but Brand didn't wait.

"You told me you were not in the habit of killing magocrats. I took you at your word."

"I said I would be more forceful if they came back." Sven frowned. "You did not expect me to be here when you returned, did you?"

Brand gave him a weak smile. "You should not have had a chance against the first attack, much less the second."

"I should have lost the second battle. The snow was higher than the level of the recon stone's scans, and they could not see the myst in the blizzard, so of course they blundered right into the traps as soon as they were under attack."

Brand shook his head, expression serious. "I do not know where you learned these magical applications, Sven, but it is not right for you to wear the green any longer. You should leave Tortz before Dux Feiglin shows up to exact his revenge on you."

"He has no legal grounds against me."

Brand barked a mirthless laugh.

Sven sighed. "You're right. That won't stop him. Still, too many of his magocrats have seen my face."

"You are my prisoner," Brand said, his tone matter-of-fact. "You acted in Tortz's defense under duress. I have been holding your apprentices hostage, and I have threatened to murder the people of your Protectorates if you do not obey me."

Sven was in no mood for levity. "Very funny. I am sure they will believe ... "

"When was the last time I let you leave?" Brand asked, removing a flask from his cloak pocket. "And is not Erbark late returning?"

Sven stiffened and stared hard at Brand, searching for some sign that this was a joke. He glanced at the closed chest of metal-studded gloves three paces away.

Brand followed his eyes. "You know why that would be a bad idea, right?"

Sven glared at him. "Even if I am fast enough, even if you are bluffing, even if you have not used Elements to disperse the spells in them, killing you will not stop Flasten from coming."

Brand smiled with satisfaction. "It is good that you remember that. If you kill me, who will you blame for all those wizards you murdered?" He waved the flask at Sven. "Drink."

Sven snatched it and took a sip of the morutsen, tasted its sickly sweetness. "Volund will not care if I am your prisoner."

"He will not," Brand admitted with a shrug, "Unless you can convince him that you are more valuable to him alive than dead."

"How do you expect me to do that?"

Brand snorted a laugh. "You can be very convincing when you try. He may hate you, but he can not help but respect the effectiveness of your traps."

"I trust Volund with my knowledge even less than I do you."

"So be it. The best you can do is to die without betraying your interest in the Protectorates. If you return there, Volund will hunt you and enslave them all just to avenge his son."

Sven seethed. "And that is where you will be. If I tell the dux where you are, he will hurt the people of the Protectorates to punish you."

"Yes, but do not think I will be idle. The defenses will give me time to train many, many adepts in the Protectorates. Even Dux Feiglin has limits to his power over his magocrats." Brand smiled at him wickedly. "You did not really expect an oathbreaker like me to stay true to a promise like that, did you?"

"At least take Erika with you, Brand. You have nothing to fear from her, and as long as she is there, you can be assured I will not betray the Protectorates."

Brand shook his head. "You missed your opportunity. She stays in Tortz."

Sven stood up and tried to call the myst before remembering the morutsen.

"None of that, now," Brand said, and a wave of Power threw Sven to the ground. "Goodbye, old friend."

Then a fist of force hit Sven in the temple, and darkness descended.

What if Brand had told you he had been instructed to abandon you?

I would not have believed him. Why would my patrons treat me so cruelly?

You do not feed an entire tree into your fireplace. You must chop it into pieces first. You do not pour soup onto a log. You fashion the wood into a bowl first.

You were shaping me to be the Guardian.

You blamed yourself for your successes. You thought yourself wor-

thy of them because of your intellect and talents. You were too proud to learn faith. Only a miracle could have convinced you. Until you lost everything, you would never appreciate anything, least of all the gifts we gave you.

Tortz was when I started to suspect. If the snow had not hidden the traps, or if Arnlaug had attacked from another direction, I would have been defeated.

Yes. Who commands the snow? Who grants the gift of wisdom? Who rules the waters? Had Volund led an attack from the north with a hundred gallons of torutsen, Marrish himself would have defended you that day. The gods wanted you to make use of the gifts they gave you. We wanted you to know that you are strong because of us.

I do not feel strong now.

No leader is stronger than those who share his vision.

I must make the Mar stronger.

"I have been ordered to kill you, Sven Takraf." The voice was Katla's.

Ordered by whom? Volund?

Still drugged with morutsen, he couldn't summon the myst. He was as helpless as he had been in Tortz.

"I will not do that, even if it means Marrishland will burn. You must act quickly. The wizards are not here. It is too late for the Domus army to intercept the Flasten army."

"Too late?" *So the deadline passed while I was ill. This will be tricky.*

Sven tried to raise his arm, but he couldn't hold it up very high. "If Flasten's army makes it here, they will not be able to take Domus. There are still thousands of people here to protect the city."

"It will not be enough. You must make peace with Flasten before they reach Domus Palus, or all is lost."

Now I can pass the amendment. Flasten will be removed.

"Have you nothing to say for yourself?"

Every one of my ten thousand mundanes will learn magic.

"It appears I will have to save you once again."

Sven did not notice Katla vanish into the Tempest.

 **22**

*"The Mass is the true reason the wizards maintain
their numbers. As the number of magic-wielding Mar
rises, the Drakes become more aggressive. Legends say
that it is the Mass that guides Dinah's Children against
us. Some say it becomes more powerful every time we
activate the myst, like a magical leech. Its power spawns
more Drakes, and these Drakes descend upon our towns
to destroy them."*

— Nightfire Tradition,
Catalogue of Drakes

"Where is Eda Stormgul?" Sven shouted, irritable.

Here he was, healthy again, sitting upright by himself — at least,
with the help of pillows — and he couldn't go out and do anything
with it. He had been wise enough that when Erika had said, "Go
ahead, dress yourself if you want," he had known he wouldn't be able
to. He hadn't even tried. But it made him angry.

Horsa answered his question. "She went with Bui Beglin and his
men as per your orders before your condition."

Sven recalled the orders. "I did not order her to go. I told her to
send someone."

Horsa remained silent.

Then Sven remembered what he had planned to do with Bui ... *Did
my patrons plan this, too?* His mind raced to trace what could happen.
Twenty thousand trained wizards against twenty mundanes and a
cyan.

Bui and his nineteen "guerrillas" will die. Eda will die with them.

He shrugged it off as a best-case scenario. *Is obedience to me for the sake of revenge pleasing to my patrons?* Sven knew he could not answer that. *Sooner discern the motives of the Mass.*

"Horsa, where is the army?"

Sven had used Horsa and another priest to create a new reconnaissance stone, one that could be transported. Horsa was adept at the use of Vitality, and the latest stone now showed a relief map of the city, every tree pulsing with life. Not quite as bright as the little figures that marked Drakes, wizards, mundanes and slaves, but with some distinction between them.

Horsa gestured. "Well within the Duxy of Flasten, as per your orders." He frowned. "They would have had to turn back several days ago to be able to intercept Flasten."

Sven waved off his obvious statement. "Where is Flasten?"

"At the border, here. Between them and us are about a hundred and fifty towns, most of which still have their residents. Very few people wanted to leave their homes."

As expected, Sven thought. *But they will slow Flasten.*

He did the vectors in his head. *The Domus army will reach Flasten Palus three days ahead of the Flasten army reaching here — and that is still a month away. Can I train enough mundanes between now and then?* He wanted to hit himself. *The Drakes would have been perfect to attack Flasten, if I could have brought them to bear.* Instantly he saw a way he could have used the Drakes, but it was too late now.

"We need the Law," Sven said. "Or we are defeated."

"I did not quite catch that, Mardux."

Sven cleared his throat. "Horsa, you need to go to the army. Can you rebuild this version?"

Horsa nodded.

"Good. Listen. We will not lose Domus Palus to Flasten's army. You will take command, and this is what you will do ..."

Horsa Verifien wore a marsord out of devotion.

Since Nightfire had taken him from Rustiford so many years ago to be a slave, and then an apprentice, he had praised Marrish for enlightening him above everyone else. Having the Lord of Wind and Fire as his patron, plus his strength with Vitality, had earned his acceptance into the priesthood, and he had achieved the highest rank they allowed there.

A yellow cloak meant one was a spokesperson for a red, but if there was glory, it all went to the red. Then again, if there was trouble, the red took the blame.

He was as big as Erbark Lasik — in fact, they were cousins — but where Erbark had black hair, Horsa had dark brown. Where Erbark had muscles of steel, Horsa had muscles like rivers. Horsa was devoted to Marrish and the priesthood, and he quietly wielded great influence in that sphere. Horsa doubted even Sven suspected his role in convincing the priests to swear allegiance to him when he took the Chair. Horsa had hoped it would delay the bloodshed between Mar longer than this, but now he held hope that it would save more Mar in the long term than letting Volund have his way.

Upon receiving the Mardux's orders, he teleported to the leading edge of the army, certain the plan proposed by his Mardux would be enough to save Domus Palus.

That afternoon, Erika helped Sven to the Council with a frown on her face. He smiled and assured her he would return directly to bed after the meeting.

Dux Gruber Ratsell of Wasfal was there. Duxes Yver Verlren of Piljerka and Borya Zaghaf of Skrem were there — if only because they had no place else to go. Dux Wolber Verden was not there — Flasten's army was too close to Gunne Palus for him to be away from his army. Duxess Glyda Zaun did not put in an appearance. Since the battle at Skrem Palus, her words that this was an inter-duxy fight no matter how you twisted it had been proven true, and she would not budge from the Bastion at Pidel Palus. Dux Volund Feiglen, though invited, had refused to come.

"Fellow weards," Sven told the Council. "The Dux of Flasten has committed an egregious sin against the Duxy of Skrem. Even now his army comes through the Duxy of Gunne. Gunne has approved the following decree, which requires only a simple majority: The Dux of Flasten is a traitor for his attack on the Duxy of Skrem and subsequent invasion of the Duxy of Gunne. His lands, title and name are to revert to the Mardux's authority until such time as this Council agrees Flasten should exist again.

"I have signed this document, and I ask all of you to, as well."

They did, for what reasons Sven could only guess. But Borya's pen nearly tore the paper, and Yver was only slightly less emphatic. Gruber looked up as he signed.

"This does not yet give you the votes you need to create your adepts."

"Pidel's absence in the previous trouble with the Drakes was marked," Sven said. "The duxy's lack of involvement to save the Duxy of Piljerka is reminiscent of the fall of the Duxy of Despar. I make no accusations against the duxess. I merely note that her isolationism is hardly in the interest of the Mar. The following writ, also signed by Gunne already, suspends her seat on the Council until she returns to Domus Palus."

"You get your unanimous vote," Gruber said. "Every duxy is involved in this except Pidel, which is too far south now, and Wasfal, which will certainly never be involved. Why should I vote in favor of stripping Pidel of her rights? Then I will be giving up my own."

In answer, Sven motioned the three duxes to join him at the reconnaissance stone.

"I have not told anyone else about this," he said, pointing to the area north of Domus Palus. "We had focused our efforts south and east, which makes the stone more powerful. Routinely, though, I do a sweep to the north."

"The Mass," Yver whispered.

Sven nodded, redirected the myst. To the north, less than four hundred miles away, was a sea of Drake life. It extended off the map.

"We must make the adepts," Sven said quietly. "The Mass approaches."

"We must make peace with Flasten," Gruber said, his voice shaking.

Skrem shook his head. "Never!"

Gruber did not seem to notice. "We need his wizards to defend

Domus Palus!"

Sven displayed the writ for Wasfal and held out a quill. "Sign this, and we will have more magic-wielders in Domus than exist in the rest of Marrishland."

In the light of tens of thousands of invading Drakes, the Dux of Wasfal stripped the Duxess of Pidel of her Council seat, to save Marrishland from a threat that didn't exist.

Falsified intelligence is more dangerous than no intelligence at all, Sven thought. *With luck, Wasfal and others who might be my enemies will not recognize the deception until the adepts are too numerous and useful to destroy.*

No single recon spell could stretch four hundred miles. Sven would have had to set up an entire network of recon stones in the Fens of Reur to see across them.

Reconnaissance can be falsified on either end of the spell.

On the map, the imaginary Mass crept forward.

In the Fens of Reur, the real Mass crept forward.

Riding on a platform on top of a striped guer — one of the largest species of guer — Katla felt like the tiniest speck of myst in Marrishland. The Wave Commander, a jabber guer, stood near her, watching the army pulse below them. He had long since gotten over the novelty of having her there.

Despite herself, she looked back over her shoulder. Of course she could not see the Second Wave. It was more than a span behind them, and east besides — the First Wave stripped the land of everything as it marched south. But it was coming. She had seen it form, and the Third and Fourth Waves. She stared back ahead, trying to convince herself she was still in control. They had not let her talk to the Delegates yet.

You had better get those wizards back to the capital, Sven!

It was the only hope the Mar had of surviving, and even with her brother in charge of the forces there, she knew it was a dim one.

So many will die in this war — Drakes, mundanes and magocrats. By Seruvus, it was not supposed to come to this!

Bui, Eda and the others from Tortz hid in trees on the edge of Flasten's army, well above anyone's line of sight. Like any Mar army, this one stretched and compacted like a snake's belly as it moved through the swamp. Occasionally, several dozen greens would drift far to one side and then trickle back in.

Slowly but surely, five were headed their way.

Bui waved two fingers at Eda, who passed the signal around to the other side.

Two minutes.

They slowly counted to one hundred twenty, until the five were below them, and then, with a holler, they pounced on the wizards. Eda countered the few spells that would have been effective at such close range as knives flashed and blood spurted.

The five wizards never stood up again.

Quietly, the mundanes stripped the wizards of cloaks, gloves, boots and rations, and then they disappeared into the swamp.

War.

The word reverberated off the trees. It flowed with the rivers. The mud sucked it up, and konig worms ate it, infected the Drakes, and they knew of it. And as the Mar rediscovered the power they had unleashed, the Mass, dark and sinister, crept south toward Domus Palus.

The Domus army tramped through the Duxy of Flasten, following their Mardux's last orders to them. When they came across Drakes, they killed them, exterminating a problem Dux Feiglin had fought for many years. During that time, they learned.

Before war, there had been battles. Battles had been individual confrontations or paid-for events for most of the army's wizards. Battle magic was limited to blasts of Power and Energy — hardly anyone spent time on defensive magic. The wizards were better healers than warriors, but they weren't skilled enough to cure disease.

Now, they were learning to work together. They had heard of Hall-gerd and Flosi and their disastrous battle because of lack of knowl-edge. They had seen how Sven had wielded a thousand wizards like a razor to an infected leg, dividing and defeating chunks of Drakes. They practiced that.

Flasten's army pulsated. On a reconnaissance stone, the brilliant blob representing the army birthed a hundred little scouts — groups of eighty, a hundred or more wizards sent to "retrieve deserters" or "hunt ravits." And interspersed with them, between them, among them, entirely invisible, were the guerrillas, abiding by their remorse.

In Domus Palus a new army formed. The priests were appointed to gather mundanes and teach them magic. There came to be three types of rotes passed on. Attack adepts learned Power or Energy. De-fense adepts learned to create walls of force and the basics of coun-tering magic. Healer adepts used Vitality to cure burns and broken bodies. All were given bright green armbands to wear over their cloaks, patches torn from a dead green, a reminder of what power could bring you.

The Duxy of Pidel heard of the war and did nothing.

The Takraf Protectorates fought a different war, a war against it-self. It was quiet, it was insidious, and it didn't show up on Sven's reconnaissance stones. What alarm would sound if groups of Mar wandered from town to town in the Protectorates where Sven had worked for years to encourage inter-village cooperation? Einar ex-plained the one red the stones showed. Anti-divination spells sur-rounded Robert, Valgird and Ari as they plunged into the Protector-ates like a boot into mud — with little or no resistance and perfectly protected by Sven's defenses from the dangerous things they might otherwise have encountered.

 **23**

"While Mar scholars are best known for their devotion to logic and empiricism, mundane Mar have always placed great trust in the interpretation of natural phenomena. It is not so surprising, then, that Sven Takraf so often sees omens and portents scattered throughout his life, guiding him on the path set for him by the gods. The thinkers of the Duxy of Pidel prize and practice both modes of thinking — one for its practicality and the other as necessary to living a good and moral life."

— Pondr,
Collected Journals, edited by Weard Asa Sehtah

The Bastion of Pidel Palus was the most bizarre structure Erbark had ever seen. Four roads led to the rise of land upon which Pidel had built the Bastion. One led to Domus Palus, another led out of the country, a third to the docks along the southern coast. The last led north into the Dead Swamps, once the road to Despar Palus. Eight spires marked the points of the octagonal fortress. Every wall was identical — perfectly level, precisely forty blocks of stone high. Amazingly, the Bastion lacked a gate. Each road led to a blank stone wall, and there were no windows — just tiny air holes.

"How am I to get in?" Erbark said out loud.

Teleportation, he realized.

The Duxy of Pidel was reputed to be the only region in Marrishland able to produce wizards as skilled as the graduates of Nightfire's Academy. Only the duxess and her closest councilors lived within the walls of the Bastion. The duxess's advisors were all powerful wizards. They did not need guards on the towers, and they did not need gates. Their magic was enough to provide both defense and accessibility.

No green's Mobility trick can get me inside, nor would a stairway of Power. Linetel requires a clear path to travel. Formtel cannot travel uphill. Memtel cannot access a place never visited.

Erbark could use none. Even ambers seldom learned these lesser types of teleportation.

That leaves hightel — true teleportation.

That was the teleportation of reds and some yellows. It was as much out of his reach as morutmanon. The statement the Bastion's design made was clear.

"Peace in the swamp," a woman's voice said in Middling Gien behind him.

Erbark whirled and found himself facing a middle-aged woman dressed in red. *"Peace in the swamp,"* he responded, the language sounding unnatural in his mouth. *"I am Erbark Lasik."*

She spoke quickly, easily. There was a poetry there. *"I am Duxess Glyda Zaun. You have come not in peace but in war. I see the Mardux's marks upon you."*

Erbark struggled to translate the words as she spoke them. He raised his right hand in salute and prayed she would not force him to argue rhetoric in Middling Gien. *Sven should have sent someone else.*

"I beg your aid," he managed, his pronunciation clumsy. *"Side with us and you will end this war. Flasten knows he cannot defeat all the duxies."*

"The Duxy of Pidel will not involve itself in the conflict between Domus and Flasten." She spoke firmly and without room for argument.

Erbark gave up, switching to Mar. "The Mardux didn't want a war between Mar. His enemy is Dinah, but Dux Feiglin has sided with the Bald Goddess against Marrishland. Mardux Takraf only wishes an end to this bloodshed."

The red continued in Middling Gien, but she spoke more slowly. *"No Mardux has won a battle against Dinah. She is a fearsome goddess when moved to revenge."*

Erbark could tell this would be difficult. He began unlacing his boots, every childhood teaching screaming against it. "The Bald Goddess is not omnipresent as is Seruvus. We Mar have feared Dinah and her curse too much for too long. The Mardux can tame her, but he cannot do that if Flasten continues to betray Marrishland."

She stretched out a hand to touch his shoulder. Her grey eyes brimmed with wonder and curiosity. She spoke Mar with a thick Middling Gien accent, evidence of the Gien Empire's influence even after centuries of freedom. "Keep your boots, weard. I have some soup. I will hear your cause in the Bastion."

Erbark obeyed. A black portal opened in front of him, and he suddenly realized Pidel Palus' stronghold could also serve as an effective prison. With a silent prayer to Fraemauna for guidance, Erbark stepped through the darkness and into the Bastion.

He passed mere minutes in the silent sense deprivation of the Tempest before arriving in a narrow hallway. The duxess stood a pace away, and it was a mark of the duxess' skill with teleportation that neither of them suffered a twinge of teleportation sickness.

To say nothing of the accuracy necessary to arrive in such tight quarters.

"If you'll follow," the duxess said in Middling Gien, beckoning.

Erbark walked with her through unornamented corridors. From the outside it had appeared as large as the citadel of Domus Palus, but the closely spaced wooden doors spoke of small cell-like rooms, not the vast, vaulted gathering chambers of the citadel.

What it lacked in physical detail, the Bastion made up in magical artistry. Energy spells lit the windowless corridors. A Power-driven draft circulated fresh air through the narrow area. They walked past many wizards going about their business, none of them below the lavender of sixth-degree. The few open doors they passed gave Erbark glimpses of vast libraries, impossible fountains that flowed backwards or sideways, a room filled with marsords and similar spectacles. Every one of them spoke of the duxy's wealth, knowledge and magical power.

She's trying to impress me, Erbark knew, but he couldn't help being a little impressed in spite of himself. *She could have brought me directly to the audience chamber or sitting room or wherever we're heading.*

The duxess stepped toward a door at the end of the hall. It opened silently without so much as a gesture from her, revealing a well-lit room occupied by three stuffed couches in a circle around a small table.

"Have a seat, Weard Lasik," she said, still speaking Middling Gien. "The soup will arrive shortly."

Erbark nodded and entered the room. She followed him. The door swung gently shut behind her and locked with a soft click. Ignoring the sensation of having walked into a trap, he sat on one of the couches. The duxess sat on a second, and it wasn't until her knee bent that Erbark noticed the shorter gouger blade of a marsord peeking out of a slot in her cloak.

Her eyes followed his, and she smiled slightly. "Does this surprise you?"

He shook his head.

"It surprises me to see a green wearing a marsord."

He shrugged. "It's a useful tool — a saw, a machete, a utility knife, a serviceable hunting device."

"A weapon," she added.

"When necessary, yes."

"Yours has killed."

"Many times, duxess. There were once many gobbels on the Morden Moors."

"It has killed Mar?"

Erbark struggled with the structure of his reply. He didn't like where this conversation was going.

"Is it so difficult to answer yes or no?"

He lowered his eyes and bowed his head. "Yes, but never without need. It is a great sadness for Mar to kill Mar, even to protect my master and his family."

She said nothing for a long time, and Erbark could feel her weighing his words. When the duxess spoke, it was in Mar, which Erbark interpreted to mean he had passed her first test. "Do you know why the Duxy of Pidel has always remained politically neutral?"

He left his head bowed deferentially and spoke in a near whisper. "I cannot know, Duxess Zaun. I can only interpret."

"Do you mock me?" she demanded.

"No," Erbark said without raising his voice, though he looked up slightly. He had intended for her to assume he was referring to omen reading, and she had risen to the bait. "Pidel's actions in times of civil war are predictable, but no one understands its motives."

After a pause, she spoke calmly, and her voice took a lecturer's tone. "Nightfire teaches that the myst is nothing more than energy — coming from somewhere ill-defined and going somewhere just as mysterious. We believe the souls of Mar become myst at the moment of death — lingering in our world to protect the Mar from Dinah and Domin."

"Watch over us, my fellow Mar," Erbark murmured, reciting the prayer for the dead. "Shelter us with your darkness and guide us with your light. By your sacrifice, we are warmed. By your sacrifice, we can see. By your sacrifice, we live on."

"Yes." She sounded pleased. "The power of the shades is limited, but Marrish grants wizards the power to guide the spirits in a concerted effort and to use their strength to aid their descendants."

"The myst and stars on the same side. The dark dead guard. The bright dead guide," Erbark recited. He looked directly into her grey eyes even as the startled look grew accusatory. "Like Pidel, the Mardux's motives are less obvious than his actions."

"His amendment is reckless. It will bring Dinah's Curse down on Marrishland."

"He wishes to fulfill the dream of Weard Darflaem — the first Guardian of the Mar."

"Or he hopes to raise an army of adepts to consolidate his power," she countered crisply.

"Weard gave Marrish's gift to anyone who came to him for instruction. Sven wishes to do the same."

"Weard did not use his power to kill those who made themselves his enemies."

"Sven's only enemies are those who serve Dinah's children."

"But they are Mar nonetheless, and he would turn the shades of the dead against the living."

"He did not begin this war. Flasten has invaded. He has broken the Law, while the Mardux wishes to obey it. Why side with Dux Feiglin?"

"Both sides are in the wrong, Weard Lasik," the duxess said with cold fury in her eyes. "Pidel will side with neither. Flasten received the same answer."

Erbark stiffened. It shouldn't have surprised him that Volund would try to win allies. Flasten had convinced no one on the Council to side with him against Sven, not even Wasfal. Erbark knew he had reached an impasse in the negotiations, so he changed tactics. "What sign would you demand of the gods before you changed your mind, Duxess Zaun?"

She frowned. "Why is the magic of deception called Wisdom?" Glyda asked without explanation for the sudden change in subject. "Why is the magic of altering magic called Elements?"

Where is this coming from? "Both are translated from farl words, so perhaps the translation is imprecise."

The duxess gave him a mysterious smile and shook her head. "Ancient histories tell of wizards commanding the weather — summoning storms, calling down lightning, guiding the winds. No wizard can do that anymore — not with Elements or any other myst. Do you know why, Weard Lasik?"

"I'd guess either the stories were exaggerated, or the knowledge was lost," Erbark said hesitantly. He had heard only a few such stories.

"The scholars of Pidel Palus disagree."

"What other explanation is there?" Erbark asked, baffled more at this sudden transition than at the statement itself.

"Magic changed. We changed it. Oh, not deliberately. Marrish gave us control over the elements, but the gods later took it from us. Maybe we used it to make war with each other, and that was our punishment. Or maybe we needed to counter the magic of enemy invaders more than we needed to control the weather, and the cyan souls changed to serve that need."

"I suppose it is ... possible," Erbark conceded without enthusiasm.

She looked at him with deadly seriousness, her fingers flicking in irritation as she returned to Middling Gien. "*You think wizards of Pidel are Fulemon sitting on the library, believing they can hear the voices of the torvekson within.*" The duxess spoke several complex sentences so quickly Erbark could only pick out the words for "magic" and "empire" among them.

He spoke in Mar deliberately. "Please, duxess. I am less fluent in Middling Gien than you."

"I am sorry, Weard Lasik. The influence of the Gien Empire still runs strong in my duxy." She paused, as though trying to find a way to speak eloquently in a foreign language. "Changes in the myst tell us where the gods are leading Mar civilization. Dinah and Domin did not topple the Gien Empire by merely sending the Mass. They changed the rules of the magic the Giens relied on to expand and control their empire. The Giens had not imagined magic could change, so they were not prepared. The Duxy of Pidel will be." A brief pause. "You look like you have doubts."

"I don't see what this has to do with the Mardux."

The duxess set her empty bowl on the table and stood up. "It has everything to do with the Mardux." She gave him a weak smile. "If it makes you more comfortable, you can continue to believe I am waiting for a sign from the gods to tell me whether or not I should side with Weard Takraf, or whether he is simply tempting Dinah's wrath. Let us see how he deals with Flasten's invasion, first. You will be my guest until then, Weard Lasik."

 **24**

*"Reconnaissance is essential to any general, but it does
not always come without risk. A scout who is spotted
tells an enemy much about the nearness of your force.
A captured scout subjected to sufficient pressure might
actually yield more information about your movements
than thirty of your scouts might learn of your enemy's."*

— Weard Gilda Kronas,
Magic and War

When Einar arrived in Todsfal, the southernmost of the Protectorate towns, to renew the defenses, a bone-deep chill seized him. According to the recon stone in Leiben, everything here was normal, but a casual glance told him otherwise. Several buildings had been damaged, and the village square was little more than a scorched patch of bare earth littered with blackened corpses.

My worst fears have come true. Flasten has invaded.

Not a soul still breathed in Todsfal, though it appeared that many had fled or been taken slaves. Steeling himself for an escape from an army of wizards, Einar teleported north.

Verfal's condition was a little better, though there was still no sign of its inhabitants. Einar frowned and swatted a mosquito as it brushed his cheek. He glanced up to confirm what he already knew. A few scans with Knowledge told him the rest.

Robert is leading this attack. A Mar could not alter a recon spell on such a massive scale. This is worse than blindness. How many villages have they seized already?

He did not know and, short of a systematic check of every town in the area, could not.

Robert's army is out there somewhere. Even if he can send misinformation through the network of recon stones, it cannot be easy to conceal an entire army from the village recon spell.

He risked a recon north. An unusually large number of unmoving mundanes occupied the village of Zerst nine miles away, but there was no sign of wizards there.

Robert might be hiding the wizards, though.

He reconned east and west. He found six more empty communities whose recon stones sent local information to the hub here in Verfal. Verfal was one of the three towns that sent local recon information to the regional recon stone in Zerst.

He teleported to one of the towns on the eastern edge of the Verfal region and stretched out with a recon spell into another region of the Protectorates. The defenses there still held, supporting his hypothesis.

Einar teleported to Leiben's observation room, the center of all the Mardux's recon spells. A large, raised circle of clay flickered with specks of color in a detailed map of every yard of the Protectorates.

"You're back early," Asfrid Staute, the cyan, commented, her lips twitching in a half-smile.

"You are," Einar corrected her. He frowned and stared at the recon stone. Everything looked normal in the abandoned villages.

Definitely Robert.

"What is it, Weard Schwert?"

"Bring the other weards here. We have a serious problem."

By the time the recon stone had gathered information about all the other villages in the Protectorates, the sixteen wizards who taught at the new academy in Leiben stood in a circle around the recon stone. Einar looked at each in turn.

"We need to stop the reconnaissance stones."

"What? Why?" Asfrid asked.

"Dux Feiglin's pet farl is leading an army of wizards that has penetrated the Protectorates. The reconnaissance spells tell him exactly which villages to strike and where to find them. Worse, it is not difficult to follow the trail of recon from village to village all the way back to Leiben, and from here to every hub and village in the entire network. If they take this town before the network is broken, it will be a small matter to find and capture every community in the Protectorates."

There were several sharp intakes of breath.

"Moreover, the defenses in every village within ten miles of Zerst must be shut down completely. The farl can certainly trace signs of large standing spells at a shorter range."

"But that includes Leiben."

"The citizens will evacuate north with the contents of the academy library. The wizards will fan out along the lines of recon and break up the village defenses."

"But what if there are Drake raids?"

"Repel them. You are all weards. You can fight alone, too, and you know the secrets of the Blosin wand — including those applications of it the Mardux never dared publish." Einar touched the gloves at his belt. "Hold the perimeter as best you can and wait for Sven or me to contact you. Stockpile wands so that if Flasten presses on after Leiben, you will have the means to protect the people of the Protectorates. A lazy wizard is a useless magocrat."

"We are to be as magocrats, then?"

"As Sven was a magocrat, yes."

"And what will you do, Weard Schwert?"

Einar smiled grimly. "Hopefully, I will be able to convince Flasten that it must capture this bastion before it can conquer the rest of the Protectorates."

"You mean to fight."

"I mean to turn Leiben into a fortress that will serve as both trap and bait, and I intend for them to know who defends this place. By the time they capture it, the network will be broken and the army will be forced to wander aimlessly across the moors in search of the other villages. With luck, they will give up before long."

"Attrition. Flasten has greater worries than the Protectorates."

"Yes."

"Will Sven send us reinforcements?"

Einar wanted to lie. He wanted to comfort these accidental magocrats somehow.

"There will be no reinforcements until after the war is over. Your greatest consolation is this: Once Dux Feiglin realizes the Mardux will make no effort to defend the Protectorates, he will withdraw his force."

"What of those Flasten takes as slaves?" Asfrid asked softly.

Einar could almost smell the anger wafting from all of them. Many of those in the room were deeply opposed to slavery.

Reformers flock to Sven. They long to change Marrishland the way he did. He never speaks of Tortz. Would they embrace his ideals if they knew?

"By the Oathbinder, those who have been taken will not be enslaved for long by Flasten. Weard Takraf will win this war, and he will not leave his people to serve as slaves."

They nodded, accepting this.

"Give the word to the people. We have little time."

He watched them leave in silence, recalling a time long ago when he had given similar orders.

I warned them of the dangers. I taught them everything I knew. How could I have prepared them for the raids they faced that year? None of us knew the insero and ravits had formed such a powerful alliance.

He had lost his wife and all her children but the youngest that year. Einar had been forced to organize and lead an army of magocrats against the invaders mere hours after losing his family. Ari had never forgiven him for behaving like a magocrat when the boy thought Einar should have acted like a father, for once.

He was fourteen already, and his siblings were grown men and women when I married Freydisa. They were old enough not to need a new father. How could I have known he wanted me to be what he had lost as a young boy?

Einar wondered idly how his stepson was doing, but he soon turned his full attention to dismantling the recon stone and planning Leiben's defenses.

"You are still here?"

Sven and Erika walked the halls of the citadel daily so he could regain his strength. It had taken some time, but after half a year, he felt stronger. He felt ready to do something again.

At the same time, he had to keep himself from touching his scarred face, and when he looked into Erika's eyes, he often sought disgust for his white, blinded eye. He never saw any.

I must wait until the wizards of Domus and its allies are fully engaged in their war against the Flasten invaders. Otherwise, the magocrats may still have enough military might to wipe out the adepts once they discover my ruse.

But as a kind of penance for the harm he had done his wife, he felt he should spend more time with her and his daughter. That was what he told himself when he smiled at them, seeing in their eyes the fear that he would leave again soon.

The Traveller turned from the window and grinned at them. "There'sa ter'ble storm brewin', an' I feel it'll be ba' fra sev'al day."

"Your effected accent grows worse by the day, Pondr," Erika laughed.

"Some Mar in the most rural areas have unusual dialects." He bowed outrageously.

Sven leaned against the wall next to him. Erika's mirth faded to a mix of concern and relief, which a quick smile did not allay. He worried that she would stop him when he had to go, but then dismissed it — how could she stop him? He grabbed her hand and squeezed it, making her smile at last.

The Traveller went on. "You said there would be bloodshed, and right enough, there is. Are you ready to lead these people?"

"Are you playing my conscience?" Sven said wryly. "You tell me stories that remind me of who I am. You torment me with my past. Is there nothing else you can do?"

"Tell me why Flasten hates you so."

"That should be a story everyone knows. Tortz." *And where will this story take us? The point of Tortz is not that Flasten hates me. The point is the lesson of the fuel.* He thought about Eda, Horsa, Erbark and Einar — perhaps his first true students — and the test they were going through. *Have they learned?*

"Volund Feiglin is fairly closed-mouthed about his defeats, Mardux. And the town was destroyed."

"Except for me, Erika and Erbark."

"Erbark Lasik? He was there?"

"Let us get something to eat," Sven said, taking his wife's hand. "Brand lied to me about Erbark, among other things."

The two hundred remaining citizens of Tortz continued their studies. Despite Sven's urging them all to return to their homes, Erika and three other Protectorate teachers had refused to leave. They made great progress, under the circumstances, but they had a lot of ground to cover, and not all were as good students as Erbark and Erika. They could hope, at least.

Just as winter came to a close — when it seemed the magocrats had decided to leave Tortz alone until the mundanes reached the proper level of education — Nightfire, Katla and two reds arrived with Erbark. Sven didn't recognize his friend, at first, because he was clean-shaven for the first time since before Sven had left Rustiford with Nightfire.

Unlike the dux's wizards, Nightfire's entourage had no difficulty entering Tortz. They simply appeared on the village green. Shackles of Power arrested the movement of several surprised warriors who had charged forward to attack the invaders. The eighth-degree wizards seemed unperturbed, looking around casually at the town without fear and utterly in control. Not one drop of blood fell in the brief struggle.

Sven marveled at this even as he emerged from his home. *One red could have pacified us with ease. What could possibly stand against three of them?*

"Askr, Geir, that will not be necessary. I surrender." He raised his hands in a gesture of helplessness. "Peace in the swamp, good weards. Come to my house. I have some soup."

He recognized Nightfire and Katla immediately. *She wears amber already?* The sour faced man following was probably Dux Volund Feiglin of Flasten Palus. But the last face was unfamiliar entirely. This fourth was ancient, leaning on a cane. He wore a ring of braided silver and gold on the first finger of his right hand.

"Weard Takraf, you stand accused of a serious breach of Bera's Unwritten Laws," Nightfire said, looking very serious.

"I want to apply the fire to this wizard personally," growled the sour-faced red.

Definitely Volund.

Sven tried to match his teacher's gravitas. "Explanations are certainly in order, and I'm all too glad to provide them."

"All in the proper time, Weard Takraf," Nightfire said. "This is now an inquisition. Every person in Tortz is to return to his or her home immediately. Once there, you will surrender your boots and submit to a regimen of morutsen until the inquisition is complete. Any attempt to resist or escape will be tantamount to an admission of guilt, and that guilt will fall also on your teacher. Erbark, you will stay in a separate home. I see there are plenty that are empty."

"The fourth man was?" the Traveller prompted.

"Brack — the red who serves Dinah and Domin among the Drakes of the Mass."

"I've heard of the Mass. It's a giant monster that will come down on the Mar if there are too many wizards, right?"

Sven smiled slightly, eyes turned to the fire, the milky bulb of the left one flickering as though the flame was within it. "You could put it that way. Some say it is more magic-wielders, while others claim it is the amount of magic the Mar use that brings the Mass."

The Traveller gaped at him. "More use of magic means more Drakes? And what are you setting up here? What will happen when your army and Flasten's army meet on the field? Then you arrange for every Mar to learn magic. The adepts. Can you see the army that will attack you?"

"The Mass is probably no more than a story told to frighten young apprentices." Sven smiled grimly over his steepled fingers. "And if the Mass is real, it is too late for anyone to stop it from invading."

 **25**

"Middling Gien was invented during the Gien occupation of Marrishland by a Mar scholar. When spoken, it is nearly identical to Imperial Gien. The Mar, however, transliterated the Giens' pictographic written language into a phonetic alphabet based on magical concepts. For this reason, the Giens disparagingly regarded the Mar scholars' transliterations of their language as Middling Gien, since it shared only a few qualities of written Imperial Gien."

— Weard Eira Helderza,
The History of Linguistics

Sven spent the days drugged with morutsen and imprisoned in his own home with Erika, while Nightfire posed question after question to each person in Tortz. For the first several days, he heard nothing. Katla delivered their doses of morutsen, staying only until they drank it and never saying anything, though Sven thought she looked more worried with each visit. Once a day, she also brought them food, water and peat for cooking.

Sven only had a passing familiarity with the inquisition, but he suspected his sister's silence reflected the rules of the process. *I never intended to break the Law, so why would I care how Nightfire enforces violations of it?* He wished a hundred times over that he had taken an interest in it when he was an apprentice. It was nearly impossible to prove his innocence if he didn't even know how Nightfire would determine his guilt. *And I am not entirely innocent, am I? Brand made certain of that.*

For the first span, they heard nothing at all, and Sven allowed himself to hope. He and Erika made the best of a bad situation. They discussed the future they would have after the inquisition of Tortz. Sven continued her education — advanced Middling Gien and myst theory. They talked about starting a family. They told stories about their childhoods. They laughed and tried to be happy. They carefully avoided talking about the inquisition.

I'll beat it. My students know what to expect, what knowledge not to admit and how to behave. When I catch up with Brand, he'll wish he had lost the duel with Tosti.

Four days into the second span, the first villager failed the inquisition. Sven watched helplessly from his home as Brack and Volund led Askr to the prison that had held Sven on his first night in Tortz. They lifted Askr with Power and lowered him inside. Then Brack summoned fire, and Askr began to scream in pain.

Sven wanted to run out to them. To make them stop. Any law that punished Askr for Brand's crime was an unjust one.

It would be useless. I have no magic, and even if I did, I can't fight them. Not even the gloves would make me the equal of one red, much less three.

Behind him, Erika wept. Askr was her student, even if Sven had known him longer. He wrapped his arms around her and made noises he hoped were soothing.

If they found even one of my students guilty, they will find me guilty, too.

But he said nothing. Gradually, Askr's screams faded away into silence, but Sven knew his perfect memory would preserve that voice forever.

Or at least until they execute me, too.

But when Katla came that evening, she came alone with the usual dose of morutsen. She said nothing, and Sven could see from her bloodshot eyes that she had been sleeping badly, weeping or both. As soon as he met her gaze, though, she looked away, and she all but ran once her duty was done.

After Askr's execution, Sven and Erika spent every moment as if it would be the last they would have together. The future was lost. The past was mere myth. Only now mattered. Neither of them said it, but even if Erika survived the inquisition, they both knew Sven would not. The execution might happen today or tomorrow or in a month, but it would happen.

Nightfire did not come for Sven in the next span, which he at first considered a mercy. It meant he could spend more time with Erika before she lost him forever. Then Brack and Volund escorted six more villagers to the prison, and Brack brought forth a chorus of their screams.

It is not a kindness. This is the way Dinah punishes pride. She misses no opportunity to hurt me, for she means to crush me utterly. When they come for me, they will find me broken. I will have no pride left. I will be eager to confess quickly so I can die.

This time, not all the people of Tortz obeyed Nightfire's instructions. Nirta, one of the teachers from the Protectorates, rushed out of Brand's house barefoot, howling in rage. The blade of the knife in her upraised hand shone white in the sun, as if she wielded light itself as her weapon.

Volund smiled as he struck her with fire that engulfed her. The heat and pain should have laid Nirta low, but she kept running, her clothes trailing flames as if she was a burning star. She struck the wall of Power the dux erected and took a step backward. Volund didn't give her time to recover. A pillar of fire descended on Nirta, and when it vanished a moment later, she was gone. Not even the knife remained intact. Volund gave the scorched circle of earth an alligator's satisfied smile.

He loves death as only Domin should, Sven thought, hands shaking in rage at the spectacle. *As only Domin can.*

Erika touched his shoulder. "Pray with me, Sven," she said softly, fighting back tears.

He knelt with her on a rug facing the fireplace, and they held hands. The fire had begun to go out. Sven fed it more peat, and it crackled and hissed.

"Watch over us, friends. Shelter us with your darkness and guide us with your light. By your sacrifice, we are warmed. By your sacrifice, we can see. By your sacrifice, we live on."

Sven recited the words, but his heart was not in them. These deaths had not been sacrifices to the gods. Magocrats had murdered them to punish Brand's crime, and Brand walked free. He would break the Law again, and maybe he would find another way to escape justice. The apprentices he wielded and expended like myst, however, would not. They would die by fire like Askr, like Nirta, like Sven.

They came for Erika in the middle of the night, waking them both up from a dead sleep. She screamed Sven's name as Brack lifted her out of the bed with magic, while Volund held Sven down on the bed. The dux sneered at him the entire time as he crushed the breath out of Sven with Power until his vision grew dark.

When Sven came to, Erika and her screams of terror were gone, but the memories of her voice echoed in his mind. Another familiar voice shouted in the darkness outside his house.

Erbark!

The shout faded soon after, leaving another terrible echo. Sven clutched his head and groaned.

Everything I have done in my entire life has been for nothing! It would have been better if I had died during the passage to Rustiford. It would have been better if I had not been born.

He looked at the fire again, held his hands between it and his face, blocking its light.

What need do I have for fire anymore? I will be dead soon and yet not soon enough. Its heat is wasted on me. I cast nothing but shadows. I should let it go out.

Sven looked at his hands suddenly, saw them again for the first time. He opened and closed them. They seemed larger, the light of the fire casting huge, distorted shadows of them on the walls. They could kill from miles away now, strike down Drakes and Mar alike with equal ease. Yet they had been too small to save Tortz, too small to aid Erbark and Erika, too small even to keep himself alive.

My dream was always impossible. If I had hands as large as Volund's, I could not have achieved it. Nightfire's hands are too small, too. A Mardux's hands could not do it. How could I hope to do it as a mere green? How big would my hands have to be to create the Protectorates throughout Marrishland?

Sven looked at the trunk of Blosin gloves, all useless, now.

With those my tiny hands can slaughter hundreds. If I had, could I have done it? But imagine how many people I could destroy if my hands were big enough to change the Law. Thousands? Tens of thousands? Millions? And with hands so large, how could I help but slaugh-

ter a hundred here, a thousand there?

Sven knew he wasn't thinking clearly. He hadn't slept soundly in nearly a month. Every day brought a new grief, a new horror.

What does it mean that Nightfire has kept Erbark away from me?

Sven ran a hand through his hair and down across his unshaven face.

They want me to know I am utterly alone — like the final stick of firewood in the house. Once I am used up, the fire will go out.

But who are they? And why are they doing this to me?

A thousand fragments of stories from his youth and a thousand histories from Nightfire's library flooded him with replies.

Even alone, I still have Seruvus's memory.

The thought hung in his mind for a long moment, hummed like a single plucked string.

Seruvus knows I am innocent. My enemies are no more worthy to judge me than Weard Darflaem's murderous apprentices.

Suddenly, he knew. Sven rose to his feet and started pacing, his thoughts a blur of fragments that he had to draw into a pattern like myst.

This happened to Weard — the first wizard, the first Guardian. He gave Marrish's gift to anyone who came to him for instruction, and the magocrats killed him for it. The Law came later. The magocrats made it to keep the other Mar weak enough to control.

Sven saw shapes floating at the edge of his vision — flickers of color and movement like after images of the myst. He hadn't tasted torutsen in spans, and the morutsen should keep him from seeing the magic, but here it was. Green motes spun around cyan, pulled away and gathered together into the shape of a man.

Sven blinked, and the vision vanished. Had it even been there?

"Who serves the mundanes serves the gods," he murmured, reciting a passage from Weard's teachings. "To serve the gods, the Guardian must serve the mundanes and bring them Marrish's gift." Warmth spread through Sven's limbs as the words left his lips. He fell prostrate before the fire. "I will serve you if you will make my hands big enough," he whispered. "I will serve you."

Sven slipped out of consciousness. In his dreams, he saw nine gods, but they all spoke with Brand's voice. Try as he might, Sven couldn't understand what they were saying, so they kept talking louder and louder until they were screaming nonsense at him. Were they warnings? Threats? Demands? He couldn't tell, and he suddenly realized he had shut them out of his house, refused them his hospitality.

An unseen hand knocked on Sven's door. His eyes opened. Outside, the sky was grey with coming dawn.

"Enter, immortal patrons. I am ready to receive you," Sven said without stirring.

The door opened, and Katla stood in her amber cloak. Fraemauna's full moon hung over her shoulder, the goddess's yellow face looking down at him.

"Sven?" Katla called in a measured voice that betrayed fatigue. "Master Nightfire wishes to speak with you."

"How many times must I offer myself as tribute to him before I am worthy?" Sven asked through dry lips even as he stood up.

Katla looked startled to see him this way. She spoke gently. "You should shave before you meet with him."

"Wizards shave because it was a way to curry favor with the Giens back in Imperial times. The Giens could not grow beards, so the wizards chose not to," Sven told her, and then he burst out laughing. "Is that not ridiculous? The Gien Empire fell centuries ago, and we are still shaving! Why?"

We cling to old ways we no longer understand — like Bera's Unwritten Laws. But the magocrats trust the traditions and will kill anyone who breaks the laws the traditions have spawned.

"I will help you, if you need it," Katla said slowly.

Sven tilted his head and studied her face. *You are no more a slave to tradition than Brand was, but do you think you can make a difference in a fight against three reds?*

"I will not refuse you. I will need all the help I can get in this battle against Dinah and Domin."

Katla looked confused, but then her eyes widened. She smiled at him — the secret smile of siblings collaborating in mischief. "It is not yet the time, Sven." Her smile grew feral, full of hate long fermented and well-nurtured. "But they will pay for Mother and for Tortz. Of that you may be sure."

Is that what this is about — revenge? No. If I would serve the gods, I must serve the mundanes as Weard Darflaem did.

Katla led Sven to a chair and started shaving him, the razor cold against his trusting throat. He sensed his vulnerability, then, knew she had him completely at her mercy. He yielded to her unpracticed hand even as she cut him half a dozen times. She winced at every mistake, but he did not.

She is doing the best she can with the hands the gods have given her.

Sven watched the fire in the hearth burn as the blood trickled down his neck. The bottommost block of peat sat on the ashes of its predecessors. The flames licked the blocks above it experimentally.

"I should not tell you this," Katla whispered as she wiped the blood off his face with a hot towel, "but Brand returned to Tortz last night. He confessed. He defended you. He ... " Her voice cracked.

He burned, she meant to say. Sven looked at her with wide eyes. *His screams were more than a dream. They were a message.*

Sven looked back at the fire, and she followed his gaze silently.

When peat burns, it brings warmth and illumination to the people around it, even as it is used up. For what purpose do Mar burn?

Her green eyes fell, and her voice softened as if she was embarrassed to speak words of comfort in the face of his loss. "You have nothing to fear from Volund, now that I am here. He has wasted too much of his energy on this inquisition."

"What a waste of energy," Sven murmured.

Katla nodded.

Heliotosis' icy breath moaned as it passed over the prison entrance outside. Katla stood and helped him up. Sven followed her numbly, took the boots from her hands and clumsily stomped them on.

The lesson of the fuel. Sacrificing itself to warm and illuminate others — being a source of energy. The name my colleagues gave me at the Academy, the name I took when I earned the green — Takraf means energy. And I am the fuel for the fire.

His own name struck him like a cold wind. It came from two words that had been a part of the language since before the Gien Invasion — tat and kraft. *The first meant "act" or "deed." The second meant "divine or magical strength or power."* Sven nodded as he began to understand.

Katla sighed, eyes wet. "Brand was the sort of idealistic fool who once thought he could get away with anything. He chose a path he could not leave. He knew it, but he did the right thing, in the end."

Everything in Sven's line of vision had faded away to a blur. *The lesson of the fuel. The lesson of the fool. Brand, brand — "a mark made by fire." Marking the Mar with the gift of magic.*

Uneheilich gave Marrish's gift of magic to Weard Darflaem.

Darflaem: "Flame in the darkness." Flame in the darkness: "Night fire." Nightfire.

Weard Darflaem taught the Mar to use magic.

A flame in the darkness, bringing warmth and illumination to all. A torch. A brand. A Brand. Weard Darflaem was the first Guardian. He died without completing his mission.

"He passed the tests," Katla told him as they left his home.

Sven was unsteady as he walked. He couldn't remember the last time he had eaten. "He?"

"Erbark. Nightfire raised him to three degrees of apprenticeship away from the green," Katla said, clearly abandoning the pretense that he was still under an inquisition. "All your apprentices passed the tests. Only some of Brand's could not."

My hands will be large enough to finish what Weard Darflaem began. I will serve the gods by serving the mundanes. I will be their Guardian. My apprentices will pass the gods' tests.

A warmth spread through Sven's limbs. He looked up at the sky, thought he perceived a face in the clouds. Her, the sun, shone down, setting the snows on fire with her light. He had the distinct sensation of being surrounded by friends and allies.

"There are lessons to be learned from fuels," Sven told her.

"Yes," Katla murmured, her green eyes suddenly distant, sad. "Fire is pitiless."

Green is for Energy.

Sven laughed suddenly, stupidly. "What a waste of energy!"

Katla looked at him, her face a mask of concern. He detected anger there, too, but not directed at him. "You have been through a lot, Sven. You may wish to let others speak on your behalf today. Come."

She led, and he followed calmly, at last understanding the purpose of his life. Softly, he whispered a prayer of thanksgiving to Marrish and his other patrons. It would not be easy, but at least he would know the reason behind the trials. *More tests sent by the gods.*

 **26**

*"When one wizard kills another, the local dux receives the
power of life or death over the wizard. If the crime took
place beyond the borders of the duxy, however, the only
compensation a dux may demand is a weregild, which
is monetary compensation paid by the murderer for the
loss of a vassal, the maximum value of which is directly
proportional to the rank of the deceased magocrat."*

— Nightfire Tradition,
Vangard's Rules in Practice

The living area of Brand's home had been converted from a school-
room to a courtroom. Nightfire's lined face looked grave as Sven entered with Katla. He was sitting in a rocking chair, which spoiled this
effect somewhat. The ancient red with the gold and silver ring sat on
a three-legged stool to Nightfire's left, leaning heavily on his gnarled
cane. Dux Volund Feiglin stood next to the stool, leaning against the
wall near the hearth where a fire burned too much peat and the remnants of ... *is that a broken crib?*

There was no sign of Erbark or Erika — or anyone else, for that
matter.

They think I am alone, but I am never truly alone.

"Weard Takraf, stand before us," Nightfire addressed him.

Sven obeyed without hesitation.

"You have been accused of very serious crimes, including capital
offenses. Do you understand?" Nightfire asked, voice deadly serious.

Sven nodded. "I accept any trial to which the gods subject me,
master." He raised his hand in salute. "By the Oathbinder and my patrons, I will be worthy of this trial."

217

Nightfire rocked back slightly, frowning. By the fire, Volund failed to suppress a small, satisfied smile. His shadow from the fireplace flickered against the wall. The ancient red leaning on his cane remained utterly neutral and utterly still, as if made of stone. *Who is he?*

Suddenly, Katla was at Sven's side. "Weard Takraf cannot defend himself in his present condition."

"Who will represent him then?" the ancient red asked.

Even in his dazed state, Sven recognized the rhetorical question. Only a wizard could represent a wizard, and all but one was already involved here. *Did Nightfire choose to bring my sister, or did my patrons?* He wasn't sure there was any difference.

Nightfire spoke. "Weard Katla Duxpite, you will speak for Weard Takraf. Dux Volund Feiglin brings these accusations. Master Brack will speak for Dinah and Domin. As Master Nightfire, I will speak for Seruvus and the Law."

That's Brack — the dark wizard who commands the Mass?

Katla saluted. "By the Oathbinder I swear to defend the accused as best I can."

"Dux Feiglin, bring your accusations against Weard Takraf," Nightfire said.

Volund stood up but didn't move away from the fire. "Weard Takraf has broken Bera's Unwritten Laws. He has broken his oath of fealty to the Duxy of Flasten. He has broken the Morden Accords by setting himself up as a dux on the Morden Moors." The dux took a sharp breath and said nothing for a long while. When he spoke again, his voice and hands shook with rage, and he had to lean against the wall for support. "Finally, he and his accomplices murdered fifty-one of my magocrats, including Weard Arnlaug Saugen."

"What of all the mundanes who marched with him?" Sven asked mildly. "Or do their deaths not matter?"

Katla gasped. Nightfire frowned.

Volund took a step forward, his face twisted in rage. "You will pay as Brand did!"

"Peace, both of you!" Nightfire said. He shot a glare at the dux. "And if you touch the myst again before this trial is over, I will administer the morutsen personally." He took in the whole room. "That goes for all of you. Weard Duxpite, speak for the accused."

"Yes, master," Katla said, sounding embarrassed, almost contrite. "I regret the outburst. Weard Takraf, please have a seat over there and say nothing without instruction from me."

Sven opened his mouth to object. He could certainly defend himself against these ridiculous accusations. Katla placed a finger to his lips and leaned in very close to him. Her whisper was so soft that he still had to strain to catch all of it.

Swind's whisper, he thought with a small shiver. *Our father's gift.*

"I will save you from this, Sven, but you must trust me."

He nodded once and meekly obeyed, taking a seat on the pile of black cloaks by the door. Perhaps they had once belonged to the mundanes who had already been executed — victims of Brand's folly and the Law that had delayed Weard's dream for so long. *Who serves the mundanes serves the gods.*

Katla turned to Nightfire and Brack. She stood tall, with shoulders back and jaw set. With a voice that flowed from gentle to hard and back again, she attacked Dux Feiglin's accusations ruthlessly — seeking and exploiting vulnerabilities like an ochre systematically testing magical defenses.

Brand, Erbark and many others had testified that Sven had not been involved in teaching magic to mundanes. He would have brought the crime to Nightfire, but Brand held him prisoner through a combination of blackmail and direct threats of force. Even as a captive, Sven had worked tirelessly to bring Tortz into compliance with the Law — an impossible task under the best of circumstances, and yet only a handful of Brand's illegal apprentices had failed the inquisition.

By the end of it, Nightfire was nodding along with her. "You are correct, Weard Duxpite. Weard Brand Halfin has already claimed sole responsibility for this."

Brack said nothing, but he watched Katla with rapt attention.

Katla struck the other deadly accusations. Sven had not sworn fealty to any duxy, least of all Flasten. Nightfire dismissed that charge as well. That downgraded the seriousness of the murder charges substantially. If Sven owed no fealty to Flasten, Dux Feiglin had no power to sentence him. It would then fall to Nightfire to collect a weregild on Volund's behalf.

"While Weard Takraf owed no fealty to Flasten, he knowingly killed magocrats who did. I cannot accept the claim that he did not know who his magical traps would harm at the time he designed and placed them," Nightfire said, rocking a little. "As those wizards' master, Dux Feiglin is entitled to a weregild from Weard Takraf as compensation for those losses."

Volund looked at Nightfire with unmasked fury but said nothing.

Nightfire met Volund's eye with a placid expression as he rocked gently. "Dux Feiglin, the next time you suspect a wizard outside of your jurisdiction has broken Bera's Unwritten Laws, you will come to me immediately instead of taking their enforcement into your own hands. I alone am arbiter when it comes to judging the Law."

Sven could see the accusation on Volund's lips — bias of a master for an apprentice. Nightfire frowned, and the dux's words died in his throat.

"If Tortz lies within the Duxy of Flasten, Dux Feiglin, justice is still yours," Brack said, casting an irritated look at Nightfire. "And if it turns out that Tortz is not within your duxy, you will receive the maximum possible weregild. That much I can promise you." The dark wizard turned his attention back to Katla. "Weard Duxpite, you have one further accusation to address before we can pass sentence — one that interests the Mass greatly."

"The Morden Accords, yes," Katla said, and she sounded uncertain for the first time since entering the house. "In accordance with an agreement with the Mass, the Morden Moors are neutral territory. Mar and Drakes may live there, but neither is to establish a duxy in the region nor add territory there to an existing duxy. Tortz falls north of the established boundary of the Morden Moors."

"Masters, that is not correct," Volund said defensively. "The Grenz Verken shifted south only two years ago. Tortz has long been a part of the Duxy of Flasten."

Brack frowned at the dux briefly. "We will save the discussion for why you did not immediately relinquish your claim over Tortz for another time. Regrettably, she is correct on this count. Weard Takraf's crimes did not take place within the Duxy of Flasten."

Sven blinked at that. *Seruvus changed the river's course just to place me beyond the reach of my enemy.*

Katla spread her hands helplessly. "The other communities within Weard Takraf's so-called Protectorates possess superior magical defenses, but they do not fit the legal definition of a duxy."

"How so, Weard Duxpite?" Brack asked, his eyes intent upon her.

"First, he exacts no tribute from the mundanes who live in the forty communities there. Second, no other wizard has sworn fealty to him as his magocrat. To my knowledge, Weard Takraf is the only wizard acting within the Protectorates."

"Weard Halfin admitted to helping him," Nightfire observed.

Katla shrugged this off. "He no doubt hoped Weard Takraf would reveal the secret of those defenses. I suppose you could declare an inquisition on every village in the Protectorates."

Nightfire barked a laugh and rocked leisurely in the chair. "There must be tens of thousands of people living on the moors, Weard Duxpite. Brack and I have better things to do than chase thousands of flimsy accusations." At a look from Brack, though, he added, "I will, of course, send some wizards from my academy to investigate. If they find anything suspicious, I will take the appropriate action."

Brack nodded at this, satisfied. "Weard Duxpite, once Master Nightfire and I have finished our business here, I would sincerely like to speak to you." He smiled at her — a knowing, calculating smile. "You may go now."

Katla saluted and left without a word.

"Weard Takraf," Nightfire said. "Stand before us and receive our judgment."

Sven rose and obeyed, deliberately ignoring Dux Feiglin, who was no doubt still fuming.

Nightfire stopped rocking and leaned forward. "As punishment for your crimes, we levy a weregild of three hundred ounces of silver, three of gold, or one ton of common metals."

"Or three hundred mundane slaves," Brack added almost absently.

Sven tensed at the word.

"Or three hundred mundane slaves," Nightfire conceded. "Can you pay the weregild you owe Dux Volund Feiglin, Weard Takraf?"

Sven shook his head.

Volund threw back his head and laughed. "Your Brand Halfin made the same mistake. Do not think I will let you guard a border town as I did him."

Sven looked to Brack and Nightfire for explanation. Brack was nodding gently, as if he saw justice being done. Nightfire looked thoughtful.

"You now owe fealty to me as surely as if you had sworn it — until your debt is paid, and a green will never pay off a debt that large."

"I am not convinced he is a green," Brack mused aloud, and Volund looked at him. The ancient red's attention stayed on Sven. "Weard Takraf faced an army of wizards and won. He has earned the right to wear the auburn, at the very least, and probably the blue. But even a blue will serve you for decades, Dux Feiglin."

Volund sneered. "If he lives that long, of course. A magocrat's life is a dangerous one."

"Master Nightfire, is this true?" Sven asked, voice flat even though he dreaded the answer. *If I swear an oath to Flasten, he will never stop finding ways to avenge his son upon me.*

"Dux Feiglin is correct," Nightfire said, leaning back in the rocking chair, arms folded into his red cloak. "However ... " He looked thoughtful, and his hands shifted in the cloak. His eyes weighed Sven carefully. "My offer from before you graduated still stands."

"Offer?" Volund repeated.

Nightfire's hands moved, and a small pouch fell to the floor at the dux's feet. Silver and gold coins rolled out. "That should be adequate compensation for your loss, Dux Feiglin."

Volund let out a choking sob. "No! This is not justice! My son ... "

Nightfire looked at him with cold fury. "Your son took tribute where none was owed. Weard Takraf demanded no tribute even though he more than earned it. Take your weregild and leave Tortz."

Sven favored Volund with a smug smile. *You cannot defeat me over the objections of the gods.*

The dux snatched the pouch without bothering to scoop up the fallen coins. He stuck a finger in Sven's face as he passed. "This is not over, Takraf. By the Oathbinder and the Bald Goddess, I swear it!"

With a groan, Brack pushed himself up with his cane, limbs creaking. "Nightfire, we will talk about this more later, but if I sit on that stool for much longer, I will never be able to stand again. Peace in the swamp."

"Am I to be your slave?" Sven asked when the ancient red was gone.

Nightfire resumed his gentle rocking and didn't speak for a long minute. "No," he said at last. "You were too young to remember your birthplace."

"I remember some," Sven told him.

"Of course. Seruvus' memory."

Sven remained silent.

"Your magocrat was a student of mine. She was a cyan sworn to the Dux of Gunne, but she also considered many of the mundanes in her care her friends, including your parents. That is why, when she asked me to evacuate the border towns to somewhere out of Flasten's reach, I agreed." Nightfire heaved a sigh. "I am not supposed to take sides or play favorites. What I did today was dangerous, but I am not like Volund. No, you will not be my slave — not now, not ever again — but I want you to come back to the Academy."

"I have obligations, now, master."

"Yes, you do," Nightfire said distantly. "The wizards I send to investigate your Protectorates will renew your defenses. I will let you choose ones you feel you can trust."

"The Protectorates will stagnate at forty towns, including Tortz," Sven said with a frown. "Also, I won't be around to teach the mundanes."

Nightfire leaned forward in the chair and spoke in a rush. "You cannot do this alone, Sven, and you cannot do it as a green. While you teach, you will be learning the higher laws of magic. You will master skills you cannot even imagine yet. You have done much with very little knowledge. Imagine what you can achieve as a lavender or yellow!"

Sven chewed his lip thoughtfully. He knew Nightfire tended to regard each student as a possible contributor to his Academy's famous library — worker bees who gathered pollen from far off flowers to make honey in his paper hive.

"Your apprentices would come with you. Erbark will wear green within two years, Erika a year or two after that, if she is diligent. If you want to spread your ideals, teach apprentices and young wizards. Some will loathe you, but others will flock to you. And a brighter colored cloak will win you more respect even from your enemies."

Sven knew he needed to go back to school. He needed to steal some of the honey for himself before he could ever defeat the likes of Volund.

"Very well. I will teach at the Academy."

"You killed Dux Feiglin's son and made him look the fool," Pondr said. "No wonder he hates you."

Sven balled his hands into fists. His voice came out as a hoarse whisper. "As soon as he found out I had returned to the Academy, Volund returned to Tortz. Well, I cannot actually prove it was him, but when Weard Staute returned to renew its defenses, she found it empty and destroyed by fire."

"He killed them?"

Sven shook his head. "He took them all as slaves. I discovered that when three of them returned to the Academy with Weard Robert Wost a year later."

"The farl."

"Yes. The enchanter. He claimed they were tribute slaves, of course, and none of them contradicted him. I thought they were just afraid of him, so I found ways to talk to them where he could not find out about it, but they did not even recognize me. He ... he did something to them. I do not regret what happened to him, but we did not exactly part on the best of terms."

 **27**

"The heroes of stories the Mar love most dearly are often those who are nearly as vice-ridden as their enemies, but possessed of an impossible number of balancing virtues."

> — Weard Eira Helderza,
> *Unavoidable Problems in Literature*

Horsa steadied himself in the Tempest, the motes of Knowledge warning him his trip was nearly finished. He gripped the hilt of his marsord, silently praying the Domus army would recognize him and not kill him.

The Tempest exploded into the swamp, and Horsa crouched down in the mud to steady himself from vertigo.

The first thing he became aware of was the sloshing of feet around him. Then there were shouts, and green- and auburn-colored arms were hauling on his bright yellow shoulders to help him to his feet.

Horsa was questioned, and only the Mardux's symbol on his cloak convinced them he was from Domus. He was brought before the four lavenders who led the army.

"The Mardux sends his respects to the commanders of the Domus army, and thanks them for their obedience so far. Here is the writ that places the army under my command. We are to turn around and intercept the Flasten army before it leaves the Duxy of Gunne and enters the Duxy of Domus."

One of the leaders stuttered. "We are on Flasten Palus' doorstep, Weard Verifien. We will crush the dux as the Mardux ordered."

Horsa prayed they would understand when he ignored the protest.

"Turn the army around now, good weard, and tell me what you have been doing."

Another lavender took the protester aside. One left to get the army moving. The fourth told Horsa about their formations, their divisions and organization.

Horsa nodded. "The Mardux said we must catch the Flasten army. Can we do that?"

The woman shook her head. "No. There are too many of us, and we cannot move fast enough."

"We could try the Mobility trick." The other two had returned, and it was the protester who made the suggestion. "Groups of four weards, or just pairs. Two of them use Power and Mobility in tandem to generate short line teleportation hops on the group. After a mile, switch. Nothing fancy, but it would quadruple our speed."

"Why have you chosen now to tell this?" Horsa's informer said.

He shrugged. "You told me to develop a quick scouting force. This is what we came up with. Groups of three can go slightly faster, but we think the safest is groups of four. The ones using magic will not be much good if they meet an enemy force along the way."

Horsa took a deep breath. *Marrish, let us not be walking into a greater danger than we face from the Mass.*

"Groups of eight will be safer," he said, and the lavenders listened. "Just as groups of four, only double for protection." He cast the reconnaissance spell. Flasten was still out of range. "Get the weards moving, but after two hours I want to stop and gather everyone. Let us use that to gauge our speed."

"Yes, Weard Verifien," they said, and the army turned around.

In two hours, they had traveled close to nine miles. In a day, they could travel about seventy miles.

Six more days, then, Horsa thought. *We can catch Flasten's army before it reaches the Duxy of Domus.*

He still couldn't believe their pace, even with himself teleporting to catch up.

Fraemauna, help me deal wisely with this situation. Let us have good soup and healthy Mar when this is all over.

The reconnaissance stone in Domus refreshed, showing the Flasten army slightly closer to the city. The Domus army had just appeared on the stone, and in a few hours, Sven would be able to gauge its speed.

Will Horsa catch up with Vigfus and Ragnar? Will the Domus army trust him? Sven could have no doubts the priest would be able to take charge. The weards lived by the system of degrees, and no one in that army was equal to Horsa's rank.

The Mardux stood patiently by the stone, well lit by the white sphere of Energy above it. Weard Devla Salt and two greens stood silently in a corner, conferring over notes under their own, muted light. Weard Salt was in charge of the stone. She had a very precise mind and could make minute adjustments as necessary to the stone. Sven felt lucky to have found her.

His right hand, fingers resting on the edge of the stone, lifted for a minute, casting a shadow over Domus and the Flasten army. It cupped the red, vibrating Mass on the north edge that represented the coming danger.

It is good that it is not real, he thought, glancing at the three weards. A green looked away as he looked up, and Weard Salt said something sharp to him. *I wonder what Katla is doing.* He had his suspicions, but no proof, and no time. There were too many people to watch.

The three other weards occupied, Sven closed his fist over the Mass on the stone. When he moved his hand, it had disappeared.

"Weard Salt," he said with some satisfaction. "There seems to be a malfunction." He left them to work it out.

In the hall outside, a runner met him with news that washed his contentment away. He hurried to his sitting room, poured himself a cup of water and stood by the fire. The door opened, and boots stopped two paces inside. Sven waited until the door was shut again, and then turned, his face half-lit by the flames.

"Weard Stormgul. Your arrival is as unexpected as your departure was."

She has changed, Sven noticed as she lifted her chin. Though freshly scrubbed, her face still looked dirty from the shadows under her eyes and cheeks — she had lost weight and stood in a manner that suggested she might run at any minute, in any direction, including right at him.

You look dangerous now, Eda Stormgul. You are like Erbark, only you were a wizard first.

"Report," he said, when she did not respond.

"Mardux," she said. "Bui Beglin, his men and I stalled the army of Flasten, led by Weard Ragnar Groth and Weard Vigfus Vielfrae. ..." She gave a full report, from when they arrived to what they did to how many supplies they stole.

Nothing I can use now, though, because it's moving. It will be harder for Horsa to catch up. His test just became more difficult. Sven felt his patience melting like iron in a forge. He tried to keep an edge off his voice.

"You swore to obey me. I did not order you to delay Flasten with a handful of mundanes."

"You were in no condition to give me any orders," she said with no apology in her voice or liquid brown eyes. "Flasten's invasion demanded action, and I took action."

"You took useless action — like firewood that gives off neither light nor heat, only smoke. If you had stayed in Domus Palus, I would have sent you with an army of wizards to delay Flasten. I would not have needed to send Horsa to turn the Domus army around, and he could have organized the adept training program."

"If I had stayed in Domus Palus, Flasten would already be at the gates!" she snapped back. "I immobilized an army of twenty thousand wizards for an entire season with twenty mundanes, and I kept all of Bui's guerillas alive throughout."

"Why return here now?" Sven asked with a snort of derision.

"The Flasten army is on the move, again. I knew you would need me in Domus Palus." She held out her hands in a gesture of helplessness, but her anger never wavered. "If you do not want me to act on my own initiative, Mardux, give me orders to obey. Send me to ... "

His look silenced her. *Does she not realize how much this has disrupted my plan? My army won't take Flasten Palus. Horsa isn't here to organize the adepts. There isn't enough time to raise a diversionary army for Eda to lead. I only have one option left, and it has consequences she cannot even begin to comprehend!* His voice rose a little as he spoke to her.

"Because of your failure, a great wizard will die, and I will lose the only advantage I have in this war." *Even with the amendment, the Law will condemn me for what I must do.*

"Mardux," she said, her face closed, wooden. "I did not fail."

"You did," he said hoarsely. "Get out of my sight. I will call on you if I find any use for you after this."

She turned and left, radiating fury at his treatment of her. He sat down heavily and launched into a coughing fit, but it passed more quickly this time. Did he need to intervene on the other fronts? Erbark was missing. Einar had not reported in some time.

Not yet, he thought. *Give Horsa a chance. Maybe I should check on Einar. And no one has heard from Erbark in months.* He shook his head. "Not yet."

"Not yet what?"

He wheeled. Erika had led Asa in by the hand. "Your daughter wants you to tell her a story about Affe's adventures."

"Or Tryggvi Fochs," Asa chimed in, smiling easily. "How he beat the Gien army by himself."

Sven rubbed a finger against one of the leather gloves at his belt. "I am very busy, Erika," he said, stepping toward them, though he did kiss Asa's forehead. *Not now. I have to convince the priests the amendment also legalizes wand-wielding mundanes, and then I have to teach them how to make them.*

Erika's eyes hardened as she looked up at him. "I worry about you," she said. "You might be healthy again, but you will get sick if you push yourself too soon. You need to wait, my dear."

"I am so tired of waiting," he said, voicing what he couldn't think in his head. "I need to act."

She grabbed his hand. "Please," she started, but he threw her hand away and stalked out of the room, her shocked stare following him.

The only applications I have kept a secret will no longer be secret.

Sven knew Robert at least suspected. The farl had taught him the principles behind the Blosin wands when Sven had been an apprentice, after all. And after Tortz, Sven had gone to the enchanter again for more instruction.

He knows how carefully I studied the dynamics of Knowledge and Elements. He knows I can design applications for both. It is only a matter of time before he discovers the truth behind all my victories, and then he will use it against me.

A portal leading through the Tempest and into the temple of Marrish opened before him.

I must do this. I must tilt the odds back in my favor.

Sven pulled his cloak tighter around him and stepped into the darkness.

Ragnar listened to the messenger's report with a frown, not quite able to believe what he was hearing. A force of ochres from the Dead Swamps had broken through the southern defenses of the Duxy of Flasten.

"Does my father know how they got past our defenses in such large numbers, Weard Spitz?"

The middle-aged cyan shook his head. "He just received news from two magocrats that their towns have been captured. He intends to send Weard Wenigar to investigate."

Ragnar frowned. "This is ill-timed. Suspiciously timed, in fact."

Odveig Spitz could say nothing to that.

"Weard Vielfrae?"

The enormous red looked up from where he was devouring a duck leg, grease dripping down his chin. He stood with effort. "Yes, Weard Groth?"

"Return to Flasten Palus."

"Ochres are slow-moving," Vigfus noted. "It will be months before they reach Flasten, if they even get that far."

"The ochres are not my worry. The Mardux is. I would not have my father face Weard Takraf alone."

"You think Sven Takraf has allied himself with the ochres just so he can assassinate the dux?" Vigfus asked, incredulous.

The cyan's eyes went wide at that.

"The Mardux is a clever opponent. He deliberately defies expectations just to keep us off-balance, wondering what he will do. He murdered my brother in cold blood without hesitation or remorse. He spared Einar, swatted Horik like a mosquito and dismembered Solvi in full view of all of us. I put nothing past him."

"Even so, Nightfire would bring the full weight of the Law against the Mardux for assassinating a dux."

"Not until after he had done the deed. Even then, Nightfire has already spared Weard Takraf once. The sage is every bit as unpredictable as his student, where the Mardux is concerned." Ragnar saluted Vigfus. "Go to Flasten. I can handle the siege of Domus Palus."

"Yes, Weard Groth." Vigfus called the myst and vanished into the Tempest.

"Shall I return, as well, Weard Groth?" Odveig Spitz asked softly.

Ragnar looked at the cyan as though he had forgotten he was there. He considered for a moment. "No, stay here. I will find a use for you."

Two days later, a scout dressed in blue reported to Ragnar's command tent. He saluted with one raised hand. "Weard Groth, the Domus army has turned around."

"They will never reach us before we take Domus," Odveig murmured, slapping a mosquito.

Ragnar took a good look at the scout. Odveig was clearly not used to being out of Flasten Palus. He was a history scholar, a teacher at the Flasten Palus Academy. He was enduring this march poorly in spite of his magic, but the mosquitos seemed glad to have him. Some of the other wizards joked that Odvig kept the mosquitos away from them by presenting such an irresistible alternative. His face and hands were a mass of bite marks.

"How far away are they?" Ragnar asked carefully.

"Three hundred miles or more. We had to relay scouts."

It would take them more than a month to move that distance, Ragnar thought. *It took them two months to get out there. They would all have to be able to teleport to reach us.*

So Ragnar put it out of his mind until the next afternoon, when the report said the Domus army was less than two hundred miles away. The same blue delivered it. Ragnar thought his name was Rolf Entsen. *Or is it Odulf Entsen?*

"A hundred miles a day?" the dux's son mused. "They will be exhausted when they catch up. If they catch up."

Odvig Spitz scratched his face. "We could move our men with Mobility, too."

Ragnar shook his head. "We would be sitting ducks to anyone who came upon us. The only reason the Domus army is not being annihilated by Drakes is because they killed all of them on the way out. They collapse into the mud every night."

But Ragnar ordered the Flasten army to stop and make camp a day ahead of the Domus army. Unless Domus had enough control over its twenty thousand wizards to call a halt with very little notice, they would arrive and be surrounded on three sides by his carefully deployed troops.

 **28**

*"Early Marduxes supported scholars researching spells
with military applications by granting them charters
to claim any village with a population of less than five
hundred as a research domain. These charters provided
the first magocrats with a place to live and work where
their basic needs could be met by the mundane population, but many wizards became petty tyrants over communities that lacked the authority to expel them."*

— Weard Gilda Kronas,
The Rise of Magocracy

Ragnar wished for one of the reconnaissance stones the Mardux's
army was rumored to have.

He wandered the north side of his army relaying messages and
listening to reports from his amber and cyan commanders. A quarter-mile south, another line paralleled this one, and to the west, the
bulk of his army waited. North and south would envelope the Domus
army. A retinue of twelve blues trailed him, eyes peeled for anyone
aiming a stick in their direction.

He was thus employed when the message arrived from the far
south edge: "The Domus army is turning."

"How in Marrish's name?" he cried, calling upon his retinue to
help him in a reconnaissance spell.

The Domus army was indeed turning, slowly, inexorably bending
to the north. But the southern side had clipped his southern flank and
spun, like a log in a whirlpool. It would slam into the northern arm.

To his runners, "West side collapse on the north flank. South side
march north. Attack Domus wizards on sight." Then he used Mobility

to run east, to beat the Domus army to his flank.

He arrived as the armies clashed.

Domus greens appeared on the edge of his vision out of nowhere. Then they vanished, and before he could blink were behind his carefully structured line, its wizards still drawing on Energy for a blast.

The Flasten wizards' spells hit empty air ahead of them as they themselves were slammed face-first into the mud from behind. Then the Domus wizards were gone again.

Ragnar drew his marsord and joined the army, shouting at the top of his lungs.

They were moving way too fast. Standing in a line is not going to work.

The generals of a thousand years of wars in his nation and others screamed tactics at him. But this kind of battle was beyond their experience; he would have to adapt.

Walls of Power met the next wave of greens. As they fell into the mud, Energy ignited their cloaks.

Now Domus will come more cautiously.

Horsa hovered out of sight with a hundred wizards.

It is my own fault. I should have stopped us an hour earlier, figured out exactly what Flasten's position was.

In any case, his order to turn the army had come too late, and now smaller groups — never more than a hundred, usually much smaller — were scattered amid Flasten's crescent defense.

He used Knowledge to ascertain where any gap was in Flasten's defenses. The north flank of his army had been able to move, but the south flank's momentum had been too great to steer it out of the way of the crescent.

Finally, it appeared a gap would open for them.

I must get these people through alive.

"Go in thirty," he whispered, and the words swept out from him like ripples in water. "Spare your magic to save your companions and to move faster."

Three ... two ... one.

The force moved as one, a school of fish appearing and disappearing every hundred yards. It paused a hundred feet before the straggling line of Flasten's army and leapt two hundred feet beyond it.

They made it.

Horsa hopped back to the line, looking for more wizards. He chanced a recon spell. Another large group of Domus wizards was ahead. He found them quickly.

"Follow me," he ordered and turned to take them to safety.

Explosions sent mud flying from the rear. Trees sailed up into the air.

Flasten's south flank has arrived, Horsa thought. "Quickly!"

An arm landed in the mud in front of him. He ran over it and prepared to teleport away. He let a few people pass him, shouting orders, as an invisible wall of Power swept up everything in the swamp — trees, shrubs and Mar alike. Ahead, another wall filled his vision from horizon to horizon.

Cannot go through it. "To the east! Move! Get out!"

They raced as the two walls came crushing down on them. Horsa jumped onto a tree limb, his cloak catching on a bramble bush. Then he was on top of a pile of trees. He could see the edge of the walls, where the motes were sparser. *It will hurt, but ...*

He slammed through the edge of the wall and tumbled through the mud. Rising as fast as he could, Power stripped the mud off him.

About a dozen had survived with him. He gathered them to himself and summoned every bit of the myst he could. Grabbing the weards, he whispered, "Marrish, help me," and teleported them all to the rendezvous point.

They appeared four miles to the north, in what was rapidly becoming a clearing. As Horsa ordered his twelve to find their division, a lavender ran up to him.

"Weard Verifien, we have a preliminary count," she said.

"Of what?" he asked, staring at another group of weards who had just arrived.

"Casualties."

Horsa received the casualty count with dulled ears. Today at least a thousand had died, those caught in Flasten's flank and reactions.

Marrish, grant me strength. Lord of Wind and Fire, keep my soul steady. He sat in a clearing designated for him while the four lavenders waited on him to give orders.

But we saved hundreds today. Thousands. More than nineteen thousand remain to fight. What do I do with them?

Take them and retreat to a town? There was no town big enough to hold them. They must meet any army on the field.

Attack Flasten? The Flasten army was at nearly full strength, and it was well-rested. They had been caught by surprise today and still killed a thousand of the Domus army. What kind of casualties had they suffered?

Horsa put his head in his hands, prayed. *I am no general. How do I direct these men?*

"Flasten's army is regrouping," the report came from the weard guarding the recon stone. "They look to be building defenses."

He raised his head. *That general knows what he is doing. But we have the advantage in leadership. I can split our army four ways, and each of those divisions can be split again, down to the very groups of eight the Mardux instructed me to make them into.*

He paused in his thoughts, looking at the lavenders.

"We could attack him in a fortified position," Horsa said.

They nodded, giving him advice on doing it. But he decided there would be too many casualties.

"When the Mardux attacked the advancing gobbels ... " someone said, and Horsa raised his hand to stop the lavender as the answer appeared in his head.

A moving army is more difficult to defend. We must find a way to get his army moving.

He nodded to himself, gave thanks to the gods. Then he summoned the lavenders before him and began issuing orders.

"How are the defenses coming?"

Ragnar had ordered traps built, trenches dug and the camp raised out of the swamp several feet so most types of teleportation would not work. He had learned enough from his first encounter with the Domus army to understand how quickly it had crossed the vast distance between them.

I will not be caught unaware again.

Shouts rose from the northeast, and Ragnar grabbed his marsord and ran there.

Domus weards clashed freely with the Flasten weards. The Domus weards appeared to flicker in and out.

"Walls of Power!" Ragnar shouted, heeding his own advice and throwing up the blue wall that hundreds of Domus wizards had slammed into during the first battle.

But those did not stop the Domus wizards this time. They dodged them. Suddenly, Ragnar realized what was really happening here, even as shouts rose from the northwest.

"Regroup! Don't follow them!" The defenses were destroyed. Many weards were singed and being healed by a comrade. And many more touched Mobility and followed the token Domus assault out into the swamp.

Ragnar swore, summoned Mobility and chased down a group of Domus weards. *Nine of them,* he noted as four of them struck his shield with bolts of fire. He targeted the ground below them with Power and Energy, which exploded, drenching himself with mud and leaving four boots behind. He moved on, trying to gather his men.

But the Domus commander had done his job well. Eight groups of a thousand had sliced through the Flasten camp, shaving chunks of a hundred or more off each time to chase and — Ragnar had to assume — die before the army they followed.

But if I did my math right... Ragnar reappeared in the center of his camp.

"Order the army to march north," he told his commanders. He pointed at a cyan. "Take a thousand north as quickly as possible and strike through the center of the Domus army."

The cyan nodded and left.

"We divide the rest of the army into seven groups, chase down those others who came in. And when I say chase, good weards, I mean hunt them as though they were gobbels who had just kidnapped your daughter."

Horsa sat in his clearing, three of the lavenders in attendance.

What can I do? he thought, staring at the reconnaissance stone. The plan had worked. The Flasten army was obviously dividing, even more than his groups had taken it. They were engaged with the slices they had drawn away from the enemy army, each a mile or more from the Flasten camp.

The divisions will attack those weards. We must get them to return here as soon as they are through.

But his gut said they should move sooner.

Then a blob of Flasten's army flickered dead toward them. It flickered again, much closer.

"A thousand approach from the south," Horsa told one of his commanders. "Make sure we don't splinter."

The lavender nodded and strode away.

Then shouts came from the east. Horsa's head snapped back to the stone. The Flasten thousand had shifted, come in from the east. He almost moved, but then, as quickly as it had come, there was silence. Then shouts of victory.

"A thousand attacked in the east," the report came. "They killed three, injured more than a hundred, who are now healed. Then they retreated."

What happened? Where did they go?

From the northwest, shouts.

Oh, Marrish, will we have to keep a watch all night of every man?

He suddenly felt anger rise in him. *This is the Mardux's battle. He should be fighting it, not me. Too many Mar will die.*

Then somehow I must save as many as I can.

The revelation hit him like a bowl of hot soup on an empty stomach.

Their general will not negotiate. Not yet. We must ... What must we do?

The shouts to the north turned to cries of victory again, followed by the sounds of battle to the west.

"Engulf them," Horsa said finally. "Mark them, and follow them. When we are regrouped, we will deal with Flasten."

It took about a span, but the two massive Mar armies were soon thoroughly entangled with each other. They were less than twenty miles south of Domus Palus. They were each about nineteen thousand strong. They both had generals whose knowledge of war stemmed from stories they had learned as children and books they had read during their apprenticeships.

The Flasten army clumped, but Ragnar had divided it into three main divisions. The first assault that divided the army would not work again. He kept them maybe a mile apart, drifting slowly east and west for supply reasons, and sent forays of a hundred or so north to check the Domus army's defenses. They had reconnaissance stones now, but Ragnar was certain Domus' were better.

In this teleport war, spreading out over four thousand square miles now, it was a serious advantage. But using the edge of his reconnaissance spells, he could even triangulate Domus' location while being more than fifteen miles from them.

The Domus army was spread much more thinly. There were nine obvious divisions, and each of those could break down, and down again, to component groups of nine.

Nonagons: Four to attack, two to defend, two to heal or rest, and one to move them all. Ragnar had seen enough of them to copy them more efficiently. *Pentagons: Two attack, one to heal, one to rest, one to move. Defense came from healing.*

But they were at a standoff. Ragnar not only had to defeat this army, he had to take Domus Palus. Despite his attempt to contact his father without heading back to Flasten Palus, Ragnar had not received a reply. Every time he made plans to move, he would barely have finished his preparations before a raid would sneak into his camp.

These were particularly vexing. Nothing he had read gave him a response against the tactics the Domus army used.

No more than thirty at a time would appear a few yards into his camp, blast his wizards in the throat, eyes and mouth with Energy, then jump a few hundred yards deeper in. They would not retreat.

Not until they had gone all the way through his men and out the other side. And then come back. His weards were hard-pressed to do much of anything during the ten or so seconds the enemy was among them.

This didn't happen just one invasion at a time. It would happen two or three at a time and then stop.

What game are you playing? He cursed the leader of the Domus army. They had good reconnaissance. He could get nine miles out of his best wizard, and if Ragnar lost that weard, he'd be lucky to find one who could manage six miles.

The good news was that only one wizard had died over the last four days of these tactics, and that was because he had passed out in a puddle. No matter how many throats were melted shut, there were always ten more wizards prepared to heal them. More would die from konig worms than would die from these magical tactics. That was certain.

Now Ragnar thought strategy, even as another raid brought screams from the west. Vaguely, he ordered a counterstrike. *Someone will break through.*

I should march on the Domus army.

He would have to eventually. Right now, he barely knew where they were. He could be surrounded.

I should teleport whoever I can into Domus Palus, force the Domus general to divide his loyalties.

And split them up even more? He would be as a bootless map-maker heading for the Fens of Reur in a striped cloak carrying only a candle.

He grabbed his marsord and a whetstone and started polishing it. The blade was nicked in places, dulled in others.

Ragnar wore a marsord because he was a leader. He had spent most of his life studying books by foreign generals who knew the strategy and tactics of their lands. He had trained himself to win this war. Or any war. A war against men or Drakes. He had studied the works of all the great Mar generals. He knew about ravit and gobbel tactics.

He knew how to lead men. He understood what he had to do. And despite that, many of his men had run off when they were attacked by the overpowering numbers of Domus troops. Still, in the thick of a fight, they listened and obeyed. Casualties were ridiculously low.

He put the sharpened marsord down. *I need to regain the advantage. I need Domus to come when I call, to move where I tell it to.* He looked at his sword. *What are the resources in this war.*

The stone rasped against the sword. In terms of numbers, the two armies were nearly the same size. As for weapons, Ragnar knew the Domus army could beat him in Mobility and Knowledge, but he had an edge in Vitality and Power. *They can dodge, but we can heal.*

He drew an oiled rag from his belt and wiped at the blade.

We need an edge, he thought, staring at the blade. *Magic tires us out; if we could use less, we could heal more. If everyone had a marsord ...*

Suddenly he grinned.

The latest report to Horsa was just as empty of promise as the previous thirty. No Flasten weards killed. For every one whose flesh was seared to the bone with energy, a dozen more jumped to save him.

Ragnar has that edge: Vitality. But we have Knowledge. Horsa's reconnaissance stones saw for five miles more than his opponents', the yellow was sure of it.

His advisers thought they could keep this up. Four or five nonagons cutting through the Flasten army would wear them down. Horsa knew the opposite was true. Domus would be worn through first.

We have been peppering him with small strikes, Horsa thought as his generals babbled on. *A hammer blow now might break him. And ... if we were to disappear ...*

He looked up, and the lavenders grew silent.

Ragnar was barely awake before he heard the shouts. He leapt from his tent in his boots and undershorts, marsord in his hand to strike down the flood that had descended on them.

This time they hadn't come in small groups.

This time the whole army had come.

But Ragnar had prepared his men, and instead of gathering myst, they all had spears encased in Power. The wet wood would have bent without, and dozens of Domus wizards, expecting hesitation as a magical assault was summoned, were speared where they stood. Many immediately got back up as healers worked, but death claimed dozens.

A few minutes later, no Domus wizards remained in Ragnar's camp, and Ragnar called for his generals. Combining their powers, they reconned. The Domus army now surrounded them — a thousand at every point in the compass and every point in between. And their line was constricting on Ragnar's army

The screams came again as the Domus army pounced through them, but this time it was with shields of Elements and Power. One minute, Ragnar's army stood, prepared, in silence. The next, there were twice as many weards. The spears broke in the hands of the Mar who held them. The silence shattered. Domus and Flasten alike sundered the ground and air with Energy and Power.

This time, when the Domus army retreated, several hundred Mar, led by ambitious ambers, followed them.

Ragnar, marsord wet with Mar blood, reconned. His men had followed the Domus men out and were losing ground on them.

Then the nineteen thousand Domus weards fragmented, grew hazy and vanished.

Ragnar and his generals glared at their reconnaissance stone for a minute. One of the men kicked the thing.

"Use everything you have got," Ragnar told them. The stone remained blank.

"Where in Domin's domain did they go?"

Ragnar scratched his beard. *They might be out of range. But they could not have move that fast.*

He shook his head. "They must have some way of clouding this. We will deal with it later. Right now we need to get our stragglers back."

"They could have split up."

"Individuals? We could see their general before."

"Resonation," a lavender said. "The reconnaissance has always been hazy around the edges. It relies on them being near each other."

Ragnar toyed with this. Then it hit him. "He will have to protect Domus. So we divide. Three armies, the outside two carve out like this." He cupped his hands and tapped his fingers together. "We will meet at Domus Palus. Do not let a single Domus wizard escape you."

"How many will there be?"

"Thousands. And hundreds of traps. But in very small groups."

The blood of the Mar knew battles. Thousands of years of history had been fraught with them. They lived in a realm more populated by Drakes than Mar, and both needed to live. Both wanted the space, the solid ground and the wild rice. They fought over any exposed rock, because that meant minerals — iron and copper, or maybe even gold. A new outcropping exposed by the grinding of water and earth could start a decades-long feud. But now their blood sang with war.

One by one, the Domus wizards altered their cloaks to be camouflaged — the colored cloaks were wise in times of peace, but they only made you an easier target for ambushes and programmed traps. Though a young deer was dappled to hide it from predators, an older deer did not glow in the dark to draw enemies to it.

The wizards reverted to mundane colors — black and dark green. They fashioned spears from hardwoods. Nine-man squads, nonagons, so equipped could conserve magic. They recalled how to move silently, to climb trees and drop down on their enemies. They devised a nonverbal communication. They learned and practiced Drake tactics against their fellow Mar.

Mar had long ago mastered the art of defending a position, for they had needed it to survive the nearly constant Drake raids. The Drakes, however, had perfected several methods of fighting in the swamps, moors and marshes. Away from the walls of a town, even a small army of wizards was at a disadvantage against the Drakes.

The Flasten army was slower to learn. Horsa had to admit that Flasten had reacted to Domus from the first encounter on. By the time Flasten learned, it neared Domus in numbers, and the war had spread out over a hundred thousand square miles.

And the war progressed, Domus squads fighting pairs of Flasten pentagons. Fight, run, heal — and forage. The land suffered more than anything. This patch of Marrishland, less than five percent of its total area, would not recover for many years. Power had uprooted thousands of plants in attempts to stop wizards from teleporting. Energy had dried out patches of mud and, in some rare cases, burned the mud to char.

Horsa glanced over the landscape after a battle where his three nonagons had pushed back four pentagons with no casualties.

Cedar, forgive us for our damage to the land. I vow if I survive this war to heal and preserve this battlefield as a memorial to the follies of the Mar during the great Teleport War.

Sven, I pray your cause is worthy of this sacrifice.

 **29**

*"Tryggvi Fochs drew his sword calmly as the eight
damnens moved forward, the claws on their hands un-
sheathed. Tryggvi spoke to them in their native tongue.
'My magic cannot harm you, and my skill is no match
for your numbers, but the first three who come within
my marsord's reach are dead.' He ran a thumb along
the blade. 'So, which three want to die?' The Drakes
hesitated. Tryggvi took a step forward, face relaxed. The
damnens fled."*

— Weard Eira Helderza,
The Tryggvi Fochs Saga

When Einar was finished, Leiben was a fortress to rival even the
Bastion of Pidel Palus. The ground had long since been raised above
the level of the surrounding moorland, and now the earthen wall
surrounding the town was a solid barrier of clay bricks baked with
Energy. To deter even hightel, Einar had warded virtually every foot
of the town with magical traps that would make short work of any
wizard suffering even a mild case of teleportation sickness.

Einar left a few small pockets in strategic locations throughout
the town where no traps lay in wait. In the thick fog of gathered myst
that covered Leiben and the surrounding landscape, it would be next
to impossible to find them. He had taken pains to memorize the location of each and only moved from one to another by means of teleportation or by surrounding himself in a strong sphere of Elements
to prevent the traps from harming him.

What had once been an otherwise unremarkable living room in
a small house was now Einar's recon chamber and last refuge. He

examined the recon stone and carefully avoided touching it. Anyone wearing red who did touch it would trigger four simultaneous applications of morutmanon on everyone in the town. And no one would suspect the trap, because the stone was already a font of used magic.

The Mardux's Blosin gloves might yet prove the most dangerous magical application developed in the last century.

He had linked the recon stone to the one in the original recon chamber, where a particularly unpleasant series of traps awaited anyone clever enough to discover the source of the recon spell. The recon scans themselves were on varied intervals ranging from one minute to fifteen, both to foil attempts to exploit the interval and to provide the illusion that a wizard was scanning the area and not just a recon stone.

Beyond the wall of power surrounding the town, the defenses were relatively sparse compared to the traps within. Only a few were more dangerous than the ones Sven had once used to protect Tortz. In part, Einar did not have the time to trap every puddle for miles around. He knew Robert and the others would not make the mistake of ignoring other angles of attack. The traps outside the walls would deter a more mundane assault and, hopefully, convince the reds to teleport straight into Leiben, where they would die.

When they finally did, Einar had no intention of being in Leiben. He examined his enemies' progress on the recon stone. They had reached the perimeter of the traps. Of the reds there was no sign, but Einar had expected that. Robert would have kept their movements hidden. The information on the recon stone could well be an illusion in itself. The farl had certainly proven himself capable of that elsewhere.

Now to let them know where they can find their damnen.

Einar gathered the myst and opened a gateway into the Tempest.

"The Mardux's minor magocrats mimic gobbel tactics admirably," Robert commented.

"That is the capital of the Protectorates, then?" Valgird asked with a frown. "With that many defenses, this could be a long siege."

Robert shook his head. "No, Weard Geir. That is what the Mardux intends for us to do. The Protectorates' reconnaissance network is no longer functional, so we no longer need to capture this town." He turned to face Ari and Valgird. "We will find and capture the other villages and let this one starve in safety. The Mardux will regret wasting his time on tricks."

Ari stopped listening and went back to watching the myst. He had picked up on Robert's technique of using Knowledge to scan the myst instead of torutsen, which was in short supply. The farl used such skills with ease, and Valgird ignored them as useless. Ari initially strained to control enough Knowledge to make it work, but he could maintain it for an hour at a time now.

He saw the pinprick to the Tempest open and explode into a ball of flame before everyone else. A dozen weards fell before anyone could react.

"One of them has come out to meet us," Valgird growled, drawing his marsord.

Robert did not move. "No. There is no wizard in the camp."

Another pinprick opened, and a wave of Power and Vitality ripped twenty greens in half at the waist, showering the sedge and ferns of the moors with blood. Seeing nearly one third of their force die in under a minute put the remaining mercenaries to flight.

"Fall back!" Valgird shouted at Ari and Robert.

Robert stood his ground, unfazed by the display of magic and the resulting carnage. Ari saw the cyan motes whirling around the three of them, blocking out all magic.

He thinks we're safe, Ari thought, heart pounding. "Robert, he is right. This is a signature tactic. The spell arrived through the Tempest, which means we are not facing a cyan or amber."

A figure in red appeared in front of them with the sun at his back. He held a marsord in his right hand and a javelin in his left. Cyan motes whirled around him as he stalked toward them with silent confidence.

"The Mardux!" Valgird gasped.

"No," Ari said in a small voice, taking a step behind Robert. "It's Weard Schwert."

Einar's javelin was in the air before Robert could dismiss the Elements shell. Valgird gestured with a hand as if expecting to deflect it, but he couldn't seize Power through the remnants of Robert's defense. The shaft slammed home in Valgird's neck in a fountain of blood, and he tumbled to the ground, too far gone even to command Vitality to heal the mortal wound.

Einar strolled closer. Ari saw Robert calling myst to form his Will-Breaker.

Ten more steps before he throws the marsord at Robert, Ari thought, calling a wall of Power to deflect a blow. *He will defend with damnen's skin until Robert wastes his Will-Breaker, and then he will use linetel to get behind one of us with his knife.*

"Weard Schwert," Robert said pleasantly. "I have looked forward to our first meeting. I suppose I should give you a chance to surrender."

"If you wish to surrender, Weard Wost, then surrender," Einar said, matching Robert's tone as he came closer. "I defeated three consecutive reds for the Chair."

Ari added yellow motes to his flow of blue. *Five steps.*

"I could have defeated six, if your laws allowed a farl to sit on the Chair," Robert said.

Three steps.

"Only six?" Einar held out his gloved, empty left hand toward them. "With this, I could take on the whole Council at once."

Ari opened his mouth to warn Robert, but the enchanter had already taken the bait. The Will-Breaker shattered against Einar's countermagic shell even as the warrior let fly with his marsord.

The two-bladed weapon turned end-over-end through the short distance between them. The long, hacking blade struck Ari's wall of Power, but the other wizard was already in motion — a split-second flicker of Mobility. Ari activated his spell just as Einar appeared behind Robert, knife moving to cut the enchanter's throat.

The Tempest swallowed Ari, and he spent the long silence of teleportation wondering whether he had reached Robert before Einar had. He arrived with a case of teleportation sickness that doubled him over with vomiting — the price of such hasty linetel. Relief flooded Ari when he saw Robert stooped over looking similarly miserable.

The enchanter's wand-wielding slaves gathered around them, their normally vacant expressions suddenly interested. Ari called the myst to defend himself in case seeing Domin overcome with nausea would somehow dispel the Will-Breaker. They made no move to attack, though, simply watching their master with impotent hate in their eyes.

"I was not expecting that," Robert said abruptly, scrubbing his face with a scrap of cloth. "We should collect our mercenaries and regroup."

"If they are not dead yet, they soon will be," Ari said, unable to keep the bitterness from creeping into his voice. "Weard Schwert is as ruthless as Volund in dealing with his enemies. He is hardly kinder to those he calls friends."

"I thought enhanced warriors fought toe-to-toe. Those attacks came through the Tempest."

"Enhanced warriors turn battles into duels whenever they can," Ari explained. "You are fortunate Valgird was killed first."

"I suspect he knew I would flinch."

Ari shrugged. Robert maintained an appearance of cool arrogance around wizards, but that was because magocrats held enchanters in such contempt. He acted more like himself around Ari, and even then, there was always a little worry behind those pale blue eyes.

Weard Takraf came to him for knowledge, and Robert obliged him. Without Robert's wands, Sven could not have built the Protectorates and would not have survived Tortz. And yet Weard Takraf betrayed his teacher as surely as Einar betrayed my mother.

"You fear Weard Schwert, but you hate him even more," Robert said conversationally.

"The same could be said of you and Weard Takraf," Ari countered with heat in his voice.

Robert laughed. "That is the Ari Faul I accepted as an apprentice! Such fire, but I'm glad to say you are less of a fool than Weard Geir was."

"So we have lost the day. What is our next move?"

The enchanter considered this for a long moment. "Do you think he was telling the truth about knowing the secret of the Mardux's Blosin glove application?"

"I cannot say. He did nothing today that he could not do before, but enhanced warriors love keeping back some of their power so they can surprise enemies." Ari scanned the crowd of slaves again. "It is possible."

"Do you think we can convince Dux Feiglin that he was?"

Ari smiled. "I see where this is going, and yes, I believe you can convince the dux of anything you wish."

"But we will need reinforcements."

"First reinforcements. Then revenge."

Einar's recon detected a new force of wizards led by two reds. The army seemed to have swollen tenfold since the futile assault by the Flasten greens. He knew immediately that the enchanter was manipulating his spell to report false information.

As if such an obvious ruse would fool me.

It would be dark soon, Einar knew, and even a red cloak was scarcely visible by night. Naked-eye reconnaissance was always more accurate than a recon spell, and he might be able to inflict some casualties before withdrawing to the safety of Leiben.

Until then, I must save my strength so I can escape when I must.

It hadn't taken Einar long to realize the Mardux intended to abandon the Protectorates.

Mardux Takraf's own creation, a sacrifice to the enemy. But had he predicted it would be conquered this way?

Any good strategist would have chosen the route Sven had. Two armies, one four hundred times the size of the other, one heading away from your army and one toward it. Which do you attack? Take care of the big one first, and then clean up the rest. You did not put out a candle when your house was on fire.

I'm on my own against this invasion.

When Her had vanished below the western horizon, Einar set out from Leiben, using as little magic as possible. The torutsen in his belly would warn him of any enemy spells before they reached him, giving him enough time to defend himself.

Einar was not encouraged to discover the wizards had not lit campfires against the night. He crept closer to where his last reconnaissance spell had detected the magocrats but saw no sign of the Flasten wizards.

I wish I could believe they've retreated.

At last, he reached the place where the wizards had been. Only a few scraps and bits of trash provided any indication that a large army had been here hours ago. He frowned. Scrutinizing the myst around him with torutsen-enhanced vision, Einar saw not a mote out of place.

It is a risk I must take. I need to know where they went.

Einar gathered myst and reconned.

Light flooded the moors around him with dazzling radiance. His marsord was out in an instant, magic already flowing around him, awaiting his orders. Two shadows in red approached. He hurled Energy at one, dove to one side and rolled, rising with his marsord in his hands and Mobility driving him forward.

The red crumpled. Einar's marsord plunged into the chest of the second, meeting no resistance. A beard tickled his hand as the red fell.

A mundane!

Einar grabbed cyan motes even as a bolt of Power slapped him to the ground. A rain of blows, blue motes gathering in hammers, struck him in the hips and ribs. Then Elements closed around him, insulating him from further attacks.

Neither of them carry a marsord. I can beat them both.

He stood up painfully, head turning from side to side, searching the darkness for his enemies. Robert approached from one direction, dragging a cloud of Knowledge and Elements with him. Another red approached from the other direction with a flask in his hand, and Einar wondered how his stepson had gotten involved in Flasten's gambit.

Regrets bubbled out of a past best forgotten even as Einar raised his marsord to strike.

Ari's eyes went wide.

You leave me no choice.

A thick hand grabbed the back of Einar's cloak and pulled him backward. Before he could recover enough to change targets, the long blade of a marsord plunged into his back. His back arched, and a booted foot kicked him toward Ari, pulling the blade free.

Einar knew immediately he would bleed out in seconds unless he healed himself. He dismissed the Elements shell, and clutched at Vitality. The wound closed even as a bolt of Power struck him in the elbow, breaking it and sending his marsord tumbling to the ground.

Ari struck him with Power then, knocking him back. Einar rolled to the ground, ducking the second thrust of the marsord. He glanced up briefly and saw not Robert, but Vigfus Vielfrae.

Robert is still out there.

At that moment, Einar saw the cyan motes closing in around him, blocking his control of the myst. Mind racing for solutions, tor grappling for any myst that would answer, he bit down the urge to panic.

Ari was close now, but his hands were shaking. Einar kicked the flask out of his hands, using a tiny flow of Mobility to enhance his own momentum so he landed on his feet.

He lashed out with simple spells, hoping to wear down the wizard commanding the Elements barrier while gradually mending bones with Vitality. Ari picked up the fallen flask of morutsen. Biting back the urge to call out to him, Einar kicked him in the groin. Ari fell over, clutching himself in pain.

Even reds have mundane weaknesses, my son, Einar thought with a grim smile.

A pillar of flame engulfed him. He gathered Energy to counter the effect. Elements ripped the myst away from him.

Einar struggled to gather myst through the barrier, but the suppression was too strong in his exhausted condition.

"Please, Ari!" he rasped, breath rattling through scorched lips.

His frail stepson gave no sign beyond a slight widening of the eyes.

Then the fire was gone, and Ari poured morutsen into Einar's mouth. The myst slipped beyond his control as the sweet liquid soaked into his body. He closed his eyes against the pain. He felt the life ebbing from his body, knew that he had been bested.

I made the enhanced warrior's mistake of fighting when outnumbered. I should have fled as soon as I saw the light.

Robert Wost's voice broke his musings. "How embarrassing that must have been for you, Weard Schwert — tricked not by farl trickery but by mundanes dressed in red."

Vitality surged through Einar. Broken bones knitted together. New flesh crept over exposed bones. Fresh skin replaced the charred remains of the old. Ari took a few steps back, and an enormous red replaced his spot in Einar's vision.

"Will you tell us how to make Mardux Takraf's gloves?" asked Vigfus, still breathless from the exertion, his marsord dripping with Einar's blood.

"No, Weard Geir."

"Yes, you will," Valgird said. "Ari. Burn him."

Einar saw his son, whom he had just kicked, beaten and bruised, turn pale at Vigfus' words.

"No," Ari rasped.

"But this is what you wanted, was it not?" Robert asked.

"Not like this. Not trussed and weak ..."

"Fine." Vigfus raised one thick hand theatrically.

The flames returned. The spell holding Einar rigid kept him from squirming in agony. Then Vigfus healed him and turned his attention to Einar's intestines, stringing them out like vines in front of him.

Vigfus looked at Robert meaningfully, who feigned a yawn at the display. Behind them, Ari turned away and vomited.

Einar gritted his teeth in defiance. He had endured more pain for lesser causes.

I will hold out, Weard Takraf. I will fulfill my oath to you.

And deep inside, Einar prayed he could.

 **30**

"Like the Tobruson who laid the foundation for the ma-
gocracy, the Kaliheron shared their magical knowledge
freely with each other to maximize the effectiveness of
their research. Before being allowed to join Kaliheron,
students and scholars swore to take no personal credit
for their discoveries while there, for no Mar could claim
to have discovered what Marrish designed and Seruvus
already understood. This would later evolve into the
Nightfire Tradition, which does not credit individual
wizards who make discoveries while in residence at
Nightfire's Academy."

— Weard Gilda Kronas,
The Rise of Magocracy

"Let us take a few days and go somewhere."

Sven and his family sat in his office. Erika sat by the fire and mended Asa's clothes. Their daughter practiced her alphabet on the stones of the floor with a piece of charcoal. Sven, at his desk, quietly read reports out loud to himself. They came in fast and furious these days: supplies, training regimes, desertions, materials requests — the endless barrels of torutsen, for instance. Sometimes he thought half the slaves in the city were pressed into making the drink for the adepts.

He had checked the reconnaissance stone less than fifteen minutes ago. Weard Salt could not find the Mass — the fake one Sven had discontinued — despite creating a new stone, but was certain the problems would be fixed soon. Sven came back to find Erika settled in as though this were her sitting room.

This is my private place to conduct this war, he thought, not looking up. Out loud he said, "Where would you like to go?" He turned a page. *Boots? Where will I find the people to make boots?*

"Let us go visit my parents in Leiben."

Boots! Cloaks! Belts! People should wear pants that fit! Sven put the report down in exasperation and met his wife's eyes.

"There is the war, love," he said casually, leaning forward. The fire made shadows across half his face. "I really cannot leave for an extended period."

"Just two days. You can teleport us there."

"Dear, the Mass is less than two spans from reaching us. I cannot take a break." His voice was a little colder than he would have liked. *And Valgird and Robert are there, seeing to Einar's test.* He could see the set of her jaw. *She will not accept this excuse.*

"There is nothing more you can do," she said, putting down her own work and placing both hands on the arms of the chair. "The war is happening well enough without you. I have not seen my family in months."

"Nor have I." Which was certainly true. Katla was the only one left alive, and no one had heard anything in months.

She misunderstood. "Of course not. You have been here the whole time, being a dutiful father and husband." She rose, took a tentative step toward the desk. "My family is your family, Sven. They are in the Protectorates, and we should go to them."

"No," he said, straightening in his chair. Then, more emphatically, "No. I cannot leave for that long."

She turned away. "If you don't want to go, then I'll find someone else to take me."

Sven went to stand next to her. When she looked back at him, he stared down at her, half his face glowing from the light, the blind orb of his left eye reflecting the dance of the flames. He saw something in her expression, some fear or confusion.

And she should be confused. She should listen to me. I am trying to protect her. She needs so much help. He thought of when he had saved Erika, when they first met. How stupid was anyone to go out by themselves in such dangerous territory? But it was her bravery that made him notice her — she chased him, not the other way around.

Maybe the only thing she will understand is an ultimatum. He knew it would not work, but he said it anyway, softly, from lips dry from the truth.

"You will not go to the Protectorates."

Her eyes opened wide. "What? Why? The war is in the south. The Protectorates are perfectly safe. You made them so."

He shook his head. "Einar has not returned yet."

"What?" The realization set in. "Flasten attacked the Protectorates?" Strain showed in her face as she tried to remain calm.

Sven tried to keep his voice normal. *She asked, and I cannot lie to her, no matter it will hurt her.* "Einar is there ..."

"Without an army." She stood, stalked to the fire and prodded it viciously with the poker. "Alone. When there are more than enough wizards in the army to spare some for the north. And your adepts, what are they doing? They could be guarding my home!"

So it was never our home like she suggested? He wanted to be reasonable. This had started out as a calm conversation. But she insisted on not understanding what was going on. *She cannot see I was trying to protect her from what I was doing.* He felt his back tense.

"Einar knows what he is doing. I promise ..."

"But you never told me there was war up there!" She hung the poker up with a clang, turned and faced him, arms crossing her chest.

Asa had stopped writing and was watching them, now. Sven spared her a brief flicker of a glance before returning to the argument.

"I did not tell you because I wanted to protect you." He felt better for saying it, but the wild look didn't leave her eyes.

"Well? What if your hometown was attacked?" she said angrily. "If Rustiford was a part of this, would you be leaving it to be conquered?"

Sven felt his temper flare. *She has not even heard me! I come right out with it and she ignored me! She should be mad at that now, instead of questioning the way the war is going.*

"What do you know about handling the war?" he snapped back at her. "Who made you a general? Would you like me to explain why to you? Why even if Rustiford was attacked I would still be here? Flasten has practically played into my hands — this huge step toward peace we can take, and you are trying to stop the river with a mud wall. You do not understand!" He felt the heat on his cheeks, felt his muscles tense in a sneer, the skin taut and wrinkled like an ancient monster's. He could barely think for Erika's stupidity. "Sometimes I think I am talking to a book, you are so dense."

"What did you just say?" she said quietly, her eyes spears.

"I am doing this to save Marrishland," he said slowly, deliberately. Spittle flecked through the air toward her. "I cannot explain why I do it. I have to."

"You have to?" Her voice was small and lost. She looked like a little mouse in front of him. And just as confused. "You can give me this one thing," she said, tears in her eyes.

"You will not go to Leiben."

"I can. I will take adepts and free the Takraf Protectorates." The words were clipped, harsh.

His hand moved, and she fell.

"You will not go to Leiben," he growled. "If I have to put you in a cell."

Sven towered over his wife, his body rigid as the building in which he stood. She lay on the floor, her hand lightly touching the red imprint where his hand had landed, her mouth a round O. And in her eyes, he saw understanding. He saw every detail, right now, as the rage turned away from her and into him. He looked away from her.

All of Marrishland will be lost if I sit here and let the generals run the war. They will not learn fast enough! They will destroy us, but I can stop it.

Everything was a failure. This was not Tortz. It was too large, but Sven should be out there helping. He looked back down at Erika, whose mouth was just closing in a snarl of hatred. He felt the burns on his face, the glistening bulb where his eye had been. He felt the tear roll down his healed cheek.

He could not take this anymore.

"I am the light that guides the Mar, Erika." He choked back a sob. "I am the fire that burns in their souls. Without fuel, though, they cannot burn. And I have given them that fuel." He stepped back, bent over, wracked with sobs. "I ... will ... burn all the sickness away. If I must amputate the hand to save the Mar, that is what will happen."

He stepped backward into the Tempest, leaving his stunned wife forming some word to try to stop him. He reappeared in almost no time in the swamp near Rustiford and roared. Fire lanced from all of his fingers at a hapless tree, engulfing it and making it vanish as though it never was.

 **31**

*"The Kaliheron developed a vocabulary for discussing
magical theory, and many of their concepts survived,
symbolized in the Mar alphabet. The letters Myst, Tor
and Ues are next to each other because they refer to related fields of magic study — mysdyn (myst dynamics),
tordyn (tor dynamics), and uesdyn (mysterious magic
dynamics). Dih, Sen, Ud and Krah literally translate as
earth, water, wind and fire, but they also relate to the
study of Power, Vitality, Mobility and Energy — the only
four magicks known to the Kaliheron."*

— Weard Oda Kalidus,
The Origin of Nothing

Sven Takraf arrived at Volund's keep even as ochres and gobbels
besieged Flasten Palus. He strolled through the halls as though the
dux had invited him in for soup, though the marsord and the trail of
fire he left in his wake spoiled the illusion. He paused at every doorway to fling a wall of fire into the room — empty, occupied, he no
longer cared.

I never wanted this to be about revenge for Tortz! he raged.

A trio of ambers challenged him, demanding his surrender. Green
fire consumed them, and they writhed and screamed as they turned
to ash. Sven did not even wait until they stopped screaming before
turning his attention elsewhere.

*I stand with the mundanes, and the gods stand with me. I will ex-
ecute their will upon Dinah's back until I am ashes in the hearth.*

The Mardux neared the double doors of the dux's council chamber. He hurled them open with Power, the violence of the spell reduc-

259

ing them to kindling, which caught fire immediately. Inside the council room stood a lone red with a naked marsord held in his shaking hand. All around him, fire burned the tapestries and rugs of the keep, filling the air with choking smoke.

"Weard Wenigar," Sven called to him without slowing his pace. "Stand down. My business is not with you."

"I should have listened to my father," Ketil said with confidence, but his eyes betrayed the terror. "I should have killed you while you were still exhausted from the duels."

Sven stopped then and tilted his head back to laugh. "Do you think you could stand against the hand of the gods? Do you think you could have defeated the Guardian of Marrishland?"

Ketil's fist of Power never landed. Sven had already anticipated the attack, was countering the spells faster than the dux's son could cast them. Ketil charged forward with a scream of rage.

Sven swatted him aside like an insect. The younger red flew into the table with a grunt and collapsed to the floor.

"Where is your father?" Sven asked him.

"Domin take you!" Ketil shouted, lifting up his marsord.

Sven moved a single finger, and the other red's sword shattered. Drops of blood welled up from a dozen tiny cuts on Ketil's hands and face.

"Where. Is. Your. Father!" Sven said, punctuating each word by breaking a bone — a rib, a wrist, a shin, an arm.

Tears streamed down Ketil's face as he clutched at his injuries. The fire was creeping along the floor toward him. Already, the hem of his red cloak had turned black.

"Please! Please don't kill him," Ketil cried.

Sven smirked at that, his blind eye a reflection of the flames flickering around them. "And why not? He would have killed me without hesitation, if I had given him an opportunity. Might I remind you that he killed Brand and Askr and Geir and Nirta." With each name Sven spoke, Energy vaporized one of Ketil's hands or feet, leaving a cauterized stump in its place.

Ketil wailed in pain, and blood trickled from the corner of his mouth where he had bitten his tongue.

"There is nothing you can say in his defense that will convince me to spare him."

Ketil squinted against the pain, tried to call Vitality that would not come. He managed a hoarse whisper. "He was right about you in Tortz." Ketil spat blood, and his voice gained strength. "You are nothing but a murderer! Anyone who angers you dies."

Sven flinched. He recalled Brand's words, his words before Tortz. *"I am not in the habit of killing every magocrat who angers me."*

Ketil looked up at him from where he lay, crawling forward on his stomach like a worm, his cloak burning merrily in the blaze. "You murdered my brother first, Takraf!"

Sven saw the rage, there, the hate. It would never die, just like his own anger at Volund for enslaving Tortz would never die. Like Katla's hatred of Flasten for taking away her mother would never die. Like Robert's rage at Sven's betrayal would force a final confrontation one day.

"This is not about revenge." Sven pointed down at Ketil, pinned him down with Power. "This is about justice."

Ketil choked out a laugh. "Dinah must have a special fate in mind for you, Weard Takraf."

"Well, I have something special in mind for her, too," Sven snarled, and then he left Ketil where he lay and stormed out of the council room.

All are fuel for the fire I have brought to Marrishland — even my enemies!

But the thought rang hollow. He steeled himself against the uncertainty prickling the back of his mind.

I will find and kill Volund, and then three others must die. After that, it does not matter what happens to me. Marrishland will be free of the magocrats' tyranny.

All around him, Flasten's keep burned. Sven slammed the marsord into its shin sheath. He changed gloves and reconned, seeking reds. He found only one. He scanned for other wizards, and the result surprised him.

Volund is alone. Have all his allies abandoned him?

A black portal opened, and Sven stepped through the brief darkness of the Tempest and into the presence of his enemy. He appeared at the back of one of Flasten Palus's open air temples. Volund knelt on a reed mat within a circle of bronze statues, praying at the feet of the statue of a bald woman with a finger pointed down to execute the vengeance written on her face.

Oh, this is perfect, Sven thought with a small smile, and he immediately hated himself for thinking it. He looked at the statue of Seruvus, who looked back at him sternly, the cold eyes seeming to follow Sven as he crept closer to the dux.

Even from the back, Sven could see how he had worn down the dux. Sweat drenched his back and face, and he shivered. A grey beard had overtaken his face, while the curls on his head looked greasy and wild. His marsord lay nearby, still in its shin sheath.

You know this is not about vengeance, Sven thought at the statues as he entered the circle. Seruvus looked unconvinced.

Sven could hear Volund's prayers, now.

"Mother of Miseries, I know I have brought your wrath upon me. I ask no mercy for myself, but spare my sons. Spare my city. Spare my duxy. Do not look upon them as you look upon me."

Sven called the myst, readying himself for the long-awaited confrontation. To Dinah's right, Domin's alligator head seemed to smile at him.

Long-awaited because he has escaped punishment for too long already, he told himself firmly.

"Dux Fieglin," Sven said in the haughtiest, most accusatory tone he could manage.

Volund scrambled, turning his body even as he fell backward. He stared into Sven's eyes. "You! You have brought the Bald Goddess's wrath upon Marrishland!"

Sven took a step forward raising the Blosin gloves, fingers splayed. "Dinah is not the one whose wrath you should have feared to provoke."

Volund scrambled backward until he sat at the feet of the Bald Goddess. He did not call the myst, but wrapped his body around her naked shins in supplication.

"Still taking refuge in her shadow? The lies you told in her name about the Mass will not protect you from the rage of Marrish. I am the Guardian. I am the hand of the gods. No longer will you deny the dream of Weard Darflaem!"

"It wasn't a lie!" Volund shrieked even as Sven stepped forward and called the myst to activate the gloves. "The Dead Swamps are at the gates. The Dead Swamps are at the gates!"

Black rivers of killing energy flowed out of Sven's hands and lanced into the Dux of Flasten. Volund looked up at Dinah once more, and then he turned to ash.

Sven forced aside the disquieting feeling of intense personal satisfaction and stooped to take Volund's marsord. The hair on the back of his neck pricked, and he looked up to find himself staring directly at the downward pointing hand of the Bald Goddess. Next to her, Domin grinned at him, seeming to laugh.

Forgetting the dux's marsord, Sven stood up and whirled. His patrons and patronesses stood in a near circle around him.

"Who I am is unimportant, now," he told them. "What I do I do for the good of the Mar and for your glory."

Domin still grinned. Seruvus remained unconvinced. Marrish seemed on the point of hurling lightning at him.

Three more to kill, Sven thought, and then he stepped into the Tempest.

 **32**

"Mysdyn (myst dynamics) is the study of what Mar magic can do and how it works. Less experienced wizards may wield magic 'by the book' (Veks) or 'by the cup' (Xil) — relying either on known magical applications or on informal experimentation. Wizards who understand mysdyn can design spells using nothing but their knowledge of the underlying principles of magic. This is wielding magic 'by the chair' (Es), because the wizard designed and built it to his exact specifications instead of simply sitting on whatever the gods or another wizard happened to make convenient."

— Weard Oda Kalidus,
The Origin of Nothing

Ari approached Einar cautiously, a flask of morutsen in hand. He squinted at his stepfather in the darkness, trying to determine if he was asleep or merely pretending to be. Einar gave no sign. Carefully, Ari approached him.

"You are weak to follow this farl," Einar said from the hood of his cloak.

Ari jumped in surprise.

"You were always afraid to stand on your own."

Blood rose to Ari's cheeks. Einar raised his head a little. Shadowed eyes met Ari's fearful ones.

"Why do you wear my marsord, Ari?"

Ari touched the marsord on his waist subconsciously. He had, indeed, taken Einar's marsord with only a raised eyebrow from Robert.

"I fear you no longer, old man," Ari said, uncorking the flask.

"You wear my sword out of bravery?" A low chuckle escaped Einar's lips. "Who taught you bravery?"

"I hate you."

"I never wanted you to fear me."

Ari's voice came out in a hiss. "You burned the skin off my body! How could I love you for that?"

"You were failing your classes. I only wanted you to succeed."

"The way my brothers succeeded?" Ari demanded bitterly.

Einar winced. "I merely wished to expand the Mar civilization, Ari."

"By forcing your wife's children to guard villages across the river from the Fens of Reur?"

"The Fens have always been the frontier of the Duxy of Domus, but you must believe me when I say they were not so dangerous when I was your age. A few tribes of guer, a handful of gobbels, maybe the occasional insero. I defended those towns from Drakes for twenty years before I put your brothers in charge of them. Not once had the Drakes attacked me in such numbers ..."

Ari suppressed his anger. "It is time for the morutsen, Weard Schwert."

Einar laid a hand on Ari's arm. "Why do you serve him? You are afraid of him."

Ari snorted. "Certainly not. He does not torture or threaten me."

Einar turned his head as though struck. Softly, from within the hood of his cloak, he spoke. "I understand, son. I am at your mercy and at his. But should you ever wish to part his company, I will offer you whatever protection I am able."

"I wear this sword, Weard Schwert."

"Will your stolen sword protect you better than I when the Mardux comes to pass judgment on you?" Einar snapped.

"I do not need your protection." Ari thrust the flask of morutsen into Einar's hands. "Drink before I drive you into the darkness where my mother dwells!"

His stepfather obeyed. "I have been a poor guide, Ari, but even into death my shade shall guard you."

Ari received the empty flask and turned away, returning to Robert's campfire. He shuddered, remembering what had happened to Vigfus.

Weard Vielfrae had wanted Robert to bring Einar back to Flasten Palus right away, but Robert had insisted on capturing the Protectorates first. Vigfus had argued and then pulled rank, and Robert had simply ... ended him — a powerful illusion had destroyed the mind and paralyzed his body. The enchanter hadn't even bothered to land a killing blow, simply leaving Weard Vielfrae curled up in a puddle, whimpering softly.

Since they had captured Einar, they had conquered more than half of the Protectorates. Only towns in the northern half of the moors were left untouched, and the most heavily fortified of them were guarded only by a magocrat and a small militia each.

"I have been thinking, Ari," Robert said without turning to look at him. "Perhaps my Will-Breaker will succeed where Valgird's torments did not."

Ari sat down numbly and said nothing. At the edges of the firelight, the captured mundanes stirred at the sound of the enchanter's voice, as if they feared he would be moved to rage, again.

"Do you have any objections?" Robert asked, turning to stare intently into Ari's eyes.

Ari shook his head, remembering Vigfus.

Einar looked into the darkness, considering. He remembered childhood stories of the afterlife. Dead Mar were burned to release their souls, which took on the shadowy form of smoke. The smoke became a part of the air, dwelling forever among the living. They were the darkness that guarded the sleeping Mar from the Drakes when Her, the goddess of light, abandoned them.

Superstition, he thought.

He lay on his back and looked up at the sky. None of the moons was up tonight, making the stars the only natural light in all of Marrishland. Einar's mind floated away, dulled by the morutsen coursing through his veins.

The mundanes believed the stars were the spirits of the fallen heroes whose deeds were lauded by the gods as exemplary and worthy of emulation. In this way, those Mar who led justly in life were also guides in death. There were thousands of stars, tens of thousands. Each one, from the dim Larena Ynvenea to the dazzling Kaliher, had a name and a story.

"Help me face my fate with dignity as you did," Einar whispered to them all.

Folk tales. There are as many stars in the sky now as there were at the beginning of the world.

The calm air grew suddenly agitated as a cool wind swept across the moors. To the west, the stars that made up the Guardian began to disappear behind the approaching clouds.

Ari lay on his back, and he, too, watched the stars, uncomfortable beneath their gaze. In the eastern sky, the clump of stars known as the Mass began to rise. The component stars were not villains, though. Villains never became stars. The stars who formed the Mass and the other constellations named for the servants of Dinah and Domin were the souls of those heroes who had once been villains.

One of those had been Tryggvi Fochs. He had been a common brigand who preyed on merchants leaving and entering Marrishland from the east, but when the Gien Empire launched its first invasion of Marrishland, Tryggvi swore to defend his country from the attackers. He led countless raids on the Gien encampments, luring the enemy deeper into the Dead Swamps while other Mar cut supply lines.

When the remaining ten thousand Giens were hopelessly lost in the swamps, the Mar left them at the mercy of the quicksand and suckmud. Tryggvi, however, wished to seal the invaders' fates. He allowed himself to be captured. The Giens recognized him as a hero among the Mar and took steps to force him to lead them to safety. Tryggvi feigned obedience and then led them into the territory of a pack of damnens.

The Gien army was never heard from again, but according to the tale, Tryggvi managed to elude the damnens. His star was Vetrator Ducor, a prominent member of the Mass.

Ari gazed at the wideness of the sky. There were so many stars, but there was more darkness than lights. In the western sky, the approaching storm cast its first bolt of lightning, illuminating the sky for just a moment before giving the swamp back to the embrace of the shades.

Eda came to a sudden stop in her exercises, panting. Something was different in the room.

The bed was splintered. The mattress was so many thousands of incinerated bits across the floor. A chair could just be recognized in the mess, and the splatters from the candles. The only thing intact in the room was the door — which hung open now.

The cyan-garbed weard lowered her sword and stepped quietly toward the door so she could see through it, watching the myst for any sign of attack.

Here in Domus? Who would dare?

Katla stood in the room, her red hood thrown back, with her hands clasped in front of her.

"Weard Katla Duxpite," Eda said, lowering her marsord but not her guard. The woman had teleported here.

"Weard Eda Stormgul."

The greetings were strained and formal — childhood friends who had sworn allegiance to very different masters. They stared at each other for several minutes, and then Katla seemed to break. She sighed.

"Peace in the swamp, Eda," Katla said. "I have not come to harm you."

Eda relaxed a bit more, but not entirely. "Why have you come then?"

"I cannot find my brother, but I am certain he is unaware the Mass will soon be upon us," Katla said, finding a chair and sitting, adjusting her cloak as she did so.

Eda sat down heavily. "The Mass?"

"Have I ever deceived you — you who know the oaths I have sworn and the name of my patroness?

Eda smiled wryly. "Brand would owe you a pair of boots if he was still alive. He never was one to make good on old wagers."

Katla managed a wan smile. "I am afraid the Mass is every bit as real as Nightfire teaches, and the Drakes are more numerous than any Mar can imagine without having seen them. It is at the edge of the Fens of Ruer, and prepared to descend on Domus Palus."

Eda felt the familiar eagerness for action. She had never intended to sit in the citadel waiting for Sven to give her something to do. That was Erbark's gift, not hers. The decision was surprisingly easy.

"What would you have me do?"

"Find the Flasten and Domus generals, and pass the word to them. They must get to Domus to protect the city."

"Weard Verifien, I think I can find," Eda said. "But why bring the Flasten army?"

"The Mass is beyond comprehension," Katla said, her hands expanding. "The first wave will be as big as all the weards in one of those armies. And there will be a score of waves after that. Domus must be protected, and the Mass ground up against it." She leaned forward. "Sven once told me that Vitharr Taffer offered to go with Nightfire, but you fed him some bad soup a few days before, and he was too sick to go — so you had to. Stormgul, they called you even then. 'The fortress that stands against the darkness, the storm that bows the trees by night.'"

Eda flushed. *And what of your name, Katla — "one who thwarts the duxes?" How have the duxes not seen the threat you have hidden there, or has Nightfire convinced them you no longer pursue your namesake?*

"What about here, now?" Eda asked. "I could be helping out here. You could go to Flasten."

"You would not be taken seriously. The Council knew me as Brack's apprentice. They will know me as Brack."

Eda opened her mouth to object. She wasn't strong enough to hop around hunting for Horsa. And to assume peace could be made! At the hands of a cyan! She stared at her own small hands. Katla seemed to sense her hesitation.

"A tongue of flame tastes every piece of fuel to find the most flammable," she said, her voice low and sincere. "The Mass seldom attacks cities, and the armies should have enough time to occupy it before it arrives, so the capital will hopefully survive the siege. If Pidel joins Domus and its allies in a battle against the Mass, they might inflict enough casualties to discourage the Drakes. It is even possible the Mass can be turned against itself, making it far less of a threat. If all these other blocks of peat are drenched in water and coated in clay, though, I must keep the Mass focused on sacking Domus Palus long enough for Sven to solve this unique military problem."

"There is not a lot of time," Eda murmured.

"You are correct. I would be asking the help of reds if there was time to argue. But I trust a fellow student of Nightfire's, someone I grew up with. Horsa will listen to you for the same reason, and there may be others. Anyone else would be suspect."

Eda nodded, blushing slightly. That had ended years ago, when Horsa was still a cyan himself. But they were still friends. Horsa would trust her.

Katla was right. Yver Verlren ran Domus now that Sven was away, and he wouldn't listen to anyone who was not eighth-degree.

"Bui," she said. "Katla, find Bui Beglin the guerilla." She rushed over Katla's dismissal. "If anyone can defeat Drakes if they attack before the army gets here, it is him. He will know how to train people."

Katla nodded slowly. "You and he stopped the Flasten army."

"Yes. He will be useful."

"I will find him. Now, Eda, you must go."

She hesitated again. "Does Sven know?"

Katla shook her head. "He will find out soon, though. About everything."

"He will be angry."

"He will be victorious together with all of Marrishland, or he will be dead. Pray my patroness is humbled this time."

Eda met Katla's green eyes, hard as agates. She summoned the myst and slipped into the Tempest, but couldn't help but think Katla had manipulated her for some other purpose. *How does she know so much about the Mass, and what did she mean when she said she is Brack now?*

"Lead me through the fearful times ahead," she prayed softly. "Lend me the strength and wisdom that set you forever in the heavens. Help me be worthy of your patronage."

Katla made her way through the enormous camp of Drakes. All around her, twenty thousand Drakes — mostly man-sized, humanoid jabber and stinger guer with a sprinkling of the larger striped and snatching guer — rested in advance of the next morning's march south. It would be a matter of days before they reached the Lapis Amnis, which marked the boundary between Mar and Drake lands.

Calling this the First Wave was an apt title. A few hundred scouts flowed up to the doorstep of Domus already, racing back along what would be the front. The swell was the twenty thousand she purposefully walked through now, which would break over the Lapis Amnis, reform and smash itself against Domus Palus. And this was the first of more than three hundred waves that would pile their dead against the defense of the Mar.

Brack, Nightfire and centuries of Mar were right to fear this enemy.

This part of the camp was primarily stinger guer, and their lizardlike eyes regarded her as they raised their arms away from her, intentionally showing her how careful they were being with the bony, poison-secreting stingers under each forearm. She kept her eyes on them warily in any case, but did not hurry.

She had lied to Eda in one respect. She had not spoken to the people in charge in Domus Palus. She did not want someone to usurp Sven's place by becoming more of a hero. Domus would fall, despite their adepts. Their training was simple, minimal. They would collapse quickly. Piljerka had always been a chauvinistic simpleton, perfect for following orders from men he deemed more powerful.

Sven will have to return to save the Mar. He will have to show them he is the torch they must follow.

They thought so differently sometimes. The loss of their mother had ignited Katla, but she had controlled the fire, had nursed it and fed it just enough fuel to keep from going out before the proper time. It would burn exactly what needed to burn, and not a stick more.

Sven had always had a fiery way about him — an enthusiasm that could exhaust those around him. Tortz had changed him, had redirected his passion along a path he never would have taken on his own. He had slipped out of the hearth and was burning the floorboards. Soon he would take the house, and then the whole town. He was blazing out of control without realizing he was consuming himself.

She did not like seeing Sven raging wildly like this, hurting those around him and seeing enemies where there were none. That had been Brand's undoing, and it would be his. Katla knew she would have to contain Sven eventually. But his was a fire more easily extinguished than controlled, and Katla had sworn not to destroy her brother no matter what he did.

An identifiable line marked the border between the stinger guer camp and the jabber guer one, but the increase in noise level was unmistakable. They were jabber guer because they always made noises. Sometimes they were speaking, but now, as they readied for sleep, it was the growing amount of uneven snoring that sounded like a cross between a cricket and an axe chopping wood. Katla passed by them without causing any stir.

She had spoken to Bui Beglin, because what kind of a hero could a mundane make? The thick rural speech was difficult to comprehend at first, but his intelligence had surprised her. He and his small band would do what they could to stop the Mass, and Katla judged he would be enough of a thorn for the First Wave to make the commander do something stupid — like hole up until the Second Wave arrived less than a span later.

Creating defensive positions would be fatal to the Mass, Katla knew. Oh, there were millions of Drakes coming in regular waves of thousands against a much smaller number of Mar. But they were not supernatural beasts. They had to eat, and drink, and defecate, and heal — one wave would strip a region to the ground. A second one in the same area at the same time would lead to smaller rations. A third one would beget starvation. When the Mass crashed against Domus, it would hurt itself as much as the weards who stood behind the walls.

She thought this as she approached the palanquin that carried the Wave Commander. Guer of all shapes gave reports to the jabber guer, who responded eloquently. She pushed through them until she stood next to him. His head turned slowly to look at her, first with one eye, then the other.

"Wave Commander, have you received word from the Delegates?"

The Wave Commander was a jabber guer — a reptilian humanoid with a short, broad tail, strong legs built for jumping and three-fingered hands with bony wrist spikes. He spoke both Mar and Middling Gien, Katla had learned, but never in front of his troops. He spoke the Drake common tongue now.

"Yee Ka Lah, I was about to send for you. The Delegates are disappointed you failed to kill Yee Seh Tah, but they have consented to meet with you."

Finally, she thought. *I can teleport there and be back in a few days.* "I will visit them directly."

"You must follow the appropriate path to visit the Delegates," the Wave Commander said, gesturing to one of his adjutants. The jabber guer produced a large skin and handed it to him.

Katla sniffed. The sickeningly sweet, faintly fermented smell was morutsen.

"I will submit to the morutsen," she said carefully, "before I visit with them."

"Yee Ka Lah will begin her regimen now." The skin was thrust under her nose. "A messenger must return to the Delegates to say you are coming. You may not arrive before him. This is the only way your kind may visit the Delegates."

"It will take spans to walk there." *Who knows what will happen while I am away!* She tried to keep complaint from her voice, but the Wave Commander grinned, showing three rows of sharp teeth.

"It will take as long as it takes," he said.

Katla hesitated, remembering Brack's travel-worn boots and cane, his long expeditions away from Tue Yee. She thought of all the Mar blood that could be spilled before she even reached the Delegates, and she felt renewed respect for Brack's patience and fortitude.

For the first time, she reconsidered her plan. *Can I do this without talking to the Delegates?* In the hundreds of square miles of Marrishland around her, four Waves poised to descend on Domus and all its innocents in the next few spans.

But in the thousands of square miles to the north, more than a dozen Waves were massing. *Isn't the choice as simple as that? To save the many, a few must be sacrificed?*

Katla lowered her gaze respectfully and took the skin. "As you wish, Wave Commander."

Erika Unschul neither owned nor desired a marsord. Despite claims that it was mostly a tool, she knew wizards seldom used it except to kill other Mar, and her parents had raised her better than that. But it seemed like everyone who served Sven wore one — even the yellow-garbed priests who stood guard in the citadel.

Pondr does not, but he is not a Mar, so that doesn't count.

She adjusted the black apprentice's cloak covering her sturdy, cotton pants and shirt. Some luxuries could be afforded the Mardux, and her clothing was one of the first things Erika had upgraded. Dux Ratsel of Wasfal had gifted her half of her wardrobe, from Mar-made leather belts, boots and vests to the fine Kafthaian cotton she wore. Smoothing her sleeves, she gestured that her visitor be brought in.

The man the yellows brought to her was the first she had seen in months who didn't have a marsord gouger peeking out from a slot in his cloak. She would have rather seen another marsord than a face that dredged up the memories his did, though.

"Bui? Is that you?"

He smiled sheepishly at her. "I'm that, Erika."

"I am glad to see you're safe. Eda told me about what you have been doing for Sven. I have some soup."

Erika had tried to forget about Tortz. It was the first time Sven had killed other Mar and the place where he lost a part of himself that she had fallen in love with in Leiben. She had nearly lost him entirely. She had spent nearly a month certain he would be executed, in fact.

Only Brand's confession spared me that grief — a confession he would not have returned to make if Nightfire had not sent Katla and Robert to track and capture him.

A wizard could not have done it, Erika knew. Even Sven's reconnaissance spells were not as precise or far-reaching as the enchanter's.

Sven owes so much to Robert Wost, but he couldn't forgive him for turning the people of Tortz into fawning slaves with his enchantment. That is forbidden by Vangard's Rules of Governance. Sven collected proof and brought it to Nightfire, who had no choice but to dismiss Robert from the Academy.

"I'll take a little, yes," Bui replied.

Erika had eaten lunch only an hour ago, so she wasn't hungry, either, but she went to the fireplace where a small pot hung and put a little soup in each bowl for hospitality's sake. She glanced down at Asa where she lay curled up on a rug nearby, the flames flickering on her sleeping face.

The only good thing to come of Tortz, Erika thought.

"What brings you to me?" Erika asked when they had finished eating.

"I need you to sen' wizards to the Lapis Amnis up north — thousan's of 'em."

Erika's brow furrowed. "Why?"

Bui scratched his beard. "We've got to keep the Mass from crossin' until the other wizards come back, an' my twenty guerillas can't fight hun'reds of thousan's of Drakes."

She realized her mouth was open. "The Mass?"

"Yes. That's why you've trained all those weards I saw marchin' aroun' the city, right?"

"They're adepts," she managed. "The Law was changed so mundanes could be taught magic, but I didn't think Sven was preparing for the real Mass."

Bui stiffened while she spoke, and his face turned red. "'Depts? Mundanes usin' magic? After Askr an' the others died for doin' that? After I atoned over an' over for doin' it? An' now, anyone can use the myst?" He spat the last word.

Erika shrank back at his vehemence.

Bui unclenched his fists and took a deep breath. "The Mass is real, an' it's comin'. We don't have much time, an' I need all the help I can get to stop it."

Pondr had told Erika that Sven had used the threat of the Mass to convince the duxes to change the Law.

Sven does not really believe in the Mass. Whatever he showed the duxes must have been some ruse. Otherwise he would not have left Domus Palus.

"You're volunteering to lead an army to fight the Mass?"

He nodded. "Someone has to. All the big wizards are fightin' Volun', an' none here believes me. The dux won't even talk to me!"

She leaned forward and clasped her hands on the table. "I believe you, Bui. I'll take your case to Dux Verlren, but I need you to tell me everything you know."

Bui stared hard at her, and she stared back, as calm as she could.

"You're sayin' he might not listen to you, either."

If he always thought it was real, he should already have a plan. If he knew about Sven's lie, though, I will never convince him. She said nothing.

"What'll we do if he doesn't?" Bui pressed.

"I don't know."

Please come home soon, my love.

Bui spoke slowly. "There're ways to fight wizards. I could teach some of these 'depts how to do it."

"No!" Erika almost shouted, and Asa stirred on her rug. She lowered her voice. "No. We need the wizards' help. There are only ten thousand adepts. That's not enough to stop the whole Mass."

But we could train more, she thought. *There are more than a hundred thousand Mar in Domus Palus. Surely they will fight the Mass to protect their homes and families.*

Bui simply nodded, but she could see the argument in his eyes. He would kill a few hundred wizards without hesitation if it would save a hundred thousand mundanes.

I am not Bui. I am not Sven, either.

"If Asa wakes up, tell her I'll be back soon," Erika said as she left the room to find the dux.

"We must strengthen the city's defenses, Dux Verlren," Erika told the Dux of Piljerka.

Yver Verlren looked up from the book he was reading, his eyes speaking volumes about the gap between his red cloak and her black. Having so asserted his superior wisdom, he returned to his reading.

Erika gritted her teeth. Yver was a dux. He had power. She was merely an apprentice who had been neglecting her education for nearly two years.

"You are as stubborn as the Mardux."

Yver finished the page, dog-eared it and closed the book.

"You forget yourself, apprentice. In the absence of the Mardux or a designated seneschal, the highest-ranking wizard sits regent over Domus Palus."

"The Mass is coming. We will need the aid of every magic-wielder in Domus Palus, Dux Verlren. We need to train more adepts — tens of thousands more."

"Domus Palus has withstood centuries of Drake invasions without need of additional defenses, Erika. Go tend your daughter. This is not your concern."

"Sven would not approve of your squandering the only advantage we have."

"The Mardux," Yver emphasized the title, "ordered the formation of the adepts to deal with this invasion that frightens you so. Ten thousand is more than adequate." His small smile chilled her blood.

He knows about Sven's ruse.

Erika plucked the book out of his hands and hurled it out a window, eyes gleaming in a challenge beyond her black apprentice's cloak. "Sven's vision is far from perfect, whatever you believe. The gods may guide him, but they can guide us as well. We can't waste time reading books when the enemy will soon be at the gates!"

He stood, calling Power to bring the book back to his hands. "Because you are the Mardux's wife, I will not harm you. If you were my apprentice, however, I would punish such insubordination. Clearly Mardux Takraf has been far too busy to properly discipline his apprentices."

"Please. This is no raid. The Mass — the real Mass — approaches Domus Palus. You must make more adepts and bring the wizards back to Domus Palus."

"We lost contact with them some time ago. Either they are out of range of our reconnaissance, or they are so spread out as to be virtually undetectable."

"What of Flasten's army?"

He shook his head. "Even if we knew where they were, we would hardly open our gates to an enemy force."

"This is a bad time for a civil war. The Mass has nearly crossed the Fens of Reur! The Mardux does not want a slaughter. I know that."

"Enough! This is none of your concern. Do not attempt to manipulate me by invoking the name of your husband. His power is not yours to command in his absence. You have no more authority here than one of the adepts."

She stiffened as though slapped. She held up her right hand. "Of course, Dux Verlren. Sorry to have troubled you with my mundane concerns."

He had already returned to his book.

She left him to his delusions and madness. Less than a thousand wizards remained in Domus Palus, and many were priests loyal to Horsa. By Sven's decree, more than ten thousand mundanes had begun training as adepts in a city with well over a hundred thousand mundane citizens.

If Sven will not protect Domus Palus and his family, I will.

 **33**

"Tordyn (tor dynamics) is the study of how Mar wizards influence the myst. Each wizard's tor has strengths and weaknesses when it comes to wielding the myst. One might find the myst moves toward her eagerly, but she struggles to shape it into complex patterns. Another can call the myst for a long time before it ceases to obey, but he cannot hold a large amount close to him. Self-improvement by practice alone takes years, but tordyn scholars have found techniques that ease the learning process if they are practiced properly."

— Weard Oda Kalidus,
The Origin of Nothing

Sven crouched in the swamp near Nightfire's Academy and studied his hands. He had had time to think about why he was here and what he was doing.

He was not looking forward to the next step, but he could see no way to avoid it. The gods had supported his desire to create the adepts. Otherwise, one of the Council would have seen through his ruse.

But they'll eventually find out, and the wands will only make them more suspicious.

In order to protect them, Sven needed to remove all potential threats to this future army of Marrishland. He must protect the future of the Mar, his Mar. What he had been and what he became were nothing compared to that.

Are my hands big enough to take on this task? He still felt the sting from where he had hit Erika, and his eyes watered with tears again.

This is the only way I can prove to her I am doing the right thing.

Sliding on a pair of gloves and drawing his marsord, he teleported again.

"Erika, I should not do what you ask of me. We Travellers are welcome wherever we go because we do not involve ourselves in local politics."

She filled his bowl with soup and handed it to him. "This isn't about politics, Pondr. You cannot get out of the path of the Mass before it reaches Domus Palus."

He accepted the bowl warily. "Of course. My life depends on your conspiracy, doesn't it?"

She picked up a second bowl for herself. "Unless you believe six hundred wizards can defeat three million Drakes, yes."

He sighed. "Where will I even find so much stored in one place?"

She blew gently on the soup to cool it. "Healers use it to ease pain and prevent sick wizards from hurting themselves. Go to the temple and ask after Weard Salt. Her reconnaissance should be able to see the Mass by now, and that should convince her of the necessity."

He tried to take a sip of the soup and burned his tongue. He sighed. "Why not send one of the adepts instead?"

"An adept is still treated like a mundane, while a Traveller is welcomed like a Traveller." She looked around the room furtively. "Try to keep your true business secret until you meet Weard Salt. We do not want to cause a panic."

He nodded and sipped his soup. Erika sighed and filled a third bowl. She stood up and went down the hall to a second guest chamber, where the Mar from Tortz waited. *The man who stalled an army. His twenty stopped Flasten's twenty thousand for days. What can he do with a few hundred against a hundred thousand?*

"Bui, have you considered my proposal?" She handed him the bowl.

Bui Beglin nodded. "We'll do what we can to slow the Mass, if that's what the Mardux wants. It'll be hard to train others so fast, but I'll try."

Erika handed him a pair of leather gloves with a metal stud at the tip of each finger. "I'll give these to as many of the adepts as I can. It's clumsy compared to one of Sven's, but it will allow even a weak magic-wielder to set proper traps. I'll teach some of the adepts here how to make them so we can replace the ones your adepts use up. I wish I could provide you with faster transportation, but the wizards seem intent upon saving their magic for a final confrontation with the Mass."

"These 'dept's'll need to walk fast to stay ahead of the Drakes. This'll teach 'em quicker."

"May the gods watch over you, Bui."

"You needn't worry 'bout that, Erika. They will." Bui raised his right hand in salute and left the room.

Hopefully, that will buy us time. I wish we could have sent him with the ten thousand adepts I promised, but even he said we need the rest here. With Pondr's supplies, the new adepts should be ready for action before the Mass crosses the Lapis Amnis.

Erika hated doing this as much as she hated that Sven had started a war between the Mar. She was not as powerful as Sven, so she had to find other ways of protecting the people of Domus Palus — in order to protect her husband. Whom she had every right to be mad at, but still could not throw to the guer.

At least my way, no one will be hurt.

Pondr grunted when Erika returned to fill another bowl for her daughter, who was reading in the library.

I think she spends as much time reading as Sven did when he was at the Academy.

She allowed herself a small smile.

Robert and Ari wore dark green cloaks as they wandered into Leiben after Einar had quietly dismantled all its defenses. The wizards and a sizable entourage of controlled citizens gathered on the green where Sven and Erika had been wed.

"The rest of your dear Protectorates have little hope now that you have chosen to serve me, Weard Schwert."

Einar recoiled, and Robert laughed. "Time to make more wands, Weard Schwert."

He nodded and did as he was told.

Ari followed Robert back to his tent.

"The Mardux will miss Einar. He must already suspect what is happening."

"Good. Volund's son is keeping Domus' real army quite busy, if the two have not destroyed each other by now. With the ten thousand wand-wielders we already have, we would crush any dregs Weard Takraf may have left to throw at us." Robert's pale face twisted in a silent snarl that turned into a knowing smile. "Eventually, he will have to deal with us personally, and that is a confrontation I have been looking forward to for a long, long time. There will be no Nightfire to spare him from me this time."

Ari took a deep breath to say something, but Robert's dark eyes bored into his own.

"Have no fear that I will hesitate to kill him. He was my pupil once, but I will not lose my stomach for revenge as you have."

Ari glanced at the silent mundanes all around them. "Once you kill the Mardux, will you set the people of the Protectorates free?"

"Why should I? With the Mardux dead and Flasten's power broken, how will I make my way in the world? Nightfire will no longer have me at his Academy. Wasfal will give me sanctuary, but he will exact a price." Robert laughed. "The Protectorate slaves are the last currency left to me."

"Stop talking," Ari said softly. *The laughter — it seemed inappropriate.*

"You asked to be my apprentice. You swore to obey me in exchange for my knowledge. You are every bit as under my control as they are. Are you still true to your oath, or will you betray me as Sven did?" Robert's eyes shone with challenge.

I can still think on my own, for now. How much longer before he takes that away from me, too?

Ari swallowed. "I obey you, Weard Wost."

Robert smiled. "Good. Now, I will show you how the Mardux defeated three challengers for the Chair with such ease."

The magic died in Nightfire's study. The fire went out. The old wizard looked up from the book he was editing when the room suddenly filled with a brilliant white-green glow. He raised his arm to shade his eyes and closed the book.

The figure slashed at Nightfire with its marsord, but his arm, clothed in Power, blocked the blade. All the same, the fire set his clothes ablaze, and Nightfire was pushed out of his chair against the wall. He opened his eyes to face Marrish, the Lord of Wind and Fire, father of the gods and lord of magic.

"Do not resist," Marrish said, striking at him again. "Your death is inevitable."

Were he truly my patron, I would already be dead. Nightfire pushed his arm back against the blade, encasing himself in Vitality.

"Am I supposed to confuse you for Marrish?" Nightfire said angrily. The marsord hurt as it bit deep into his arms, but he healed almost immediately and maneuvered out of the way. "I have done nothing but my duty as arbiter, and you owe me your life twice over. Striking me down would be the end of your rule in the eyes of the Council. They could not forgive that." He ducked a vicious blow aimed at his head.

"The Mardux's order will prevail. I will see to it."

Nightfire nodded. He was certain who it was now. "When have I stood in your way, Sven? What have I denied you? Are you as ungrateful as Domin to threaten your master?"

The marsord drew away from Nightfire. The glow faded, and Sven stood there, marsord in one gloved hand.

Nightfire suppressed a sigh of relief, waited for the pain to subside and let down his shield. "It seems a waste of its energy to keep that fire burning. Look at what you did to my floor."

"Nightfire, I swore an oath for you twice before. Now I need you to swear an oath to me."

"May I ask why?"

Sven did not move. This time, Nightfire did sigh.

"Then let me guess. You wish your order to prevail. What is your order? Teach the mundanes magic. You have done that. You have changed the Unwritten Laws. Seruvus knows the truth. But you may also know that this will bring the Mass upon us. How will you win this war you have started?"

Sven raised his gloved hand in mute response. His eyes burned.

Nightfire nodded, thinking fast. "Can you handle a million Drakes? For if there are more than twenty million Mar in the southern half of this subcontinent, there are certainly as many Drakes in the north. No matter, you have this in your plan."

"The Mass is not real."

Nightfire sat down. "It is very real, and your sister cannot quench its thirst for blood."

The Mardux hesitated, back stiff. "Brack is dead?"

"No more than the Nightfire Tradition is. Katla is Brack now."

Sven's eyes widened, but then he set his jaw. "Then I must kill her before she can order the Drakes to march."

Nightfire stared back at him in shocked horror for just a moment before shouting at him. "Are you my apprentice, Sven Takraf? Sven Gematsud?" His face was purple with rage. "Did you learn nothing of reason or ethics at my Academy?"

Sven said nothing.

Have Katla and I made an enemy now, like Volund and everyone but Einar seems to have? Nightfire thought.

Nightfire regained some of his composure. "Killing her would not help. That Brack sometimes has the ear of the Mass is the closest thing to a treaty we have with the Drakes. Correction, had. They have crossed the Fens of Reur by now." He clasped his hands together on the desk and met Sven's one-eyed gaze with his own two green eyes. "You had nobler goals when you started. There was no talk of changing the Law. Remember our conversation when you became a green?"

Sven threw his marsord into the charred wood of the floor in irritation. "Another story! I know my life!"

Nightfire spoke evenly. "Then tell me about it, Sven. Remind me why you became a wizard."

Sven's stillness answered Nightfire's question.

"The Mass is real and invading," Nightfire said. "How can you move the army to intercept it?" The aged wizard sat down heavily.

"Becoming my student meant you would not be a slave. And you had a larger goal, one which I did not entirely approve of."

"I taught my people to read," Sven said quietly.

Nightfire nodded and began to talk.

 **34**

*"The mentor-student relationship is one of the most
important. If it is strong, the student never forgets
the mentor's advice. If it is poisoned, the student still
remembers the lessons, but may look upon them with
disdain."*

— Nightfire Tradition,
On Apprenticeship

Sven finished packing, readying himself for the journey home. At last he was ready. At last his debt had been paid. Shortly after dawn, he would be a wizard. As soon as he donned the green, he could return to Rustiford.

"Are you sure you will not consider staying on as one of my assistants?"

Sven jumped. He had not seen Nightfire step into the room.

"You know what I have decided, master. I go now to my people, to defend my home from the Drakes and Dinah's Curse."

"You have the potential to be a powerful wizard, perhaps wear a red cloak one day. Your contribution to scholarship could be a great one, Sven. You think ... differently than most other wizards."

Sven grinned, but Nightfire did not. He rarely did.

"You excel at finding uses for the information that already exists. I look at a series of observations and draw the conclusions to which the data point. You, however, see results that seemingly have no bearing on those observations. With the discoveries of others, you are capable of constructing new practical applications."

Sven beamed at the compliment. "Thank you, master."

"Innovation is not your only gift. You discovered how to see the myst without the aid of torutsen. Most wizards do not use such magic. It is almost unknown among apprentices."

Sven shrugged. "A crutch. It took me a long time to abandon it and to trust timing."

"Yes, but a very unusual crutch. It seemed to your teachers that your skills were undiminished in spite of the additional strain of calling Knowledge. Either you are stronger with Knowledge than most Mar or you have greater stamina wielding the myst than many."

"Knowledge has more uses than simple reconnaissance, master. Weard Wost speaks of farl applications common to enchanters but nearly unknown to us. Not all of his hints can be exaggerations."

"It sounds like an interesting area of specialization for a student pursuing higher education," Nightfire said, smiling encouragingly now. "Weard Wost speaks fondly of you. I am certain you could learn much from him if you stayed. We are also losing three of our adjunct faculty to other pursuits, and we have more applicants this year than in the last four. If you would like to teach a few classes at the Academy, we would welcome the help."

"I have other people I want to teach. They need my teaching more."

Nightfire sniffed dismissively.

"Rustiford is my home. I have friends there, a family."

"Do you intend to become a magocrat over your own family? They may not welcome you as warmly as you might expect. In truth, I can assure you they will not. You will be wasting your time and energy."

Sven rolled his eyes. This was not the first time Nightfire had tried to turn his determination. "I will not be a magocrat. I will teach them to read, master. I will take apprentices from among them."

"I wish you would consider staying on as a teacher or research assistant or something. You are very talented. Do not waste your education on a handful of mundanes who may not appreciate your efforts."

Does he intend to keep talking until I give up?

Sven's voice hardened. "You exacted no oath of fealty from me in exchange for your knowledge, Nightfire. You taught me because I showed promise as a wizard, not because I shared your interests."

Nightfire matched his tone. "And I encourage you to follow your own path, wherever it may lead. I am merely offering my advice as I would to any of my students. You are not the only one of your peers I have invited to stay at the Academy, you know."

Sven felt a pang of frustration that his master could not see his vision.

"We are wizards, master. We are a tiny minority of the Mar population, yet we rule wherever we go in Marrishland." He tried to keep calm, but his passion burned too fiercely. "Mundanes fear us. We are little more than Drakes and Dinah's Curse to them, yet another obstacle for them to survive. Most are forced to pay tribute to a magocrat, and in turn magocrats do little to improve the quality of their lives. They live in communities built of sweat and blood. And they survive it all without magic. Yet, despite their tenacity, they will go from the cradle to the grave without knowing anything of the world beyond their home towns."

"And they will never miss it," Nightfire added. "Did you? You wanted to live the life of a mundane — never wielding the power of magic and never leaving home until Domin at last called you into his burning duxy. Do you know why I test mundane apprentices?"

Sven said nothing.

"Those mundanes who pass the test have a chance of success, and even they struggle. The others lack the curiosity and determination to become serious students," Nightfire said. "Having struggled so desperately in your own first battle with ignorance, can you honestly believe that you can rescue an entire town as easily as one might rescue a friend from quicksand?"

"At least I will try."

Nightfire grabbed him by the shoulders. His green eyes flickered with fury. "Do you think that I have not tried, Sven? Every professor in this school is fighting the ignorance of his or her students. Many will produce students with a new understanding of the universe and their place in it. But the battle leaves many casualties. As a mass, people do not want to be enlightened. If you attempt to expose them to a new understanding, they will reject it."

"What do you suggest I do?" It seemed important to ask, though Sven felt he knew the answer.

"Do as I do. Help the ones who want your help. Enlighten those who seek enlightenment." Nightfire was preaching now. Here was his passion. "As a healer cannot bring life to the dead, so even the greatest teacher in the world cannot bring life to the mind that is dead. Help those who can be helped, or you will merely end up wasting a lot of time fighting a losing battle against someone's comfortable ignorance. One at a time, Sven. Bring enlightenment to one person at a time. Nothing else works. Trust me."

Sven turned away, looking out the window of his room at the enormous kalysut that grew at the center of the Academy. Its branches were bare — stripped by the hands of a hundred apprentices and the cold winds of the coming winter.

He is partially right. I will have to be patient.

"Eight years ago, you were wrong about me, master. Becoming a wizard has not made me forget what it means to be a mundane. I will return to Rustiford to serve my friends and family."

Nightfire stared at him for a long moment before nodding slowly. "So be it. Some lessons can only be learned from hard experience. I must finish preparations for tomorrow's ceremony. I will see you at the temple in the morning."

The open-air temple sat in a broad clearing, on a rise of land just west of Nightfire's Academy. A long, broad trunk split cleanly in half served as the altar. A circle of tall, lacquered wooden statues of the gods surrounded it. The trees beyond them were not the cypress and cedars which were the most common in Marrishland, but kalysuts — hardy, thick-limbed trees that seemed almost out of place here in the swamps, despite the myriad stilt-like roots protecting the trunks from rot.

Kalysuts grew everywhere, in every nation, across the planet. They thrived in the warm, wet climate of Flecterra. They endured the dry, barren heat of Turuna. They broke the otherwise treeless landscape of the Aflangi plains. They even survived the cold deserts of the mountains of northern Huinsy. The huge trees managed to grow tall and thick in the depths of the swamps and marshes of Marrishland.

Their presence here, in a temple to the gods, was no accident. The eight-pointed leaves, once dried and boiled in water, produced torutsen — the bitter brown drink that allowed an apprentice his first glimpse of the myst. Its sap, a golden liquid extracted by trimming branches or drilling a hole in the trunk, was morutsen, which, when consumed, prevented the wizard from using any magic.

Power and powerlessness, beginning and end.

More than eight years had passed since Sven had begun his apprenticeship. He stood before the altar with nearly fifty other first-degree apprentices, most excited to receive their green cloaks. Heliotosis' icy breath tugged at their black cloaks and dragged the heat away from their bodies as the sky spat icy rain at them, but they endured it without complaint. It was nothing compared with the years of apprenticeship and grueling tests of their magical and mental abilities.

Nightfire stood opposite the apprentices on the other side of the altar, the wizards who lived and taught at the Academy spread out around him. There were also several graduates who had returned to attend the ceremony and wizards who belonged to the families of those assembled for promotion. Their cloaks were every color of the myst.

The master of the Academy spoke. "Today we recognize the graduation of forty-eight apprentices to the rank of wizard. It is a time of endings and of beginnings.

"Long ago, when this temple was new, before Weard Darflaem discovered magic, the Mar made sacrifices at this very altar. It began as sacrifices of food — a symbol of the Mar's willingness to trust the gods to provide for their needs. By surrendering more food than they could afford to lose, the Mar placed their lives in the power of forces beyond their control and comprehension. If the gods did not answer these prayers, the Mar would die. As eighth and seventh-degree apprentices not yet worthy of your first taste of torutsen, you were forced to have faith that your instructors — who could slay you with a thought — were wise and merciful, and wished for you to prosper and learn.

"As the Mar grew less dependent on the gods for their basic needs, the sacrifice of food lost meaning. Live animal sacrifices replaced food gifts. A Mar could not capture a deer or rabbit alive unless the gods brought fortune and wisdom to his hunt. The flesh of the sacrifice was not burned, as before, but roasted and given freely to a neighboring family. The gods became providers again, and the Mar tradition of hospitality was born. As sixth and fifth-degree apprentices, you tended the mundane needs of the entire Academy, giving generously to your instructors and fellow apprentices without expecting them to repay you.

"Over time, the Mar forgot the truth behind the sacrifices they made out of habit. Some priests argued that no sacrifice without surrender was worthy of remarkable intervention. They demanded human sacrifices — children, friends, wives, those dearest to the Mar. A supplicant was made to suffer great emotional loss to receive an answer to his prayers. Though it was a dark chapter in Mar history, we can learn something about ourselves from it. As fourth and third-degree apprentices, the lessons you received were almost universally harsh — demanding so much of your time and energy that it was no surprise to see tears on your faces. You grieved over lost sleep, over surrendered time with friends, and over the term breaks you sacrificed to long tomes and elaborate projects.

"By the time the dark period of human sacrifice ended, Weard Darflaem had received the gift of magic. Within a few generations, wizards became the rulers of Marrishland and set about learning the secrets of magic — inventing the applications that are now standard instruction for apprentices. As second and first-degree apprentices, you learned those applications and many more. You observed less experienced apprentices and brought bad behavior to the attention of your instructors for disciplinary attention.

"After many centuries, Marrishland's magocracy emerged. In it, the Mardux ruled the duxes. The duxes ruled the magocrats. And the magocrats ruled the mundanes. Wizards do not seek to bribe mysterious gods with gifts of food. The wizard seeks to become like the god or goddess he or she serves. As new wizards, you will shed the trappings of a mundane Mar and swear your allegiance to your immortal patron."

Nightfire joined the other observers beyond the ring of statues. The graduating apprentices removed their boots and walked to the altar as one body, stripping off their cloaks and clothes as well. Even though all of them knew the ground had been purged of Dinah's Curse, including konig worms, there was some hesitation as they removed their boots.

When the apprentices reached the altar, they threw their clothes on it until the pile flowed over the sides and created a wall of cloth around the table. Naked in freezing air, the graduates diffused slowly, walking toward the statues of the gods they were choosing as patrons. Sven let his peers reach the altar ahead of him and tarried at the center of the clearing, waiting to see which statue each would choose.

Most migrated to the more commonly declared patrons — Her, the goddess of the sun; Heliotosis and Swind, the gods of the north and south winds; Sendala, the goddess of fertility and the blue moon, and her twin brother and consort, Niminth, who ruled the green moon and the loins of men; Fraemauna, the goddess of wisdom and the yellow moon; Cedar, the god of plants; Seruvus, the god of water and the Oath-binder; and Marrish, the father of the gods, the Lord of Wind and Fire, the god of magic and storms. Marrish and Fraemauna were especially favored by those who intended to continue their educations.

One, however, picked Domin, the god of death and the dark moon. *Arn's father is in charge of cremating those who die in Domus Palus. He always spoke of learning the trade. He does not fear Domin as much as most Mar do.*

None of the apprentices picked Dinah, but that was not unusual. Rumor had it that only three new greens had sworn themselves to the Bald Goddess since Sven's arrival at the Academy more than eight years ago. Sven had his suspicions, but it would have been impolite to ask.

Two merely prostrated themselves near the center of the clearing, signaling that they were not worthy to boast the patronage of a god. They would instead swear to follow the path of one or more of the heroes that lit up the night sky — whether it was a single star, a constellation, or all the bright dead in the sky. Those who swore fealty to the stars would never be allowed to join the priesthood, but they were often favored as military officers.

When almost all his peers had chosen patrons for themselves, Sven climbed onto the altar and lay on his back on the mundane trappings they had left behind. It was a measure of the severity with which the audience treated the ceremony that no one speculated aloud about what he intended it to mean. At last, the rest of the apprentices must have finalized their choices, for Nightfire spoke. There was no hesitation in his voice.

"Do you swear to live your lives in the service of your patrons?"

Every apprentice swore to the Oathbinder and to his patron that he would. In the cacophony, no one could hear Sven's oath clearly.

"Seruvus and your patrons have heard your oaths. Woe to the wizard who breaks his oath or betrays his patron. Rise, apprentices, and go forth as wizards."

Sven stood up even as Nightfire and the other instructors made the rounds with green cloaks and new boots. Then Nightfire came to Sven, wrapping him in a bright green cloak.

Sven welcomed the garment. For its warmth. For its dryness. For its protective weight. For the power it represented. For the rank it bestowed. He welcomed it, summoned his magic to return heat to his numb limbs, and joined the procession of new wizards as it returned to the Academy.

Sven interrupted his master. "You never asked why I lay down on the altar, instead of picking one patron."

"Seruvus knows why you did it," Nightfire began, but the Mardux kept speaking.

"I had a dream, master. I chose the altar because it was the center of the clearing. I swore my oath to nine patrons."

"And you thought nothing of the hubris of claiming nine gods as your own?"

"I did not claim them, master. They claimed me. Remember how I began my apprenticeship, recall the events leading up to Tortz. All of my patrons accepted my oath and took pains to show me they had accepted it."

Warning clouded Nightfire's response. "Omens are wishes wanting fulfillment. Much wrong has been done by great men in response to an omen."

Sven paid no heed. His passion, his belief rose again. "If any of my patrons had failed to give me a sign, I might have believed as you do, master. I have Seruvus's memory, as you well know, but my patrons withheld my other gifts until I passed their tests."

He stared at Nightfire's blank expression, and then continued.

"For volunteering myself as payment of Rustiford's debt, Marrish granted me great magical power."

Nightfire gestured dismissively. "Above average, I would say. You make much of what you have, but you have those gloves of yours to thank for most of your victories."

"As a reward for returning to Rustiford as a teacher, Her granted me the gift of moving speech."

"You have a certain charisma, especially among the idealists of your generation, but you did not lack it before you graduated. Have you forgotten the slaves in the house you befriended so easily?"

"My courage and generosity at Zerst earned Niminth's blessing. They named me war leader the day after I arrived."

"You saved the entire town with your magic," Nightfire said, his voice more quiet. Sven was not really listening. "Magocrats have led in war for centuries for the same reason."

"Because I sought to aid villages beyond Zerst, Sendala sent me Erika. Because I defended Bera's Unwritten Laws when Brand took me prisoner, Swind granted me miraculous skills as a teacher. For defending Tortz even though it might mean my death, Heliotosis granted me the gift of weather that always favored my cause."

Nightfire seethed, not even bothering to refute his arguments, clearly thinking them ridiculous.

"Because I did not use the people of Tortz as weapons but, rather, championed them, Fraemauna granted me her gift. She whispers no words of wisdom into the ears of my enemies. And because I did not abandon Tortz when Brand did, Cedar granted that my allies should multiply like wild rice."

"Are you finished?" Nightfire asked irritably.

"The night before my inquisition at Tortz, my patrons sent me a new vision. This time, they told me I am the Guardian. They promised I would unite Marrishland, subdue Dinah and prove to the world that the Mar are the greatest of all peoples."

Sven inhaled deeply.

"This is why I am here, master, and this is why I need you to swear to serve me and acknowledge that I am the hand of the gods."

Nightfire stood and walked around his desk, stopping not a head's width from the Mardux. His voice was as quiet as Swind's whisper, and he sounded like an old man for the first time since Sven had known him. "I will not take that oath, Sven Takraf. It is not the place of the arbiter to swear fealty to anyone."

Sven's face registered his surprise, but it vanished as quickly as it showed. His posture changed, becoming less regal and more sinister. The light slid across his face, darkening his good eye.

"Then the arbiter must be removed."

Nightfire pushed down Sven's shaking arms.

"Whether you swore an oath to the mundanes or to nine divine patrons, killing me now serves no purpose. I am no threat to you so long as you can command the power of the Council to change the Law whenever and however you wish."

Sven opened his mouth, but Nightfire's stern gaze forced it closed again. He went on.

"The Mass approaches Domus Palus, and Weard Wost marches against the Protectorates. If you are the Guardian, then your patrons will see you and your people through these dark times. If you are deluded, the knowledge I live to protect will be preserved, and there may yet be hope that the Mar will escape a dark age. If you kill me, and it turns out that you misread your omens, Mar civilization will be at an end. All Marrishland will burn because of you. Are you so certain of your vision that you would rather kill every Mar in Marrishland than consider a contingency plan to save your people in case you are terribly wrong?"

There was a very long pause as Sven considered this, weighing Nightfire with his one good eye. Nightfire stepped back, blocking the light entirely from his student's face.

At last, Sven stripped off the gloves and stuffed them in his utility vest. "I spare you, Nightfire, because even now, I can still learn from you."

"I have some soup."

The Mardux shook his head. "Not today, master. I must ready the Mar to repel the Mass." He gathered the myst and vanished into the Tempest.

Nightfire sat down, hands shaking. Within the hour, he rose to give orders to transport the library to Wasfal Palus, where the Academy would wait in exile until this war was over.

 **35**

*"It is very difficult to avoid master-servant relationships
even in the most egalitarian organization. Leaders rely
upon their apparent superiority to maintain authority
over their followers. Without leadership, civilization
dies. However, a leader who forgets he is not superior to
his followers becomes a threat to civilization, instead.
These are the tyrants."*

— Weard Hakan Ebutor,
Power Structures

Erika watched her daughter read the magical primer her husband had written during his early years as a teacher at Nightfire's Academy. The green-eyed girl spoke each word as she read just as her father did.

Does she have Seruvus' memory, as well?

She smiled as Asa struggled with the pronunciation of some of the more difficult words near the end of the book. Sven would not approve of this choice of reading material, but Erika did not see why it mattered anymore. Thanks to Sven's new law, the most illiterate among the adepts were now allowed to learn to use magic. What did it matter if their daughter studied a little magical theory? Asa certainly seemed fascinated by the subject.

Asa stopped reading in the middle of a page. She looked up with a deeply serious expression.

"When is Dad coming to take us home?"

"Soon, Asa."

The girl frowned. "I understand if you don't know, Mommy."

Erika jumped slightly.

So like her father.

"I'm sorry, honey. I don't know. I hope he'll come soon, though."

Asa nodded, seeming to accept this, and returned to her reading.

Pondr entered quietly. Erika walked over to him, a questioning look in her eyes.

"It's over, Erika." He brushed past her and collapsed into her rocking chair.

"Was there ... ?" Her gray eyes flickered toward Asa.

Pondr followed her gaze. "Some. Six of theirs, nearly forty of yours, ours. A trio of lavenders discovered the morutsen in their meal. It took time to suppress them."

Forty-six Mar killed because of me.

"And the other three?"

"Reprisals. Those responsible are now in custody."

She clasped her hands over her belly in fear. *Sven overturns some of the old laws, and his people cast down others because I asked them to.* She gently closed Asa's book. The girl looked up at her, then hopped down and left without another word. Erika watched her go with sadness. *She probably understands.*

"What is to become of them?"

Pondr outlined the punishment tersely and gruesomely. Slavery, death if they resisted — a lifetime of morutsen. Whatever they did in their lives, that was done now. Erika clutched her belly harder.

"Mar don't fight Mar, Pondr. Being even remotely responsible for the murder of magocrats does not come naturally to me. It makes me no better than they are."

"You didn't kill those wizards, Erika. Those adepts just took advantage of the situation you created. Maybe they even deserved what they got. Magocrats have taken advantage of mundanes for centuries, especially slaves."

"I don't care, Pondr. This isn't about making mundanes get along with magocrats. You know why we needed to gain control of the city."

"Yes, but not all of the adepts do."

"What do you mean?"

"I've already said more than a Traveller should. You told Sven you wanted to go back to the Protectorates, and the Mardux often spoke of them as a safe haven. I've decided to go there."

"But the Mass."

"Weard Salt's calculations say I can get to the Protectorates before the Mass reaches Domus Palus. Companions make any journey
safer, and this is an especially dangerous time and place for travel."

"I don't know what to say, Pondr. Such an abrupt departure
might..."

"Think on it," the Traveller insisted, and then he hurried away.
Before the door closed, a heavy man with a strip of red cloth tied on
each arm entered. She could just see a handful of similarly dressed
people outside. Her eyes drifted to the studded Blosin glove hung on
his belt. He raised his right hand.

"Fraemauna's blessin's be upon you, Weard Unschul."

Erika's voice was little more than a whisper. "I'm not a wizard,
adept ... "

"Finn Ochregut, Weard. An' I mean the title in its original sense —
guardian."

"Wait, aren't you a ... ?"

"Mapmaker? Yes, Weard Unschul. We're not all as mad as the stories say. I joined th'adepts at the very beginnin'. I knew we'd over-
throw the magocrats once a leader showed himself, or, as it turned
out, herself. Thanks to your gifts of torutsen, morutsen and Blosin
gloves, there are now a hundred thousand adepts in Domus Palus, all
loyal to you. With such an army of magic-wielders at your command,
you have the power to take the Chair."

They want me to take the Chair? She fell into the seat abandoned
by Pondr, thinking on his last words. *No wonder he wanted to leave!*

She met Finn's eyes. They were perfectly relaxed. He had no fear
of her. A little spark ignited in her. *They want me to be Mardux as an
apprentice weard and they have no fear for me?* Fire tinged her voice.

"What would I want with the Chair, adept? If you mean open rebellion against the wizards now, as the Mass marches against Domus
Palus, then the tales of mapmakers are all true."

Finn's face hardened, but she spoke over him, past him, to all the
adepts straining to hear in the corridor. "Overthrowing a few hundred lazy magocrats when you have a hundred thousand magic-
wielders and the element of surprise is hardly a victory worthy of a
Mardux. You have no time to waste puffing yourselves up and playing

at being heroes in an epic."

The murmurs behind him made the mapmaker-turned-adept soften.

"Then what'll we do, Weard Unschul?"

"Take the opportunity the magocrats refused. Ready the city for a prolonged siege against enemies beyond counting. Let all of Marrishland know what we face and pray the gods move them to send us reinforcements." She met Finn's eyes again. "What?"

"Will you organize the defen'ers of Domus Palus?"

Erika could no longer contain her frustration with the mapmaker. "I'm not Sven. You're more qualified to lead the adepts than I am."

"You'll just sit and watch then, like the magocrats would've done?"

Erika gaped at him. *Suddenly I'm a magocrat? These adepts are dangerous men!* She searched for a solution, thinking as hard as she had ever done. After a moment, she spoke. "I will go to the Protectorates. The wizards there know more about Blosin gloves than I do. They might even be able to send reinforcements." She stood up before he could interfere. "I will leave in the morning. Be sure to send messengers to the rest of Marrishland to warn them of this threat. Whatever you and the other adepts think of them, we need the wizards to win this war."

A hundred feet back from the mud-crusted shore of the Lapis Amnis, Marrishland's largest river and the southern border of the Fens of Reur, Bui Beglin instructed his army of adepts in preparation for a battle against the Mass even he felt they could not hope to win.

They had arrived a day earlier. The city-born adepts were exhausted after the march, but they had learned the hard lessons Bui had. Leaving Domus, they had no concept of how to look for suckmud willows or snakes, and each was terrified of every drop of water or glob of mud. To fend off those fears was the work of a half day of giving them something worse to fear: their commander, the mundane guerrilla Bui Beglin.

He had given them six hours to rest when the river was in sight, and, leaving the ones he deemed most reliable in charge, had crossed the river to scout alone, intent on discovering if his worst fears would come true.

Bui had learned something of their numbers, and other knowledge that had borne some fruit he could use. He had not seen any insero, the oversized, mantis-like fliers that could carry a half-dozen of the smaller, rat-like ravits and their deadly rain of poison darts.

Weard Duxpite had spoken of the Mass as coming in waves. If we fend this one off, how many more will come? I won't have time to recon every wave.

Returning, he ordered a mud wall built to raise them higher above the river; there was already a rise the Mass would have to run up after the river, but a few extra feet could make a difference. Trees were stripped to make a slatted roof for the army to hide beneath in case the insero did show up.

And, most importantly, the Mardux's traps were laid, as many as the adepts could, for a mile-long stretch of the river. The adepts were hardly strong enough to make them, but neither was Sven at Tortz, Bui knew now. Almost half his army had spent the past day enchanting the gloves that could make the traps, which triggered when a Drake's tor approached them, while the other half had bled the gloves dry planting the spells in the river and mud.

More than a hundred feet of death would greet the first wave of the Mass, and Bui could not think, watching his four thousand exhausted adepts, that they would be able to hold off another wave of this magnitude.

And if they hesitate, and move around us, we will be food for Dinah.

"Dinah's shriveled teat, that's too many!" someone cried.

On the other side of the river, a quarter-mile of mud, bedraggled scrub and weathered rocks ended at a pathetic row of trees, but those had been enough to block the first line of the Mass. Bui watched the first Drake run to the river's edge, and a half-dozen followed sporadically behind that first scout, but now they poured out onto the mud flats like a flood.

Mostly guer of two types — jabbers with their sharp, bony forearms and powerful legs, who would leap for their first assault; and stingers, geared with weapons, shields, and whip-like tails covered in poisoned spikes — led the First Wave. Both could swim, and while the Lapis was sluggish here, it was also wide, and the Mass would stop to rest, exhausted from their march, before crossing.

They are organized, though that isn't exactly unexpected, he thought, as the First Wave stopped and started gathering itself, jabbers in the front ranks and stingers behind, and scores of the giant, shambling striped guer beginning to appear from the back. Bui had counted more than fifty of them in his scouting, and knew that if they made it across the river, the adepts would be in trouble.

He turned to the adepts near him.

"Ready bows, but don't shoot until I say. The rest of you, stop gawkin' and keep buildin'. We'll use every minute we have to build walls and roofs. You twenty."

The team of adepts looked at him like mice staring into the eyes of a snake.

"Spread out evenly alon' the line an' watch for anythin' i'th'air. You see insero, let us know. They'll have ravits, but we'll have bows an' roofs."

They remained frozen in place until he waved a hand at them, at which point they scampered off. The other adepts nearby caught the look on Bui's face and resumed preparations. The relay team carried the order, using Mobility to hasten their movements.

The First Wave finished its deployment. Bui counted eighteen places they would likely cross, jabbers first probably, then stingers, and he pointed to the five groups in the middle, which appeared to be the largest.

"The leader's there," he said. No standard marked it, but every general would want to have the most protection. More than half of the visible striped guer were concentrated there.

"If we kill their leader, they will run," someone said, to general approval.

"No," Bui said. "They'd fall apar', sure, but they'd still come. No one would order a retrea', see, and we'd rather have that."

"So we should let it live?"

Bui didn't answer. Fighting against the Flasten army, the leaders had been predictable. They had stopped moving when the situation was confusing. The Drakes were more adaptable. But if they left the leader alive, and forced him to hesitate, it would be enough for Bui to order a retreat of his own.

They waited tensely, watching the Mass, until a shout rose. The front ranks of the Mass had entered the water, running into it with howls and screams, splashing up so much water it looked as if the river was parting for them. Bui did a quick count. The First Wave was crossing from all of its positions, and all were within the range of the traps.

He felt a sting of fear for his adepts, looking at him for instructions. Thousands of Drakes waded into the water in front of them. They should turn and run back to Domus now.

He knew the adepts couldn't win. This was the first battle of a war of attrition, and he was prepared for high casualties before the day was done. He did not intend to allow the Drakes to rout them, though. Tortz had been defended by a militia no more skilled with magic than these adepts, and Brand had organized them into a sturdy fighting force.

As the howls of the Drakes grew louder, Bui raised his own voice to his adepts.

"I need another team to come here. The rest of you teams, coun' off by four. We'll star' with the middle an' go east an' west. Ones an' threes'll make a wall with Power to keep them in the river. Twos, you'll watch the magic traps an' use the gloves to fix them until they run out, an' then attack with fire when the Drakes come out of the river. Everyone else, give them the gloves. Fours, you'll save your magic to heal the woun'ed. Remem'er — arrows when I say."

They had trained a bit. Each adept knew his strength, in Power or in Vitality, trap-setting or glove-making. Bui hoped it was enough. So far, everyone listened. Numbered by those same strengths, they distributed as they were told.

Bui waved to the team of adepts he had singled out.

"Stay close to me. You're my special escort force. You'll do what I need you to do."

They shot him confused looks but followed him as he walked up and down the line, adjusting people's positions and keeping an eye on the enemy.

The Mass filled the river halfway now, some swimming and some trying to walk across the sticky mud bottom. Their gray, brown and black heads and bodies moved determinedly, the shouts fading, eager to start this fight. The Mass came with the confidence that for each who died, a hundred more would replace him, and Bui realized that the leader would not order a retreat at all.

Somewhere down the adepts' line, an arrow took flight, followed by a hundred more before Bui could react.

"Don't shoot! We'll need those arrows later!" Bui screamed, but someone had already put a stop to it.

A few arrows hit, however, but the premature attack only seemed to spur the jabbers forward. Enough jabbers were in the river now that the stingers began their march forward, and the river was more than three-quarters full of living bodies.

Dinah's shriveled teat, it's like leading an army of mapmaker children across the Fens of Reur.

A fountain of water flung a few jabber guer up into the air, and Bui was about to shout at his adepts again when a dozen more explosions appeared up and down the line — the Mass had reached the traps.

Ten seconds later, the entire river seemed to be in the air, and jabber guer rained on the First Wave. Some hit the mud beach with thumps and cracks, setting off more explosions of mud and fire.

Through the rain of river water, some of which was turning to steam, dozens and then hundreds of jabber guer broke through in great leaping bounds, hardly touching the ground. But the mud beach was so littered with traps that most of them set off something.

"Fire! Fire at anything you can see!" Bui screamed as a particularly fast and lucky jabber took one final leap and landed among the stunned adepts. It was quickly dispatched as arrows filled the air, and someone was dragged away to be healed.

Bui stared back at the river, rushing in on itself again. Most of the traps had been used. Jabber corpses floated downstream, and jabber bodies littered the mud beach. More than half their traps were gone now, and the stinger guer swam deliberately toward him.

This will soon be the safest place to cross, Bui thought woefully, trying to see through the steam for the striped guer. A gust of wind cleared the air for a minute, and he suppressed a shout of shock.

Across the river, the striped guer and two large bands of jabbers and stingers were moving upstream.

He had no time to think. A score more jabber had leapt across the last line of traps and scrabbled at the wall to reach his adepts, and skirmishes were breaking out up and down his line. Gesturing to his special escort, Bui grabbed his spear to help in the nearest fight.

The jabber had killed someone, and it launched itself at a fear-stricken adept as Bui cast his spear into its side, knocking it into the ground. The guerrilla was on it immediately, stabbing at the throat with a knife. He wrenched the knife and spear free and looked at the terrified adept.

"You. Go down the line, and order everyone back one hundre' yards. Go now!" he barked, and the adept fled. He pointed with the blooded spear at two of his escort. "Follow him and make sure he does it. An' order a line of traps set atop the wall. Quickly, the stingers're almost upon us."

"What about us?" someone asked.

"You're comin' with me. The striped guer are headed upstream."

They jogged upstream behind the wall, ordering the adepts down and setting explosions along their mud wall. Bui killed two more jabbers and passed nearly a dozen guer corpses before the ground started shaking — the stingers had reached the traps on the mud beach.

Their view north disappeared in mud and guer as the body of the stingers hit the traps. Bui risked a glance back down the line. As far as he could tell, the adepts were retreating. A few ran up and down the wall, randomly setting traps and pocketing the used gloves.

Someone grabbed his shoulder, dragging him to a halt, and a stinger corpse landed a few feet in front of him with a crunch. It started to move, and one of his escort stabbed it with a spear.

"Thanks," he said, breathlessly.

"You're always tellin' us to watch where we're goin'," the blood-and-mud-covered woman said. "You should do the same."

He grinned fiercely at her, and they passed the last of his adepts.

Up here, more jabbers had made it past the traps, and with no one to fight, were milling around. Bui made note of this as, covered in his own explosions, he speared one and knifed a second. His escort, which had somehow grown to more than hundred, fell on the unsuspecting jabbers, and real battle ensued.

Maybe their boss died crossing the river, and they had no idea what to do, he thought, stepping to one side to avoid a leap and hamstringing a guer attacking someone else. *Maybe they had orders just to cross and then wait.*

Suddenly he was fighting a stinger guer, and brought his knife up to block the tail. They had made it past the traps, and he had no idea where they were.

"Press forward!" he shouted. "We need to stop the striped guer!"

Most of his small army disengaged and ran east, conserving their magic to heal themselves. Glancing around, Bui saw all of the jabber were down or too injured to run, and the stinger he had killed had been one of only a handful.

More will come. He risked a glance toward the river.

The mud beach was gone, the river permanently rerouted, shallower and slower. But the river was red, too, as far as the eye could see, and thousands upon thousands of the First Wave of the Mass drifted slowly toward the great delta of the Lapis Amnis. More littered the chewed and torn shallows where the beach had been, and more among the ruined wall behind him. A few Mar cloaks could be seen among them, and shouts from the west suggested more skirmishes had ensued.

Someone near him shouted, and his head whipped forward. The striped guer had entered the river, a few hundred yards above the traps.

How can we stop them? We have no traps; most of my army is downstream. Then he remembered the milling jabbers. *They have orders.* And he thought he knew what they were.

"Stop," he ordered, looking back down the line. The exhilarated adepts around him gathered in confusion.

"We're winning," one said, and they all began to cheer.

Bui nodded. "We've won," he said. "But that pocket we just passed through? There's one on the downstream flank. And this is their leader. We may have killed more than half of them, but that was because we had the traps. There are no more traps."

He gestured back the way they had come. "But we know they had orders, that they're followin' a plan. That gives us time. So we retreat, and let the rest of them by us, you understan'? We send a messenger to the weards at Domus and let them take care of this."

He looked north, across the river.

"There's another Wave we have to prepare for."

 **36**

*"Mardux Sven Takraf did not invent the wand. The Kali-
heron taught their apprentices how to wield magic 'by
the staff' (Ies). Nor did he pioneer mystalton (spell-shap-
ing spells), which were an innovation of farl enchanters.
But the Blosin gloves are his — marrying mystalton
with Ies in a way that did not violate Bera's Unwritten
Law. The Blosin gloves allowed him to overcome the
limitations of his tor and focus on mysdyn. With them,
as long as he knew the pattern of an application, he
could wield it simply by designing a series of wands that
would build increasingly complex mystalton until he had
a mystalt that could generate the pattern of the desired
application. With the Blosin gloves, no spell — not even
morutmanon — was beyond his ability."*

— Weard Oda Kalidus,
The Origin of Nothing

Horsa was praying when they brought the cyan to him.

"Weard Verifien," the cyan said. "It's Eda Stormgul. I know you remember me. The Mardux sent us to ..."

"Eda?" It was like a dream. The reality of the battles he had fought, trying to outthink and outpace Ragnar, had made him forget the rest of Marrishland. "Oh Marrish," he moaned, as though waking from a deep sleep suddenly.

"Horsa," Eda snapped. "I've come to warn you. The Mass is marching against Domus Palus. If the Drakes find it undefended, you will have no temple left to pray in."

The severity of her expression froze his blood.

"You are serious."

She nodded.

"How many Drakes? Thousands? Tens of thousands?"

"At least a million," Eda said, trying to look as certain as she could.

Another chill gripped Horsa in spite of the summer heat. "The Mass ... Sven said it was myth," Horsa whispered in fear. He glanced at the weards who had brought her to him, saw the looks on their faces range from disbelief to outright disgust. Did no one really believe?

But Eda does, and she would never lie to me about something like this.

"Call together my council," he said, though he heard his own voice as if it came from very far away. "We need to discuss this immediately."

"We are less than fifty miles east of the coast," a lavender reported, "and at least part of Flasten's force is twelve miles east of us."

"How close are we to Domus Palus?" Horsa asked.

"Less than a hundred miles. We cannot be certain because every village looks the same out here, and the Mar in the area have long since fled."

"And the magic our recon spells noticed just to the north?"

"I do not think it is Flasten. They would be headed north, not south."

"Unless they are as lost as we are." He hated the bitterness in his voice, but he could not keep it out. His men were long used to his dour nature, though. They knew he wouldn't lead them on a mapmaker's folly.

"We are not lost, Weard Verifien. We are not sure of exactly where we are. Most of the landmarks have been destroyed. Surely even Flasten would be able to guess the way to Domus Palus."

"If it is Flasten, they are in our way," Horsa said.

"We could break through their eastern arm and creep up along their flank," the lavender suggested.

"That will take too long, and Flasten will suspect your destination before you reach it. Domus Palus would face a double threat from Flasten and the Mass," Eda said.

The lavender sneered at the cyan's speech. "We do not know that the force to the north is Flasten. Perhaps the Mardux is sending reinforcements."

"Send a dozen nonagons," Horsa said. "I want eyeball recon this time. We need to be sure of who they are." *Cyan Eda might be, but I will listen to her as much as a lavender.*

"Yes, Weard Verifien." The lavender would not even think of questioning his general.

They were on the move within minutes. In addition to the nonagons, the Domus army had experimented with several formations. V formations for some assaults, jagged lines for others. This time, the detachment would travel in a tight circle used in pinpoint strike missions against vulnerable points — quick strike and, if necessary, an equally quick retreat even in the face of heavy losses.

An hour later, they returned with dire news. Flasten's army stood between them and Domus Palus. Horsa listened to the report with an impassive expression.

"Weard Verifien?" one of the lavenders asked.

He turned to them. "Pass the word to every nonagon you can find. And every pentagon. This war is no longer important. I need to find Flasten's general. We will need his help."

Once their protests were defeated and they were gone, Horsa went to his tent. He sent everyone away, threw himself onto the ground and wept. He was not alone in his grief, for throughout the camp, the veterans of the Teleport War also wept for the victory they might have had.

A year in the mud, and Ragnar had lost his marsord. Somewhere in the muck and grime of their magical battles, Dinah was taking the weapon back to the minerals that had made it. The Domus army had lost almost a third of its number, and Ragnar had lost less than a tenth. He outnumbered them now — dramatically outnumbered them.

But with the news he had received of his father's death only a few hours ago, the red found he did not care.

At least I have a marsord once more, he mused blackly, staring at the gilded blades in his hand.

"Weard Groth, we have taken a prisoner."

Ragnar looked up. A yellow stood between two cyans.

Ragnar walked forward.

"I am Weard Horsa Verifien, general of the Domus army," the yellow said, "I have come to negotiate surrender."

"Surrender?" Ragnar was astounded. *After a year in this muck, surrender?*

"The Mass approaches from the north. We would side with you to defeat it."

Ragnar scowled. "If we accept your surrender, you will be prisoners and may not use magic. You will all become slaves according to Bera's Unwritten Laws."

"This war among Mar must stop, otherwise Domus Palus will soon be no more. Our war already has destroyed a third of the Domus army and a tenth of yours." Horsa took a deep breath. "We may be the last wizards remaining who can stop the Mass before it consumes Marrishland."

"What trickery is this?"

"The Mass still lies beyond the range of your recon spells and mine, and I could easily falsify the result. You must trust me."

"Why?"

"I am a priest, and by the Oathbinder and Marrish, my patron, I swear the threat is real."

"I accept your surrender. Assemble your army for my inspection. Then we shall consider our options. Do not even consider a mapmaker's stratagem, or I really will take you all as slaves and sell you to the likes of Weard Wost."

Horsa bowed and wiped sweat from his brow.

If I can save even one more Mar, I will surrender the rest of Marrishland.

Katla chafed at the timing. By now, the First Wave was across the Lapis Amnis, maybe halfway to Domus Palus. But because the Delegates would not see her directly if she just appeared, she had to come with the messenger. She had to take a periodic dose of morutsen, as well. Brack had done the same things, and now Katla respected his patience with Drake politics. It made Mar politics look blissfully simple.

The Delegates normally met deep in the Drake territory north of the Fens of Reur, but with the Mass invading, they had moved their tent capital closer to their border with the fens. Despite having to ride the back of a striped guer with a handful of messengers and guards, Katla did not lose as much time as she thought she would have. They dismounted and walked when they reached the edge of the city.

The traveling city was followed by its own guards. Each Delegate had an entourage, varying from dozens to thousands of their own peoples. The city could be compared to Flasten Palus in size, but with many times the number of people. And nearby, the Fifth Wave amassed. Staging points for the Sixth and Seventh waves were marked within five miles east and west. This was a political city, but it was bent on war now, to move at the whim of those who spoke behind the gargantuan tent wall at the north edge of the city.

As her party approached the massive space reserved for the Delegates, she counted more than a thousand armored striped guer with spiny-tailed guer atop their backs, keeping watch. Jabber, spiny-tailed and snatching guer filled the streets, not all were warriors but certainly each was capable of wielding a weapon. Most intimidating, though, was the deep buzz of the five stick-limbed, dragonfly-winged giant insero sweeping periodically over the town with blow dart-wielding ravits mounted on them.

The spiny-tailed messenger pressed his hand against her belly to make her stop; he had refused to speak with her the entire trip. He disappeared through a well-guarded gate in the twenty-foot high tent wall, looming in front of them like a cliff stitched together from the hides of thousands of deer. Next to her, another one silently handed her the skin of morutsen. She tipped a drop onto her tongue, deciding she was sick of the flavor.

"The Delegates welcome Yee Ka Lah and bid her welcome to the Delegates' tent."

Katla entered. She remembered Brack's distinction of the Mar, as opposed to those the Drakes called Yee.

The Mar are proud, ruthless and savage, but the Yee are humble, polite and eager to serve.

Inside, twelve of the hundreds of Delegates were there, each with at least a half-dozen retainers. Across from the entrance, hand clasping an ancient, carved staff, stood the Overseer — first among equals, according to their rules. This was Doh Zue Sah, a striped guer. If the males of her species were large, intelligent and trustworthy, their female counterparts were huge, brilliant and generally considered incapable of lying.

Katla stepped into the circle of Delegates to present herself, bowed slightly to Zue Sah, then stepped back. The Delegates would finish their current agenda before introducing her issue, so she had time. Zue Sah gestured to the spiny-tailed delegate, Tee Rah Rue, to continue, while Katla considered how to speed up the proceedings or interject her own issue into them.

"The Tee have finished refurbishing the arms and equipment of the Thirteenth Wave, but Tee Rah Rue humbly asks the Delegates to give these Tee soldiers more time to prepare for the march from Tee Province, for the journey is long and not without perils." He gestured to the snatching guer delegate, and his voice took on a snide tone. "All the Hoh lands stand before us. The Tee have heard the Hoh forced the Twelfth Wave to find another, lengthier route or be attacked. The Thirteenth Wave will be of no help to the Mass if the Hoh attack them!" He glared at Zue Sah. "The Tee request a delay of half of a yellow moon."

The Mar Council would be shouting over itself at such silliness, Katla thought. The Hoh were the snatching guer who had chosen not to join the Mass — a blessing, as far as Katla was concerned. The snatching guer delegate here, Hah Po Ket, bridled at Rah Rue's suggestion that the Hoh were his responsibility, but he did not step forward when Zue Sah asked for comments. Instead, Joh Zoh Ta, the jabber guer delegate, stepped forward.

"The Delegates recognize Joh Zoh Ta," Zue Sah said, the staff twisting in her hand.

Katla suppressed a sigh. The news was good for her — dissent. But she had to get back to the front, to see what was happening. *Has Sven returned? Is Domus prepared?* She had to know.

"The Joh don't like Tee Rah Rue's suggestion. The Joh of the Thirteenth Wave are ready to march now, but the Tee are not? While the Joh wait for the Tee, the warriors of the Da and the soldiers of the Za win glory and territory for themselves in Yee lands. By now, the First Wave has reached the Yee's great city, and the Second Wave cannot be far behind. The great Yee city has never endured more than five waves! The Tee are not assigned to any of the first ten waves! The Tee would not have to ask for more time if they had readied their soldiers sooner!"

Tee Rah Rue snorted derisively. "If Five Waves of Da, Za and Joh cannot take down the Yee, then one wave of Tee will have to."

Zoh Ta's entire body turned bright crimson from its normal gray, which all jabber guer did when extremely embarrassed or enraged.

"Enough!" Zue Sah shouted, before Zoh Ta could leap on his fellow delegate. "Tee Rah Rue you are out of line. You may leave, or remember the pact you agreed to." Rah Rue did not move, but lifted his chin slightly in acknowledgment.

"Now," Zue Sah went on as Zoh Ta faded to his usual shade and stepped out of the circle. "Are there arguments that do not challenge the plan of attack, or shall the Delegates make their decision regarding this matter?"

Finally, Katla thought, but another spiny-tailed delegate, the aged Zeh Goh Soh, stepped forward, a silver chalice held urbanely in one clawed hand.

"The Delegates recognize Zeh Goh Soh."

"The Zeh thank Doh Zue Sah and all the Delegates for hearing their concerns. Long has Zeh Goh Soh represented the Zeh among the Delegates. It has been a time of peace and prosperity, and the Zeh are saddened by the grim necessity of mobilizing the Mass against the Yee, for it means fewer Zeh working in the fields and shops of Zeh Province."

He shot a brief glance at Katla before continuing.

"Joh Zoh Ta is right to say the great city of the Yee has never resisted more than five waves. Therefore, the Zeh humbly ask the Delegates to consider whether it is in the best interests of the Drakes they represent to fully mobilize the Mass."

Katla could not have hoped for something better, even as the rest of the room rumbled its thoughtful dissent. Zue Sah raised the staff to silence them, but Goh Soh raised his voice, outlining his argument.

"No matter how strong Yee Seh Tah has made the Yee, it will not take three hundred waves to defeat them. It will not even take a third of that. The twenty waves the Delegates have already ordered mobilized will crush Yee Seh Tah's armies!" A brief cheer, mostly from the younger retainers. Katla was impressed that the Drakes held Sven in high enough appraisal to name him. *It is funny that Seh Tah, means Stubborn Fire.* "Any other mobilized wave will have to be recalled, and while they mobilize, wait, march, return and disband, our fields and shops are empty."

He stepped back. Katla stepped forward before any other delegate could consider a response.

"The Delegates recognize Yee Ka Lah, bearer of Domin's Favor."

"Yee Ka Lah thanks Doh Zue Sah and all the Delegates for this opportunity to speak." She nodded to Goh Soh, and spoke loudly and clearly. "While it is true the Yee's great city has never endured more than five waves, much has changed. Yee Seh Tah has convinced the Yee that he is the chosen one of their gods — the one who will defeat the Mass. Every Yee wields magic, because of Yee Seh Tah."

She pointed to one of the gobbel delegates, Hue Ta Heh, drawing his complete attention. The Hue had lived in the Morden Moors, what became the Takraf Protectorates. "The Hue well know what magic Seh Tah teaches his students. Drakes will die without ever seeing their enemies, and those who reach Yee towns will not find them easy prey."

"Yee Ka Lah speaks truly," Ta Heh said. "Yee Seh Tah as a child invaded us and pushed us out of our homeland. If all Yee children are as him now, we are in danger."

Zue Sah glared at Katla and Ta Heh, thumping the staff against the growing uproar.

"Yee Ka Lah and Hue Ta Heh are out of order!" she cried, but Katla pushed forward.

"The Tee and Zeh might think sending twenty waves is a waste of energy! The Joh may fear the Thirteenth Wave will never know battle! But I warn you that Yee Roh Yeh was right to fear Yee Seh Tah, for he wields power far greater than you can imagine."

Yee Roh Yeh. Brack, my old master. You did well, Katla thought.

The room calmed down, and even Zue Sah lowered her staff. The glower remained, though.

Now to set them on fire. Katla raised her hands. "He has united the Yee in common cause against the Mass and given them magic! Do not send a mere twenty waves against the Yee capital, Delegates. Do not send a third of your strength."

She lowered her hands into the silence, and spoke in barely a whisper as sweat streamed down her own brow.

"This time, the Mass will need to send all three hundred waves against the Yee."

She paused. The murmurs began again: A Yee asking for all Yee to be destroyed? And she thought, *Hopefully, at least some of them recognize my bluff.*

Doh Zue Sah, in calm anger, raised her staff to question Katla.

"And should the Delegates choose not to, Yee Ka Lah?" she asked. "If we send only twenty waves, and they are defeated, how will the Yee react?"

It was a ridiculous question, and the Delegates all sat in shock. The Mass, defeated? At all? Katla smiled grimly. *Yet they entertained the idea of it.*

"Delegates," she said. "If such an impossibility were to occur, the Yee would not rest until the Mass is never a threat to them again. Do not let it happen. If you are not willing to spend every drop of your people's blood in this war, then allow me to negotiate a peace with Mardux Sven Takraf."

Her choice to use his Mar name proved powerful as again the room filled with the whispered discussions of the Delegates and their contingents.

"The Delegates recognize Hue Ta Heh."

"The delegate from the Hue thanks Doh Zue Sah and all the delegates for granting him this audience. ..."

After that, the meeting progressed quickly. Of course the situation had been oversimplified: The waves would not all be directed at Domus Palus. The Hue and their gobbel brethren, the Gue, of the Twentieth Wave, would attack the Protectorates as the farthest east assault force. The Tenth Wave would move earlier, thus forcing the Tee's proposal for more time from the floor. The Tenth Wave would attack along the Domus-Protectorate front, to push south and cut off any other aid.

Nor would they heed Katla's advice for a peace treaty or bring the whole Mass to bear, neither of which she had really wanted anyway. She left the meeting with some sense of accomplishment, though they had also called for the mobilization of the next twenty waves. The factions within the Drake species were easy to push and pull, and while she was here she would push and pull them.

The greatest weapon I have is encouraging dissent.

 **37**

"Perhaps the greatest irony of the marsord is that those who can afford to own one are those least likely to use it, and those who would put it to the use for which it was clearly designed are not likely even to see one. A weard must not be like a marsord. Power serves no function if it is not employed to a constructive end."

— Nightfire Tradition,
Ethics of Magic

Finn Ochregut wore a marsord because he had been at the right place at the right time. He had taken it from Dux Yver Verlren when the adepts had drugged and captured the wizards in the citadel of Domus Palus. Finn had ordered Piljerka's ruler confined to a tower cell — he had overheard something about teleportation being limited by height. The weapon pressed uncomfortably against his leg now.

I am probably the only mapmaker who has ever taken a marsord from a vanquished red.

He sat in the Chair and sweated, waiting for the endless line of advisors and petitioners who would soon come to him. Finn knew it was an empty gesture. The adepts who sought to counsel him knew no more about readying a city for war than Finn did. They would tell him the same things today as they had every other day.

Mardux, come back. Someone needs to rule these people! I have no idea what I'm doin'!

The reports began, and they were the same, no one sought a solution.

Weard Salt spoke of the reconnaissance stone. A sizeable Drake army, possibly the Mass, would arrive in three days. A small force of adepts harried it from the flanks, but remained near the Lapis Amnis. Someone suggested this meant more Drakes were coming, and the room erupted in discussion, punctuated with the normal, unalterable news.

As soon as word got to the general populace that the Mass was approaching, the riots began. Tens of thousands of slaves quit working, stole, looted and tried to flee. Finn had asked the adepts to stall them, to put them back to work harvesting kalysut leaves to make the torutsen the adepts needed. Several thousand on both sides had been injured, and hundreds killed, before someone decided to just let the slaves go, unprepared for the trek before them.

The Black Road leading to Pidel Palus was flanked by so many funeral pyres for those who had died in the panicked flight south that it must have appeared to observers a hundred miles away as if Domus Palus was burning down.

Not much later, the desertions began. A sizeable group of adepts left en masse after raiding the torutsen and Blosin glove supplies. No one knew where they had gone. Most deserters took only the cloaks on their shoulders, luckily. Finn listened tiredly to the argument in the room, estimating what they had left and no one suggesting they actually count. He had tried, surely. It was just his throat got so dry and too swollen to speak sometimes.

Just when things had seemed under control again, when the worst of the riots were quelled and most of the adepts were staying, someone brought the news that Verlren had escaped or been freed. That was yesterday. Finn had not slept.

He's going to kill me! I don't want to die.

The great doors at the far end of the room swung open, and a wizard in a red cloak swept inside. Shocked and relieved adepts as well as mundanes followed in his wake.

"Mardux Takraf!" Finn said, leaping to his feet.

Sven marched up the stairs of the dais until he was standing before Finn. The mapmaker stepped to one side before the glare, taking a moment to wipe off the seat before the Mardux sat down in it. Instead, the red-cloaked weard turned to face the suddenly quiet room.

"How many adepts do you have?" Sven barked.

"I don't know," Finn said.

"How much torutsen?"

The mapmaker shook his head.

"Blosin gloves? Surely some have been prepared."

"Since the slaves left ..."

"How many weards are around?"

Finn felt his throat go dry and swell again.

The Mardux turned his eyes to the rest of the room. "Find out," he said quietly. "Our lives, our country depend upon intelligence, and I see little of it in this room."

Finn slunk to a corner of the vast room to watch and listen. As far as he could tell, Sven was pleased with the number of adepts there were in Domus Palus, and the Mardux seemed delighted to learn they had made Blosin gloves for the defense of the city. Sven was much less cheerful about the looting and lack of discipline, and he seemed genuinely concerned about Dux Verlren's mysterious disappearance.

The Mardux never asked about Pondr, Erika or Asa, however, and Finn did not want to risk his wrath by mentioning them.

A mist rose in the evening on the western edge of the Takraf Protectorates. Erika rose and peered through the dreary twilight at the empty walls that had once been the village of Erscht, water droplets forming on her chilled face. A sip of torutsen confirmed its defenses no longer scanned and protected it. By the look of it, the town had been abandoned for at least a month.

What is left of my home? She stared east in the gloom. *Oh, Sven, how could you have let this happen?*

It was worse than Erika had imagined. They found the burned and savaged bodies of the militia in the last town, and adepts had spotted bands of gobbel raiders at least three times since they crossed the border into the remnants of the Protectorates. The Drakes had kept their distance. The adepts on perimeter duty wore a strip of bright green cloth around each arm, and the gobbels of the Morden Moors still feared Mar wearing that color.

Around her, the camp stirred to life. Adepts started fires, often fueled entirely by magic. Forcing them to use magic for nearly everything had led to incredible growth in their ability to use the myst. This close to the Fens of Reur, it was a necessity. Drakes were certainly not the only reason only the maddest mapmakers braved the Fens.

Power shielded legs from Dinah's Curse when they were forced to wade or dried and cleaned clothing splashed with water. Even with good boots, foot rot could force amputation. Vitality, then, helped heal blisters, scratches, rashes and other results of daily hazards. Without wood or dry peat, the adepts were forced to cook with Energy. In the desolate, war-torn landscape, magic fed them and sustained them.

"Weard Unschul, there is smoke to the east."

Cook fires or funeral pyres? Erika wondered with a shudder.

"Shall we investigate?" one of the adepts asked, her wiry grey hair snarled from spans of travel.

Erika quickly placed the face with its name.

"I will go, Nanna. The Protectorates are my home, and even if I do not know everyone who lives here, everyone on the Morden Moors will know me as Sven Takraf's wife."

"We should all go, Weard Unschul."

Erika shook her head. "I will take six adepts. More, and they might think we are with the invaders who did all this. Asa, honey, you stay here with Pondr until I get back."

"Okay, Mom, but when are we going to stop walking?"

"Soon, I hope."

"How about if I tell you the story of your father's trip to Nightfire's Academy from Rustiford, Asa?" Pondr asked.

How does he know about that? Sven never even mentioned it to me, Erika thought as she left them.

Asa leaned forward attentively.

"Nightfire came early i'the mornin', a year after Sven told his father, Pitt Gematsud, he'd offer himself as a tribute slave to Nightfire for savin' Rustiford ..."

 **38**

"Choosing an apprentice is serious business. Magic is power, and not all people are capable of employing power responsibly. Before choosing an apprentice, it is essential to learn something of the potential candidate's character. To do otherwise is as irresponsible as leaving a large stockpile of weapons in Drake territory."

— Nightfire Tradition,
Ethics of Magic

A hand touched Sven's shoulder. His head stirred and rose up to look at the cold ashes in his hearth. An empty pot hung on a hook in the chimney.

"He's here, Sven," his father told him, voice soft. His green eyes did not brim with tears, but tears were not Pitt's way. All the pain of his loss lay in the circles under his eyes from lost sleep.

Sven's black hood bobbed once, and he stood up slowly, the hem of the cloak sweeping down to his booted ankles. He turned slowly to look one more time at his home, committing its appearance to memory.

He had given away everything he could not take with him except for his plain rocking chair, and that would be his father's now. Someone else would live here soon. There was no reason to leave a house empty for eight years.

Sven picked up his travel pack and marched through the open door and outside.

The people of Rustiford waited for him on the green, keeping a safe distance between themselves and the aged wizard in red. Sven walked along the aisle in the crowd that had been created for him. As he approached Nighfire, he realized Erbark was not there. For a moment, anger flashed through Sven, but it passed.

He probably feels guilty that I'm going in his place. Lori and Hauk can't even look me in the eyes.

A great deal had happened in the last year — ravit raids and fatal accidents, weddings, births and homebuilding feasts. Sven had seen more joy than sorrow in his last year of life in Rustiford, but some sorrows fell harder than others.

Lori had not fallen in love with Erbark as Sven had expected, despite Sven's advice to Erbark and pleading with Lori to reconsider. Looking back, he had embarrassed himself in front of the entire town, but no one criticized him for it. They knew why Sven had volunteered to go with Nightfire, knew that this seemed to invalidate his reason for offering himself as tribute. They also knew Sven was too stubborn to reverse his decision and too proud to ask anyone else to go in his place when he had already let others know his choice.

Sven passed the village green where the remains of the Weardfest bonfire still smoldered and occasionally released a flickering tongue of flame.

Nightfire stood before him expectantly, red cloak spotless in spite of the mud that permeated Marrishland. Sven thought back to previous tribute slaves, recalled how terrified they had been of this moment. Eda had practically poisoned Vitharr mere days before her Weardfest in order to go in his place, but she could not hide her fear that morning. He understood that now.

Every step was a burden. The weight of cloak and boots threatened to pull him to the ground. He wanted to flee, to run into the swamps — away from this wizard, away from the altar upon which he was about to sacrifice himself.

Sven never fully understood what kept him moving forward. Perhaps it was the men and women of Rustiford, faces beaming with pride at his courage. Perhaps it was the children who peeked at him with curious eyes, begging him to teach them by his example to be brave. Perhaps it was his father — green eyes red from sleeplessness — who helped steady his son's steps. Or maybe it was the force of the hardened eyes of Nightfire himself — eyes that concealed untold knowledge and power — drawing Sven to himself with unspoken promises of new experiences and adventures he could never have here in Rustiford.

For whatever reason, Sven moved forward resolutely until he stood a few steps away from Nightfire.

"This is Sven Gematsud," Pitt said. "My son who comes to pay Rustiford's debt to you."

Nightfire nodded slightly and beckoned Sven to follow him away from the green and through the gate. As they reached the edge of earshot, Sveld, Rustiford's elder, cleared his throat.

"Let's remem'er Sven Gematsud volunteered to go with Nightfire to pay the debt we owe i'the ninth year after the Foundin'. We'll never forget his love for his frien's."

Sven only barely heard the last sentence, but it was enough. He pulled the hood of his cloak close to his face to hide the tears that slid along his unshaven jaw line as he left everyone he knew behind. He had told himself he would not look back, but his resolve broke as he followed Nightfire into the swamp. The black hood turned and looked at the walls of the town he was leaving.

"You will never see your town like this again. We will be traveling far from here. Keep your eyes focused on where you are going, not where you have been, or you will fall."

I will never forget where I came from, Sven thought fiercely. An unsettling thought occurred to him. "Where's Brand?"

"He is making his own way home," Nightfire said simply.

Sven waited for the wizard to elaborate, but he didn't. Nightfire made no other remarks that morning. He nimbly climbed over and crawled under fallen trees, ignoring the mud and briars that clung to his cloak. Sven struggled to keep up, even though he was younger and smaller.

As the sun rose higher in the sky, Sven's stomach growled, and he realized he hadn't eaten since before the Founding Festival the night before. Confident Nightfire would call for a midday halt, he said nothing.

Nightfire led the way through a much more tangled part of the swamp. Trees were less common here, giving the underbrush a better chance to flourish. The wizard produced an unusual sword from a shin sheath beneath his cloak. It had two blades, one on each side of the pommel. The front blade was more than a foot long and about two inches wide, curving in at the very tip to create a very sharp and abrupt point. The second blade was considerably shorter, about three inches, with the same abrupt point. One edge of the longer blade was toothed, while the other was smooth and sharp.

He only had enough time for wonder before Nightfire raised the weapon and sliced through a patch of thorny shrubs. Again the cloak stirred as the blade moved upward and then the arm of the red cloak brought the blade into the brush on the other side. Nightfire began cutting a narrow path into a deeper portion of the swamp.

"It is called a marsord," Nightfire explained in a lecturing tone. "It is the weapon of powerful wizards forged entirely by mundane means. No magic may go into the creation of a marsord."

Why is he telling me this? Sven wondered.

Nightfire instructed Sven on the best way to use the dual-bladed weapon so as not to cut himself. He described the ideal angle for swinging to chop brush down with the sharp side. He explained how to saw through thick vines with the toothed edge. He emphasized the angle of the wrist so the shorter, gouging blade would not cut the wielder. He illustrated all as they went.

The water grew deeper, and the mud stickier, sucking at their boots and dirtying their cloaks. The mosquitoes and biting flies became bolder, flitting up sleeves and down hoods for a chance to eat. For almost three hours they traveled in that manner, swatting away insects as they progressed deeper and deeper into the wilder parts of the swamp. Sven followed Nightfire closely, uncomfortably looking over his shoulder for any sign of Drakes.

Perhaps the wizard's red cloak would keep them at bay, but it might also attract the attention of an over-confident ravit with steady aim and poisoned barbs. Sven felt a dull stinging sensation between his shoulder blades at the thought.

Nightfire stopped abruptly. Sven only barely kept from running into him. The wizard held the marsord out to him. "Here. Show me what you have learned. Clear our path."

Sven looked at the weapon in surprise, unsure of how to react. *Is this a test to see if I will attack him? A trap to make me break some law so he can extend my slavery?*

"Take it." The face had hardened in challenge, daring Sven to disobey or attack him.

Sven took the weapon cautiously, almost as though he expected it to transform into a poisonous snake. When it did not slither in his hands, he held it firmly in his left hand. He swung the blade experimentally at a patch of vines. The clump shuddered with the first swing and came apart on the second. He smiled to himself. *No one in Rustiford has ever held a weapon like this one.*

"You will regret having it soon enough," Nightfire said with a smirk, rubbing his arm through the sleeve of his cloak. He pointed forward. "Keep moving. Night is coming."

Sven moved forward and took an experimental slash at the underbrush in their path. The vines and thorns gave way. He raised his arm again and brought the blade through the vegetation. Soon, he was moving through the swamp almost as quickly as Nightfire had.

The wizard talked endlessly as they walked. He identified every tree and herb they passed, explaining their medicinal properties in great detail. The only exception was the kalysut, which he simply named without further comment. Nightfire did the same with the animals they encountered, describing each one's anatomy, habitat and behavior.

Weary from the lack of food and the exertion of walking through nearly a foot of water, Sven barely heard him. His boots were caked in thick layers of mud, adding several pounds to each step.

He will stop soon for sure.

But the wizard did not pause for a rest and made no suggestion of doing so in the near future. So Sven continued leading him, sweating, gasping and waving away insects futilely. The sun set, and the wizard's ceaseless explanation of the world around them only grew more spirited.

Sven cut through underbrush and sawed through vines more slowly, praying to Marrish for a second wind of his own, one that would make the journey end before he died of exhaustion. Dinah must have been jealous, for at that moment, black spots clouded Sven's vision, and his head grew light. His knees buckled and he fell earthward.

When Sven woke, he could not tell if he was awake. He saw nothing, heard nothing, smelled nothing. He felt no hunger or pain; he had no physical sensation at all. Not only could he not feel the ground beneath his body, he could not discern up or down. He was disembodied thought floating in darkness. Time had no meaning in this non-place, but Sven thought for sure that days had already passed, if not years or centuries.

Then the hallucinations began. His family. His friends. They worsened. Ravits and gobbels. Drakes without names. They changed. Faces of gods. Mysteries of a world unfolding before his blinded eyes. There were voices, too — the whisper of Swind, the thundering voice of Marrish, the laughter of the Bald Goddess.

Am I dead? Sven thought. *Is this Domin's duxy? Is that why Brand didn't return?*

But no. There was no cleansing fire here, no pain. Broken images and breaths of sound pressed in on him like memories of dreams forgotten even by Seruvus. Sven's consciousness flickered like lightning in a storm — sometimes aware and sometimes not. Sometimes he dreamed, and sometimes he merely saw and heard things that were not there.

Years later, Sven would recognize it as his first experience with teleportation. The darkness through which he had passed was the Tempest, whose deprivation sometimes inspired visions in those traveling through it. He would recognize the intense overstimulation of the senses and resulting disorientation and nausea that seized him when he returned to the material world as the symptoms of teleportation sickness.

Nightfire provided him with no such explanations as Sven dry-heaved on hands and knees, however. "Rest for awhile. It will pass." Then the wizard took a seat under a tree and calmly sharpened his marsord with a small whetstone.

Once his stomach settled, Sven noticed he was no longer hungry or tired. He lay on his back and looked at the sky through the canopy above. The moon and stars were too bright tonight, their colors too vivid. He blinked, waiting for the sensation to pass, softly reciting the names of the constellations he knew to keep his mind off the strange experience of having a body again.

He could see Kaliher, the brightest of the stars, quite clearly from here. Kaliher never moved in the sky the way the others did, showing travelers the way north. The Guardian had just begun to rise in the east, most of its stars still well below the trees of the swamp. The Lone Thief wandered across the autumn sky. Right behind it chased the Corrupt Judge. The other constellations were foreign to Sven. He knew the Wild Prince and the Generous God were somewhere in tonight's sky, but he wasn't sure where to look for them.

Every star had a story, and he had heard almost all of them. His flawless memory could recite them for him at will.

A dark shape flickered across Niminth's green face, and a cold wind blew from the north. He could not help but shiver in the icy breeze. He pulled his cloak tightly around his neck. A tree creaked overhead in the wind, and leaves plummeted from the treetops.

Then Kaliher winked out as an approaching storm consumed the night sky. Niminth's light disappeared. The Lone Thief faded away and the Corrupt Judge vanished. Even the gleaming stars of the Guardian submitted to the growing storm clouds as they seemed to heave with their burden.

A flash of lightning lit the clouds, their light burning the image of a face into Sven's vision. A few seconds later, a distant rumble sent ripples through the still pools in the swamp. The wind grew stronger, and leaves began abandoning their homes by the thousands — just in time, for a fork of lightning struck a tree on the horizon and laid it low. The first raindrops fell heavily, helping the wind bring the trees to their knees before the power of the storm. Many of the trees acquiesced, bending low in preparation for the god who would soon walk among them. Those that rebelled were slain by forks of lightning from the storm god's fists.

Sven lay in silence — fascinated, afraid, invigorated. Water streamed through the opening of his hood, dousing his face and hair, the concreteness of it like sweet pain against his nose and cheeks. Wind tore at his cloak, trying to rip it from his body. Lightning arced into the ground from the clouds, threatening to burn him to ash. Then the storm's fury subsided, and it turned its attention to the lands to the south and east, leaving the land changed by its passage.

Sven said nothing, merely gasping for breath and willing his heart to slow its terrifying pace. *Was that Marrish's face? What interest does the Creator have in me?*

A bright white light bathed him, and this time Sven didn't wince. He lifted his head and saw Nightfire standing, his red cloak the source of the light.

Imagine what it must be like to wield power like that, Sven marveled, and for a moment he wasn't sure whether he meant Nightfire or Marrish.

"What happened?" Sven asked. "We weren't in a clearin' before."

Nightfire quirked an eyebrow at him. "You fainted. I brought us elsewhere."

"Those dreams ... that was magic, wasn't it?" Sven's tone was almost accusatory. *Like the passage from my birth town to Rustiford, with the wizards helpin' us move faster.*

"Why do you think that?" Nightfire asked with the hint of a smile.

Even though Sven's eyes had adjusted, it was difficult to look directly into Nightfire's aura of white light. "If you'd walked to Rustiford, there'd be a path to follow, an' we wouldn't be cuttin' a new trail through the swamps."

Nightfire's smile crept farther into his cheeks, but he didn't answer Sven's question. "It is not far now. Follow me."

Sven stood up, only a little dizzy, and staggered after Nightfire. The trees and underbrush seemed to bow down before the glowing wizard, making a straight path for him and the slave who followed in his wake. An hour passed, and then two. The swamp abruptly gave way to a rise of land. Nightfire's cloak of light made it difficult to discern distant shapes, but Sven could just make out the massive shadow of a large, walled town far to the west.

Nightfire stopped, and whirled on Sven, all secret smiles replaced by an imperious frown. "You have sworn by the Oathbinder to serve me as a slave for eight years. Is this correct?"

Sven was a little taken aback by this sudden challenge. "Yes."

"Address me as Master Nightfire," the wizard commanded.

"Yes, Master Nightfire," Sven said.

"Remove your cloak and throw it to the ground at my feet."

Sven couldn't keep the confusion off his face, but he did as he was told. The cold of autumn bit into his already chilled flesh.

"Now kneel before me."

Sven did as he was told, but it rankled him. *Doesn't he trust me enough to believe I will keep my oath?*

"Now take off your boots."

Sven hesitated, not certain he had heard correctly, Seruvus's memory or no. "What, Master Nightfire?"

"Your boots. Take them off. Then you will walk on the earth with bare feet. I command it of you."

"But Dinah's Curse," Sven stammered, suddenly afraid.

Nightfire pointed down at Sven, expression imperious, voice cold. "Does your oath mean nothing to you?"

"Please, Master Nightfire. I'm your slave, but you've no reason to take my boots!"

"If you will not obey, you will suffer," Nightfire said sharply.

Sven felt a great pressure around his body as though a huge hand had grasped him. Suddenly, he was kneeling several inches off the ground.

"And even as you suffer, you will still obey."

A gout of flame burst from the earth below Sven, engulfing him. His clothes caught fire. His boots burned away, the leather peeling away from his feet like wood shavings. With a foul whiff of smoke, his hair burned and the skin all over his body blistered from the heat.

Sven screamed in pain. The flame vanished. The invisible hand released him. He fell naked to the ground, writhing in pain through the mud. He moaned in agony. The blisters burst, sending new fires of pain along his nerves.

"I am an eighth-degree wizard!" Nightfire thundered, pointing down at where Sven squirmed on the ground. "I can reduce you to ash with as much effort as it takes you to scratch an itch. If you displease me, I can inflict such pain as you cannot even imagine." The wizard crouched down and whispered into Sven's ear. "But I am not without mercy. I can heal as well as kill, soothe as well as torment. This is what it means to be a wizard — choosing how to wield power."

Sven could only manage a whimper as he quietly prayed for death. He had heard that a deep enough burn was painless, but these certainly were not.

"Will you obey me as a slave should obey his master?"

"Yes," Sven managed, and his blistered skin became whole again. The pain vanished.

Nightfire touched his shoulder. He no longer glowed, but the first rays of dawn lit his face. The black cloak in his hand was clean as though newly washed. He no longer looked imperious and terrifying. If anything, he looked slightly embarrassed.

"Come with me, Sven," he said gently. "We will reach my home before nightfall."

Sven pulled the black cloak around his naked body and obeyed.

 **39**

"I think everyone who spent time around Sven Takraf experienced what I did — the unshakeable feeling that your presence in his life is part of a plan to guide him on the path to his destiny. From the first time I heard a story about him, I knew I wanted to be a part of it, even though I didn't know what role I would play."

— Pondr,
Collected Journals, edited by Weard Asa Sehtah

Glancing at her six companions, who were by turns scanning the horizon and fidgeting, Erika turned her eyes ahead and walked away from camp, toward the town. Shadows moved in the mist within fifty yards of the open gate. As she drew near, they became black-clothed Mar.

She grinned. Perhaps Einar had driven off the invasion the way Sven had claimed, and only a few towns had fallen.

"Peace i'the swamp," Erika called to them, raising her hand in greeting.

The approaching Mar did not respond.

Maybe they can't hear me.

She trotted ahead of her escort a few yards before coming to a sudden halt. Something was not right here. There were too many of them. It was difficult to count them in the fog, but she guessed at least a hundred Mar had appeared. They approached without conversation. A lone hunter or forager might remain quiet to avoid attracting the attention of gobbels, but a hundred Mar had nothing to fear from Drakes in a Protectorate town. There would be no reason for silence.

She squinted at them, trying to discern what might have brought them here.

"This's strange," one of the adepts whispered. "We should leave, Weard Unschul."

The Mar moved as though chained with whips lashing their backs. They moved as if defeated. All of them held twigs, their hands shaking. Two of them attracted her eye.

Her breath caught. They were her parents. She raced toward them, abandoning the adepts.

"Mother! Father! What is going on here?"

As she neared them and saw their eyes, saw the screams they couldn't sound, they raised the twigs in their hands. Flames engulfed her, and she fell to the soggy ground wondering why her parents would hurt her so. Behind her, the adepts screamed. She closed her eyes in pain.

Sven, you were wrong. They've conquered the Protectorates.

Less than an hour after Erika left the camp, the wand-wielders came for the adepts. Pondr could see a thousand Mar with vacant eyes in the clearing fog, and he could see the wands in their hands. The adepts formed in ragged ranks, trying to remember the finer points of magical combat they had been taught.

"What's going on?" Asa asked. "Where's Mom?"

Pondr grabbed her by the hand and pulled her to the back of the small army of adepts. He looked desperately for somewhere they could hide, but this part of the Morden Moors was treeless and fairly flat. Nor would black cloaks hide them among the reds and purple of the sedges that covered the landscape.

At the front of the adepts, Nanna took command of the situation as best she could. "Power adepts to the front to defen'."

The shuffle of bodies began.

"Energy adepts, center ranks. When I give the order, attack. Vitality adepts, rear ranks. Keep the others healthy. An' spread the line out. We'll want to use ochre tactics — surroun' them."

Like we have the numbers for that, Pondr mused sadly.

He knew this wasn't everything they had been taught, but only a few of the adepts had ever seen combat before. Best to keep the strategy simple.

It will do them no good. These are mapmaker's odds.

Pondr squatted in front of Asa and brushed away her frightened tears awkwardly, feeling at least as out of place here as she must. He commanded no magic that could burn or pummel men into submission. He didn't even have a real weapon — just an eating knife.

A roar rose from the adepts' ranks, shattering the mist and shaking the earth. Pondr felt it to the core of his being, felt the water shudder under the primeval war cry of the Mar. It did not die out for several minutes, and the enemy's returning silence proved powerfully effective.

"Hold your ground!" Nanna shouted, but her voice was lost in the din.

By a mutual consent akin to that of migrating birds or stampeding animals, the adepts charged.

"Climb onto my shoulders, Asa, and I will tell you another story."

She did. Pondr walked away from where the armies gathered as quickly as he dared. This was no place for either of them. The screams of rage and pain followed him as he fled. The Traveller began to speak, trying to keep himself and the girl calm.

There was a time, Asa, not too long ago, when there was no war. Mar did not fight Mar. Many of them never left their own homes. The duxies were strong and stood apart from each other except in Council, and they kept a tight rein on their provincial magocrats.

Oh, surely, the land was dangerous. Drakes abounded. Dinah's Curse was as deadly as ever. Towns were necessarily small, generally unhealthy, and people died from disease and starvation and stupidity. But they didn't die at the hands of their protectors, like the armies in the field now.

Into this time of peace, your father was born, the second child of Pitt and Tyra Gematsud. His older sister is your aunt, Katla Duxpite.

Like you are your mother's daughter, Katla and Tyra shared a strong bond — one that she carries to this day. Flasten took Tyra as a slave, though, when your father was your age, and this story began there.

Your grandmother was a remarkable woman, Asa. In those days, a mundane was as roots under a magocrat's boot, a slave as mud. With noses high and gloved hands to ward off diseases from even clean Mar, no weard would help except under duress. I didn't say it was a better time — just a peaceful one. Everyone had a place, and everyone knew it.

But Tyra Gematsud made a friend of her magocrat, who respected her reputation for beauty, charm, friendliness and willingness to help her neighbors. Tyra's spark kindled minds and lives for miles around her village, and those who knew your grandmother tried to be like her. Yes, Asa, like your father, but she never became as powerful as he is. She never had the chance.

Flasten sent magocrats to snatch people from Gunne to sell as slaves in Wasfal. Her magocrat couldn't drive them away on her own, so the wizard had to leave to go get help. She went to the Dux of Gunne, who made promises for a year but kept none of them. Meanwhile, Tyra's village ran out of food and wood, as Flasten kidnapped more and more of their hunters and foragers.

Your grandparents held their village together throughout the long and terrible winter. They kept them from arguing with each other or giving up. They took turns risking themselves on expeditions to find food and fuel for the village, so of course everyone who knew Tyra did, too. Though many people didn't survive, most of them did because your grandparents wouldn't let anyone give up and wouldn't let anyone starve or freeze.

You may wonder, Asa, where was the kind magocrat in all this? When she finally decided the dux wasn't going to help, she went to her old teacher, Nightfire, who agreed to move all the people in the magocrat's care to a place beyond Flasten's reach.

By the time Nightfire arrived with all the wizards from his Academy, though, a Flasten magocrat had kidnapped Tyra. Everyone was very sad, especially your dad and your aunt, but they couldn't find Tyra no matter how hard they looked, and they had to leave. The passage was long and hard, and the magocrat and many other people died along the way. But because of Nightfire, they eventually made it safely to Rustiford.

And what happened to your grandmother? That is a sad story, but an important one. She endured many humiliations on her long journey to Wasfal Palus, where the magocrats of the Duxy of Flasten sold her to Aflangi traders from beyond the great plateau. For twenty years, she worked as a slave to a foreign dux who did not speak her language. Life was harder than she could have ever imagined, and she missed her friends and family terribly, but she tried to be a comfort to those around her who were also suffering, for the foreign duxy was always at war with its neighbors.

During one of those wars, her dux was killed. In the confusion, Tyra led a handful of the slaves in a daring escape, but she suffered a mortal blow during the chaos. On her deathbed, she made one of her companions swear to the Oathbinder that he would go to Marrishland to tell her family what had happened to her and to help her children as much as he could.

The oath-bound slave died of fever long before reaching Marrishland, but he told Tyra's story to the healers who tried to help him. The healers told the story to their neighbors, and a trio of young mapmakers set out to carry out the dead slave's last wish. Two of them starved to death before reaching Marrishland, and the third fell prey to Dinah's Curse within a span of his arrival in Wasfal Palus. The tale passed from person to person as a curiosity, but no one set out to carry out Tyra Gematsud's final wish.

At last, the tale reached the ears of a Traveller who, though not in the least interested in carrying out the wishes of some slave woman he had never met, could not resist the lure of finding out how the story ended. It took years of research in the deepest parts of Marrishland's swamps to discover what happened to Sven and Katla — that they had both become powerful wizards. The Traveller couldn't find Tyra Gematsud's daughter, but her son had recently seized the Chair, so he went to Sven Takraf to learn the story from the man's own lips.

In picking up the ragged end of Tyra Gematsud's story, the Traveller found himself ensnared by it. He was a part of Tyra's story now, and it would give him no rest until he told it to someone who could carry out her final wish. Though he had sworn no oaths to help Tyra's family, he found the urge to do so irresistible. So long as he kept her story to himself, no harm would come to him, but he would also find it impossible to escape from the role it assigned him.

The sounds of battle faded into silence as they left the armies behind them. Pondr knew how it would end. It did not take a veteran general to recognize a hopeless battle or a merciless opponent when he saw one. Some adepts had tried to surrender, no doubt, but they would have received no quarter from the glassy-eyed Mar.

There is surely enchantment at work here, Pondr thought.

"Your grandmother was very brave, Asa. Now it is your turn to carry her story and your turn to tell it. She would want you to tell her story to your father. I'm just a stranger to him."

"You know it better, though."

He smiled sadly. There had not yet been any sign of pursuit, but Pondr had encountered wizards and enchanters too many times to think he could escape the one who turned innocent mundanes into an army of mindless wand-wielders.

"I'm a Traveller, Asa, and I know how stories work — whether I hear them, see them or live them. Your father's enemies will come for us soon. Tyra Gematsud's story cannot save me this time, but it will protect you, if you're brave like she was."

"Where is Mom?" she asked suddenly.

"She'll be safe, but your father. ... I know you have his kind of memory. No matter what happens, tell him the stories I told you, and I might still be able to help."

She tensed, but Pondr felt her right hand leave his shoulder. "I swear by the Oathbinder to tell Dad the stories."

"Good girl, Asa."

It was nearly dark before the wizards came for them.

"Did you really think you could outrun a wizard?"

Pondr had only met Weard Wost a couple times — not enough to recognize his voice — but his Flecterran accent gave him away. The

Traveller stopped in his tracks and very gently set Asa down without turning to face Robert.

"What you have done is forbidden by the laws of your land and theirs, Weard Wost." Pondr shrugged off the rucksack where he kept his journal and handed it to Asa.

"Do not lecture me about laws, Traveller. You surrendered your immunity when you aided the Mardux."

Pondr turned slowly to face the farl, raising his hand in the Mar gesture of salute and surrender. "Don't be so certain, Robert. I'm as entangled in this tale of gods, heroes and fire as you are, but at least I recognize it."

"Sven is not the Guardian!" Robert snarled. "The Mar love their epics and legends, but I know a myth when I hear one. I do not believe in that one any more than I believe in their gods!"

Pondr lowered his hand so no one would notice how much it was shaking. "Or in the power of a Traveller's stories?" He met Robert's gaze and struggled to keep his voice from cracking. "I have heard stories from your history, as well. Your teacher was a priest among the farls, was he not? Oh how you must have hated him for how he treated you."

Robert took a step back, and his lip curled. "Shut up," he said, pointing at the Traveller.

Pondr heard Asa screaming at Robert as he collapsed into the mud. Then a final silence fell upon the Traveller, and his journey came to an end.

"You should have let the Traveller go," Ari said softly, handing Robert a bowl of steaming soup. "Have you never heard of the Traveller's Curse?"

"Of course. I have also heard of fire-breathing guer called draxi." He sneered. "They are just as mythical. I was less concerned about his Curse than his stories. A dead Traveller is less trouble than a living one."

Ari sighed and sat down on a wicker chair. "Marrishland saw

many kinds of magic before the Mar were born. It is said some of our ancestors could only wield magic when they were dead."

"Nonsense. You Mar did not even have a written language until the Gien Empire crushed your army like so many irritating mosquitoes." He closed a fist in the air in front of him to capture an imaginary insect. "Half your history is myth, and the other half is extrapolated from myth."

Ari said nothing. *You farls share territory with two other races whose magic behaves nothing like mine or yours. And you know Mar do not see the myst the same way you do.*

"How are our hostages?" Robert asked, sipping.

"Einar continues making gloves," Ari said. "I see what you mean now. No wonder Weard Takraf took the Chair so easily."

"Volund was a fool not to see it. Takraf's mystique blinded him to the obvious."

"The Mardux's wife has recovered, though we are dosing her with morutsen. She might only be an apprentice, but she has long been close to powerful wizards, so it is likely she can wield magic well enough to escape."

"She would not get far."

"Well enough to inconvenience us, then. Her daughter has quieted considerably now that her mother is safe. She is reading some books the Traveller carried with him."

"Good. I have finished preparing our welcome. Send the messenger to Domus Palus and offer the Mardux our terms."

"Yes, Weard Wost."

Ari stood up and left the large hut that served as their headquarters in Leiben. Once he had been pacified, Einar had removed the defenses so they could use it as a base of operations.

Sven would not accept Robert's terms, Ari knew. Eighth-degree wizards were not known for their devotion to family, and Sven was ambitious even among his peers. He glanced in the direction of the hut where his stepfather labored on Blosin gloves for Robert's conquest.

Ari reached the small hut where Erika's parents stayed. They cringed when they saw him. All the Mar of the Protectorates did, making Ari wonder what Robert had made them see when they looked upon his Mar apprentice.

"I am sending you with a message for Sven Takraf. Tell him Weard Robert Wost has captured his wife and daughter, together with the Protectorates. If he does not come to Tortz alone, we will sell everyone here as slaves, starting with his family. Do you understand?"

They sobbed as they scraped and bowed before him, assuring him that they certainly did. Ari recoiled in a mixture of horror and disgust even as he called the myst and sent them both into the Tempest.

Is Robert's enchantment truly unbreakable?

The enchanter claimed that only proof of his death could break his hold on the slaves he made, but that was a convenient fiction. Ari knew enough about the mysdyn of Presence and Wisdom to recognize that.

Of course he would want us to believe that our army would turn against us if we killed him. If it is a spell, it is self-sustaining, but it can be broken. If it is nothing but a form of elaborate torture, then it can be resisted.

Ari removed a flask of morutsen from his cloak and went to renew Robert's less brutal hold over the Mardux's wife and daughter.

 **40**

*"We hear, tell and live stories, and those stories shape
each other. The stories we hear change the stories we
tell and live. The stories we tell change the stories we
hear and live. The stories we live change the stories we
tell and hear. My gift lies in sometimes knowing how one
story will affect another, but every story I tell changes
me as surely as it alters my audience."*

— Pondr,
Collected Journals, edited by Weard Asa Sehtah

It took two spans for Ragnar's wizards to inspect and assimilate
the Domus army. He demanded sworn oaths of each of them — to
obey him without fail until the Mass no longer threatened Marrishland. Volund's last remaining son swore no oaths in return.

If Ragnar had doubted that Horsa Verifien was the same person
who had thwarted him at every turn during the Teleport War, a few
war councils pushed aside all uncertainty. The priest was unflag-
gingly loyal to the Mardux and to the Duxy of Domus, but he was also
a competent strategist and a skilled magic-wielder. Now that he had
allied himself with his rival general, Horsa had put all his knowledge
at Ragnar's disposal. The range of their reconnaissance had already
doubled, and the Flasten army even adopted some of the Domus wizards' formations and small group tactics.

At last, the united army was ready to march on his command. Ragnar
stood before the highest-ranking wizards in the command tent. Horsa
and the most powerful Domus wizards were among those assembled.

"I bring grave news from Flasten Palus. Dux Volund Feiglin and
Weard Ketil Wenigar are dead — assassinated by Mardux Takraf or
one of his close allies," Ragnar said.

It was all he could do not to sneer at Horsa's shocked expression. *You see now the kind of master you serve?*

"The ochres of the Dead Swamps, sensing the weakness of our duxy, have invaded the Duxy of Flasten and have laid siege to Flasten Palus. As my father's sole heir, I lay claim to his lands and title — Dux of Flasten. My first loyalty is to my people." Ragnar paused, watching his allies' faces. Only Horsa's eyes grew wide in rage.

"We will return to the Duxy of Flasten to drive out these Drakes that threaten our homes and families. We will hasten our march east using the applications that served us so well in the Teleport War."

Horsa could contain himself no longer. "The Mass marches on Domus Palus, Weard Groth. This was not a part of our agreement!"

"Our agreement, as you call it, was your oath before the Oathbinder and your patron that you would obey me as an apprentice does his master until the Mass's invasion comes to an end. You surrendered to me, Weard Verifien, not the other way around, so unless you wish to add 'oathbreaker' to your long list of titles, as well as 'slave' and possibly 'shade,' I suggest you get used to obeying my orders."

Horsa glared but kept his silence.

I may yet come to your duxy's rescue, Weard Verifien, but not at the expense of my own, Ragnar thought.

"Are you still a priest of Marrish?" Ragnar asked.

Horsa's teeth were clenched as he spoke. "Until I die in his service, yes. I respectfully disagree with your strategy and ask that you at least let me lead the wizards of Domus to defend their own homeland."

"A surrender, once accepted, is not simply withdrawn by the loser. I will need your wizards to deal with this threat. I leave it to you to see that they obey the oaths that bind them as they bind you."

"As you command, Weard Groth."

"Not Weard Groth. I am Dux Groth now."

Erbark waited restlessly in the tiny bedroom provided for him in the Bastion. He had waited for Nightfire to agree to initiate an inquisition of Tortz, and that had proven worthwhile. But the duxess had refused him an audience for a year and had refused to let him leave. Actually, strictly speaking she hadn't told him he couldn't go, but she hadn't offered to have anyone teleport him out of the Bastion, either, and Erbark didn't have the mastery of mysdyn and tordyn that would have required.

They hold me prisoner unofficially, because their code will not allow them to do it officially. Like their ancestors invented the marsord to let their assassins get around duxy rules against killing Mar with magic.

The wizards of Pidel were polite hosts, but none of them seemed to have any knowledge or interest in the world beyond the windowless walls of the Bastion. Having spent several years living in the Takraf Protectorates, Erbark was not used to information vacuums. While he waited on the pleasure of the duxess, the Duxy of Flasten could have invaded Domus, for all he knew. There was a timid knock on the door.

At last!

"Enter."

A yellow with a shaved head and a small grey beard peeked in as though expecting Erbark to cut his head off.

"The duxess has agreed to an audience at your convenience."

Erbark was on his feet before the words were out of the man's mouth. He followed the priest through the labyrinthine corridors of the Bastion. Even after nearly a year, he still got lost. All the doors and hallways looked the same, and the entire fortress was largely unornamented, leaving him with no way to get his bearings. A mapmaker would have preferred the Fens of Reur on a foggy night to this. The priest opened a door into a room Erbark remembered from his first day at the Bastion. The duxess was waiting for him.

"Good afternoon, Weard Lasik."

"Good afternoon, Duxess Zaun. Have you come to a decision?"

"Yes. I am sorry for making you wait so long. I received a report hours ago that Domin himself could not fail to recognize as a clear sign from the gods."

Erbark felt a chill pass through his body. He froze rigid for several seconds before speaking. "What sign is that, duxess, and how do you interpret it?"

"The last wizards of Domus Palus have sought refuge here in the Duxy of Pidel."

Erbark shook his head. "What do you mean?"

"The Mardux's adepts broke their oaths and rebelled against their rightful rulers. Mar have spilled the blood of Mar, and Domus Palus is a place of anarchy and barbarism where once it was a center of law and order. Dux Verlren only barely escaped the city to tell us of Mardux Takraf's terrible deception."

Erbark clenched his fists. "Adepts? Rebellion? Deception? What has been happening while I have been here?"

The duxess smiled slightly. "I see your master has not told you all his plans, Weard Lasik. Dux Verlren told me everything. The Mardux took advantage of Flasten's invasion to create an elaborate ruse to convince the duxes the Mass was invading. Under this false pretense, they stripped the Duxies of Flasten and Pidel of their seats on the Council. This allowed the Mardux to pass an amendment to Bera's Unwritten Laws that permits mundanes to learn the rudiments of magic. He has raised an army of these magic-wielding mundanes — which he calls adepts — and now they have driven all the wizards out of Domus Palus."

Erbark spoke slowly, hoping his voice was not shaking. "And how do you interpret this turn of events, duxess?"

"The Mardux's claim that he is the Guardian is a false one, and he will be punished justly for his crimes. His adepts are apprentices who wield magic beyond their knowledge and station — a crime whose penalty is death by fire. Weard Takraf and his closest conspirators will suffer the same fate. Though a staunch supporter of your master in the past, Dux Verlren has asked me to help him raise an army to crush the adepts' rebellion and oust the Mardux by force, if necessary."

The first time Pidel takes a side in any war in centuries, and she sides with Sven's enemies. What does that say about the duxess, and what does it say about Sven?

"Clearly the Mardux was not completely frank with me on certain details of his plan, and I do not agree with all his methods of accomplishing his objectives. Nevertheless, if he claims the Mass is invading, I would believe him. March to Domus Palus with all your legions of wizards, Duxess Zaun. You will provide welcome reinforcements as the Mardux's adepts face the Mass."

"If indeed the Mass besieges Domus Palus, it is because the increased number of magic-wielding Mar drew the Mass down from the north. If the Mass has come to punish the Mardux for his pride and recklessness, Pidel will not interfere with the will of the gods."

I see faith and cowardice go hand in hand! Erbark fumed silently, but he didn't dare speak his mind.

"We are wizards, and it is difficult enough to convince two weards to agree on anything, much less an entire nation of us. You are clearly already decided on this matter, so there is nothing I can do to change your mind. I will fight the Mass until my body is spent, and then I will fight it until my soul is used up, too. Send me to Domus Palus so I can resume my service to my liege."

"And let the Mardux know we march against him? I do not think so, Weard Lasik."

"I will march with your wizards, duxess. I go to fight the Drakes, not to warn the Mardux."

"I insist you remain an honored guest in the Bastion."

"And there is no condition under which you will release me? I am not without my uses or resources."

"There is one condition under which I will gladly teleport you back to Domus Palus."

"Name it."

She did, and it was all Erbark could do not to bear steel against her, duxess or not.

"You would have me make an oath to violate yet another of my oaths. Domin take you, then, and may the dark dead rebel against you!"

She shrugged. "Then do not tell me I did not give you a choice, Weard Lasik."

Sven, I've failed you!

He stormed out and headed toward his cell of a room. A familiar wizard in red sat in a chair near his bed. This time, Erbark really did draw his marsord. His limbs froze before he could attack, though.

"Peace in the swamp, Weard Lasik," Arnora said, smirking. The door slammed and locked behind him. "It would be best if no one knew you had a visitor."

"How dare you!" he snarled, wrestling for Elements to counter the magic holding him.

"I mean you no harm, Weard Lasik," she assured him. "I cannot imagine how, shall we say, creatively the Mardux will deal with me if I kill his most trusted friend. If I release you, will you put up your weapon and negotiate with me? You will find me more malleable than the duxess."

"Very well," Erbark said, and the pressure on his limbs instantly vanished. True to his word, he slid the marsord back into its shin sheath.

"What do you want from me?"

"Straight to the point. I can see why Weard Takraf likes having you around. Very well, I ask for nothing more than a full pardon."

"For aiding Volund's rebellion? You do not seem the type to be troubled by conscience, Weard Stoltz."

"Volund is dead and his rebellion with him. The Mardux has killed most of the reds who were loyal to Flasten, and it is only a matter of time before the others suffer the same fates. Perhaps you have noticed how he treats those whom he considers enemies? I would rather not die for a cause I know to be lost."

"And in return, you will send me to Domus Palus to fight the Mass?"

Arnora sighed. "If you think it is the best course of action, yes, I will."

"You do not believe it is."

"Do not misunderstand me, Weard Lasik. It is a good course of action, but why bring just a warning to the Mardux when you can bring a warning to the Mardux and his enemies at once?"

"I am no assassin."

"I know that. Weard Takraf sent you as an envoy, and his envoy you will be — just to a different duxy."

"Why would they help Sven?"

"Why? For the same reason as I would — self-interest. The Dux of Wasfal borrows as much as he lends, and if the Mass wipes out his debtors, his foreign creditors will quickly lose patience with him. So, have I earned that pardon?"

 **41**

"Recognizing the shape of a story is not the same as knowing the future, for every story heard or told changes the lived story. Sven Takraf lived a stubborn story, but I thought that with the right stories, I could save him from his fate. His tale has ensnared me, and I fear I may have absorbed some of his hubris. Can I still see the shape of his story well enough to change it, or has his pride become mine, blinding me to the damage I am doing to him with every tale we share?"

— Pondr,
Collected Journals, edited by Weard Asa Sehtah

"Weard Staute, come to the recon hut quickly!"

Asfrid Staute, the cyan who had been coordinating the Protectorates' defenses since Weard Schwert had gone to deal with the Flasten invaders, put the finishing touches on the Blosin gloves she had been enchanting and stood up.

"What is it, Sigrun?"

"Drakes from the north. Stinger guer, from the looks of it, but it's hard to tell at this range."

Asfrid broke into a run. The town leaders were waiting for her, staring worriedly at the stone at the center of the hut that served as Heliowache's recon chamber.

Drakes here in the Protectorates?

She knew the Mardux had fought hard to drive the gobbel tribes and other Drakes out of the Protectorates when they were just as often called the Morden Moors — a region long thought indefensible and unworthy of contest, as well as technically neutral. But for as long as Asfrid had lived there, she had never seen so much as a mote on a recon stone that represented a Drake — at least not one that hadn't vanished as suddenly as it had appeared.

Now, though, a swarm of red characters swam within the reach of the Protectorates' outermost defenses and were not diminished by the spells set to ward the Morden Moors against them. The swarm extended north across the river and off the map. As Asfrid examined the characters more closely, she saw mostly stinger guer, but accompanied by jabber guer and gobbels.

"Is it ... ?" Sigrun Zwei asked.

"Don't be ridiculous, Weard Zwei. The gobbels have made an alliance with some guer. The Mass is a story told by magocrats to maintain their monopoly on power."

Sigrun did not seem completely convinced, but she didn't argue.

"Send messages to the other wizards. We will need to be ready to shore up the Protectorates' defenses quickly in case the Drakes wear down the defenses by pure body weight. They do not have reconnaissance like we do, and a guer fears an enemy it cannot see no less than a Mar. The Mardux designed the Protectorates to repel Drake assaults, but we must not let them find any of the towns. A march of a few miles is but a journey, but razing an enemy town feels like a victory, and we must give them none of those."

"Yes, Weard Staute."

Asfrid watched the recon stone as the Drakes pressed against the Protectorates' defensive perimeter, idly enchanting more Blosin gloves as she did so. The red characters touched the boundary and vanished by the dozen, but more Drakes pushed forward, goaded by whatever dark power commanded them. She imagined the stinger guer with their tails of poisonous spines, jabber guer with their strong legs and bony hand spikes, and gobbels with spears and shields — all marching on and dying in fire as they hurled themselves against the wall of force that barred their paths. Mobility sapped their speed, making their attacks too weak and sluggish to penetrate the walls that stood in their way.

She knew they would never see a Mar or even the smoke of a town. A dozen Drakes died and then a hundred, until those that followed had to press through a wall of their allies' charred corpses before even reaching the magical wall that halted their advance. But at last, the Protectorates' defenses weakened, and the red dots spilled beyond the outermost wall.

Asfrid put on a pair of studded gloves and touched Elements. The spell of the Blosin gloves flowed into the recon stone, and from there, to the buckling northern perimeter defenses. She shed them and put on another. And another. And scores more, until she had used up nearly sixty pairs — a tenth of her stockpile.

The Drakes north of the wall found their path barred once more, and those south of it discovered the second line of defenses — a mere hundred yards south of the outer perimeter — and died swiftly.

Asfrid estimated the Drakes's casualties at a thousand when the wave shattered against the Protectorates' defenses and rolled back from the walls.

One thousand Drakes slain. And no Mar wounded or slain. No towns burned. No wild rice fields disturbed.

Asfrid stripped off the Blosin gloves and restarted the process of enchanting them. It would take spans to replace the exhausted gloves, which meant fewer remained to deal with the Flasten army that was almost certainly still absorbing the southern towns of the Protectorates.

If I didn't know any better, I might think the timing of this attack was orchestrated by Flasten to weaken us.

"Gobbels and guer fighting together in formations," Sigrun remarked. "This is unheard of except ..."

"If it had been the Mass, we would not have driven them away with a few traps."

"Unless it was a scouting force testing the strength of the Protectorates' defenses, Weard Staute. This might have been a mere test. If so, the next attack will be far worse."

Asfrid digested this for a long minute without comment.

"If you are right, what can we do about it? We've had no word from Weard Schwert, so it is likely Flasten's invasion continues unabated. The Mardux faces Dux Feiglin's army in the field, so he cannot spare reinforcements. Even if we were to violate the Unwritten Laws, we hardly have enough torutsen to train our apprentices, much less the mundanes at large."

"There is no hope, then?"

Asfrid shrugged. "Only the hope of the fallen. We can die like Mar on the fringes of civilization always have when the Mass invaded — outnumbered and under-equipped but fearless. If we inflict enough casualties, we might discourage future incursions. But that is all we can do, Sigrun."

Sven sat on the Chair, but he did not sit in the citadel. Rather, he sat at the top of a stone tower on the northern side of Domus Palus. Nine priests of Marrish dressed in yellow attended him — one for each of his patrons. He had chosen them for the task from the nearly four hundred priests in Domus Palus for his own reasons — three women and six men of varying ages and appearances.

The cries and howls of the Mass rushed through the surrounding swamps ahead of the terrible forms of the Drakes as they appeared north of Domus Palus. No one raised an alarm, for they were not as numerous as Sven had expected. According to the recon stone in the citadel, slightly more than eight thousand had survived the journey from the Lapis Amnis. Such a small force was no threat to the 75,000 adepts in Domus Palus.

Even if only one in five has actually had tactical training and we can't train the rest without endangering our torutsen supply.

Bui's guerilla-adepts had launched dozens of raids in a few short days — striking swiftly with magic attacks and retreating just as quickly. After this battle, Sven intended to send him reinforcements. He knew he would have no trouble finding volunteers for the force the adepts had started calling Bui's draxi — named for a mythical race of guer that could fly and breathe fire. Given the origin of Bui's signature tactics, it seemed a fitting moniker.

Sven surveyed the gathering army from the northern wall of Domus Palus. Whatever ruin the rest of the capital's buildings might have fallen into, the Mar had carefully maintained its outer wall.

If they overwhelm that, though, the citadel is in no condition to weather an assault.

The wall had once been taller, for even the relatively solid ground upon which Domus Palus was built was soft by the standards of other nations, and layers of rock had to be periodically added to the top of the wall to compensate for the layers that had sunk into the ground. "Fifteen feet high and a hundred feet deep," the residents of Domus Palus joked, and there were plenty of stories about invaders who had tried to tunnel under the wall only to find themselves foiled by the impenetrable barrier of centuries of slowly sinking stone.

Tens of thousands of mundanes had been evacuated from the outlying villages that lay beyond the city walls — mostly harvesters who tended the wild rice fields that helped feed the vast population of Domus Palus. Only food levies exacted by the duxy's magocrats normally prevented the city from starving.

No mundane had stayed behind in those villages. Sven's recon stone had made sure of that. It wasn't entirely out of concern for their safety. Drakes were perfectly willing to eat any Mar they caught. Unsavory though it might seem to the Mar, even an army of Drakes needed to eat something, and a sufficiently large army of Drakes could not live off the land for long.

The Drake army came to a halt, and a company of jabber guer charged into the outermost northern village.

My, but they learn quickly, Sven mused.

The air burst into flames around the scouting force, which quickly switched from a charge to a withdrawal. A quarter of an hour later, companies of jabbers tested the perimeter a little to the east and west. The Drakes knew ravit tactics, so they would probe every point in the Mar defenses in hopes of finding some weakness. Sven almost pitied them for having to rely on such crude methods of reconnaissance.

Their siege equipment will not be up to the task, either.

Bui's draxi had been surprised to learn that the Mass had not wantonly burned down captured Mar villages in their path the way Drakes usually did. Instead, they collected every stick and scrap of metal they could find to build scaling ladders and battering rams for the siege that inevitably awaited them.

Armed with this knowledge, Sven had ordered all the buildings of the outlying villages burned in advance of the Drakes' arrival. There would be no siege towers to bring attackers into the city — only the tough striped guer.

But not until the jabbers and stingers clear the magic traps around the city the hard way.

Sven ate his lunch of wild rice, venison and mushroom soup on the wall. The most opulent of the priests — the Mardux named him Cedar in his mind but never addressed him as such — brought it to him. It was saltier than Sven preferred, but they had already run out of fresh meat and would have to subsist on cured meat from here on. While he ate, he watched the Drakes snake farther around the western edge of the defenses, aiming for the gap between the city and the docks along Domus Palus Bay.

As I expected, they seek to cut off our supply lines quickly so our foraging parties won't be able to bring us the food, fuel or kalysut leaves we need.

"Weard Snelfus," he said to the priestess he thought of as Frae-mauna.

"Yes, Mardux?" Guthrun Snelfus was remarkably young for a yellow — barely twenty-five — but her small size and girlish voice made her seem even younger.

"Send out the adepts of the Swind Legion at the west gate. Put the priests and the other eight legions on alert."

If the Drakes throw their full weight at the legion we field, none of them will live long enough to regret the mistake. I'd rather save the morutdyjiton for a larger assault, but it is more important for the adepts to win their first battle against the Mass.

There were now more than thirty different kinds of Blosin gloves and Blosin wands in use in Domus Palus, and each variety produced a different magical application. Sven had therefore been forced to distinguish them from one another. Names helped in conversations. Morutdyjiton were the most powerful offensive Blosin gloves at his disposal, for they allowed any magic-wielder to use morutmanon. Painted bands on wands and the shapes and color of the metal studs on the gloves allowed even illiterate adepts to recognize which wand would heal an ally rather than roasting him alive.

With a nod, Fraemauna — Guthrun — vanished into the Tempest to deliver his orders.

"What is the word on the search for my wife?" *Erika ... forgive me.*

Sven knew she was in the Protectorates, with Asa. The recon stones did not stretch that far, so he had sent someone to find out what was going on.

"No word," someone said.

He felt a tear sting his eye. He wished he could go, but look at what happened when he left last! Thousands of adepts running away, taking over the city as if they knew how to run it. His own wife and a mapmaker had duped Verlren, and who knew where that coward dux had gone? No one had had his patience. Now they would learn from his example, though it chafed to not seek his own wife.

Eight years ago you would have done it and been back before anyone knew you were gone.

Eight years ago it was just the Protectorates.

He took a deep breath and turned to give more orders.

Erika, forgive me.

An hour later, Sven and the Chair sat on the western wall with his escort of nine priests.

The Swind Legion — a force of about a thousand adepts armed with spears and Blosin wands — marched through the west gate. The Drakes began their charge before the four wide ranks came to a halt.

They were jabber guer, known for being able to leap dozens of feet in the air and rain down on their foe with pinpoint accuracy. Sven smirked as they did such now, jumping his traps. Against their normal foes, the jabber ability was deadly.

Against his adepts, it was fatal.

Fire rose from the ranks of the adepts, and the guer rained down over the traps, springing a few of them.

Spiny-tailed guer sent companies of archers and slingers to support the struggling jabber guer. Missiles frayed the adepts' left flank, killing some and wounding many others. The adepts lacked the range to return fire, but those on the left flank soon erected walls of magic that rendered arrows and stones harmless. True, arrows could penetrate walls of Power as surely as a mundane shield, but not at long ranges, and if the spiny-tailed archers moved closer, they would be within range of the adepts' attack wands.

The wand-wielding gobbels were a bigger threat than this.

Sven estimated the Drake losses at nearly five hundred when the striped guer made a low, groaning sound that must have been some kind of signal, for the jabbers and stingers gave up on the western flanking maneuver and withdrew to join the main body of their force. Sven considered what would have happened if he had thought to cut off the flanking force but quickly recognized it would have been a waste of resources.

A cheer rose from the adepts as the Drakes retreated. They showed enough discipline to not chase their enemies. Sven felt a surge of pride.

Today's first battle had only cost the Mar a handful of adepts and probably as many Blosin wands as the adepts could make in a day. That didn't even cover the priests' daily production of Blosin gloves, a mere span's production of which was represented by all the traps around the city. There was still enough torutsen in Domus Palus to replace wands like this one for ten days before they would have to dip into their stockpile of Blosin wands and Blosin gloves. Eight thousand Drakes was a small threat, at best, against so many magic-wielders, but how many Drakes did the Mass command?

Sven thought of Domus Palus' outer wall. A single layer of stones would have provided no protection at all, but with enough layers, it presented an impossible obstacle for an enemy. Eight thousand Drakes was nothing to the defenses in place at Domus Palus, but could they endure a hundred thousand?

"Weard Sigwyrd."

"Yes, Mardux." That Ing Sigwyrd had been a magocrat in a village near the Dead Swamps for two decades was betrayed by his enormous muscles and numerous scars. Only an enhanced warrior had any hope of defending himself in the event he faced a damnen in combat, for those terrible Drakes were immune to the touch of magic. Ing reminded Sven of Erbark, sometimes, but mostly he reminded the Mardux of Niminth — the god of hunters and warriors and, above all things, maleness.

"I want you to gather together some of the greener adepts — two legions should be more than adequate. Have them sort all our Blosin wands and gloves by application and load them into barrels, crates and any other easily portable containers. Make sure they are labeled, complete with the number of wands or gloves they contain. I also want an account of all the wands and gloves before dawn."

"Yes, Mardux Takraf." Ing slipped into the Tempest.

"Weard Marspar."

"Yes, Mardux." Rig Marspar had a constantly stormy complexion, and his grey eyes betrayed his mood to any onlookers. Sven thought the priest very much resembled the god he served, both in appearance and temperament.

"Send the rest of the west gate legions to refresh Swind Legion. I would have the priests ensure victory, if necessary. I will lead the eastern legions myself."

"Yes, Mardux." Rig vanished into the Tempest.

"Weard Eisaug."

Surd Eisaug made no sign, but Sven knew he had heard him. The tall priest's hearing was sharp, and his memory was as good as the Mardux's. "Seruvus's memory," the Mar called such gifts as Surd's.

"Prepare a mobile recon stone and meet me north of the city."

Surd slid into the Tempest without comment.

"The rest of us will go to the east gate."

Guthrun was already waiting there when they arrived. Adepts stood in lines to take a spear and eight wands each — four with a single green band, two with a pair of blue bands, one with a trio of braided amber lines, and one with four red dots that looked like drops of blood.

Furos to shoot flame. Murus to create a wall of force. Repud to move quickly. Medis to heal injuries. A dozen or so uses in each. After that, the adepts will have to wield their own magic, however weak it might be.

"Adepts, assemble!" Sven shouted.

They didn't leap to obey his command, but neither were their movements as leisurely as those of a typical army of wizards. He kept talking while they formed in ragged ranks in front of him.

"West of Domus Palus, the Swind Legion alone has given the Mass its first defeat in its long history. It will not be the last!"

Many of the adepts cheered.

"The Mass came from the Fens of Reur thinking to storm Domus Palus and kill every Mar who lives here, but now that they realize we are numerous, well-fortified in defense and deadly in our attacks, they are less eager to meet us in battle. The five thousand adepts of the Seruvus, Cedar, Fraemauna, Marrish and Swind Legions intend to force these cowardly Drakes to fight. Today, the Mar will hand the Mass the first rout in its history!"

The cheers were even louder, this time.

"And what will we do? We will come upon the Drakes from the rear as they are routed and give them yet another first — the complete annihilation of their invading force. Too many times has the Mass invaded Marrishland. They showed our ancestors no mercy. They spared no one — not even elders and children — slaughtering whole cities in a vain effort to slake their unquenchable thirst for blood."

A sudden hush fell over the adepts, and Sven could not be sure if they were afraid or enraged. He paused for several seconds before shouting.

"Let us return the favor!"

The adepts roared their approval, waving spears in the air.

Sven drew his marsord and held it aloft, calling Mobility to him. "Repudon out and follow me!"

The landscape blurred around the eastern legions as they ran around the north side of the city, their movement aided by magic. The Mardux stopped them a few hundred yards north of the Drake army, which was still engaged in a bitter struggle against the slow advance of the western legions of adepts.

"Repudon away. Form up staggered ranks."

While the adepts formed four long lines that stretched from the edge of the city's magical defenses all the way to the shore a quarter of a mile to the west, Sven watched the battle to the south unfold. The Drakes were pressed against the adepts' walls of Power, daring magical fire and hurled javelins to force their way through the lines. Concentrated magical strikes toppled two of the striped guer, and three others lost their riders to force and fire and now withdrew.

A hundred stinger archers supported by jabber infantry stayed out of range of the wands as they picked their way around the left flank. With a nod from Sven, the priests reminded the Drakes that wizards still ran the army. A wall of fire roasted scores of these flankers and forced the rest to return to the main body of their army with howls of outrage.

"Niminth's crescent!" Sven shouted to his eastern legions.

Those adepts at either end of the lines moved forward first, followed by those a little closer to the center until the army formed a crescent that was wider than the enemy force.

The Mardux stood at the midpoint of the adepts' formation when the crescent was complete. He waved his marsord and shouted. "Heliotosis! Her! Niminth! Sendala!"

The adepts of the eastern legions answered him, shouting the names of their legions. Beyond the army of Drakes, the western legions answered them with cries to Marrish, Seruvus, Fraemauna, Cedar and Swind. As if the gods themselves had answered, the priests among the western legion unleashed morutmanon. Thousands of tendrils of black and white fire snaked through the ranks of adepts and swept a hundred yards into the ranks of the Drakes, reducing jabber, stinger and striped guer alike to ash in an instant while leaving the Mar untouched.

There were no screams of pain — for morutmanon killed before its victims felt its touch — but there were many shrill cries of terror as the surviving Drakes realized that the front two-thirds of their army had vanished. They broke and fled in every direction, dropping anything they were carrying.

Those that fled north or south met their end against the adepts. Those that ran east burned in the perimeter traps like insects in one of the Mosquito Shields of the Takraf Protectorates. Those that fled west found themselves pinned against ocean, and those that did not throw themselves into the sea stood their ground and fought the advancing adepts. Some Drakes had not moved from their place at the center of the circle of adepts, where they gestured and chattered what might have been pleas for mercy. They received none.

Sven singled out one spiny-tailed guer and let the adepts slaughter the rest. He wanted to send the Mass a message — to demand they break off the attack or suffer horrible consequences. Unfortunately, he did not speak the Drake's language, and none of those begging for mercy had spoken Mar, so he settled for teleporting this sole survivor north of the Fens of Reur.

His tale might be message enough.

Surd Eisaug arrived with the mobile recon stone. Sven sent him with the adepts of the Seruvus Legion. They would hunt down and kill any Drake that had not come to the battle or that had somehow hidden itself during the confusion. The Marrish Legion had the task of ensuring that any wounded Drakes never recovered from their injuries.

If not all the stragglers received a swift death at the hands of the Mar, it was only because the adepts chose to exact a thousand years of vengeance upon them. Mar of all nine legions stripped Drake corpses of weapons and jewelry, and many took more grisly trophies, as well.

Enjoy your easy victory today, Sven thought as he watched them. *Tomorrow, we all become draxi.*

 **42**

*"Some mapmakers tell tales of Drakes that live beyond
the Fens of Reur — so far from civilization that certain
tribes don't even recognize Mar as an enemy or threat.
The most common creature they describe is a wholly
remarkable guer race, which they call fire-breathing
guer or, more commonly, draxi. These remarkable guer
are almost certainly fictitious."*

— Nightfire Tradition,
Catalogue of Drakes

Bui counted the ranks and columns of Drakes. His adepts — draxi, they were calling themselves now — were much more organized now than they had been when they faced the first wave of Drakes. They had replenished their supply of torutsen, filled quivers with arrows and javelins, and increased their output of Blosin gloves. Had they been this well-prepared a month ago, Bui was confident the first army of Drakes never would have made it across the Lapis Amnis.

We harried twenty thousand before with minimal casualties, but can we repeat our success against the same number again?

And suppose they learn, and increase the size of their waves? What is next — thirty thousand and then forty thousand? How long before we break?

The draxi had spent nearly every waking hour for the last three days preparing for the second assault. This time, the traps did not wait for the Drakes to cross the river. Rather, they started a hundred yards into the Fens of Reur.

"Arn Besen says th'adepts on th'east flank're ready," one of the relays said.

Bui nodded. Arn Besen had swept the corridors of the citadel before becoming an adept. He was no hero, Bui knew, but he knew the Drakes would kill him if they defeated the draxi, and so Arn fought valiantly to ensure victory.

Surround me with men who want to live, Bui prayed silently. *For they won't throw away their lives on a mapmaker's folly.*

Bui meant to live, too, but he knew that would not happen unless he fought.

For now, though, there is little more I can do except watch.

Bui watched the Mass halt. Drake scouts came out, methodically and precisely seeking the edge of the Mar's magical traps. They made little sound as they burned — a finger sacrificed for the sake of the body.

The war wasn't fast. Bui preferred it that way. He was tremendously outnumbered. He needed time to build these complicated traps. The first wave of Drakes had given him a feel for how much time he would have.

The field of traps ended two miles to the east of the adepts' fortifications. Eventually, the scouting jabbers reached the edge of the magical defenses and picked their way closer to the river.

"They mean to leave our traps unsprung," said a member of Bui's escort, his accent as stilted as a magocrat's. "Either they mean to ignore us or flank us."

Brok Gelasen had once stoically endured a thousand outrageous demands from his wizardly clients as a cloakmaker. He was one of the best of his trade, but no matter how fine the cloth, how small the stitches, and how well-placed the pockets, some magocrats would never be happy. He had weathered a thousand dire threats and countless insults in the course of his trade while still managing to turn a profit on his wares. The cloakmaker had brought the same patient endurance to his duties as one of the draxi.

"We'll outrun them, still," Bui assured him. *I hope the Mardux has beaten the first army. It would be really bad if the draxi were pinned between the first army and the second.*

The Drakes systematically checked the path to the Lapis Amnis on the eastern front, jabber guer weaving back and forth along a swath almost a mile wide until they reached the river's bank. Bui hoped they hadn't noticed that the part of the river they were scouting was now more of a lake.

If even the Mar mapmakers can't keep the maps of rivers up to date, why would the Drakes notice a difference?

The striped guer at the rear made low trumpeting noises, and the Drake army entered the Lapis, jabber in the fore and spiny-tailed flanking them. The striped guer waded in soon after. Bui encouraged his men to taunt the enemy, enrage them. Make them commit. He eyed the place where the lake narrowed, a few yards within the range of the Mar traps.

A handful of spiny-tailed guer were close to the narrows, and they swirled around, screaming at each other. They had bumped into the Mar's trap, a plug made from Power, damming the river. Bui saw several striped guer, partway into the water, turn their heads to listen.

"Tell Arn to do it now," he told the relay, who sprinted off to deliver the message.

The striped guer trumpeted again, and the thousands of Drakes in the river doubled their speed. The jabber, past halfway, raced for the south bank. The spiny-tailed, smaller and weaker, turned back. The tall striped guer pressed on with spiny-tailed archers on their backs.

The Mar fell back, and a handful appeared on the south bank from under the obstruction, led by Arn. Behind them, the tunnel of Power they had built vanished much faster than it had been created, and the lake began its swift return to river, taking the Drakes with it — into the two-mile swath of traps that the adepts had set up earlier, and that the Drakes had carefully avoided.

The Mar faded away as the Drakes drowned. Spiny-tailed died first, then jabber, and finally the striped guer, who could brace themselves for some time but tired. The river ran with fire as it funneled its writhing, screaming load into the traps.

"They didn't expect that," Brok said dryly.

"I'm not complainin'," Bui told him, unable to resist grinning broadly. He turned to a relay. "Tell Arn that was great work."

The relay ran to comply even as another arrived, breathless.

"Some of Arn's didn't make it out in time."

"How many?" Bui asked.

"He's still countin', but at least twenty, so far."

Twenty Mar compared to a lakeful of Drakes. Any general would consider that a bargain.

"Sen' some 'depts downstream to fish out their bodies. I'd like to burn as many as they can fin'. We'll remem'er their sacrifice."

The relay nodded and ran west.

Bui gave orders to rebuild what traps they could while keeping an eye on the edge of the Drake army for their next charge. The enemy waited just long enough for the Lapis to return almost to normal, and then the trumpeting began.

The splash of the first thousand howling jabbers sent a chill down Bui's spine.

We can stand and hold them off, or we can turn and run. But I don't know what's behind me right now.

"Glovers, stren'then the traps. Guardians, be ready to push them."

Rank after rank of Drake pushed into the river and died — each pushed into the traps by the rank behind it, all the way to the rear of the army.

"More than half the gloves're gone," reported one of the runners.

"Striped guer've crossed the river three miles east," reported another.

"Brin' all the 'depts to the fortifications," Bui ordered. "We're goin' to run soon, an' I don't want to leave anyone behin'."

The guer had reached the guardians' walls on the south bank. Soon, they broke through the line in half a dozen places, forcing the draxi to resort to spears, knives and desperate fire magic to close the breaches.

"Th'east flank's collapsin'!" a breathless runner told him.

"We've spotted stingers comin' from the west," warned another. "They must've crossed out of sight downstream."

"Let's leave," Bui said. *We should've left after the first wave.* "South. Leave traps to slow them."

Another runner arrived from the eastern flank. "The Drakes've turned the other way. They're goin' east, now."

Bui raised an eyebrow but didn't rescind his first order.

What are they doing?

The adepts had begun to evacuate, leaving a trail of traps in their wake. When they were several miles south of the Lapis Amnis, Bui ordered a head count. They had only lost twenty adepts. The best estimate of Drake casualties was close to five thousand.

Without magic, we couldn't have hoped for battles as successful these have been. We can attack our enemies with impunity and escape before they ever come close to us. Every battle, they must storm a fortress made of fire.

The draxi turned east, moving quickly using Mobility. Abruptly, they found themselves looking upon a column of adepts armed with wands and spears marching north.

Bui sighed in unmistakable relief, and many of the draxi wept openly in their joy.

The Mardux has come, and he has brought us reinforcements.

Without the reconnaissance stones, the wizards would have lost the Duxy of Flasten. The ochres were perfectly camouflaged and able to shape themselves as if made of soft clay, which, as far as Horsa could tell, was exactly what they were. Torutsen by itself wouldn't allow the weards to see them, for whatever part of the ochres was alive was buried deep enough under their muddy coats to conceal the dispersion of myst. Horsa had been able to modify the recon stones to track them, though, and now the ochres fled from their path.

Many Mar would go hungry until the next crop of wild rice could be planted and harvested, however. To eliminate the ochres lurking beneath the water, the wizards had boiled away hundreds of marshes and wild rice fields, leaving only steaming patches of scorched, cracked clay. Even the Teleport War had not created such total devastation in the areas it touched, but the wizards could tell from the lack of friendly casualties and the vanishing number of ochre motes on the recon stones that they were winning.

They had met no Mar in two spans of sporadic clashes with the ochres. Every town was empty, and the decomposing corpses were too few to account for all the disappearances. Ragnar seemed certain that the mundanes had fled ahead of the ochre invasion. The strange Drakes were disconcertingly difficult to fight without magic, after all.

Horsa had his doubts, though he prayed desperately that they were unfounded.

The army of more than thirty thousand wizards came within sight of Flasten Palus. This was the first place any refugees were likely to go.

"Weard Verifien, recon the city. I want a full account of its condition," Ragnar said.

Horsa nodded and did as he was told — obedient as he had sworn to be.

"There are no signs of magical defenses, Dux Groth. No ochres, either." On a hunch, Horsa made one more sweep of Flasten Palus. "No Mar, either — at least no living ones."

Ragnar frowned. "Set the recon stone for regular sweeps of the surrounding area and leave it here to help our sentries keep watch. Weard Verifien, I am bringing you and a hundred of my magocrats with me into Flasten Palus. I cannot wait until tomorrow to learn what has happened to my city. The rest of the army will make camp here for the night. Keep a sharp watch. There could still be ochres in the area."

"Not within nine miles," Horsa reminded him. "And ochres do not move quickly. Set sentries, as well. The reconnaissance stone can be fooled by enemy wizards, but only an enchanter can completely hide from enemy eyes."

"Agreed."

Ragnar gave orders to the wizards. Soon, the army's fires burned everywhere on the open marsh. When the generals were satisfied that the rest of the army could operate without them for a while, Horsa, Ragnar and eleven nonagons disappeared into the Tempest.

Flasten Palus's southern gate hung open. Several dozen Mar corpses lined both sides of the dirt road that led to the entrance as if they had been moved out of the path of a marching army. Scavengers had already rendered it impossible for Horsa to guess at a specific cause of death, though most showed battlefield injuries of some kind — a twisted neck, a severed head, a missing limb and even one whose torso faced the opposite way from his feet.

"Still reconning, Weard Verifien?" Ragnar murmured.

Horsa reconned but found nothing — no Mar, no ochre, no Drakes of any kind. He said as much to Weard Groth. The news relaxed the dux no more than it had relaxed him.

The wizards cautiously entered the city. Flasten Palus looked nothing at all like Domus Palus. Mud daub and sod huts dominated, but there were a few wooden structures here and there. The outer wall was little more than a very large palisade, and Horsa knew the central keep was yet ahead.

It has more in common with Rustiford than with Domus Palus, he reflected. *In fact, Rustiford probably has more wooden buildings than Flasten Palus. The city is just bigger.*

"Split into nonagons and spread out," Ragnar said. "Look for signs of what might have happened here and where the people might have gone. Weard Verifien, you are still with me. We will head for the ruins of the keep."

Ruins? It must have been destroyed before the ochres reached it.

Groups of wizards wound through the streets and away from each other. Horsa, Ragnar and a nonagon of Flasten magocrats walked down the central street — if a trampled dirt path a couple of paces wide could be called a street. The corpses piled up outside the gates were not the only signs of struggle they saw. The stench of death that hung in the air was strong enough to make some of the wizards sick, and none of them talked about food. Weapons and corpses were strewn helter-skelter wherever they went, but the dead were all Mar — some wizards, but mostly mundanes. Huts had been burned down in some places, though the fires had long since gone out.

Burned by the attackers or by the defenders? Horsa wondered.

They reached a small public square, and Horsa almost gagged at the sight and smell. The ground a hundred feet across was covered in dried blood, and someone had raised a pile of corpses at the center of the square. Decomposition had already begun, but Horsa could tell that these were no victims of battle. There were no weapons in the area, and the victims in the pile appeared to be mostly old men and women. Many looked like they had been savaged by the sharp teeth of some large predator.

"Ochres do not leave marks like those," one of the greens pointed out.

No one responded. They didn't need to. Everyone feared they

knew exactly what was responsible for this carnage.

Damnens.

"Burn it," Ragnar growled.

"Dux Groth, won't that just attract their attention?" asked an auburn.

"Do it. I am not in the habit of letting dead Mar rot."

The wizards summoned fire and turned the pile of corpses into a funeral pyre.

"Weard Verifien, will you give us a prayer?" the dux asked.

Horsa did not respond right away, surprised as he was by the request in such grim surroundings. He nodded to acknowledge he had heard and tried to compose himself.

"Watch over us, my fellow Mar," Horsa murmured to the sparks and thick smoke that rose up from the pile. "Shelter us with your darkness and guide us with your light. By your sacrifice, we are warmed. By your sacrifice, we can see. By your..."

A snort from one of the huts at the edge of the square interrupted him — a sound like laughter but lacking any human mirth.

"To arms!" Ragnar snapped, drawing his marsord.

Horsa had his marsord out an instant later, and the nine wizards with them were not slow to ready their spears. They stood there in silence for what seemed like at least a minute, but nothing leapt out at them.

Horsa reconned and found no Drakes in the city. With a second quick spell, he noted that two of the nonagons had vanished, and three others had suffered losses.

"This was misguided," he whispered to Ragnar. "We must withdraw."

The dux had no chance to respond before a tall humanoid stepped into the square. The damnen had a body that looked like a shadow and claws as long as knives. It snorted and strolled toward them, betraying no fear of their weapons and bright cloaks.

Ragnar stood his ground, but his magocrats shied away from the dread Drake, pushing Horsa back with them. A sudden wall of fire sprang up in front of the damnen as one of the wizards panicked, but it vanished when the creature ran through it.

"Look out!" Horsa shouted at Ragnar, but it was no use.

The damnen passed through the fire without a mark on it. Ragnar lashed out with his marsord, but the damnen parried it at the hilt, knocking the weapon out of his hand. A small line of crimson appeared on Ragnar's wrist where one claw had grazed it. Before anyone could react, the damnen grabbed the red by the neck and lifted him off the ground.

The Flasten wizards rushed forward to strike it with spears, but the damnen did not wait for them to engage it, fleeing with surprising speed. One thrown spear grazed its thigh as it ran, but no other came close as it widened the gap between itself and its pursuers. Two of the wizards used magic to keep pace, moving out of sight of their companions in seconds. Only the muffled cries informed Horsa that they had caught up with their prey.

One damnen did not kill everyone in Flasten Palus. If there are damnens here but no Mar survivors, either the Drakes killed everyone in Flasten Palus or they have taken prisoners.

Mar told terrifying stories about the fates of those whom the damnens took prisoner, and Horsa did not intend to learn the truth of them first-hand. He called the myst and escaped into the Tempest, only belatedly realizing he was leaving a hundred wizards to die.

Katla did not wait quietly in the Delegates' tent city for an end to the war. Her incessant lobbying made few friends and more enemies, but most of the words she planted led to dissension between the delegates, which was all to the good.

She had started with the spiny-tailed guer, who wanted a swift and easy war with the Mar and not the agonizing sacrifices she had promised on Sven's behalf. By this point, they could see that was not going to happen.

Most of the Hue — those gobbels from the Morden Moors — had gone to invade the Takraf Protectorates along with the Nineteenth Wave of the Mass, but they had left a hundred of their best warriors with Katla, ostensibly to protect her from stinger coercion in future meetings of the Delegates, though she noted that they were quick to point out the advantages of supporting the Hue in every meeting since she had supported their attack on the Protectorates.

The Gue delegate spent most meetings opposing any measure the ravits — and especially the Koh — supported, even though his lone vote had no weight compared to the ten votes carried by the ravits and their insero allies. The jabber guer seemed largely uninterested in her, though they seemed glad to fight a Mar civilization worthy of their race's glorious reputation and had mobilized their forces more eagerly than any other Drake race.

Katla knew Doh Zue Sah — the leader of the Delegates — did not trust her, but it was impossible to read the striped guer's reptilian features for any sign beyond her tendency to find arguments against anything Katla said, even if the guer ultimately supported the Mar when it came to a vote.

I wonder if she trusted Brack more.

Katla almost pitied every Drake tribe that had no delegate present for the meetings of the last few months. Whenever the Delegates needed someone to do an unpleasant or impossible task, they immediately handed it to a tribe that lacked a representative to protest. The spiny-tailed guer delegates were the worst offenders by far — quick to find excuses for delays in the mobilization of their tribes' shares of the Waves. The jabber guer were bad in their own way, but rather than avoiding battle, they seemed eager to place their warriors in battle.

The stinger delegates waste no time in delegating the dirty work to other tribes, Katla mused.

A spiny-tailed guer arrived in her tent with a vial — her regular dose of morutsen, which was the only thing preventing her from slaughtering the Delegates or escaping to inform the Mar of the limits of the Mass's intelligence. Even with insero-mounted ravit messengers, it took a month or more for any information to get to a Wave from the Delegates, and Katla suspected any messages the Waves sent back took just as long.

Katla seized the container and drank without comment, but she instantly had to force herself not to screw up her face in surprise. She eyed the departing stinger, looking for some mark of its tribe but found none.

One of the spiny-tailed guer tribes is preventing them from dosing me with morutsen, and they're being subtle about it. But which tribe and why?

Katla had little time to consider the possibilities, much less how she should react, before another spiny-tailed guer arrived.

"The Delegates call Yee Ka Lah to the Delegates' Tent for a meeting," the guer said.

"Did they mention the subject of the meeting?" Katla asked as she rose to follow him.

"Word has reached the delegate of the Ko that the Twenty-first Wave has been mobilized and awaits the Delegates' instructions for its deployment."

Katla tried to remember the composition of the Twenty-first Wave, but it eluded her for most of the walk to the Delegates' Tent. She was only ten paces from her destination when the realization struck her.

The Twenty-first Wave is made up of ravits mounted on insero, and is no smaller than any other wave.

Suddenly, the Mass's shortage of military intelligence did not seem like such a handicap.

 **43**

*"Less often celebrated but ultimately more important,
Mardux Sven Takraf used takstuf mystalton exclusively.
Unlike ordinary mystalton, which eventually expired
and needed to be rebuilt each time, takstuf mystalton
could be renewed simply by adding Energy to their existing reservoirs — like adding fuel to a fire while it still
burns instead of letting it go out and rekindling it anew.
Without takstuf mystalton, the Protectorates would
not have been possible, because Weard Takraf would
have spent all his time replenishing his supply of Blosin
gloves. Later, it allowed him to send allied wizards and
even apprentices on rounds of spell renewal — all without revealing the secret of his Blosin gloves to them."*

— Weard Oda Kalidus,
The Origin of Nothing

When Horsa finished describing the events in Flasten Palus, Eda shrugged.

"We should leave this duxy to the damnens. It certainly seems like divine retribution to me. The Mass is the real enemy, and Sven needs us."

Horsa was glad none of the Flasten magocrats were close enough to hear them.

"It is not that easy, Eda. If we march north, the Flasten wizards will not follow us. In fact, they might attack us outright if we try to leave. They still outnumber us, remember?"

"Yes, but besieging a city occupied by damnens sounds like a mapmaker's adventure, and chasing an unknown number of damnens into the Dead Swamps seems even more suicidal, if that's possible. You said yourself that our recon can't see them."

"It cannot, but we can find the Mar they are herding." The last word came out as a snarl. After a brief pause, he spoke more softly. "You are right to be afraid."

"I am not afraid."

"Most of these magocrats do not even have weapons, and forces and fire wizards are useless against damnens. Our chances would be better if they were all mundane warriors like your guerillas."

"They are not mine. I'm just their magic support."

"But we both know why we must stop the damnens from taking slaves among the mundane Mar. We were both born in Grun and lived in Rustiford. We both swore to stop slave-taking among the mundanes, if we could."

Eda bowed her head and said nothing.

"I have saved many lives since the Academy, but I caused many more deaths in the Teleport War than ever I prevented as a priest."

"Sven needs us, Horsa," she said softly without raising her brown eyes.

"Yes, but the magocrats of the Duxy of Flasten need us more. Their mundanes need us more. If we ignore that, the entire Duxy will hate us."

"They already do, and I don't think we can end that enmity. Sven just killed their dux in advance of a Drake invasion. And you just left Ragnar to die in their capital city."

"He was already dead. Magic cannot get within three feet of a damnen, so I could not even have teleported him with me."

"You are right to invoke Grun and Rustiford, though. Leading the Flasten magocrats against the damnens is not prudent, but it is the right thing to do. I'll lead half the wizards south to deal with the damnens. The guerillas might prove their usefulness yet again before this is done. Lead the other half in a siege of Flasten Palus. Both groups will need to have a mix of Domus and Flasten wizards. We'd better make some kind of announcement soon, though."

"Yes. I do have one concern. How will the Domus wizards take this? We are ordering them to assist an enemy army instead of returning to their home duxy."

"I never said it wouldn't be messy. In the end, the damnens might be the least likely to kill us." She kissed him on the cheek without warning. "Watch yourself out there, Horsa."

Great gods, please grant me the power to keep peace between these wizards, Horsa prayed.

Finn Ochregut sat on a stool at the foot of the dais leading to the Chair, listening to the reports of Domus Palus events. He no longer had any illusions about his importance or power. He knew Sven had left him in charge of the administration of Domus Palus because Sven was leading the adepts at the Lapis Amnis, his closest advisors were scattered across Marrishland and the city magocrats had gone with Horsa to make war with the Duxy of Flasten — in short, because Finn was the only one left for the job whom the Mardux could actually spare. Sven, of course, had not explained it that way — citing instead Finn's rapport with the adepts and his proven loyalty to the Mardux.

Day in and day out, the reports were the same, from the same people. Supply figures — weapons growing, food shrinking. Desertions and new recruits — plenty of the former and few of the latter. A group of former slaves stealing a handful of wands and threatening their old masters. Complaints from the imprisoned, drugged magocrats.

Finn invoked Sven's name in everything he decreed. He didn't want anyone to look back at this time and remember his mistakes.

Today there were two unlikely faces, though.

Rig Polchef approached first. He had been the chief cook in the kitchens of the citadel, and for his role in Erika's conspiracy, Finn had put him in charge of city security. The job had proved too big for him, and his assistants did most of the real work now, but he occasionally learned something useful.

"We've foun' two mun'anes i'the square near the citadel — the one where wizards appear. They're sayin' they're kin of Sven's an' have a message for him."

"What're their names?" Finn asked.

"Brita somethin' and Erlend Littlehart. Mardux ever talk about such?"

Finn shook his head. "The Mardux has lots of frien's an' lots of enemies. What's their message?"

Rig flushed. "I didn't ask."

"Well, fin' out. Sven'll want to know, but he doesn't like his time wasted. If it soun's important, sen' them with the next legion of adepts that goes to the Lapis Amnis."

"I'll do as you've said."

The other was a very impatient Weard Salt, the keeper of the recon stone.

"Tell me it's still workin'."

"It is working, adept," she said, always unsure how to address him. At least she had no problems with who was in charge. "But a new army has appeared, to the south."

"The south," Finn muttered. "Not the Domus army returned?"

"We are not sure. It is about the correct size."

"Sen' someone to fin' out. Give them morutdyjiton just in case, but make sure they don't start a fight if they don't have to."

Finn went to bed that night comfortable with his position and decision-making. He woke to a nightmare of battle and smoke. He dressed in the dark and strapped the marsord to his shin. Taking a sip of torutsen from a flask, he opened the door to face the horrors outside. The sea of myst danced before his eyes, allowing the mapmaker to make his way through the darkened corridors of the citadel. It gave him no sense of texture or color, but he could at least see solid objects as silhouettes among the colored specks of magic flowing through the air.

Dead and dying Mar lay in the hallway not far from his room. Finn caught a glimpse of two Mar wrestling on the floor in a side room, weapons drawn and seeking blood. Neither was using magic.

One of Bui's tactics for fighting wizards. Get close enough, and your tor buffer makes it a little harder for your enemy to wield magic. If he tries to do it anyway, he's almost as likely to do himself harm.

Finn approached them as quietly as he could, though they were obviously too locked in their own struggle to notice him. He summoned Energy to create a small light that lasted long enough for him to identify the adept and stab the wizard in the neck with the short blade of his marsord. Blood pooled rapidly on the ground as the green crumpled and clutched his neck, calling Vitality to heal himself. Finn and the adept never gave him the opportunity to recover, stabbing the wizard repeatedly with knife and marsord. When it was done, the mapmaker let his light fade, fearful that it might attract the attention of more wizards.

"What's happenin'?"

"I don't know. There're wizards i'the citadel — hun'reds of them. I don't know how they got in, but they're killin' everyone."

"You've torutsen?"

"Yes. He'd've killed me, otherwise."

"We need to rally th'adepts an' make formations like Sven told us."

Finn wiped off the blade of the marsord and slid it back through the hole in his cloak and into the shin sheath. The adept said nothing, following Finn out of the room and closer to the source of the commotion. They turned a corner into a corridor leading into the Mardux's audience chamber and found at least three dozen wizards waiting for them.

Never mind then, Finn thought, ducking back around the bend.

The adept reacted differently, summoning myst and hurling fire at the wizards. There was a brief cry as the magic scorched one, but the retaliation from the others reduced the adept to a smoking corpse.

Fool! These aren't Drakes. A few burns don't kill them.

A woman's voice called from the audience chamber. "Surrender or die, adept."

Finn knew he could flee. Those adepts who had once been slaves knew of hiding places in the citadel that were beyond the knowledge of the wizards.

In the swamps, swift movement kills more surely than caution.

Finn raised his hand in a gesture of helplessness and stepped over the adept. The woman who had spoken wore a red cloak.

"Peace i'the swamp. I'm Finn Ochregut — actin' leader of th'adepts in Domus Palus. You've bested me, an' I submit."

The red opened her mouth, but Yver Verlren stepped out of the crowd beside her and spoke first.

"I know this mapmaker, duxess. He led the adepts' rebellion." Yver sneered and turned his attention to Finn. "Return what is mine to me."

Duxess? Why is Glyda Zaun involved in this?

Finn drew the marsord and walked toward the duxes. A pair of auburns intercepted him.

"That's close enough," one growled.

Finn shrugged and slid the marsord closer to the Dux of Piljerka. "We don't want to fight wizards. You're not our enemies."

Yver seized the marsord and inspected it as if expecting it to vanish.

"Then why do you unlawfully hold wizards prisoner and teach mundanes to use magic beyond their understanding?" the duxess asked with false sweetness.

"We saw the Mass comin' on the recon stone, but the dux wasn't doin' anythin', so th'adepts the Mardux made to fight the Mass had to do somethin'."

"Three duxes have sworn to me that the Mardux deceived Dux Ratsell to change the law so he could turn Domus Palus into a new Tortz. The Mass was not invading until Weard Takraf made his adepts."

"They're lyin', then, or they're wron'," Finn said.

"That is a very serious accusation, Finn. What proof do you have?"

"Take a look aroun' the city, duxess. The Mass sent twenty thousan' guer against it about a month ago, but they never even got to the wall before th'adepts an' the priests killed them all. Th'other Drakes were takin' too long to get here, so Sven's taken fifty thousan' adepts to the Lapis Amnis to fight the Mass, an' he's winnin'. They've killed two hun'red thousan', last I knew."

"That is impossible!" Borya Zaghaf cried from where he sat on Finn's stool at the foot of the dais.

"They have Blosin wands," Yver reminded him. "Weariness is less of a factor."

"Even so, I cannot believe this mundane's lies!" Borya raged.

Finn shrugged again. "It must be a miracle, then. They say the Mardux has nine patrons who help him succeed at everythin'. After seein' Drakes kneel on the groun' an' beg Mar for mercy, nothin' seems impossible anymore."

"Tell your adepts to surrender, if you are their leader," Glyda said.

"We are taking control of the capital."

"I'd welcome your counsel, duxess, but I can't make you anythin' but an advisor."

"It was not a request, mundane. You will yield the capital to us."

Finn risked a small smile. "Do you know how to tell an adept from a mun'ane, duxess?" He pointed at the strips of red cloth sewn onto the sleeves of his cloak. "Just these. Without them, I still have magic, an' I know how to make wan's an' torutsen. Take Domus Palus away from me, an' all the adepts'll stop wearin' bright colors. Your magocrats'll be livin' in a city filled with Mar who want to kill them, but they won't know which're loyal an' which're traitors waitin' for a good time to strike."

"They would kill Mar even though the Mass is the greater threat?" Glyda asked coolly.

"We want all the help we can get, duxess. If you've come to help the Mardux fight the Mass, you're allies to th'adepts, not enemies. An' if you've come to help the Mass beat the Mardux, then you're listenin' to the wron' gods, same as Flasten."

The duxess laughed without mirth. There was an uneasy silence as everyone waited to see the true nature of her reaction to the adept. The duxess sobered, and her eyes were like unseeing gemstones when she stared into Finn's.

"I see the Mardux's henchmen are blocks of peat cut from the same bog. Weard Lasik said the same things you just did, though he argued the points more diplomatically and eloquently than you could dream of expressing them. I should admit that Weard Takraf is the Guardian chosen by the gods and ignore all signs to the contrary."

"The outrage of the people's the surest sign of the gods' will they'll ever give you."

"I have heard enough. Finn Ochregut, I accuse you of violating Bera Branehilde's Unwritten Laws for wielding power beyond your understanding and for teaching magic to those who are not properly educated."

"I deman' Nightfire judge me," he said, thinking of the story of Sven and Tortz.

She smiled faintly. "You are mistaken. That is the right of wizards, not mundanes. Do not worry, though. You will have plenty of company in the execution chamber." Then to the auburns in front of her. "Take him to the prisons and give him morutsen until his trial."

"No!" Finn cried. "You're makin' a mistake! You have to help the Mardux, or the Mass'll win, an' all the Mar'll die!"

"If that is the will of the gods," she said softly. "Then so be it."

"Weard Staute," a voice called, and Asfrid jerked awake.

"Yes, Sigrun?"

"They've breached the perimeter defenses."

Asfrid's heart leapt into her throat. Without speaking, she pulled on her boots, threw her cloak over her shoulders and followed Sigrun to the recon hut at the center of the town. What she saw did not present any immediate solution.

A mile-wide column of red icons representing at least eight thousand stinger guer, gobbels and jabber guer stretched fifty miles from beyond the range of the Protectorates' reconnaissance to within a league of the northernmost town. Each community had its own defenses, but they had never been intended to stop an entire army of Drakes, much less one of this scale.

"What is the estimated body count?"

"Ten thousand Drakes, Weard Staute, and all the gloves are used up."

Asfrid shook her head. "We are too few to stop that many with our magic. Ten thousand casualties without meeting an enemy in the field, and the Drakes march on. This can only be the Mass."

Sigrun laid a hand on her shoulder. "It is up to the mundane army now."

Asfrid looked at the swarm of green dots gathered within the walls of Amboth — the small, walled community the Drake army was rapidly approaching. They had worked hard and without magic to fortify the town as well as they could. The wall was now too high for jabber guer to leap onto it, much less over it. The last of the civilian population had fled spans earlier, and almost all the warriors in the Takraf Protectorates waited there with stockpiles of food and water in preparation for what they hoped would be a swift victory — or at least a long siege.

If I were a Drake with access to our reconnaissance, I would avoid Amboth entirely and strike our other towns — damnen tactics. Right now, the warriors believe they fight to prevent the Drakes from killing their families and destroying their homes. If they could be convinced that staying in Amboth only increased the danger to what they care about, they will either despair and give weak battle or act rashly and march against an army larger and better-situated than their own.

"What can we do?" Sigrun asked.

"Weard Schwert is captured or dead. The Mardux is no doubt fighting the Mass elsewhere — probably at Domus Palus. The Domus wizards fight the Flasten wizards far to the southwest. The other duxies are both neutral and far away, so we can expect no help from them. There is only one army close enough to influence the outcome."

"They are the cause of our current predicament. Otherwise, we might have withdrawn even farther into the Protectorates and let our standing defenses wear away at these invaders."

"Who knows what fate we will suffer at the hands of the Mardux's enemies? Will they even honor a truce or accept a surrender? Even if they come to our aid, what price will they exact, and will we ever be citizens of the Takraf Protectorates again?"

Sigrun didn't respond immediately. The recon stone updated, and the line of Drakes pushed a little farther south. There was still no sign of an end to the approaching column.

"You don't know what will happen, but you're willing to take that risk."

Asfrid nodded grimly.

"If the farl is going to make us all his slaves and use his magic to prevent us from ever disobeying him, many Mar would rather die — myself among them — and you would have chosen that fate for us. Do you really think this is the right thing to do?"

"I don't know, but if the Mardux wins this war, I have faith that he will not let us remain slaves to Flasten. And if he loses, either Flasten will annex the Protectorates, or the Mass will destroy them. Three possible outcomes of surrender — one that will preserve us, one that will destroy us and one that will do much worse than destroy us."

"And if we accept no enemy's aid and meet the Mass in the field?"

Asfrid gestured to recon stone. "Do you see more than one outcome? Because I certainly don't. Given the choice between death and a chance to stay alive, I will take my chances that the gods will smile upon me."

On the recon stone, the column of Drakes moved closer.

 **44**

"Only a fool dismisses an enchanter. They might not be as skilled in combat as we are, but they are quite capable of protecting themselves against our attacks. More importantly, a skilled enchanter can decide which side of the battlefield you will stand on before the battle is even begun."

— Nightfire Tradition,
Nightfire's Magical Primer

"Our eastern flank is beginning to fray again," Sven commented to Fraemauna — Guthrun — pointing at the recon stone. "Send Swind's legions to sweep those Drakes back into the Lapis Amnis, and bring Sendala's legions out of the battle. Her children have fought valiantly for the past span and deserve a few days' rest."

The Mardux barely noticed the concerned looks his escort priests shot each other. He hadn't slept in four days — not since he had railed at Heliotosis — Weard Aesir Schnee — for wasting magic sending him into the Tempest to rest. They needed all the magic they could muster to keep the adepts armed with wands and Blosin gloves, and sleep was a luxury the Mardux could no longer afford. He couldn't shake the feeling that he had misread all the signs pointing him on his path.

How could I have overlooked this possibility? I should have crushed Volund earlier. Horsa and the Domus wizards would be here to help hold the Lapis Amnis. I could have passed my amendment without dividing the Mar when they needed to be united.

He enchanted a pair of morutdyjiton idly as he watched the seemingly endless battle unfold on the recon stone in front of him. Sven enchanted Blosin gloves whenever he had the magical strength to do so. Most days, a green could have slain him, though he suspected his escort reserved more of their strength than he did.

"Another two hundred striped guer are approaching the ford near the midpoint. Make sure Niminth's men are ready for them. The fighting has been intense, and I do not want them to run out of wands before the Drakes cross."

Sendala — Weard Frig Blauge — nodded once and vanished into the Tempest.

"Mardux!" Bui shouted behind him. "Messengers from Domus Palus. Bad news."

Sven turned as the guerilla approached. Bui's draxi acted as scouts and messengers between the far-flung Mar legions that now held a stretch of the Lapis Amnis five hundred miles wide. The army certainly was not spread evenly across that area, as they needed to focus their attention on parts of the river the Drakes could conceivably ford.

"Bring them, Bui."

The guerilla was clearly out of breath. "They'll be here in a minute. People're fleeing Domus Palus an' comin' north. They say the Duxess of Pidel has seized Domus Palus. She's goin' to kill all th'adepts there for breakin' the law."

The only indication of his consternation Sven gave Bui was a slight frown. When it became clear the Mardux was not going to respond, the guerilla continued talking.

"The other part of the message is. An older couple claimin' to be your wife's parents say they've a message from Weard Wost." Bui spat. "He's got your family an' wants you to meet him alone in Tortz, or he'll sell them as slaves."

Sven's face locked into a sneer, and his blind eye flashed in the sun.

It always comes back to Tortz, doesn't it?

"This fire will end where it started," he murmured as he stuffed several pairs of Blosin gloves into his vest. Bui squirmed in obvious discomfort.

"Mardux," Cedar — Weard Kiarr Bukaltar — said softly. "You need sleep. We are worried about you."

"Marrish, send me to Tortz," Sven said imperiously to one of the priests.

Rig Marspar looked at him with deepening worry.

"Forgive me," Sven murmured. "Rig, please send me to Tortz."

"I do not know where it is, Mardux. You are in dire need of sleep, and you are definitely in no condition to face the farl enchanter alone."

Sven casually removed a pair of gloves from his utility vest and slid them onto his hands. "I am never alone, Weard Marspur. The gods are with me always."

"If you wish to aid your family, we will go with you, but please sleep awhile first," Cedar said.

Sven touched Elements and felt the Blosin gloves seize the myst all around him.

"Mardux, no!" cried Marrish, but Sven was already gone.

On the recon stone near them, a new group of Drakes appeared to the north. Kiarr squinted at the symbol.

"Those are not guer."

"Insero," Rig said.

Eda stood in an open area between two hills and waved her arms at the damnen scouting party.

Six of them this time. I think they are learning to fear us.

They approached her with uncharacteristic caution, but they only stole occasional glances in her direction, clearly on the lookout for any Mar archers hidden behind the hills. As they came closer, Eda backed away slowly farther between the hills, drawing her marsord.

Tryggvi would laugh at me, she thought. *Here I am a wizard, and I'm just the bait.*

The damnens surged forward, thinking to catch her off-guard. Eda flickered, and she was suddenly several yards behind them. Suddenly, ten nonagons armed with javelins surrounded the Drakes and filled the air with wooden shafts guided with Power and hastened with Mobility. Even though the magic died before the javelins reached the damnens, the momentum drove the shafts home.

One damnen survived the initial rush and attacked desperately, raking at the wizards with sharp claws. Eda rushed to join the killing frenzy. Magic could not touch a damnen, but her marsord was perfectly serviceable. Surprised and alone against a hundred opponents, the damnen soon fell to a flurry of spears and knives.

When it was done, the Mar hacked off damnen heads and set about healing the wounded. They had only lost two this time.

Just like in all the stories about mapmaker expeditions in the Dead Swamps, except this time, we're the predators at the edge of vision, Eda mused with a feral smile.

So far, Eda and her company of ten nonagons had killed fifty damnens in raids and ambushes like these. In the informal contest to take the most heads, her company was a long way from first place, but she was marshaling a force of Flasten and Domus wizards 10,000 strong, ranging from greens to cyans, and the damnens had worked together much longer. By striking the damnen slavers without warning from every angle at least dozen times a day, they had reduced the Drakes' march to a veritable crawl. Even the mundane guerillas had made a few kills by emerging out of the mud and hamstringing damnens before they even knew the Mar were there, though the guerillas lacked the mobility of the nonagons and couldn't cover as much ground.

The only irritation was that the Mar still did not have a good estimate of the damnens' numbers.

The Mar presented the damnen corpses to her. Two greens improvised a comedy using the freshly severed heads as puppets. Eda shook her head in amazement.

"Let's get back to camp," she said. "Two nonagons will take the severed heads and put them on spikes in the damnens' path. The rest of you have leave to forage for food."

Eda called the myst and flickered across the landscape until she reached her base of operations in the south of the Duxy of Flasten. Other company captains waited for her.

"Bad luck," one Domus lavender — Olvir Bedaulich — spat. "Two of theirs and six of ours. If I didn't know any better, I'd think they knew we were coming."

"One of ours, three of theirs. We've given them a tough choice," noted an unusually perceptive Domus green. "They can stay close to their fellow damnens with the herd of mundanes where we concentrate our raids, or they can keep their distance to reduce the chance of being attacked while increasing the chance that any raiders that find them will kill them."

"Five of ours, eight of theirs. There is safety in both numbers and obscurity, but it is almost impossible to have both at the same time," a Flasten auburn said, summarizing her fellow captain's analysis.

"Two of ours, one of theirs. They will adjust their tactics," warned a Flasten cyan. "Damnens are terribly clever, and I am certain they recognize we do not know how many they are. They will find some way to use that to their advantage."

A Flasten blue arrived late to their daily meeting.

"You look troubled, Weard Entsen," Eda said, frowning. "What happened?"

"None of ours, one of theirs," he said automatically. All the captains had fallen into the habit of providing a casualty count before addressing all other orders of business. "But I bring troubling news. My company struck from the rear today, and while we saw only one damnen, it looks like they have left us a grisly gift of their own — eighty-six impaled and elaborately eviscerated Mar men."

Damnens are herders, Eda thought grimly. *Men are less valuable to them than women.*

"The same as the number of damnens we killed yesterday," Eda said softly. "They're adjusting their tactics."

"It could be the ploy of desperation," the same Flasten cyan said — Odveig Spitz, Eda recalled, was his name. "Or they are trying to distract us from their intentions."

Eda shook her head. "I'd say that's a fair guess, Weard Spitz. Wizards wear bright colors to frighten away less courageous enemies, but their entire strategy does not hinge on their cloaks. They cannot catch us, and we cannot see them — at least not with magic."

"They might be sending scouts farther afield in search of our base of operations," Weard Entsen suggested.

"Unlikely," the observant Domus green — Oysten Klarein — countered. "We can move our camp almost instantly. We could be a hundred miles away before their scout returned."

"Small scouting parties are more vulnerable than larger bands," Weard Spitz said. "Even with surprise, we suffer far more casualties against fifty damnens than we do against five."

Eda chewed her lower lip, listening to the discussion. "They might be trying to force us to meet them in the field. The more damnens we kill in ambushes and raids, the more innocent Mar they torture and kill in retaliation."

"Then that is the last thing we should give them," Weard Spitz growled.

"I disagree," Eda said. "That's exactly what we should give them — or, at least, that is what we should make them think we are giving them. They don't have a good count of our numbers, either."

"But why throw away troops on a pitched battle with damnens?" Weard Bedaulich asked.

"Because we didn't come here to kill damnens," Eda reminded him.

"A rescue," Weard Klarein murmured. "Field one or two thousand wizards to hold the damnens' attention, and while the battle is raging, the rest of the army snatches the mundanes away from them."

Weard Spitz snorted a laugh. "Sounds like we are paying them back for Despar Palus. I cannot argue against that. Once that thousand is engaged with the damnens, though, there is no escape for them. It is a terrible sacrifice to ask a Mar to make. After all, if the damnens win — and they probably will — some of those wizards will be taken prisoner by the Drakes. Everyone knows what damnens do to their captives."

"I'll lead the diversion force," Eda said. "I'd rather have volunteers than wizards who are only following orders."

"You'll need naked eye recon to make sure the plan is working," Weard Klarein said. "My company will circle around to see that they aren't guarding their captives too closely when the time comes. If it's too dangerous for a rescue, we'll try to warn you before the battle is joined."

"I will be with you, Weard Stormgul," Weard Spitz said, expression deadly serious. "I am not about to let a Domus magocrat make me look like a coward in my home duxy."

Other Flasten wizards voiced their agreement, and several Domus wizards, not wanting to be shown up by their old rivals, soon did the same.

Eda tried to appear calm in spite of the deep terror threatening to strangle her.

Diplomatically, that was the right move. Because I'm willing to die for their duxy, they will love the Mardux a little more. I wanted to be on the winning side, Sven, and so I will be, but I won't be alive to see it.

Sven sailed through the Tempest, his mind swirling with visions and memories. Living and dead Mar spoke to him, whispering endless advice into his ears, and he had followed none of it. His patrons appeared to offer dire pronouncements about his failure.

How wrong I was about the Mass! How terribly I underestimated Dinah and Domin! How badly I misinterpreted the signs the gods gave me!

Then Sven heard a new voice in the murmurs of the Tempest's dark as Pondr told his story for the first time. "Sven Takraf was born i'the wild'ress of Gunne, a secret child of Marrish an' Fraemauna. Seekin' to spare her lover from the wrath of his wife, Dinah, Fraemauna aban'oned her son. Seruvus, who sees all, took pity on the babe, blessed the boy with his own memory an' gave him to Pitt Gematsud to raise as his son."

He knew my story before I told it to him. He knew everything ... up to Tortz. He did not know the lesson of the fuel, that I am the fuel the Mar's fire would feed on. And Katla ... she said, "Fire is pitiless." The Mar will not be pitiless. I brought Marrish's gift of magic to the mundanes, I am the fuel their fire consumes, and each will be fuel for the next.

"An' Sven Takraf stepped forward an' volunteered to pay Rustiford's debt to Nightfire with his own life, never thinkin' of his own fate, but only that of his people."

But is that wrong? Nightfire just said, "All Marrishland will burn because of you." He thinks I am the fire, that our country is the fuel ... He thinks it is the lesson of the fire. Katla does too. The country cannot be consumed; the fire will always burn.

I did lose my way. I tried to sacrifice others to the gods as proof of my devotion, but it only proved my arrogance. As long as other Mar are out there, as long as Marrishland stands, I can still emerge victorious.

He remembered Dux Fieglin huddled at the feet of Dinah, begging her to show mercy to his people.

Dinah has called me out, too, but she will not bring me to my knees. If she lays me low, she will fall with me.

Sven exited the Tempest and arrived in the ruins of Tortz. The air was so thick with the odor of wetness and slow decay that his nostrils flared.

Have I forgotten what it means to live in the swamps and marshes?

Most of the buildings had vanished under years of Marrishland's winter and summer storms. The town wall was little more than a broad hurdle, and even the adobe prison had begun to return to the earth.

All things in Marrishland fade away. Nothing we build ever lasts for long.

"I have been waiting for you," Robert Wost said, his red cloak seeming to glow in the morning mist. To one side of him, Ari stood, watching. "You are too late, Mardux. Your mundane rabble will be destroyed by your old friends, the Protectorates. You cannot defeat me."

Sven sent bolts of Energy at the red from seven sides. Elements appeared and dissolved each bolt.

Robert laughed. "Did you really think it would be that easy?" His cloak became a halo of flame.

It is not real. He excels at illusions.

"Your efforts have been futile. I will swallow Marrishland, and there is nothing you can do to stop me."

A shell of Elements surrounded Sven, blocking all but a few motes of the myst. Sven yanked the metal-studded gloves from the back of his belt and yanked them onto his hands. He summoned Elements with all the force he could muster.

"Give up, Sven Takraf. You cannot break through my shell."

Sven dragged the tiny trickle of Elements to his fingertips. The magic concealed in the metal studs came to life, bursting forth and blending together to produce the most powerful attack magic any wizard could wield — morutmanon. Each finger sent forth a crackling bolt of raw magic built of each of the eight magicks. Without the gloves, Sven could never have gathered so much myst, much less control it.

Ari gaped and even Robert looked surprised as the rivulets of killing power lanced toward them. The black tendrils seared through Robert's shell of Elements and passed through the enchanter's desperate defense like water through air, wrapping itself around the two wizards. The two men evaporated at the touch of the magic, their bodies becoming as insubstantial as smoke.

"I am the hand of the gods!" Sven shouted at the smoke, stripping off the spent Blosin gloves. "If I fall, you will fall with me!"

"You are not my hand," Robert's voice said from the cloud.

A creature with the head of an alligator stepped out of the haze.

"Nor mine," said Katla's voice. A bald woman clad in layers of mud came forward to stand next to the alligator-headed creature.

"Domin? Dinah?" Sven's voice was unsteady. "But that's impossible."

"You have already received visits from nine of the gods. Why should two more surprise you, Weard Takraf?"

Sven drew his marsord and let out a scream of fury. "Marrishland is yours no longer!" He charged.

 **45**

"The source of Mardux Takraf's incredible magical power introduced a fatal weakness. He became utterly reliant upon the takraf mystalton in his Blosin gloves. His long neglect of tordyn discipline meant he could barely wield three magicks at once, even as a red. The same tactic his Duxy of Domus army used to neutralize the gobbel invasion rendered him nearly as helpless."

— Weard Oda Kalidus,
The Origin of Nothing

Sven collapsed to the ground while Ari looked on in shock. "How did you do that?"

Robert sneered and wiped his hands on his cloak. "My triggered spell countered all the magic in his gloves the instant he arrived. I am much more powerful than he is without those."

"He is a red, though. He still should have put up some fight."

"Perhaps it was teleportation sickness," Robert suggested with a shrug. He gestured to Sven's twitching form. "Regardless, he is now living the worst nightmare he is capable of imagining — a situation with no choices and no hope. Soon, he will surrender to terror and die, without ever waking from that dream. Nothing any Mar can do will break the spell without killing him."

Ari frowned slightly. *The Mardux must have been suffering from extreme tor weariness, which means he has been using a lot of magic recently. What is happening at Domus Palus?*

"Come, Ari, we have an envoy to bend to our will." Robert gestured, and Einar came out of the myst like an obedient slave. When they returned to Leiben, a cyan waited for them — one of Sven's ma-

387

gocrats named Weard Asfrid Staute. She looked up at them with eyes clouded by morutsen, and one side of her face was a swollen mass of bruises.

"Thank you for your patience, Weard Staute," Robert said sweetly. "I must say that the terms of surrender you have offered us are quite attractive, but you will excuse me if I cannot accept them. So here are my terms."

Ari turned away as Robert began his Will-Breaker. He knew that in the prison Robert had made for Sven's family, Erika and Asa would soon be weeping. Ari found himself missing his mother.

Eda Stormgul chose a wide, flat expanse of Flasten's marshes surrounded by deep pools in key locations. The damnens would not be able to sneak up on the Mar here, but nor would they have an easy time reaching their prey. The thousand wizards with her stood in rough lines just barely within recon range of the southernmost prisoners.

The magocrats had cast aside the drab garb of the Teleport War and donned the bright colors for which Mar wizards were known. There were more greens than any other single color of cloak, but there was also an abundance of auburn, blue and amber. Here and there, cyan and lavender cloaks marked the most powerful wizards — magocrats who could crush a dozen greens at once in magical combat. Against damnens, though, they were only slightly better than their skill with javelin, spear and marsord.

Across the field, the damnens gathered, their tall, muscular bodies looking like the shadows of monsters instead of the monsters themselves. The Drakes carried no weapons, for their claws and teeth had served them well enough. Their hides, Eda had learned, were far from impenetrable, but they were immune to magic. That alone made every wizard fear damnens. Eda could almost hear all the Mar behind her silently counting the damnens as they appeared in front of them.

Hundreds. We have killed several score in a span. No wonder they wanted to meet us like this, Eda thought. A nagging doubt crept in. *Unless this isn't all of them, of course.*

Weard Klarcin appeared abruptly next to Eda. "Weard Stormgul."

"Fight or flight?" she asked without turning her attention away from the army of damnens.

What answer do I really want to hear? she asked herself.

"Fight. There are less than a hundred guarding the prisoners. Our attack will be swift and deadly, and our withdrawal will be silent and untraceable."

Eda nodded slightly and turned to face the wizards behind her.

"We stay and fight."

There were nervous murmurs and a few grim laughs but no cheers. Odveig Spitz summoned Power and raised himself off the ground so everyone could see him.

"Hear me, my fellow Mar," he said, and his voice carried farther than was possible without magic. "Our ancestors believed that the gods answered no prayer without sacrifice. These were not the painless libations of alien lands — a wasting of food without fear that it might bring starvation. No, their sacrifices were of a sort that might mean dying for their faith — whether it meant destroying food they could not spare or giving the last of their food to a stranger.

"Thousands of years ago, the mapmakers of the Affe Expeditionary Force prayed to Marrish for deliverance from the Drakes that threatened to wipe out the Mar. Instead of risking starvation, those brave mapmakers performed daring reconnaissance missions in Drake lands. In those dark times, the Drakes ruled all of Marrishland except for Domus Palus, and so for every mapmaker who returned from such a mission, nine others did not. The Affe Expeditionary Force faced every mission unflinchingly.

"Now it is our turn to stand on the altar, resolved to pay whatever price the gods demand of us. We pray that they will accept this offering and restore the Duxy of Flasten to even greater glory. We pray that they will accept this offering and bring an end to the war between Domus and Flasten. The people who bleed together are truly one people, and we are Mar!"

There were cheers this time, and Weard Spitz lowered himself.

He turned to Weard Klarein.

"Return to the Mar and tell them that we will fight the damnens — not as Flasten magocrats and Domus magocrats but as Mar. Any further violence between our duxies — or any duxies — is an abomination in the sight of the gods and all the heroes who have bled for the Mar."

"I want to stay and fight with you."

Odveig placed a hand on the green's shoulder. "Allow us this one conceit, Weard Klarein. Live today. Tell our story. Die in another tale."

Oysten Klarein raised his right hand in salute. "By the Oathbinder and by Fraemauna, my patron, I will do as you command, and the epics Mar will write of you will place you among the stars."

To the north, the damnens approached the Mar army. Nonagons of magocrats flickered in and out in flanking maneuvers.

"Go," Eda told him.

Oysten obeyed, flickering away in a flurry of green cloth. As she watched him leave, she knew that her part in the story had come to an end.

"We should go to the Protectorates and bring back the Mardux," Weard Kiarr Bukaltar said.

"The Protectorates're big," Bui reminded him. "An' we've got insero comin'. They'll have ravits with them, an' that means poison darts an' fallin' rocks."

"We still have Blosin gloves, including morutdyjiton," Rig Marspur said.

Bui examined the recon stone. The insero and ravits were not as numerous as the other Drakes in the Mass — a few thousand all told — but they had apparently already been warned about the morutdyjinon, for they kept their distance from each other. Morutmanon might knock down two or three at a time, if it was well-aimed enough. Worse, they were carefully avoiding the front of the army, creeping around on either flank.

"Guard the flanks, an' be ready for them to attack our rear," Bui told them. "We'll need mobile roofs and Power 'depts to keep the darts off our heads."

Bui thanked Her that the priests never thought to question him. By the time the insero reached the Lapis Amnis, the army of adepts was as ready as they could be. After that, there was little he could do except watch the recon stone and adjust tactics as needed.

The ravits and insero rained poisonous darts and large stones on the adepts. The Mar retaliated with morutdyjinon, reducing insero and ravits to floating dust. When they had sustained a hundred casualties, the Drakes broke off the aerial assault and flew north to regroup.

At that moment, thousands of jabber and stinger guer pressed across the Lapis Amnis to engage the Mar there, and the adepts — distracted as they were by the presence of insero — barely repulsed them before they gained a beachhead.

"Get those gloves to the back ranks!" Bui called to the priests without looking up from the recon stone.

The insero surprised them by flying south toward Domus Palus. Meanwhile, the guer continued pressing the assault on the river. A hundred striped guer risked another crossing, and in the confusion, the Mar failed to stop them. Stinger guer flooded onto the south bank in half a dozen places. Bui called his draxi to him and sent them to break the assaults.

"What are the insero doing?" Rig asked.

"They're cutting our supply lines, such as they are. They know the Ian's out here're dead, an' think if we don't take back Domus Palus soon, we'll be, too. They're not wron', either. We need to get Domus back or die tryin'. The Drakes likely don't know the wizards there've decided they're our enemies."

"They intend to split our loyalties," Guthrun Snelfus noted. "They might also think the adepts are actually wizards and expect to face less resistance from the city's defenders."

"Even worse," Bui murmured, still looking at the recon stone. "They inten' to surroun' us. Look."

On the recon stone, three more groups of a thousand insero and ravits moved into sight — one directly to the north and one on each flank. Bui knew the adepts were about to lose control of the river and started considering how to minimize casualties.

Domin deflected Sven's marsord with a casual movement of his hand.

"Whatever Guardian you think you are, surely you do not think you can defeat a god."

"I can, and I will!" Sven snarled, hurling the deity backward with a wave of Power.

He spun around to strike Dinah with the shorter of the two blades. The steel struck the mud on her skin. Sparks flew as the attack glanced off.

"You think steel can strike the goddess of the earth? What I made I can unmake."

The marsord rusted rapidly, aging centuries in mere moments. Sven tossed it aside, and it burst into a small cloud of red dust before sinking in the mud. He called Energy and Power, knocking the Bald Goddess backward with a bolt of lightning just as Domin's black hand reached forward to touch his face.

If he touches me, I'm dead.

He took a hasty step backward and flung up a wall of Power.

Dinah stood up, patches of her muddy skin blackened by Sven's attack. "You cannot fight us forever, Sven Takraf. You are mortal, and we are gods. Our Mass walks the land. Soon, Her will set on the Mar for the last time."

He tried to take another step backward, but the mud had grabbed his boot, rooting him to the earth.

"You, too, are my creation. Who else could have given us free reign to destroy Marrishland as you have?"

He felt himself beginning to sink.

"And now that your usefulness has ended," Domin said as he reached out to touch Sven's face, "we will destroy you."

"Divine patrons, my life is yours," he whispered. "Without you, I am nothing."

"They cannot hear you, Mardux," Dinah snarled. "I have silenced your voice to their ears."

Domin's fatal fingers brushed against the left side of his face. Death crept into his flesh.

Seruvus, I know you can hear me. I am ashes in the hearth. Preserve the fire.

 # 46

"Uesdyn (mysterious magic dynamics) is a catch-all category for the study of things that affect Mar magic but are neither myst nor tor. The clearest example is the kaly-sut, the tree from which both torutsen and morutsen are made. Another is the Tempest, an inhospitable darkness accessed only during teleportation. Some uesdyn topics have passed into mysdyn and tordyn, however. The Kali-heron never discovered how to use Elements, Knowledge, Wisdom and Presence, which they regarded as shadows or echoes of Energy, Mobility, Power and Vitality."

— Weard Oda Kalidus,
The Origin of Nothing

Horsa sat on a small bench in Flasten Palus's walled garden, which had been one of the few places in the city the two sieges had not touched. All around him, the flowers of summer were beginning to fade, but they were still more colorful than any place on the marshes of the Duxy of Flasten. It was said the magocrats who first built the city, weary of the drab browns and greens that surrounded them, had collected flowers and flowering trees from across Marrishland to plant here, creating a refuge of vivid color amid the marshes.

It was also one of the few places in Flasten that did not reek of decaying Mar and damnen corpses. Horsa had set the army to work burning the dead, but it was a slow task, both because there were so many dead and because of the damnens still prowling the city, killing any stragglers they found. The Mar were gradually rooting out the Drakes, but even three spans after the magocrats had taken back Flasten Palus, no one dared travel in groups smaller than a company.

He stared down at the marsord in his hands — Eda's marsord. The steel shone in the sun now, but when Wcard Oysten Klarein had found it among the dead on the battlefield, so he said, it was covered in the blood of a hundred damnens.

"Eda Stormgul lived her chosen name," the green had assured him. "Odveig Spitz brought Flasten and Domus together and bound their wizards together with his own blood. Three hundred damnens died on Mar spears and marsords. The Mar of Stormgul's legion fought to the end, and while they sacrificed themselves, the rest of us stole the entire population of Flasten Palus from the damnens. By the time we reached the place where Stormgul's legion had been, the damnens had fled the field without leaving so much as one grisly totem of Mar corpses. We spent the day erecting a great pyre of the dead. That night, a thousand new stars shot across the sky, and I thought I saw two new stars in the sky — one in the Guardian and one in the Slave."

Horsa blinked away the tears. Eda had lived and died bravely, but he couldn't help but remember the playmate he had teased since they were both children — his first love. And now she was gone from him forever.

Watch over me, my friend. By your sacrifice, I am warmed. By your sacrifice, I can see. By your sacrifice, I live on.

"Weard Verifien, we have recovered the dux's marsord."

Horsa looked up from his reverie. The lavender held the blade out to him.

"Forgive me, good weard. I seem to have forgotten your name."

"We have not been introduced. I am Olvir Bedaulich. I was with Weard Stormgul in the south."

Horsa accepted the marsord numbly.

I have too many marsords and not enough hands to wield them.

"Do you come from Domus or Flasten?"

"I am loyal to you as I was to her," Olvir said fiercely.

Horsa suddenly recalled a time when Eda had played a prank on Katla and arranged for him to take the blame. He laughed softly and wiped his eyes.

"Have I said something funny, Weard Verifien?"

"Of course not. Forgive me, Weard Bedaulich. Eda was an old friend, but I suppose everyone has lost someone dear to them."

"Grief is no sin, Weard Verifien."

Neither of them spoke, but Horsa noted that more wizards had joined them. He looked around nervously, suddenly painfully aware that his face was flushed with grief. He stood up, trying to look harmless even with a marsord in each hand and a third peeking through the hole in the front of his yellow cloak.

He looked over the heads of the dozen weards waiting his words. All were Mar who had proven their leadership and loyalty — to him, to Ragnar, to the Mardux, Flasten and Marrishland. Any one of them could lead the army now. He felt proud to know them, and sad to think how he had come to know them.

"Flasten needs a dux," Olvir said. "Dux Feiglin and his children are dead. Magocrats on both sides agree no one deserves it more than you."

The yellow focused on the younger man closest to him, ignoring the murmurs of the rest of his advisers.

It could be you, Olvir. You could lead these magocrats and be a dux. I have only tried to follow Sven's example. So did Eda. And you are only trying to follow her example. There is something to be learned, here.

He shook his head. "I am a priest of Marrish."

"Every Duxess of Pidel was once a priestess of Marrish," Olvir reminded him.

"I am not an eighth-degree."

A yellow stepped forward and thrust a red cloak at him. "Take it, Weard Verifien. The Mardux himself will not dispute your right to wear it."

Horsa set the two marsords on the bench behind him took the cloak from her, but he did not put it on. He stared into her brown eyes.

Or this woman, whose name I cannot remember. She is like a jug, filled with the water overflowing from my jug. Or like a torch, lit by my fire. She could make a great leader.

But I hold this cloak.

"This is not how wizards ascend to eighth degree."

"Perhaps it should be," the yellow said. "Reds were rare enough a few years ago, and most of them are dead now. Those who survived Dux Feiglin's dispute with the Mardux are not fit to rule a village, much less a duxy."

The other wizards voiced their agreement.

"I have sworn to serve Sven Takraf," Horsa reminded them. "If you make me your dux, peace will not come swiftly to Flasten. The Mass has crossed the Lapis Amnis by now, and it was always my intention to lead the Domus army north to provide reinforcements to the Takraf Protectorates as soon as we had finished dealing with the damnen and ochre invasion."

"The Mass is a dire threat to Flasten's safety," a cyan declared. "Lead, and we will follow you, Weard Verifien. Time enough for peace when the war is won."

The words of agreement were even louder this time.

Weard Klarein did not wait for Horsa to answer. "The Stormgul Legion prayed fervently that their deaths would bring an end to the war between Domus and Flasten. What better way to show our duxy's good faith than to aid the Mardux's own homeland in its battle with the Drakes?"

Several wizards shouted their agreement. Horsa opened his mouth, but the yellow that had brought the red cloak spoke before him.

"We have heard that Weard Wost has taken slaves of those who owe him no tribute and who have broken no oaths. We must bring him to justice for his crimes. Perhaps we can undo some of the damage he has done there, as well."

Horsa bowed his head as magocrats of two duxies called for him to rule them as the Dux of Flasten.

They need a leader, and I am the best figurehead they have left. It isn't what I expected, but both Eda and Sven would want me to accept this opportunity. Who am I to argue?

When he lifted his head, they quieted.

"When I became a priest of Marrish, I vowed to obey the commands of my patron. It seems clear to me that he is manifesting his will here, and I will not break that oath."

Horsa removed his yellow cloak and put it aside reverently on the bench behind him as the crowd looked on breathlessly. He forced himself to put on the red cloak of an eighth-degree wizard. His breath caught when he noticed the embroidery on the breast of the cloak was not the broken, burning marsord of Sven Takraf but a grey tower being struck by a bolt of lightning.

The fortress that stands against the darkness, the storm that bows the trees by night. This cloak was meant for Eda, not me.

Horsa looked at them with eyes brimming with tears. He raised his right hand in a gesture of salute, choking back sobs as he spoke, "I accept the power and duty of Dux of Flasten. By the Oathbinder and Marrish, my patron, I vow to lead its magocrats, serve its people, and protect its territory from all foes, be they Mar or Drake, internal or external. I serve at the pleasure of the people of Flasten, and I swear to uphold the Law to which I remain bound."

The yellow raised her hand to him. "By the Oathbinder and Fraemauna, my patroness, I vow to serve and obey you, Dux Horsa Verifien. May Fraemauna grant you wisdom."

The yellow withdrew, but the other magocrats formed a procession, each one swearing fealty to him and offering him the blessings of their divine patrons. Horsa accepted their loyalty numbly, torn between shock and grief.

What a sad sight I must be, he thought. *Dux Weinen, they should call me — "the weeping general."*

The oaths and blessings continued all afternoon and late into the night. Shortly before dawn, a thunderstorm swept down from the north, and the magocrats all declared it a sign of Marrish's approval of the new dux's rule.

Horsa wasn't so sure.

The Delegates were locked in a power struggle, though Katla doubted any other Mar would have been able to tell. The courtesies were there — the little rituals that held the Mass together in an allied whole — but every suggestion sparked a fierce debate between those who supported Doh Zue Sah as chair of the Delegates and those who opposed her decision to continue the war against the Mar.

She wanted to gloat. She had helped foster this chaos.

The Delegates' Tent was much more crowded today than it had

been when Katla first arrived. In the past months, delegates had trickled in to voice their concerns before Doh Zue Sah, who manipulated the Delegates deftly at this point — this was her war now. Katla had burned many torches to stubs to make sure everyone was aware of that.

All of their losses, all of the death, rests at the hands of Zue Sah.

She smiled grimly at the striped guer as she entered the tent, escorted by her Hue honor guard. Today, three more waves had begun the march south, and the Thirtieth Wave had begun mobilizing.

The tent was full: all thirty-five tribes of spiny-tailed guer had delegates in the Delegates' Tent. The regular doling out of unpleasant duties to those tribes who had no delegates present had seen to that. One jabber guer delegate was here, for the others had been eager to join their armies in war. Both gobbel delegates — Gue Gue Jue and Hue Tah Heh — had stayed to oppose Koh Zue Ja and the five other ravit delegates who had joined her.

The delegates from the other four tribes of striped guer were today's surprise, and their presence was a sure sign that Zue Sah would soon have her authority challenged, or so the captain of her Hue "honor guard" claimed.

Zue Sah returned Katla's smile with a flat stare of her own, and rammed her staff firmly into the ground.

"The Delegates recognize Zoh Lee Zah," Doh Zue Sah intoned.

The emaciated spiny-tailed guer stepped forward, and there were murmurs among the delegates. Zoh Lee Zah was dressed in the military uniform of his tribe with badges that marked him as a member of the First Wave, which meant he was the lone survivor of the Mass's first battle with the Mar — the one the Mardux had ordered teleported back to the Drakes.

"The Zoh thank Doh Zue Sah and all the Delegates for hearing their concerns. My people are deeply troubled by the events outside of Domus Palus. They have sent me to humbly request that the Delegates intensify the attack on the Yee lands. Yee Seh Tah killed every soldier of the First Wave with an army much smaller than our own, and he did it with few casualties. Zoh Lee Zah lives because Yee Seh Tah wished to use me to convince the Delegates that we cannot win this war. The Zoh believe we can still achieve victory, but we must send all the Waves we can muster."

Most of the delegates had stepped forward to speak before Zoh Lee Zah returned to his place among them. If the Zoh had intended that Lee Zah's speech convince the Mass to redouble its efforts, and Katla wasn't sure they had, it had the opposite effect.

Zue Sah allowed another spiny-tailed guer delegate to speak. Of the thirty-five there, Katla knew more than half wanted an end to the war. Zue Sah had to know she was outnumbered. The almost daily votes were getting closer and closer. The arguments were never new.

But she wielded her staff with brisk, vicious motions, and the spiny-tailed guer delegates opposed to the war spoke one after the other, interminably, until even Katla was bored with their monotonous arguments. Then an eloquent supporter of the war — and Zue Sah — woke everyone up with a crafted, impassioned speech.

The tactic was brilliant, but Katla, watching the striped guer delegates eye each other, felt it would be too little, too late.

Hue Tah Heh and Gue Gue Jue had stepped forward to speak when the spiny-tailed tirade had tired, but Zue Sah chose another veteran of the Mass' invasion: the lame jabber guer Jah Ta Jee. The gobbels held their ground but exchanged glances with each other.

What is Zue Sah planning here? Katla wondered.

"The Jah thank Doh Zue Sah and all the Delegates for this audience." Ta Jee looked around at all the attentive eyes on him. He raised a fist into the air. "The Jah are without fear of death! We have been warriors for as long as the sun has risen and set! The Jah gave five thousand to the First Wave and forty-five thousand to the next nine Waves — our strongest, proudest and bravest warriors." He glanced at the badged spiny-tailed survivor. "Unlike the Zoh, no Jah warriors tried to surrender to the Yee when the First Wave attacked their great city."

Tah Heh and Gue Jue, as well as the other handful of delegates waiting to speak, abruptly stepped back. A spiny-tailed delegate placed a hand on Lee Zah's shoulder to hold him back, whispering ferociously in his ear.

Those are the waves that are known to have been destroyed. The next ten, at least, are at the front right now. Ta Jee will call for more waves, again, like Lee Zah did. Except he called out the Zoh.

Ta Jee was alone in the center of the tent, staring at everyone as his words faded into silence. The rage on his face was marred by the tears in his eyes. He turned to face Zue Sah and squared his shoulders.

"The Jah are the fiercest of warriors," he said, his voice hoarse. "Jah Ta Jee cannot offer the Delegates more warriors, because the Jah have no warriors left to give. We are bled dry."

He shook in his boots in rage or sadness, Katla couldn't tell. The jabber had so much pride, and even that had been defeated. In the thick silence, the only sound became the wracking sob of the lone delegate.

Zue Sah raised the staff, possibly to order Ta Jee to leave the ring. She did not look happy. Before she spoke, two striped guer delegates stepped forward. One quietly bent to remove Ta Jee. The other met Zue Sah's eyes with a look of imperious arrogance.

She has no choice, Katla thought. *She has lost.*

"The Delegates recognize Due Goh Rue."

"The Due thank Doh Zue Sah and all the Delegates for this rare opportunity to speak."

The tone was as flat as Doh Zue Sah's had been, but Katla heard volumes of irritation in her choice of words. Katla had long suspected the striped guer were not capable of a lot of vocal variation, and this confirmed it, in her mind.

"Due Goh Rue thanks the Jah for their nobility and strength in these dark days. The Due, the Dah and the Doh are troubled by the news coming from the war with the Yee and are disappointed that the Delegates have not, in our opinion, been allowed to do enough to resolve this situation. If the Delegates are restrained in their actions, the blame lies with the Overseer. Before this debate on wartime strategy can continue, Due Goh Rue feels it is necessary for Doh Zue Sah to step down as Overseer of the Delegates."

The striped guer stepped back even as one of the other striped guer stepped forward. None of the other delegates moved. Though they had few votes, a striped guer had sat as Overseer for as long as the Drakes had kept records of the Delegates' membership. No one would think of interfering with a dispute between the leaders of the striped guer. Zue Sah was left with no choice, then, but to give Doh Yue Dee — another delegate from her own tribe — the floor.

Yue Dee seconded the request, and Zue Sah had to open up the matter for debate. Lee Zah was the only ally the Overseer had left, but he attempted to drag out the debate for as long as possible. After nearly an hour of exalting Zue Sah without presenting any new arguments, Yue Dee interrupted him.

"Stop speaking. You insult the Delegates and the process by which we reach decisions, and if Doh Zue Sah has grown so lax in her duties as to allow you to do so, Doh Yue Dee must put an end to it instead."

Zue Sah should have reprimanded them; instead, she stood stiff and righteous. Lee Zah's imploring look was met with the side of her head, and he trailed off and stepped back into his place in the circle as much out of surprise as out of a desire to comply. After that, no one stepped forward to defend Doh Zue Sah, forcing her to call the question. The Delegates removed her and put Due Goh Rue in her place.

Goh Rue leaned heavily on the staff.

"The Delegates recognize Yee Ka Lah."

Katla jumped. She had not even stepped into the circle. No one had mentioned her name yet today. She stepped forward, unsure as to what the new Overseer wanted. The rest of the delegates stepped back, but Lee Zah bounded forward.

"The Zoh must insist that this breach of protocol be overturned," he cried. "The Yee delegate was not in the circle to speak!"

Goh Rue lifted the staff. "The Zoh delegate will remove himself from the circle."

"The Yee are savages who are not interested in truces and refuse to take prisoners!" Lee Zah shouted to anyone but the Overseer. "If the Delegates do not destroy them, what will keep the Yee from invading? We must kill them all! We must kill them or die!"

Goh Rue gestured, and two striped guer stepped forward to apprehend the raving stinger. Shouting and kicking, they dragged him from the circle.

All eyes turned to Katla.

"Yee Ka Lah thanks Due Goh Rue and the Delegates for this chance to speak. The Yee are not savages. The Yee follow their ruler, Yee Seh Tah, with devotion and loyalty. If a truce is made with him, it will be honored."

"You may bring him here, to negotiate."

Katla smiled wanly and shook her head. "I am here to negotiate on his behalf. You may send one Delegate with me to negotiate with him in the Yee capital."

She raised a hand into the silence. "The Yee will continue to kill your peoples until the truce is made! You must call back the waves that left today, cease mobilizing the Thirtieth Wave, and order a retreat of the invading waves from the Yee lands. With this sign of good faith, Yee Seh Tah will be more amenable to a fair negotiation."

"And he will not pursue us into our lands?"

"The Yee will not," Katla said. "You have my word on that."

The debate raged until after sunset. When Due Goh Rue at last called for a vote, the gobbels and ravits were the only ones other than Doh Zue Sah who opposed the truce.

"By a vote of forty in favor and thirteen against, the Delegates have chosen to offer the Yee a truce so both parties can discuss terms of a more lasting peace," Due Goh Rue announced. She then turned her attention to Katla. "The Delegates expect Yee Ka Lah to remember that while peace is desirable to them, they will not agree to terms that will harm their constituents."

Katla met her gaze. "Yee Ka Lah will work diligently to ensure that both parties find the terms of any treaty agreeable to them. Among the Delegates, I represent the interests of the Yee, but among the Yee, I represent the interests of the Delegates."

"Then go with the Delegates' good will, Yee Ka Lah. We will send insero messengers to order the Waves to withdraw from the lands south of the Lapis Amnis. Order your wizards not to pursue them."

Katla looked at each delegate in turn and left the Delegates' Tent. She did not teleport until she was out of their sight, for though all of them knew she was a wizard, some might have regarded it as threatening if she wielded magic in their presence.

"You should not have killed that Traveller," Ari said, finally breaking the morning silence.

Robert frowned at him from across the table where the enchanter had set up a recon stone of their own.

Ari continued. "The Drakes are invading from the north. Wasfal's army approaches from the east. Does it even matter if they are invading or rescuing? And now a third Mar army from the Duxy of Flasten is less than a day's march south of here. Someone will certainly have seen the last recon sweeps and triangulated our positions by now. Westward is the Duxy of Domus, and I do not think much of our chances there, either."

Robert's voice betrayed no small amount of annoyance, and given the farl's usual unshakable demeanor, Ari was certain the enchanter was more worried than he wanted to admit. "Do I have to break your will the way I have broken the others'?"

Ari looked away, unable to meet Robert's gaze. "No, Weard Wost."

Robert stood up and paced from one end of the room to the other. "Weard Faul, we have been over this a hundred times. We have Mardux Takraf to use as a hostage. His friends and allies will not risk his life by killing me. I am the only one with the antidote to the strange poison that plagues Weard Takraf."

Perhaps not the only one, Ari thought, but he stayed silent. The spell nestled beneath the tor buffer, which meant a simple Elements counter couldn't reach it. It would take both Elements and Presence, which most Mar wouldn't dare attempt. *But I've watched you and I've learned, and maybe I can wield it well enough to undo your enchantment.*

The victims of the Will-Breaker were easier to free. Robert's enchantment would only last a span or two without renewal. The enchanter's mastery of Energy was not nearly as complete as an eighth-degree wizard's. The spell would fade, and the victims would not, thankfully, remember anything they had witnessed while they were enchanted.

There may be hope for Einar and Sven yet, which means there may be hope for me.

Robert turned suddenly to look at the recon stone. He smiled in that way that made Ari uncomfortable. "Come, Weard Faul. Our guests are arriving. Einar, bring me those fine gloves you made for me, and make sure these visitors do not attempt anything foolish."

Einar handed the farl a pair of Blosin gloves, which Robert pulled on as he strode out of the large hut. The aged border guardian trailed the enchanter's steps as if a short rope connected them. Behind them, Ari fingered the gap in the front of his cloak, just above his knee.

When they reached the village green, four reds and a green — Dux Gruber Ratsell, Horsa Verifien, Nightfire, Arnora Stoltz and Erbark Lasik — waited for them.

"Weards Wost and Faul," Arnora said in a level tone. "I accuse you of violating Bera's Unwritten Laws. These duxes and weards stand as witnesses to this accusation, and Nightfire will try you for your crimes under Mar law."

Robert laughed. "Such exalted company we have, Weard Faul! The priest has become a dux, now? Did you kill Ragnar and Volund the way your Mardux killed Horik?"

Ari's cloak rustled as he lifted one leg, plunging the short blade of the marsord into the back of Robert's thigh. The enchanter tried to pull away, but Ari wrapped his left arm around Robert's shoulders, holding the farl's back to his chest as he reached for the marsord.

"I am not sharing your fall," Ari whispered.

Gruber and Arnora summoned fire to strike both of them, but Einar stepped in front of them before they could find their marks. He countered most of the attack, but fire licked his cloak.

Robert snarled in pain and fury and lifted up his hands.

"Counter the gloves!" Ari shouted at them all.

It was too late. Erbark moved only a few steps, marsord already out. Nightfire and Horsa did not even move, but they had no doubt begun gathering myst. In mad desperation, Ari reached around Robert and grabbed his wrists.

Then black tendrils of killing magic lanced out of the Blosin gloves, sweeping and twisting in the air as they chose their targets. Ari closed his eyes, waiting for the inevitable.

Abruptly, Robert's body crumbled in Ari's arms. He risked opening one eye.

The wizards stood staring at him, unharmed by the deadly magic. Einar lay on the ground, healing himself. The light had returned to his eyes.

"What happened?" Ari murmured.

Everyone turned their attention to Nightfire, who cleared his throat.

"It would seem the close proximity of Weard Faul's tor somehow interfered with Weard Wost's application of morutmanon. This is an unprecedented series of events, but as repeating the experiment in a more controlled environment would be ... problematic, we may never know the cause of what we just witnessed. I will make a note of it for future generations, though."

"If Weard Wost's morutmanon harmed only Weard Faul's enemies," Horsa said, "then I suppose that means we are not his enemies."

"Had my son not acted when he did, Weard Wost's morutmanon would likely have killed us all," Einar said. "According to Vangard's Rules of Governance, he could demand eight years of service from each of us."

"This is true," Nightfire mused. "In light of that, it is my judgment that Weard Faul was enslaved by Weard Wost's Will-Breaker and cannot be held responsible for the crimes he committed while under its effects. In exchange, no one serves anyone for eight years. Weard Faul, is this acceptable to you?"

Ari nodded and drew the marsord. "This is yours, Weard Schwert. I was wrong to take it from you."

"I am sorry, son, for everything."

"The rightful order is restored and justice reigns again, yes?" Gruber said with mock cheerfulness. "Then we should join our armies and march before the Drakes come any farther south. These two will no doubt bring reinforcements soon, yes?"

The wizards murmured their agreement and, one by one, vanished into the Tempest, leaving Einar and Ari alone with Robert's army of confused mundanes armed with wands.

"Father, even if I had not been there, Robert's Blosin gloves would not have killed anyone, would they? The morutmanon attacked your enemy instead of his, didn't they?"

"Which would you rather believe, Ari?"

"Whichever is true."

Einar shrugged. "The truth is I do not know. Maybe it was your tor. Maybe morutmanon knows its creator's enemies better than the scholars realize. Maybe one of the gods intervened. Maybe it was the Traveller's curse. Believe what you wish and be glad you are alive and free."

Einar pulled the last strap of the shin sheath tight. He frowned at the mundanes standing around them. "It seems the morutmanon freed me from Robert's Will-Breaker, but I'm not sure what to do about the rest of the Protectorates."

"I think I can free them. If not, the enchantment will eventually pass."

"And the Mardux?"

Ari took a deep breath. "That will be harder. It is a different enchantment, and unlike the others, he will remember his nightmare."

Einar went silent at that, remnants of his own torment perhaps not yet fully faded. "Then let us get started, son."

 **47**

*"Every story has its end. The mortality of storytellers
alone makes this true."*

— Pondr,
Collected Journals, edited by Weard Asa Sehtah

"Would you like me to tell you one last story about yourself, Mardux?" Pondr's voice whispered in his ear as Sven floated in the frozen
darkness.

What is happening?

Then Pondr spoke, and Sven felt himself transported.

Sven Takraf stood on an altar at the center of a vast host of Mar.
Adepts, wand-wielders, mundanes and wizards stood in a circle
around him, and the Mass pressed in all around them, trapping them,
suffocating his people.

From his vantage, he could see clear to the horizon. The swamps'
giant trees, with their thick, hollow roots and soft moss, were gone.
The moors' and fens' grasses and stunted, rotting growth had vanished. No wild rice fields remained. The rivers themselves had disappeared, replaced by countless Drakes.

Guer of every species, gobbels and ravits had swallowed his country, and their fierce cries and waving weapons and arms were a wild,
ungodly creation before them. Even the reclusive ochres could be
spotted among the fray.

The Mass truly *was.* Unlike the first Waves of it, the Drakes did not
separate by race. Here, two gobbels and three distinct types of guer,
united, launched spears at his Mar, who deflected with their magic
but as yet did not attack back. There, a lone ochre was enmeshed
with jabber and spiny-tailed guer, waving spears and screaming in

disarray. They moved in many directions, but as one, as if the Mass wasn't a singular collection of all the Drakes, but had acquired its own mind and person in Domin's favor, with millions upon millions of hands, preparing to take Sven's last island in Marrishland.

And its largest hands were the damnens, who had come from their seclusion to finish off their largest competitor. They towered above everything except the insero and ravits, Mar-length claws reaching for Sven's people and jaws wide, screaming as incoherently as the rest of the Mass.

It was a nightmare. It was everything Sven had feared it would be, but everything he had prepared for, as well.

We have placed the last of our food on the altar as a sacrifice. If the gods do not provide for us, we will die.

The buzz of inseros' wings shadowed the sky to the north, and the darts of the ravits on their backs rained deadly poison on the adepts and wand-wielders.

"Stand fast! We will still carry the day!" the Mardux shouted.

It was no use. No one could afford to turn and look at him. No one could waste the energy to raise a cry. The south and east continued their collapses, meeting the remnants of the west. The damnens roared again.

"Stand fast!" Sven called again, more desperately. "The gods are with us!"

A few eyes in the back ranks searched out the Mardux. A hand pointed. Someone said his name, maybe. But the wizards who had joined his cause gladly and the magocrats he had ordered to bleed for him knew the battle lost, and yet they fought to stay true to their oaths. The screams of adepts and wand-wielders — people from the Protectorates who entrusted their lives to him and those from Domus Palus who blindly followed him — filled the air.

"Immortal patrons — Marrish, Niminth, Fraemauna, Sendala, Heliotosis, Swind, Seruvus, Cedar and Her — we are lost without your aid. Help your people!"

Still, the Mar hesitated.

"Her, give us a sign of your presence!" Sven shouted.

Please, gods.

Horsa and the last remnants of his priests took up the cry, unleashing fire and force and morutmanon. The sun stood still in the sky.

"Cedar, give us a sign of your presence!"

The Duxess of Pidel and the Duxes of Gunne, Piljerka and Skrem shouted oaths of fealty to Sven, and massive trees sprang up from the ground, their branches shielding the Mar from the insero and ravits above. Sven felt a slight shift in the battlefield as both sides hesitated slightly in light of this unusual phenomenon. Even the damnens, on the edge of another roar, took a collective breath.

"Fraemauna, Sendala and Niminth, give us a sign of your presence!" he shouted just as the damnens' roar came again.

Erbark, Eda and the Dux of Wasfal drew marsords in unison and assailed the damnens, driving them back for the first time in memory. The moons danced in the sky. The armies of Flasten and Domus cheered. The Drakes renewed their assault without the damnens or insero, compressing the remaining Mar into a tiny ball.

"Swind, give us a sign of your presence!"

Einar, Erika, Asfrid and Sigrun reconned, and a dome of Energy like the Mosquito Shields of the Protectorates sprang up around the Mar. The Drakes who tried to pass through it burned, while the wounded Mar within it healed. A warm south wind stirred Sven's cloak and drew water from the pools to splash on cloaks and corpses alike.

"Heliotosis, give us a sign of your presence!"

The Dux of Wasfal came from the east with Ari and Arnora and all the other Mar who had opposed the Mardux. The gobbels and guer grinned, welcoming them as reinforcements, but Dux Gruber Ratsell gave the order to attack, instead, and the stingers and jabbers were unprepared for this abrupt flanking maneuver. An icy gale blew from the north, forcing Drake and Mar alike to grab shrubs and tree trunks to keep from being knocked over. The gobbels fled, and the guer trembled.

Sven screamed over the din. "Seruvus, give us a sign of your presence!"

Bui and Finn and all the adepts, wand-wielders and mundanes in Marrishland rose up from the mud of the swamp and struck down tens of thousands of stinger and jabber guer, and then hundreds of thousands. Thousands of humanoid shapes formed of brackish water rose with them and struck down Drakes with liquid fists.

"Marrish, Lord of Wind and Fire, God of Magic, Father of the Mar, show us a sign of your presence!"

Nightfire took the field with all the professors and apprentices of his Academy. Cold rage flickered across his features as they hurled striped guer around like clods of clay. The sky turned black with thick clouds. Lightning struck the ground in a hundred places, blasting Drakes to ash where they stood.

Sven fixed his gaze upon the Mass and stretched out with both his hands. The black storm clouds broke open, dropping balls of fire that sucked the moisture from the air. The water of the swamps rapidly evaporated. The air became choked with the stench of death as the Mass crumbled before the onslaught of the gods.

"Praise the gods!" the Mar shouted over the deafening thunder.

The myst appeared to plain sight, and Sven blinked, lowering his arms. It stood still, the colors separating and gathering. Suddenly, it shifted. Cyan and lavender motes illuminated the dark cyclone, spinning around as though chasing one another. The pools of water radiated an amber glow and red motes danced around the grasses and wild rice. The clouds struck the Drakes with bolts of green lightning.

The Drakes, finally overwhelmed by the combined attacks of Mar and gods, broke and fled in every direction. At the north, where most of the Drakes still lived, nine figures dressed in green, auburn, blue, amber, cyan, lavender, yellow, red and white cloaks waited for them. The nine gods each glowed with light corresponding to the color of his cloak, and each held hands forward, fingers outstretched.

Every wizard on the field of battle recognized that gesture. Even the mundane — none of whom had studied the careers of such wizards as Nightfire, Brack, Olaf Weisht, Asfrid Gegnart and the bare handful of other wizards who had possessed the power such a gesture represented — had heard the stories.

The gods' auras dimmed for just a moment as the tendrils of black flame leapt from their fingers, the deadly rivers of magic twisting and shifting like angry serpents as they struck the fleeing Mass.

The divine morutmanon crackled like bolts of lightning, held its victims fast and reduced the army to hot ash that sizzled and steamed as it struck the water below. Then the spell ended, and stars appeared in broad daylight and fell from the sky. Where they landed, the legendary hero for whom each star had been named rose from the swamp and marched forward to join the line of gods. Sven followed them, surrounding himself with an aura of flame. Ten thousand heroes formed a long line behind the retreating Mass.

The Mar blinked in unison at the miraculous vision, knowing this could not be a mere dream. As they watched, the gods and stars joined hands, with Marrish at the center of the line. The two heroes on either end of the long line — Weard Darflaem and Uneheilich — took a step toward the center, their bodies merging into their neighbors'. Gradually, all the fallen heroes became one with either Fraemauna or Cedar. Then the deities did the same, until Marrish (or was it Nightfire?) stood alone.

Three figures stood before the gods, barring their way. One was either a farl or a man with the head of an alligator who held a marsord to Sven's throat. The other was either Katla or a woman clad only in mud.

"We have come to beg the gods to show my children mercy," Dinah — Katla — said, kneeling before Marrish — Nightfire. "In return, we have spared Pitt Gematsud's son — the Guardian who leads all Mar."

Domin — Robert — did not kneel, but nor did he voice any objection.

Marrish held out a hand. "Your offer is acceptable to me, Dinah. Trouble my people no more, and I will consent to a truce between us."

The clouds dispersed. The sun shone down. The winds stopped. The water and grasses grew still. And the moons looked on in silence. On the battlefield, the Mar had fallen to their knees on the dry and cracked ground, shouting prayers of thanksgiving.

Sven felt the blade move away from his throat, and then the darkness devoured him.

Did I truly fight Dinah and Domin, or was that another of Robert's illusions?

"Why can't both be true? The moons are lights in the sky but also gods — crescent or gibbous, but still the same moon. Life is full of paradoxes. The storyteller is dead, but the story is alive. Open your eyes, Sven Takraf. Use your energy. You are not the fuel that everyone feeds on; you are the fire in the hearts and minds of all Mar."

The lesson of the fire. I brought Marrish's gift of magic to the mundanes. Marrishland is the fuel, not me. I am the fire who touched each Mar, and now they are fire.

Sven saw the fire in the hearth first as the room came into focus around him. He sat in a rocking chair, swaddled in blankets like an infant, and someone had taken his boots. Sven touched the wood of the chair's arm and recognized it immediately as his.

They've brought me home. To Leiben.

"Pondr, are you there?" Sven said, his voice softer than he expected.

There was a whoosh of cloth behind him, and Erika was at his side, clutching his face to her chest. Sven felt a child crawling into his lap. He clutched both of them to him with fingers too weak to hold them tight.

"Erbark," Erika began, but the warrior was outside before she could even finish her sentence.

"How long has it been?" Sven whispered urgently. "The Mass..."

"Has withdrawn, Sven, so don't set yourself on fire," Erika said, easing her hold on him somewhat. "It has been a month. Ari and Horsa tried everything they could think of to break the enchantment — magic, morutsen, torutsen. Asa spent days upon days reading to you and telling you stories. Something worked, but by all the gods, we have no idea what."

"Papa," Asa whispered in one ear. "It was Pondr's stories."

Sven opened his mouth to respond, but the heavy clomping of many boots interrupted him.

Erika stood up. "Can't you give him some time to recover?"

"We will try not to wear him out too much, but some matters require his immediate attention," Einar said behind him. "Is that acceptable, Mardux?"

"Weard Schwert, I am in your debt. Please, call me Sven, and let me know how I can repay you."

Sven couldn't see Einar's expression, but he could all but hear the embarrassment. "I took an oath, and I fulfilled it. You owe your life to Ari and Horsa more than to me."

"I owe more debts than I can ever repay," Sven murmured.

"Are you strong enough for a brief audience, Sven?"

"I think so. Turn me around so I can see."

Erbark did so, and Sven scanned the crowd for familiar faces. He saw many.

Nightfire and Bui seemed unchanged, and Erbark had lost some more hair but otherwise was as he had always been. Einar looked older, as did Asa, who was much heavier on his lap than he remembered.

When was the last time she had a chance to sit on my lap?

Erika and Finn looked fiercer than before. Duxes Borya Zaghaf, Wolber Verden and Yver Verlren, his vassals, looked vaguely guilty, but Duxess Glyda Zaun looked upon him with a mixture of reverence and relief that seemed out of place on her face. Dux Gruber Ratsell was all smiles, making Sven wonder how much he owed to Wasfal, after recent events.

Then came the surprises. Horsa wore a red cloak now, and once Sven determined that Ragnar was not among the assembled crowd, he felt he already knew the cause. Arnora Stolz seemed out of place, but she stood at Erbark's side. Eda Stormgul was absent, as was Pondr, and Sven wept inside for what he knew that must mean. Katla was all business, as always, though she betrayed her nervousness by fiddling with the braided silver and gold ring on her finger.

He cleared his throat, commanding their attention. "Who is first?" he croaked.

As the others were looking at each other, Katla stepped forward, raising her right hand in a gesture of salute.

"Weard Duxpite, I have yet to repay you for Tortz, and now I am doubly in your debt. How can I serve you?"

"I come to you as a representative of the Delegates — the ruling council that commands the Drakes of the Mass — to discuss terms for a long-lasting peace. The Delegates will withdraw from all the lands south of the Lapis Amnis, which will serve as a natural boundary between the Mar and the Drakes. Neither side is to violate this boundary by building settlements on the wrong side."

"This is a matter for the whole Council to approve, but I would vote in favor of it."

Sven looked to the duxes and saw no objections there.

"The Delegates have one other small request. They would like permission to send an envoy to Domus Palus to represent the Drakes to the Council as I represent the interests of the Mar among the Delegates."

Again, Sven looked to the rest of the Council. "Is this acceptable to you? A permanent envoy from the Delegates might help head off future conflicts."

"It is unprecedented," Pidel said. "But as the rules of magic have changed, so too may some of our customs."

The other Mar murmured their agreement.

"Let it be as the Council wills," Sven murmured, nodding his head.

"I will inform the Delegates," Katla said as she stepped back.

Several others stepped forward, but Erika interposed herself between them and Sven.

"The Mardux needs to rest. The other petitions can wait until he returns to Domus Palus. Weard Schwert, you will rule as seneschal in his absence, as the law describes. Erbark and Arnlaug, rebuild the Protectorates' recon stones. Bui, have your draxi set up a visible boundary along the Lapis Amnis. The war might be officially over, but that doesn't mean all the Drakes know that yet. Until the Mardux returns, mourn your dead, tend your wounded and visit your families."

Dux Verlren opened his mouth to object but closed it after a brief glance at Nightfire and the other duxes. The Mar filed out of the house. Erbark was the last to leave, closing the door behind him.

"Asa, go to your room. I need to talk to your father for a little while," Erika said.

Asa seemed on the point of refusing.

Sven kissed her on the cheek before the words could leave her mouth. "Do as your mother says."

Asa stared at him hard as if calculating the probability of successfully arguing her case, but in the end, she obeyed. When she was gone, Sven met Erika's gaze.

"Nothing I say will convince you that I only did what had to be done," he said flatly.

"And nothing I say will convince you to give up the Chair and settle for a quiet life teaching at Nightfire's Academy," she countered with a surprising lack of venom.

Sven cocked his head.

"Volund is dead, and Flasten has chosen your friend Horsa to rule them. None of the duxes oppose your rule. The Mass has broken off its invasion and agreed to a truce between Drakes and Mar. The adepts have proven their value, and it seems unlikely that magic will ever be the secret power of the wizards again. What is left to do?"

"Deal with the Drakes out of the lands south of the Lapis Amnis — the damnens, the ochres, the ravits and the gobbels. Nurture the diplomatic relations between Mar and Mass. Put a stop to slave-taking or, at the least, prevent the kind of slavery that steals a mother from her family."

Erika stared at him with tears in her eyes, her emotions conflicted. He looked away, watching the shadows cast by the fire flicker and twist on the wall.

"You know my head is always filled with grand schemes and far-reaching plans," he said. "I cannot lay that part of me aside no matter how hard I try."

"I don't want you to give up your vision. It's why I married you, remember?" She laid a hand on his arm. "But let me be a part of it. I helped Finn plan the adepts' revolt and showed them how to make Blosin gloves. I'm not completely useless, you know."

Sven noted the bitterness in her voice. He replayed a thousand conversations and found no such statement. "When did I ever say you were useless, Erika?"

"Whenever you hid us and pretended we didn't exist. You never even tell me what you're doing anymore. I like hearing about how you mean to give everyone magic, Sven. It comforts me to know you are working to make Marrishland a better place for Asa and her children."

Sven considered what to say next, and when he spoke, his voice was soft. "I have treated you unfairly, my love, and I will make use of your talents in the future. As to my plans, let me lay them out plainly. I plan to declare an amnesty that frees all current slaves. I will use the good will my victory has earned me to change the Law so that all Mar can wield magic. I also intend to prohibit the possession of Blosin gloves enchanted with offensive spells so that only those licensed to wield them may have them. If the Mar are ever moved to fight each other again, I would not have them all wielding morut-manon. I expect to acknowledge Horsa's claim to the Duxy of Flasten, and I will pardon those duxes who attacked Domus Palus while the adepts fought the Mass."

He looked up into her eyes. "And while the Mar rebuild the country from the ruins I have left it in, I intend to finish your apprenticeship and take Asa as my apprentice. Even if all Mar wield magic, those who also hold the title of weard will always have elevated status in this country. Besides, I have never known a child more eager for or deserving of an education as our daughter is. You have taught her well in my absence, and it is past time I was a part of her life again. Is there anything you would like to add to my list, Erika?"

"Let me take the test soon. I have known magic too well to wear black any longer. You should begin teaching Asa now, before you return to Domus Palus."

He smirked at her. "You say that because you know that once she finds out she is my apprentice, she will hound me for knowledge day and night until she wears the green, too."

"Until she wears the red, and you know it." She leaned over and kissed him impishly. "Welcome home, Sven Takraf." Then she shouted up the stairs. "Asa, honey, your father has something he wants to tell you!"

Asa raced down the stairs and drew to a halt in front of him. He watched her eyes as he began her apprenticeship, and sometimes, he could see the reflection of the fire behind him.

The fuel turns to ash, but the fire lives on.

 Afterword

When the Takraf War ended, it had become the most violent period in Mar history since the Fall of the Gien Empire centuries ago. Tens of thousands of wizards and adepts, hundreds of thousands of Drakes and as many as a million wand-wielders and other mundanes died as a direct result of the conflict or in its aftermath.

Although widely considered one of the most successful Marduxes in the last several generations, Sven Takraf did not achieve all of his stated objectives in the years he held the Chair. Today, the damnens still control the Dead Swamps. The sale of slaves to foreigners, although now illegal, remains a problem. Dangerous Blosin gloves and wands have proliferated at an alarming rate, doing much harm to innocent Mar in spite of all the laws the Council has passed to curb crimes involving them.

In the end, Sven Takraf's frustration with his inability to prevent Mar from abusing the magical tools he created drove him out of statecraft. He handed over control of the Duxy of Domus to Einar Schwert by means of a no-contest duel for the Chair and returned to Nightfire's Academy to teach.

Certainly, much good also came to Marrishland in the aftermath of the Takraf War. The peace between Mar and Mass remains — forged in fear, but as yet unbroken. The Takraf Amendment to Bera's Unwritten Laws still stands. The proliferation of adepts and wand-wielders it allowed has resulted in a safer, healthier and wealthier nation. But, was it worth the price Marrishland paid? That is for later generations to decide.

The comforts we Mar enjoy today depend on never allowing anyone to overturn the Takraf Amendment. Some magocrats still wish to snatch away Marrish's Gift from the Mar, and they have tried many things in and out of the Council in hopes of accomplishing this. All the blood and fire and madness of the Takraf War were for nothing if we do not remain vigilant in our defense of its most important achievement.

— *Weard Asa Sehtah, editor*

 # Acknowledgments

The Takraf War affected virtually every corner of Marrishland, and no one person could have written a complete and accurate account of its history without the testimony of its survivors. The editor and contributors would like to thank the following witnesses for their commitment to this work: Mardux Einar Schwert, Duxess Glyda Zaun, Dux Gruber Ratsell, Master Brack (Weard Katla Duxpite and Yee Ka Lah), Master Nightfire, Weard Ari Faul, Weard Arnora Stoltz, Weard Erbark Lasik, Weard Erika Unschul, Weard Asfrid Staute, Weard Devla Salt, Weard Olvir Bedaulich, Weard Oysten Klarein, Weard Sven Takraf, General Bui Beglin, Adept Finn Ochregut, Due Goh Rue and Tee Rah Rue.

 # Contributors

As no one person could have provided a complete account of the Takraf War, no one scholar could have written it, and I owe my colleagues a greater debt than I can pay in this life.

Weard Eira Helderza: A historian of Pidel Palus Academy specializing in the Gien Invasion and the oral tradition of pre-literate Marrishland.

Weard Gilda Kronas: A historian at Pidel Palus Academy specializing in the military history of Marrishland, especially from the time of Weard Darflaem to the Fall of the Gien Empire.

Weard Girdag Langat: A veteran mapmaker who served the Duxy of Pidel for twelve years before he turned scholar. He now teaches at Nightfire's Academy, specializing in documenting aspects of the everyday life of mundane Mar.

Weard Oda Kalidus: A historian at Domus Palus Academy specializing in the study of magic in Marrishland prior to Weard Darflaem, especially that of the Kalkorae, which is the subject of her book *Wind Fans and Waterwheels*.

Weard Olga Fydelis: A priestess of Marrish and theology professor at Pidel Palus Academy, she specializes in Mar religious literature.

Weard Sigrath Brennan: A senior professor of governance at Flasten Palus Academy, she is most famous for *Guard and Guide* — an instructional manual aimed at wizards who wish to become magocrats in the lands at the edge of Mar civilization.

 # Special thanks

Weard Ottar Verunsigud: The editor's editor, my beloved husband. Thank you for keeping me honest when no one else dared my temper. You know who I got it from!

Pondr: The Traveller and storyteller who never told us his real name. His journals inspired and informed this work more than I can express. Watch over me, my friend. By your sacrifice, I am warmed. By your sacrifice, I can see. By your sacrifice, I live on.

Four Moons Press

Invites you to read a sample
of a forthcoming novel

By Eric Zawadzki and Matthew Schick

available at

fourmoonspress.com

COMING SOON

ABOUT THE AUTHORS

Eric Zawadzki

Eric spent his Midwestern childhood reading fantasy, so it probably isn't surprising that he came to idealize stories of going to a far-off land. When no wizard showed up to tell him he was the heir to some otherworldly throne or the only one who could defeat the nefarious designs of a dark god, Eric took this whole questing hero thing into his own hands.

While backpacking alone in Poland without so much as a phrasebook, he met many strangers who gave him advice and directions. One family even took him in for the night, feeding him and asking him about his travels. No bandits or wolves, but that's probably for the best. He still has nightmares about that wolfman from The Neverending Story.

He lived for a time among the majestic mountains of Colorado before seeking his one true love, Beth, on the frozen wastelands of Minnesota. They married on a beautiful spring day and are in the process of living happily ever after.

Matthew Schick

Indiana had a slogan in Matt's childhood: "There's more than corn in Indiana." Driving around the state, he agreed — there were also soybeans and vast, flat skies. He found inspiration because there was so much room for it, inspiration to explore, to fill himself with variety, and to write with them in mind.

He now lives in Charlottesville, Va., with his lady, whom he met while working as a journalist in Hawaii. He ended up in Hawaii after doing similar work in Colorado and Virginia, and going to college in Wisconsin. In his explorations, he has found people, food and experiences that made each place an inspiration for the worlds in which he writes.

. . .

The words of a prophecy brought Matthew and Eric together for the first time when they were only fourteen. Not ones to fight destiny, they quickly began a collaboration that has endured for nearly twenty years — flourishing even after they discovered girls, went to different colleges, and lived half an ocean apart. Fate briefly brought them both to Minneapolis, only to fling Matt away again, but they concocted a scheme to finally publish their works and throw off the prophecy altogether.

www.ingramcontent.com/pod-product-compliance
Lightning Source LLC
Chambersburg PA
CBHW071220250626
47163CB00001B/49